MOONLIT ECSTASY

"Yes, you are beautiful, Crislyn. More beautiful now than the first time I saw you," he said.

My head turned to see the dark shape on the bank, and my heart pounded crazily. I was aware of how vulnerable I was in the moonlight, the water still glistening on my naked body. And the thought of Lord Blackheart seeing me like this brought a tingling to my loins that made me unshamedly aware of how much I wanted him to make love to me....

He didn't take his eyes off me as he stood there, poised on the bank, and I took a deep breath, feeling the anticipation of what was to come.

"You're beautiful, too," I breathed softly. And he was beautiful, with his lean muscled strength emphasized by the curling gold hair at his chest and loins. He was ready for me; I could tell that at a shy glance. I stood still as he approached me through the shallows.

Without words, we sank into the rippling stream, our mouths locked together and our bodies tightly clasped. . . .

Other *Leisure Books* by Nelle McFather:

ECSTASY'S CAPTIVE
WOMAN ALIVE

LOVESPELL

NELLE McFATHER

*For
Mother and Aunt Rita,
great southern ladies
who love me and my stories.*

Book Margins, Inc.

A BMI Edition

Published by special arrangement with Dorchester Publishing Co., Inc.

Printed in the United States of America.

LOVE SPELL

Prologue

It's my wedding night, and I awaken to the sound of the monastery bells tolling midnight. I count silently with them—*nine . . . ten . . . eleven . . .*

Twelve. My tension leaves me, and I smile happily as the man sleeping beside me stirs but doesn't waken. I move his arm to a more comfortable position across my breasts and wait for silence to return to the castle and the Kent countryside.

But sleep is no longer possible. The bells have reminded me of all that has happened.

I look around the tower room, thinking how it must have been the same in medieval times. Bloodstones Castle had taken on Tudor changes, but very few, I was told. This room, often referred to as the King's Tower, is almost exactly the way it's always been.

Even the great bed in which I lie has been carefully restored and kept the same. The linen hangings have been refurbished, of course, but they're copied from the original ones. I shiver a little when I think of the first bride of James Gerald Linwood dying in this very bed.

My restlessness can't be stilled, and I ease my new

husband's bare arm from my body, which still tingles from earlier hunger. Carefully, so that the bed's leather springs won't squeak, I leave my warm place, taking care not to disturb my peaceful bridegroom. There'll be time for renewed passion later, but now I want to think about the events leading up to this, my wedding night. I need to think about my cousin Cassandra and about Phillip.

The memories are too painful. I delay what I know to be a necessary exorcism by wandering around the room, looking at things as if I'd never seen them before. There are few appointments: an old chest or two, a few wooden hooks, a rough stool. I touch the faded tapestries hung to catch castle drafts and left hanging from olden days. The moonlight streams in through the room's one window, actually an arrow-slit or *meurtriere*, catching a movement. It is my own image in a full-length mirror which, like the cleverly hidden W.C., was added in the twentieth century.

For a moment I stare at the woman I see reflected there, still and naked and somehow ghostlike. Objectively I acknowledge the figure falls short of classic beauty. The breasts are too full, the belly too flat. The long neck seems too fragile in contrast to a heavy, dark mane with its wide streak of silver, while the face is too strong with its wide-set eyes and stubborn chin.

I move away to finish my restless tour, stopping in front of a small, framed sketch of this room's most famous occupant. I suspect the lightly-done drawing is a contraband Holbein, a misplaced preliminary sketch of the famous portrait of Henry VIII, and belongs to The British Museum. Someday we'll share it with the public, but for now it shall remain a part of Bloodstones' personal history.

The broad-shouldered, strutting figure who set the fashion for much of his era leers at me good-naturedly, reminding me he too once put our bed to good use. "You royal rascal," I whisper to the picture. "I wonder how many wenches you had up here while poor old Anne was waiting for you to come wooing her at Hever?"

My imagination is running away with me again. As I look at the sketch, I can almost hear the slip-slap of bricks being laid at the foot of the stairs leading up here. The poor old paranoid king couldn't even spend the night in a friend's castle without worrying about assassination. But the fascinating story about Henry's bizarre demand to be sealed off in the tower when visiting isn't the part of Bloodstones' colorful past that affects me.

I hug myself against the chill, knowing the goosebumps are for another reason. How can I ever get used to being here, in the castle once occupied by my own ancestors? How many American women can say their wedding night was spent in the center of their own beginnings?

The monastery bells are ringing again. No doubt they're signaling early prayers, since the first light is creeping in through the archer's slit.

Memories are stirred once more at the sound of the bells, though these I've just heard have nothing to do with me.

Eleven bells ringing out the eleventh hour for a soul departing the castle forever—an ancient ancestral tradition. Like the other stories my uncle told Cassandra and me about Bloodstones, it was just another deliciously scary fairy tale, but the affect on me the first time the eleven bells rang out in the ancestral context, at Uncle Porter's funeral, was astonishing.

A psychiatrist I talked to recently tried to explain it in a logical way. I was deeply affected by my uncle's death, he told me, and the eleven bells triggered an emotional escape from the sad present into the past. All the stories heard by a lonely, imaginative little girl were ready to provide a welcome escape from reality. He said a lot more, about genetic memory and the like, but I know that what started happening to me the day of Uncle Porter's funeral can't be explained away in psychiatric terms.

I always go back to the day of the funeral as a starting place. As a student of history, I know you can't ever begin at the real beginning. You pick an event that's important for some reason, something that sets off a chain of other events, then you work your way forward—and backward—from that point.

So I start with the funeral. That's when I heard eleven bells. That's when I watched a lonely hawk circle the sky, with the sun breaking through the grey clouds. That's when Phillip came back into my life.

Let the memories come freely now in this wonderful old tower, while my husband sleeps. Let the past seep in like the grey dawn's light this last time.

When the morning sun comes in and my love holds out his arms to me, there'll be no more time for memories, only the joy of the present.

1

As I looked up at the cloudy Alabama sky and felt the drizzling rain on my face, I had to admit it was the proper kind of day for a funeral. Being a novelist, I couldn't help having an appreciation for the right setting for an event, even when that event was my beloved uncle's burial in the tiny Manning cemetery on the old homestead. The circle of mourners, with their scalloped row of umbrellas surrounding the dark, hollow grave completed the picture.

I hoped they hadn't thought badly of me for slipping away from the final part of the ceremony, elderly·southern gentility feeling strongly about its funeral customs. The soft plops of dirt falling onto my uncle's coffin had been too unbearably sad. I knew Uncle Porter wouldn't mind if I sought a quiet spot away from the measured thumps of damp sod.

In a moment there would be a special farewell from the bells in the tiny chapel near the cemetery. It had been an impulse on my part, arranging for the eleven bells to peal out a final farewell. Somehow it seemed fitting, since Uncle Porter had loved drama when he was alive. He had told me about the centuries-old custom among our English ancestors

—when a member of the family died, the castle bells would knell eleven times.

I was in charge of my uncle's funeral. The bells would be rung, as they had been at the castle in England.

The peals began from the little belfry, and I found myself counting silently as they rang out.

. . . three . . . four . . .

My eye caught the movement of a large bird circling overhead, dark against the breaking sunlight. I followed the graceful motion of the lone creature and thought of its wonderful freedom, alone in the sky. As the tolling continued and my eyes followed the swoops of the hawk, my brain started swirling in rhythm with both the bird and the bells.

. . . nine . . . ten . . .

Were the bells inside my head, making me feel this dizzy? The swirling sight and sound grew swifter till I wondered if I were losing consciousness. Unexpectedly, there was the new sensation of distant hoofbeats. I tried to hold onto the present, but it seemed to be slipping away from under me like one of those gravity-defying rides at an amusement park.

The hoofbeats were real, no longer pounding just inside my head, and coming closer. Before I entered a strange new world, I thought my last conscious thought: *How odd! Uncle Porter hasn't kept horses since Cass and I were little.*

Surely and steadily the sound of galloping horses moved away. I let out my breath and reached for the whistle made of a crane's larynx. Once I caught my breath, I would call my falcon down from the sky. It could be that the king was visiting and hunting his private chase next to that owned by the lord of the castle. It was said Henry was courting the Bullen girl and liked to hunt when he stayed overnight.

I looked up through the trees anxiously. I'd get in terrible trouble if my falcon were sighted. Even though Lord Linwood liked his villagers to have meat on their tables and allowed small prey to be hunted on his chase, it wouldn't do for me to be caught at my secret hunt. Gerfalcons were reserved for hierarchy, not girls of the working populace.

"Oh, come on, Penfeather, I know you heard my whistle, you stubborn creature. Get back here right now; the animals are all scared off anyway, silly girl." I blew again, praying anyone hearing would take the ridiculous sound for a real crane. "Come down, I say!"

The sun was boiling. I wiped my heavy hair back from my forehead and yanked out my neckcloth to dampen it from the nearby river. "Damnable silly clothes! If I could hunt in my breeches like I want, people would forget I'm a girl and no good for anything but kitchen work." The rippling water cleared to show my image, and I knelt to get a better look. The wide streak of silver at my hairline made me stick out my tongue at the reflection. How I hated it, though my grandmother said it was a sign from the heavens that I was born with special ways.

The soft roundness swelling above my bodice seemed to about to burst. There was a blue spot from where one of the young upstarts in the village had grabbed me. As I squeezed cooling drops of water onto the tender bruise, I couldn't help smugly recollecting that the blow to my assailant was much worse.

"Blast Roark anyway! He's the one going about the village making sly remarks to his friends' sons about my being ripe for the plucking." Roark Scotney was my father, but I had little reason to feel filial respect for him. In fact, I despised him for his insinuating crudeness regarding me.

The whirring of wings made me forget my resentment. I hurriedly filled my mouth with water and received my falcon on my wrist. Penfeather nervously bit at her jesses but quieted when I sprayed her gently with the river water. I hooded her, cooing all the while, "There, there, my sweet. You're a wonderful bird, a beauty in the air. We'll kill us a crane next time, love. Don't worry."

"I don't think I've ever seen anything quite like it—a beautiful wood nymph putting the king's falconers to shame!"

I whirled around, and Penfeather tensed on my wrist as an involuntary gasp escaped from me at the sound of the mocking words. The man who stood there watching me was like someone out of a fantastic tale. At first the details of the foppish costume escaped me; I was too busy staring at the feathery bird mask which gave its wearer a frighteningly sinister appearance, like that of a half-human hawk.

Finally, I recaptured my power of speech. "What . . . who are you?"

The laugh was low and definitely human. "Don't tell me a pretty little thing like you has never been asked to one of the castle's famous masked revels. The silly little peacock I was chasing escaped me and what do I find instead? A beautiful falconess!"

I stiffened at the hidden mockery and drew myself up, my hand calmly stroking Penfeather back into stillness. As my falcon's bells jingled restlessly, I spoke very softly, hiding my agitation at being caught in a place I had no right to be. "The sport does not belong to our king alone—nor to men. Have you never seen a girl hunting in the forest before?"

Though edged with mocking laughter, his words were solemn. "Never. And certainly not with a falcon. You must admit it's a bit unsual. By God, you're lucky it was I and not Henry who came up on you like this. He's rather proud of his mews and wouldn't like to know of a provincial rival, much less one who was trained by a girl. How did you get such a fine bird, a girl like you?"

I blushed at the insulting inference, knowing he was aware by my shabby dress that I was from a lowly family who certainly couldn't afford to buy a hunting hawk. "I didn't steal her, if that's what you mean." Carefully, so the man wouldn't see my trembling hands, I put Penfeather in her cage with its dark covering and pushed the latch. "She was put out by someone from the King's party a year ago, all crippled in one wing."

"And you nursed her back to health, pretty girl?"

The derision in his voice was hateful. I stood up and looked at him defiantly. "With the help of Nana, my grandmum. She knows a bit about healing herbs and mending broken bones, even in creatures like this one."

"Oh, ho." I saw then that he knew the family connection and I regretted my indiscretion. There was talk about Nana's healing talent, most of it from the village midwife and her daughter Meuriel—the former jealous of Nana's powers and the latter of my own beauty. "Then you're Crislyn, the miller's daughter." Mockery gave way to curiosity. "By heaven, I see now what I've heard is true about the young bucks poking through their beds at night for thinking about the miller's daughter who's returned." I lifted my chin high, not letting him see how it shamed me to be scorned by the town's mothers and daughters at the same time I was lusted after by its fathers and sons. "But it's not true about you being so pretty."

Before realizing I'd fallen into his trap, I spat at him. "Oh, it isn't, is it?" Except for the hated white streak in my hair, I was somewhat vain about my looks.

"No." He came closer and smiled at me. I could not see his eyes behind the half-mask for the sun that was beaming into my own eyes. But incongruously I found myself thinking how white his teeth were. "No, you're not pretty. You're beautiful. And do you know what makes you beautiful, Crislyn? The way you hold yourself. You're like a queen, with no man her master." He bowed deeply and asked sarcastically, "Are you certain you are not the off-shoot from some royal play-prince? The mill is no fit reign for such as you."

I hated being made fun of and matched his sarcasm with my own. "And where do you come from, with your fancy clothes and perfumed beard, hiding behind that silly mask? Is that how men from the London courts dress to go hunting in our provinces?" My contempt for the idle classes represented by this man and his host could not be contained. Lord Linfield was rumored to hate solitude and country entertainment and was known to be fond of importing companions from London—soppy young men and simpering young women from what I'd heard. I looked my tormentor up and down, not hiding my disdain. Even without the ludicrous hawk's mask that topped them, the clothes were ridiculous. On a less muscular, shorter man they would be laughable. I'd heard how our monarch had influenced the styles since he was so proud of his own physical breadth, but how could a man dress in the slashed doublet and ruffled undershirt without blushing? Or pull on an embroidered overjerkin with sleeves puffed like a toad's throat and feel well-dressed? At least, I said to myself after my scathing appraisal of my unwanted company, he doesn't pad his breeches or wear those ridiculous shoes shaped like shovels.

I shrugged and told him airily, "Never mind, I'm really not interested in who you might be or where you come from." I turned my back on him, preparing to leave with my huntress. I could feel the man close behind me, and I tried not to breathe, suddenly and uneasily aware I had, as usual, gone too far in my rudeness.

"Are you a witch, too, Crislyn, like they say your grandmother is?" The soft question sent a chill down my spine. If such talk started about us again, here in my father's village . . .

"Like her, I do what I can for the sick. But what you might call witching, I call human kindness."

"Whatever you call it, your spell is on me and I yield to it. Stay a while, lovely witch, and let me feast my eyes on you. Turn and look at me, Crislyn. I've never met any woman like you."

I whirled around and gave him the grim smile I'd often practiced on taunting village youngsters, at the same time puffing out my cheeks, crossing my eyes and making gurgling sounds. "There," I told him. "Does that convince you that it's best to leave me alone before I turn you into a braying jackass?"

He threw back his head and laughed heartily. "By heaven, you're not a witch, after all." He stopped laughing and said softly, "You're an enchantress and a female devil. Could I have just one kiss from those bewitching lips?"

I tossed my head and said haughtily, "How stupid that would be of me, to kiss a man whose face I cannot see. Besides, I kiss no one except those I choose myself."

I could sense his growing anger. Perhaps Roark was right for once: my years away from obedient habits to higher classes had sharpened my pride and tongue to equally sharp edges. Though the miller, by early Kent tradition, was not bound to villein's boon to his lordship, insulting his guest (or whoever this man was) certainly would not do us any good.

"You refuse me a simple kiss? Do you really think I'm a besotted village boy begging you for favors? I'm not used to being turned away from what I want, Crislyn."

I decided it was time for distraction of a different sort. "Shh, I hear the baying of the hounds. The hunters might ride up on us at any moment."

He laughed at me. "Our games of hide and seek started atop the castle allure along the north parapet. From up there I saw the king's party headed in a direction opposite from the one I took and also spotted your fine bird in the sky. Think of another lie."

."Why would you be intrigued by my falcon?"

"Curiosity. Simple curiosity about who would dare hunt at the same hour on the chase next to the king's. Henry is jealous when it comes to his private sports." His face changed suddenly and he wrinkled his nose. "My God, what is that awful smell?" He saw my hand go to the sack at my waist and he laughed. "Is that how you keep men at their distance? Well, my sweet, if that lure gets any warmer and smellier, we *will* have the king's hounds down on us."

I'd forgotten about the rabbit pelt stuffed with meat that I'd brought in case my falcon forgot her training and needed luring. "You wear your scent to attract those silly castle women; I wear mine to my own purposes." I turned to leave, but he caught me lightly by the arm.

"Don't go, beautiful Crislyn," he whispered. "You're not my falcon. Her I trust to return to me, no matter how much she wants to fly away forever. But you, I feel, would never come back to me, no matter what the lure."

I didn't struggle but looked down at his hand on my arm in a way that told him it was not welcome and never would be. "I may be one of your precious friend Linwood's tenants, but that doesn't mean his guests can make free with me."

The man's hand slid reluctantly away. "There's a rule about the castle chase here, but perhaps you don't know it. It says that any creature except the deer that's run to ground within the bounds belongs to the hunter."

"I'm not a creature to be hunted," I said tartly. "And I suspect you're not much of a hunter, when it comes down to it."

He laughed but without much humor. "Delicious, sharp Crislyn—like a pudding tart, all crusty and tempting outside and so sweet and tangy inside."

"How would you know?" I asked sweetly, my confidence back now that I perceived this London fop to be no real threat to me. "You don't know me or what I'm like inside."

"I know that it's incredible that a nasty lout like Roark Scotney could father a girl like you. It's like seeing a rose—with thorns, admittedly—sprout from a bog."

I looked at him, startled. How would one of Lord Linwood's friends know my father? The fact is that I shared his low opinion of Roark. How many times had I asked myself, since coming to live in the cottage by the mill, why I'd been cursed with an ale-rotted, mean-minded lump for a father! I'd lived away from him since infancy, so it wasn't strange that I felt no love for him. But it was strange that my mother, whom Nana had described as a beautiful noble-woman, would have married a dull-witted miller.

Nana had always side-stepped my questions when we lived away in the Cotswold (before our little cottage burned, throwing us back on Roark's mercy). She said only that the miller had hardened toward me because my birth caused my mother's death. He was strong and handsome once, she told me, and kind to take us both in when we had no place to go.

My unwanted companion was saying something that brought me back sharply. "I'm surprised, after seeing you, that some jealous woman hasn't given your name to the royal witch-hunters. Or your grandmother's."

The veiled threat was made lightly, but it evoked real fear in me. God knows how many innocent women had died horribly because someone's cow had dried up in their vicinity. And I knew my grandmum's ability to heal was as real as her power to read a sheep's entrails after the slaughter.

I knew, too, that I had a special way with wild creatures that some would find strange indeed. That was why my granny and I kept up the farce, even with Roark, of my using traps to hunt, though I had no need of them. "Why would anyone listen to a word from you?" I blustered, not wanting him to see my fear. "And how do you know so much about all of us? About the miller, my grandmum and me? I've never seen you in the village."

"You might say I'm Linwood's closest confidante. He often tells stories of the villagers when he's in his cups, and I've heard most of them since I'm frequently at the castle. I tamed the wildest falcon in Linwood's mews, which endeared me to him for life."

"My Penfeather could pluck your falcon midflight and never lose a feather. Don't boast about the Linwood mews; they're ill-kept and full of chickens."

His eyes, never wavering from my face, grew speculative. "I'm not the one doing the boasting. Would you care to back up your claim?"

I frowned, uneasiness returning at the thought that I may have misjudged this man. "Penfeather's tired. It wouldn't be fair."

"I didn't mean right now. Tomorrow. At this very place." He wrinkled his nose at the drifting smell of ripening meat from my pouch. "And leave your lure at home, if you will. No tricks and props—just your falcon against Linwood's finest." He added softly, "That is, if you're not afraid you'll lose."

"I'm not afraid of that, but you must be right out of Bedlam to think I'd agree to such a ridiculous contest. What possible gain would winning bring me except to call me to Lord Linwood's attention—probably unfavorably." I had never laid eyes on the master of the castle but had heard enough stories about his excesses to dampen any curiosity I might have had.

"Gain?" The man's lip curled. "I was getting to the wager, but first it's best you remember that I'm close to Linwood's ear. Agree to the contest between our falcons and I might be persuaded to keep silent about a rumor in the castle that concerns your grandmother."

I stared at him. "Rumor?"

"Last Old Hallows, someone gave certain mysterious potions to one of the kitchen maids. I believe the girl died shortly afterwards."

I was aghast. "The girl was half-dead when she came to Nana. All my grandmum did was mix some soothing herbs to make the pain easier."

"Nonetheless, there was some talk about it. A word to the constable and your grandmother might be called upon to make certain explanations."

This was no London fop. This man was my deadly enemy, and the unwilling attraction I felt for him must be thoroughly quelled. Though my heart thudded painfully in my chest, I reminded myself that the contest could only have one ending. Penfeather could fly rings around any falcon in the Linwood mews and I knew it. And my beloved Nana's safety was at stake. The man's threat was no idle one; I knew that with cold certainty. "You spoke of a wager. A wager has two parts."

"The wager is simply this: if my bird dies or runs, I lose and you'll never have to be concerned about your grandmother coming up before the authorities; if your bird dies or runs, I win."

There was a rustle inside Penfeather's cage as if she understood and was eager to start. It restored my cockiness. "Win what? My worldly possessions?" I laughed. "You see before you everything I own except my deerskins and awl."

His words were like a cold wind, cutting through my levity. "I win you, how and where I choose. A proper bedding, one without biting and scratching."

I stared at him, feeling stupid for not knowing all along what he wanted. "You're crazy," I whispered. "I could never agree to that."

He looked at me, then picked up a loose feather that was the same color as Penfeather. As I stood there, still stupefied, he blew it up in the air. We both watched it make its slow spiraling descent to the ground. The man said softly, looking from the still feather back to my face, "I think you can. Otherwise, tonight when King Hal asks Linwood for his favorite pasties, I'll be forced to bring up the fact that the pastie cook isn't around to pamper his majesty's splendid palate any longer. The story of why she's no longer with us will make interesting supper conversation."

"Damn you to the devil," I said softly. "It will be a pleasure seeing my Penfeather tear your bird to bits. I only wish she were trained to attack people instead of creatures!"

My tormentor smiled. "I'm grateful her mistress has concentrated her training on attacking the helpless. Otherwise, disaster would result. As it is, I admire your confidence but look forward to my post-victory which shall be celebrated in Linwood's cozy little stonecutter's house. Its privacy should prove suitable for our becoming . . . properly acquainted." He bowed, his eyes never leaving mine. "So, my lady, shall I be seeing you here tomorrow?"

"Damn you to the devil," I hissed at him. "I'll be here, but on one condition." My voice sounded as though it were fading in and out. The hawk face in front of me was wavy and seemed to be circling me. I struggled for my words. "You will wear your mask tomorrow, as I despise you and have no wish to ever see your face. And if by some freak of fate I lose to you, our . . . our liaison in the stone cottage will be in utter blackness—like that of your heart." There was a confused ringing in my ears that was making me dizzy. Leaving my challenger staring after me, I picked up the falcon's cage and ran through the forest, toward the voice I heard calling inside my head. How strange, I thought amidst the whirling dizziness of my flight, why should I feel the need to answer to the name *Alix*?

2

What had happened to me?

Dazed from the strange trance, I was aware of my black dress clinging to me damply. How could a daydream seem so real? And how long had I been in my startlingly real world of fantasy?

The answer to the last was evident. Though it had seemed I was fully living the girl Crislyn's life moment by moment, I had only been "away" for a minute or two. The people at my uncle's grave were only now dispersing.

Many of the mourners looked over at me as if hesitant to intrude, and I was glad when they decided to allow me my solitude since I was still shaken by what had happened to me.

Then I again heard the voice that had recalled me from the strange dream. That part, at least, had really happened.

"Alix! My God, it really is you. They said you'd left before the service was over and then I saw you standing over here by yourself."

He stopped, surely because of the look of astonishment—and then anger—on my face. I thought my mind must be playing more tricks. Phillip Coleman wouldn't have the nerve to come here today. It was a cruel joke of some kind. I'd prayed Cassandra would come. How could she not, loving Uncle Porter as I was sure he still did in spite of Phillip? How could she stay away, turning her back on the golden summers spent here basking in the warmth of Alabama's sun and the devotion of Uncle Porter and Aunt May? Those summers had meant as much to her as they did to me.

How could she have let Phillip come in her stead? It was a slap in the face to me and insulting to Uncle Porter's memory.

My hands clenched at my side, I glared at the man I'd hated steadily for a dozen years. The banked fires of hate leapt into flames at seeing him again after all this time. My feelings had not changed.

Neither had Phillip, I observed. Oh, there had been no greying temples when I saw him and less thickness to the wide shoulders.

And there hadn't been such visible signs of a rich life, I thought with contempt. Cassandra's money had paid for the luxurious suit, the Gucci shoes, the expensive tan.

"How *dare* you come here! How *dare* you, Phillip Coleman!"

"Alix, please, keep your voice down; people are staring." He held his hand out to me. "For their sake, at least, accept my sympathy."

I ignored the outstretched hand. "And let those people think you possess a heart? Or that you're here because of noble reasons?" I asked bluntly, "Why *are* you here? Because you want to contest Uncle Porter's will? I begged him not to leave Cass out, but he insisted that I inherit all he had. Which," I added, "is peanuts compared to your wife's fortune."

"Alix, for God's sake . . ."

"Where is she, by the way? Why didn't Cassandra come? Even if she and I haven't spoken all these years, she owed Uncle Porter the decency of attending his funeral. He still loved her, you know, right up until he died, and

24

worried about hurting her feelings with the will."

"Alix, Cass doesn't give a damn about your uncle's estate. My God, we've . . . .she's got four of her own scattered all over the world. And I certainly didn't come here to raise a stink about you being the sole beneficiary. As a matter of fact, I think it's wonderful. Even though," he smiled the old Professor Coleman boyish smile that charmed many a freshman in his classes at Harris College, "I understand you're doing quite well on your own."

"You haven't answered my question. Why didn't Cass come today?" This was my cousin's husband, not the shabby, handsome English teacher who'd given Wordsworth and Keats the appeal of popular rock stars. This was a man who'd heartlessly exploited a sensitive young girl. No—two! His presence today had to have a cold-blooded reason. Phillip Coleman never did anything without a selfish motive. I'd do well to stay on my guard.

"Believe me, Alix, Cass would have been here if possible. She never stopped loving your uncle for a moment. Nor you, either," he added softly.

I didn't want to hear that from him, even if it were true—not in this place where two small girls had played and fought and loved each other more like sisters than cousins. I dabbed at the fresh tears on my cheeks, not caring that my face was probably a mess. Anyway, Phillip Coleman no longer had any right to expect me to be beautiful for him. "Then why the hell isn't she here?" I asked him, feeling the disappointment keener than ever. I had counted on Cassandra coming; I'd even pictured the two of us falling into each other's arms and ending our long estrangement with tears and laughter. I'd pictured sharing our grief over Uncle Porter and tried to imagine the look on her face when I told her this place would be hers as much as mine, in spite of the one-sided will.

But my cousin had stayed away. Apparently she couldn't bear to see me again, even if she had to miss our uncle's funeral. I cried out to Phillip. "It's because of you, damn you! The Cass I knew and loved, before you got hold of her, would have gotten here through hell and high water. Nothing would have kept her away from the man who was kinder and dearer to her than her own father."

"Alix, you weren't listening. I've been trying to tell you that Cass is in England. There's no way she could have gotten back here in time, even if the wire I sent ever reached her."

"England! Cassandra is in *England*?"

Phillip nodded. "And thanks to the Gatwick airport strike, she couldn't get a flight back here." He looked at me anxiously. "Alix, what's wrong? I'm sure you'd have heard from her by now if she knew about your uncle."

"It's not that, Phillip. It's just that I'm surprised." At his words, something had turned over inside me. Cass and I had promised each other that someday we'd go to England together and that one wouldn't go without the other. Together we would find the castle in Kent where our roots had begun. From our distant relatives, the Linwoods, we would hear the stories about Bloodstones' murders and witches and ghosts and lost treasures. The stories at Uncle Porter's knee had been wonderful but only had whetted our girlish appetites for more.

Another childhood promise broken, another dream shattered, another betrayal. Cassandra had gone to England without me. The cold knife in my heart gave another turn.

"I'm surprised you didn't go along. I've heard you travel a lot, with and without Cass. There was something in the Alumni Quarterly about the book you've been researching in Oxford."

Something stirred in his eyes, an odd intentness. "I'm surprised—and pleased—you've kept up with me that well."

I examined a wet leaf clinging to the toe of my black pump as if it were more important than the man I was talking to. "Oh, I suppose you could call it a kind of cold war reconnaissance of an old enemy. I didn't like to think I might run into you unexpectedly, like today. I travel a good bit myself."

"That's pretty hard to take, your saying you think of me

as your enemy," he said.

"A few things went down pretty hard with me, too, Phillip."

He wiped his brow with a handkerchief bearing a famous designer's initials. Incredible, I thought. "Damn, it's hot here. Couldn't we go inside and talk? Maybe have a drink together?"

"I don't think Uncle Porter would care for the idea of your being in his house. And I know I don't."

He looked at me. "Boy, since you've gotten to be rich and famous, you certainly do speak your mind, Alix."

"I'm not rich and famous; I'm a novelist whose books happen to appeal to a lot of women and sell fairly well."

"Writing romantic novels wasn't what I would have chosen for my top English student."

I said coolly, "Don't pull any academic snobbery on me, Phillip. I'm very proud of the modest success I've enjoyed at something I like to do and am good at doing."

"Heaven forbid you should think I'm putting you or your novels down. As a matter of fact, your books have a lot to do with my being here."

"I was wondering when you'd get around to explaining why you came."

He smiled. "You just won't buy my coming as a civilized gesture of respect?"

"No, I won't. You mentioned my books . . ."

"Oh, yes. Cass left in such a hurry she forgot to mail a package to you. She said it was all of your books that she wanted you to autograph for her." He grinned. "If you're thinking that it's a farfetched excuse to see you, my bringing them from Nashville personally, you're right."

The ice was melting and I wanted to cry, but this time because I saw some hope of a reconciliation with my cousin. If Cass had read my books, if she were breaking the long silence between us in a way that would make it easy for both of us to say that all is forgiven . . . I looked up to see that the clouds were almost all gone and suddenly felt happy. "You're right, Phillip, it is scorching out here. I'll go up and have the housekeeper make some lemonade. There'll be people stopping in this afternoon, but there should be a few moments before that for you to cool off before the drive back." I started off toward the house, calling over my shoulder, "That's your Mercedes parked out front, isn't it? You get the package while I—"

"I'm sorry, Alix, but I got a room at the hotel last night. Sorry to say, your package is back there and not with me."

I turned to face him, suddenly suspicious. "Tell me the truth, Phillip. Is there really a package from Cass, or is this one of your tricks?"

He managed to sound indignant. "Of course not. Alix, I realize you have good reason not to trust me. But it's ridiculous to imply I manufactured all of this just to get a chance to talk to you. What kind of a man do you think I am?"

I looked at him with a slight smile. "Are you sure you want me to answer that, Phillip?" I didn't give him a chance to answer. "Because it gives me great pleasure to do so." I took a deep breath. "I think you're a man who could seduce in cold blood a vulnerable young student whom you mistakenly thought to be the heiress of Manning Steel Enterprises. I think you're a man who, when your first target turned out to be penniless and possibly a bit smarter than you thought, went after the cousin who was the true heiress."

His face was losing its tan, but I went on relentlessly, all the bottled hate pouring out at last. "How much of what I told you about my cousin, Phillip, when we were lovers and I filled your ears with story after story of two lonely little girls, did you use to win Cass? She was smart, too. The fortune hunters had been after her for years, but you knew the soft spots and had an inside track. You even knew where to start with her—with horses, her deepest passion."

Phillip paled. "That was honest, Alix, and you know it. I've always loved horses. My God, woman, stop it!"

"No, I've started this and I'll finish it. You got through to Cass when all the others didn't because you knew what

I'd already told you about her. You knew how her parents left her out of their lives because she wasn't beautiful and glamorous like they were. It was easy for a smooth operator like you, wasn't it, Phillip? After all, you'd been picking my brains about Cass for weeks once you found out about her money. And once you had all you needed from me . . .''
I took a deep breath. "I think we both know what kind of man you are, Phillip.''

He was angry but trying not to show it. "Now that you've got that out of your system, let's get back to the present question. When can I see you?''

"Never" was on the tip of my tongue, but I wanted to see Cass again. Phillip could keep us apart as he had before. "You can come by around four. Most of the visitors should be gone by then. Of course, Mrs. Goody will be here till five.''

"That old biddy of a housekeeper? Is she still around?''

I said coldly, "I don't know what I would have done the past few days without 'that old biddy.' Four, then?'' "And, Phillip . . .'' I said quietly, ". . . . don't forget to bring that package. Without it, you won't set one foot inside that house.''

I didn't wait to hear his answer and didn't even look around when I heard the powerful engine of the Mercedes start up.

It had been, all in all, an incredible day. Not to mention the simple grief of burying a loved one, the string of unusual occurrences was baffling—the bells, the hawk, the paralyzing realness of my hallucination.

As if those things weren't bizarre enough, here was Phillip Coleman popping back into my life after all this time. And then to learn my cousin had gone to Kent alone, breaking our solemn promise to each other . . .

I looked down at the tiny white scar where the two of us had pressed our wrists together, after drawing blood.

We'll go to that castle together, so we won't get scared.
Promise! Cross my heart and hope to die.
Promise! Cross my heart and hope to die.

I stared past the gracious veranda wrapping around the old house, knowing with certainty that whatever had taken Cassandra to Kent had to be of the utmost importance.

As Mrs. Goody welcomed me, beaming as always even in times of sadness, I had another sudden thought.

What if somehow all of today's odd events were connected?

"Miss Alix, are you sure I can't get you something? A drop of sherry, maybe? You look all tuckered out."

I smiled at her, for the hundredth time noting that she looked like the Pillsbury doughboy in gingham. "That would be lovely. I'll have it in my room."

She looked at me a little anxiously. "Are you sure you'll be all right? I feel terrible about leaving early and all, but there's enough food stacked up from all our visitors to feed an army."

So I would not have my comfortable chaperone while Phillip was here, after all. Maybe it was better this way. I wasn't afraid of Phillip Coleman or of being alone with him. It would bring me great satisfaction to be totally impervious to the man I'd once loved.

"Wonderful! And please set out an extra place, Mrs. Goody—the old Royal Doulton and the heirloom crystal, come to think of it. Never mind about the sherry; I'm fine now."

She knew me well. "Just who's this visitor that gets cold chicken on your aunt's best china? What're you up to, Miss Alix?"

I laughed. "The guest, dear Goody, is a man who coveted this place and all the gracious living it stands for from the moment he set eyes on it—twelve and a half years ago."

The housekeeper's chin dropped and then the blue eyes kindled. "You mean that . . . that scalawag husband of Miss Cassie's is coming here, after your uncle told him never to darken the door again?"

"Yes," I told her softly, "and I'd appreciate it if you didn't poison the potato salad. Goody, he's up to something,

I just know it, and I've got to find out what it is."

Her face brightened. "I'll get out the good wine, too, and the best linen and . . ." She stopped and looked back at me. "You're a beautiful woman, Miss Alix. Why, folks around here can't believe you never got married. If that man's after something, it might not be this place; it might just be you."

I honestly hadn't thought of that. "You forget that Oakhaven and I are a package deal now, but Phillip wouldn't stand a chance, even if there weren't Cassandra in the picture."

"Well, anyways, you be careful."

I would indeed.

After the last gentle good-byes were made to visitors paying their respects, I went up to bathe and change for my meeting with Phillip. He'd called to say he'd be late, so I had a leisurely hour ahead of me. I bathed and dressed in a simple voile sundress that was neither seductive nor unflattering. Brushing out the loose chignon I affected on formal occasions like today's, my eyes went to the unusual streak of silver that sprang from my forehead. The girl Crislyn had had the same hair.

I resumed brushing, still pondering that hallucinatory daydream at the cemetery.

Phillip would be here at any moment. I looked at myself as I brushed out my hair, down loose on my shoulders. Not one to change hair styles with the fads, it dawned on me I'd been wearing my hair like this when Professor Phillip Coleman first showed an interest, one that was far from academic, in the young Alixandra Manning, who was one of his college students. . . .

"Miss Manning, wait up a minute!"

I felt my heart beat faster as I stopped on the colonnade path leading to Biology lab. "Professor Coleman, what are you doing here? I thought you had another class."

He smiled at me and ran his hand through his tousled hair, adding to his boyishness. "I do, but they're working on an assignment. I caught sight of you out the window, rushing by as usual, and decided it was time we had a little talk.''

I clutched my books tighter. He was my advisor but I'd been avoiding the necessary conference for reasons I wasn't sure of. ''Now? I have a lab.'' I made a face. ''Some poor pickled frog cadaver is lying in wait for me.''

He laughed. ''I'll let you get to him if you'll promise to stop by to see me this evening.''

''This evening? I've got phone desk in my dorm, but I could stop by your office on my way from—''

''I thought it might be better if you came to my house.'' He didn't seem to notice that I was open-mouthed with surprise.

''Professor Coleman, I couldn't do that. Your cottage is off-campus and first-quarter freshmen aren't allowed to . . .''

He picked up the book that had fallen from my arms and replaced it. The light grazing of my breast as he did so might have been accidental. ''That's all taken care of. I've spoken to the resident dean in your dorm, and your phone duty has been assigned to another girl. You don't even have to sign out, since this is a special situation.''

''Professor Coleman, I don't know what you're talking about. What 'special situation'?''

''You're staying in my aunt's house next door to mine on Friday nights, starting this evening. The regular nurse is off, so we need someone to stay in the house.'' He looked at me with dancing eyes. ''Don't look so worried. Aunt Dora sleeps like a rock, but she just likes the idea of someone being around. It was her idea for me to arrange for someone from one of my classes. I thought of you at once.''

''Why me?'' I asked. ''And why couldn't you stay with her that one night a week?''

He shrugged. ''She likes the idea of another female, and I thought of you because you're mature. Also, you wrote in your application bio that you assisted your uncle part-time in his medical practice. Besides . . .'' The eyes held mine, challenging me to deny the mutual physical awareness that had crackled between us from the first day. ". . . I want to know you better, Alixandra Manning. I look at you sometimes in class and see a beautiful, mysterious goddess in the middle of a sea of nymphets, and I sense you're someone extraordinary."

He was mesmerizing me. I pulled myself sharply up and blurted, "You never even asked me what I wanted." I added more calmly, "I realize Mrs. Coates is generous to the school and has a lot of influence, but you should have asked me about this before you talked to the Dean."

"She thinks I did and that you said 'yes.' I didn't want you to have a chance to say no, Alix. Forgive me?"

"I'll think about it," I answered.

"But you'll come this evening. Promise me."

"I'll try."

"Promise me, Alix!"

"All right—I promise!"

It wasn't until many months later that I was to learn that Phillip's desperate maneuverings had to do with a deeper passion than attraction to a young student. He'd come to live near his aunt to charm her into leaving her estate to him. I suppose he found her will and learned that the school, not Phillip Coleman, was to be her sole beneficiary. No doubt that's when he remembered that one of his students came out of the wealthy Manning Steel family. He had to move fast, since after less than a quarter term, I already was getting heady rushes from men at the nearby colleges.

Phillip knew it was only a matter of time before I exchanged my schoolgirl crush on a handsome professor for an ardent tumble with some persistent football hero in the backseat of his convertible.

His seduction of me, therefore, was swift, relentless and thorough.

That first evening when I showed up at his cottage, he was polite and reserved, escorting me over to his aunt's bedroom in the big house with proper gentlemanliness. He explained to his sweetly drowsy aunt that Miss Manning would be next door giving student assistance for a short time and to sound the buzzer connected to the cottage if she were needed.

Aunt Dora hardly knew when we left. From the hefty snores, I was sure she didn't care, though I protested about leaving her alone.

"Don't worry. I only wanted to let you hear a couple of my Eliot recordings, and the sound might disturb her."

So there we were, back in his shabbily cozy cottage. I became too interested in the vintage recitation of "Ash Wednesday" to notice that the wine glass put quietly in front of me was emptied and refilled several times.

"More?" He held up the decanter as he replaced the concluded Eliot reading with a stack of Mantovanni records.

I shook my head. "Let's discuss my project for the Pitts Award." I heard the slurring in my voice with mild shock. "On second thought, maybe I'd better leave now and go check on Aunt Dora."

"She has her buzzer, remember." He went over to the fire and put on another log. "You could be at her side in two minutes, if anything happened." He came over and sat on the rug at my feet. "You look so stiff, sitting there like a scared little girl. Come down here beside me and let's look for snapdragons in the fire." With his help, I slid down off the sofa, knowing as I did that there would be no turning back from the inevitable.

"You realize, don't you," I asked him as I watched the hypnotizing flames and felt a mixture of fear and excitement at the nearness of him, "we'd both be kicked out of school if anyone found out I was here with you like this."

He set his wine glass down and turned to me, whispering, "I won't tell anyone, if you won't." His hand lightly stroked my chin. Then unexpectedly, his other hand tangled in my hair from behind, and my head was pulled down to rest on the sofa's edge. The handsome face came over mine, so close I felt we were breathing the same air.

His hand tightened on my chin, parting my lips, and his whisper was warm on my mouth. "Such a beautiful mouth. It was the first thing I craved about you, that strong, sensual softness."

The kiss that followed left no doubt about Phillip's expertise at lovemaking. His mouth was demanding but unhurried, and there was no fumbling at my blouse or skirt zipper. Before I really knew what was happening I was aware of the fire's warmth on my bare flesh. He gave me time to catch my breath from the intensity of our kisses before concentrating on my breasts with leisurely ardor. "My God, you're beautiful," he murmured, each hand circling a breast before he kissed slowly and lingeringly the tip of one and then the other.

In a voice that sounded very far away, I said, "My cousin said I was too full-bosomed to be truly aristocratic."

"Your cousin can go to hell," he whispered and once again possessed my mouth. I could feel my nipples swell against his warm palms as he gently massaged them in concert with the deeply thrusting tongue that was boldly imitating the more intimate penetration to come.

The ache in the lower part of me was unfamiliar. I'd never felt like this before. Oh, I'd experienced the usual little puberty urges and had my stomach lurch in a funny way when I read spicy passages from raunchy novels, but it had never been like this.

Phillip knew exactly how I was responding to his unrelenting arousal of every part of me. He raised his head and smiled into my eyes, then gently took my hand in his. I inwardly flinched, thinking he was going to guide my hand to his male hardness, like the backseat jocks who always turned me off at that point, but Phillip's sensual creativeness was unending. Ever so gently he placed my hand on the soft heat between my own thighs, whispering, "Feel your wanting me, Alixandra. The Snow Queen is melting, as I knew she would."

I shyly pulled my hand away, leaving his there alone to make more daring exploration.

Then I was lying back on the soft rug and he was as naked as I, kneeling to trail shivery kisses up the length of my body. His lips reached mine, staying a breath away as his tongue traced the outline of my mouth. I felt the hardness between my thighs as it circled like the tongue tantalizing my mouth. The gasp as he suddenly thrust into me may have been mine, but I think it was Phillip's.

I don't think he really believed I might be a virgin.

The pain was sharp and brief, not at all what I'd always imagined. And before the first rays of dawn filtered in on us, I was arching my body against his as passionately as he moved inside me.

Whoever said that virgins can't expect fulfillment on their first night obviously didn't have a superb lover like Phillip.

I've wondered since how I managed to keep quiet about Phillip and me and those love-drugged Friday nights in his arms. I even, somehow, came up with all A's at the end of winter quarter and was said to be the favorite for the coveted Pitts Award for Excellence in English. Since Phillip was on the committee to select the winning student, it was even more vital that we keep our affair secret.

There were two things important to me at that time—loving Phillip and winning the Pitts Award. With Phillip, I could fill in some of the emotional voids of a orphaned childhood, and by winning the substantial scholarship attached to the Pitts citation, I could be independent of Uncle Porter's financial support. Though generously given, his money spent toward my education was still charity and touched a raw spot in my pride.

Since we couldn't possibly announce our engagement until long after the possibility of any bias about my being chosen for the Pitts honor, our weekly rendezvous assumed even more excitement and romance. My lover was an able instructor in the art of sensuality, introducing me to every form of sensual rapture, drawing out undreamed-of nuances of sexual passion. After one such night, I lay in his arms and murmured, "You'd be a wonderful gigolo, darling. You're a man who recognizes that every woman wants romance above all else." I pointed out the various subtleties that he unerringly provided our love scenes—candlelight, an occasional poem read together with punctuating kisses, always a flickering fire.

"By pleasing you, I please myself," he told me.

I can translate that statement more truthfully now: by giving a woman what she wanted, Phillip thought he could get what he wanted.

And what Phillip wanted was money—lots and lots of money.

The day finally came when he discovered I could not give him what he wanted. It came as a shock to him, I know now, but he restrained it beautifully.

"Why does this award mean so much to you, Alix? I've never seen anyone work so hard for a meaningless certificate with a gold seal. You sure as hell don't need the scholarship, with all your family's money."

I stared at him, then broke into peals of laughter. "What are you talking about? Of course, I want that scholarship. With that and what I can earn during the summers, I can finish up only a few hundred dollars in debt to Uncle Porter. He swears I don't have to repay him, but . . . Phillip, what on earth's the matter?"

He was staring at me with disbelief. "But you're a Manning and I assumed . . . I mean, I thought there was the steel business and that you'd . . . darling, I'm really confused." How much effort the loving smile cost him, I'll never know.

I chuckled. "Boy, you certainly are. It's my cousin Cassandra who stands to come into all that money when she's twenty-one. I thought I told you what a poor business-man my father was."

"I suppose you did," Phillip said in a choked voice, kissing my shoulder so I couldn't see his face, "but even gambling and poor investments wouldn't make a dent in all that steel money."

I touched my lips to his hand, still not aware that I had just sealed an end to our flaming romance with a chance remark. "Maybe not, but poor daddy sold his stock for practically nothing, long before the mills grew into the giant industry they are now. Cass was luckier than I; her father had a ticker-tape for a heart and hung onto everything. He even bought my father's stock—very cheaply, I seem to remember." I said this without bitterness. I knew Cassandra would give me all the money I wanted if I asked her. It was like that for both of us—an honest lack of competitiveness. *You've got the looks, Alix, and I've got the money. Together we'd make some fortune hunter a lucky fellow.*

"This cousin of yours—Cassandra, isn't it?—will get it all?"

"Every last dime," I said cheerfully.

"Isn't that a bit unfair? For her to inherit everything and you nothing? I'm not surprised you two split up when it came to college. I suppose there's a lot of bitterness."

I sat up and looked at him with astonishment. "Bitter toward Cass because she'll be rich and I won't? Phillip, that's like saying you envy your sister because she has brown eyes and you've got blue." I snuggled up to him and closed my eyes, never once sensing the tumult in his brain. "She chose another college from this because she doesn't like to study, not because the two of us might be competitive." I giggled and snuggled closer. "It's like two kids—one chose vanila, one strawberry, then we swap licks when we get together. Next to you, Cass is my best friend. We tell each other everything."

"Even about boyfriends—and lovers?" He was caressing my breast, and I admit I had more things on my mind than my cousin. "I take it, then, you've broken your promise and told her about . . . us."

I pulled away and truthfully said, "Phillip, of course not. I've never even mentioned your name."

He drew me back into his arms. "Sorry, darling, I'm just so afraid of nasty gossip getting back here and hurting you."

"And you," I murmured. "You could lose everything

you've worked so hard for."

"Yes, I certainly could," he told me, before making love to me with an intensity that made me forget Cassandra, the Pitts award, everything but Phillip and the delicious things he was doing to my body.

It was then that Phillip began his subtle campaign to find out everything he could about my cousin—her likes and dislikes, her quirks, her thought patterns, everything.

And somehow, through it all, he managed to keep me from becoming suspicious that his questions had to do with anything except a loving interest in me.

The leak about us came, I have no doubt, from Phillip himself. When the Chairman of the Pitts Committee came to me privately and said there were some unflattering rumors floating around about the lengths to which I was going to win the award, I was dumbfounded.

"Professor Coleman tells us he regrets it very much, but that he feels you should be disqualified from consideration."

"Disqualified!" I couldn't believe it.

"Alixandra, we've had a meeting with the Dean about this ... unfortunate matter. Considering Professor Coleman's reluctant evidence that you've tried to use your special privileges as his aunt's part-time companion in a way unbefitting a Harris student ..."

"We're planning to be married," I cried, still not believing that Phillip was my betrayer. "We love each other."

The pity in the Chairman's eyes was terrible to see. "It's not the first time a young woman has contrived a romantic fantasy, Alixandra, especially around an attractive faculty member like Professor Coleman."

"Ask Aunt Dora," I cried desperately. "Mrs. Coates, I mean. She'll tell you that all those Friday nights I was supposed to be with her I was actually with Phillip."

"My dear, I'm so sorry about this. Professor Coleman said you were a student inclined to dream up extraordinary fantasies, but I never realized ..."

"Ask her! Ask Aunt Dora!" I screamed at her.

"My dear, you're getting hysterical. Perhaps we ought to . . ."

"Ask her, damn you!"

The Chairman pulled my file toward her and wrote something inside, then closed it ominously, before looking at me with sympathetic but unyielding scrutiny. "We already have, Alixandra. Mrs. Coates spoke highly of you and said you were always at her side when she went to bed and there when she awakened. Your responsibility in that case makes it even more difficult for us to tell you our decision."

"Your decision? I don't even get a chance to tell my side?"

The gaze was serene and still full of pity. "I think," the Chairman said gently, "it would be better all around if you quietly transferred to another college. You're from a fine old southern family, Alixandra; I don't think you want them embarrassed anymore than we do by a scandal."

I thought of Uncle Porter and Aunt May and knew I was beaten. I would leave Harris and I'd leave quietly. Those two gentle people would never understand what had happened to me even if they believed it.

As for Cassandra, I shuddered to think of her disgust if she ever learned I had let myself be taken in by someone like Phillip. Hadn't she warned me about the men out there who were lured by the smell of the Manning Steel fortune?

That made me feel even more stupid—that there was no fortune and that I had let myself be blinded to Phillip's real motives. Never again, I vowed. In the meantime, I could never bring myself to tell Cassandra what occured.

As it happened, I never had the chance to tell Cass everything. She transferred to a school in Switzerland and we didn't even get to talk until almost a year later. By then, it was too late.

But right now, my family was not foremost in mind.

"Very well," I told the Chairman stiffly, never letting her see that my world had just fallen in bits around me. "I'll leave without making the stink I should. I'll pack my things and be out of this hypocritical place before morning. But forget about a transfer," I said coldly. "I think I'd rather take my chances with the real world than some new bunch of self-styled moral witch hunters."

She had the grace to blush. "If we can be of any assistance . . ."

"You can." I stood up. I'd learned what I needed to learn here. Trust was a four letter word, and you couldn't depend on another person for your happiness. You had to carve that out for yourself. "You can go to hell, all of you, and let Phillip Coleman lead the way."

I walked out and never set foot on the sheltered campus of Harris College again.

3

Again I was in the present, with the older and wiser Alix looking back at me from the mirror.

"You're a damned fool," I told her, "letting Phillip come here tonight. Even if you are curious to learn more about why Cass went to Kent, you're a damned fool for seeing him again."

"You're the fool," the present Alix replied. "After all, living well is the best revenge. Nothing would please you more than to have Phillip see that you're the lucky one, the one who didn't marry Phillip and is just as desirable as you were back then."

Just to show her, I yanked my hair back into its prim chignon and scrubbed off the bright lipstick.

It was almost time to go downstairs. I paused at the light switch, smiling at a picture of Cass and me together, snaggled-toothed and pigtailed, with our arms entwined.

And then my smile faded, as I remembered. How could she have fallen in love with Phillip so quickly? The horses probably had helped; they'd first met at a racetrack where Cass was entering her first thoroughbred. Phillip would have been convincing, since he sincerely did love beautiful horseflesh.

While Phillip was wooing Cass, I had found a poor-paying but satisfying job as flunky to an editor of a tough-minded regional magazine. He fathered me, pulled me through some pretty serious personal crises, and later nagged and goaded me into starting a writing career.

We both realized before long that feature and article writing wasn't for me. "You've had enough real life, dammit, Alix. Start making up one—and put it on paper."

With his help, that's exactly what I did. And fate, used to its jollies from me, decided it was time for a new twist to my life story. I sold my first novel to a publisher Max knew in New York and after that it was a whole new ballgame.

By the time I was 22 I had two promo tours under my belt, a healthy bank account, and an apartment in Westport, Connecticut.

On my 23rd birthday, I signed with a top New York literary agency and went back to my apartment to celebrate. There was a wire waiting from Cassandra that took some of the fizzle out of my champagne.

Getting married in two weeks to one of your old profs. Happier than I ever dreamed possible. Phillip sends his best.

Feeling sick inside, I noted the date on the wire. At the time I was reading it, Cass was on her second day of honey-mooning as Mrs. Phillip Coleman.

I called Uncle Porter and blurted out the whole sordid story. He convinced me I had an obligation to Cass to tell her about Phillip, even though the marriage already had taken place.

My mistake was in trying to make the story less painful for Cassandra, who was apparently even more besotted by Phillip than I'd ever been. She listened to my stumbling account of what he'd done to me and what I thought he might have done to her, then all hell broke loose over the phone.

"Phillip warned me not to tell you about our relationship. He said you might pull something like this, Alix, but I couldn't believe it. I just couldn't believe you'd carry a grudge after all this time, just because he refused to compromise his ethical standards, just because he was kind to a student with a crush on him . . ."

There was more, a lot more, and the harsh things that were said on both sides brought about the estrangement that lasted over six years. And when Uncle Porter took my testimony about Phillip's unwholesome motives as truth and Cassandra stood firmly loyal to her new husband, the family was permanently split with no hope of reconciliation.

Until tonight. With the package of books Phillip was bringing, my hopes of resuming a loving friendship with my cousin were revitalized.

I sat on the veranda, watching the fireflies put on their phychedelic show and waiting for Phillip's Mercedes. He was even later than he'd predicted, but finally there he was, looking about the gracious wicker and greenery-bedecked setting with appreciation, and then at me where I sat in the semi-darkness at the end of the veranda.

"This place is even more beautiful than ever. And so are you, Alix."

I pointed toward the wicker cart Goody had set up before she left. "Thank you. Please help yourself to a drink, Phillip. We'll have a bit to eat in a little while, but right now I'm enjoying this peace and quiet."

He brought his bourbon on ice over and sat in the Hong Kong chair opposite the glider I was using. "It *is* peaceful here. I remember that time I stopped by here at Christmas to see you, pretending I was just making a casual call on a student as I drove through to Gadsden. I fell in love with this place—or maybe with the idea of living like a gracious country squire, like your uncle."

It was probably the only honest statement he'd ever made about his secret longings. The life I'd taken for granted must have seemed tempting to an ambitious young man brought up in a mill village, who had to scratch his way up the hard way.

But I had no real sympathy for him. "So I gathered from Uncle Porter. He was pretty indignant when you tried to buy this place from him when you and Cass stopped by on your honeymoon." I didn't add that Uncle Porter's anger had come partly from the fact that Phillip had made it clear that his new wife's wealth could get him anything he wanted.

Phillip got another drink. "I'm sorry about that. I just thought with the two of them getting old and this place being so big . . ."

"Never mind that. Cass should have known better even if you didn't." I stood up. "Do you mind bringing that in with you? I don't know about you, but I haven't eaten all day. And I've had a pretty full day."

Phillip followed me into the house, putting the brown paper-wrapped parcel under his arm on the table in the foyer. "The books Cass sent you. You see, I really did have a legitimate errand coming here."

I led the way into the dining room, noting Goody had set a table that befitted royalty. "So you did." I handed him a plate. "You won't mind serving yourself?" As we sat down to the opulent table adorned with generations-old china, crystal and silver, I said solemnly, "If I'd known there would be a guest for dinner, I'd have made Goody trot out all the good stuff."

I readily admit it—I can be petty about taking my revenge.

Phillip was making free with the wine and getting very, very drunk, and I decided it was time to question him about Cass and her unexpected trip to England.

"You said she's never missed one of your horse shows before, Phillip. This Dark Satin you mentioned, that you say is one of her pets . . . if he's so sure of getting a ribbon at Celebration, why would Cass leave right now?"

"Dark Satin Two. The first one died." Phillip stared down into his wine. "Damned if I can understand it, either. Cass has been working on the family gene . . . geneology for years. Maybe you didn't know about it."

"It doesn't surprise me. Both of us loved hearing all the old ancestral yarns, and Cass always had a passion for organizing things."

"Well, she got pretty excited about it when she heard from some old woman in Kent."

"There was some crazy story about a lost jewel," I mused.

Phillip reached for his napkin which had fallen to the floor and his voice was muffled. "You really believe that stuff, about the 'Devil's Eye' ruby? I kidded Cassandra about it, telling her old Porter was pulling her leg and yours, probably."

"I don't think so. He thought we were too imaginative already. I don't think he would have made it up."

"Then why the hell would he fill your ears with all those crazy stories?"

"Maybe because he knew I never felt I belonged anywhere, and that Cass didn't, either. Maybe because he was a kind and sensitive man he thought it might help us to know we had a solid past, rooted in history."

"Maybe. Anyway, that stuff got to be more important to my wife than anything in the present, which doesn't make a helluva lot of sense to me."

I raised my eyebrows. "You don't share Cass' passion for the family history?"

Phillip's face took on a cautious look. "Uh-uh. Now you're trying to pump me about my relationship with your cousin, aren't you? Let's put it this way. Cass is crazy about horses and so am I. It's a very deep bond between us, Alix, very deep."

I couldn't hold back and said, "I thought it was her money that was the deepest bond between you, Phillip."

He colored. "There you go, digging into me about that. Go ahead, Alix. Go ahead and stick the knife in. I know I deserve it."

I smiled without meaning it and refilled my own wine glass, ignoring his. "At least you admit that . . . now. Too bad some of that honesty didn't show up a long time ago when it might have done me more good."

He made a hopeless gesture. "I'm . . . sorry, Alix. What more can I say?"

"Nothing. Except possibly 'good-night.' I'm very tired, Phillip. I realize you didn't care anything about my uncle or his dying, but the strain has begun to get to me." The strain of talking to Phillip was beginning to tell on me, too. I wanted nothing more than to be rid of the man who had made a good stab at destroying my life at a very vulnerable age. "Please go."

He sighed. "Very well. But I had hoped bygones would be bygones between us, Alix."

I led the way to the door, holding it open for him. I hoped Uncle Porter, God rest his dear soul, wasn't lingering on this plane. He would hate knowing that the man he despised was on his beloved premises. "They can be, once I see my cousin face to face and things are right between us again." By that point, maybe Cass would have had enough of Phillip Coleman, too.

"Well, good-night, Alix." Phillip seemed to want to linger, but I would have none of it. I practically pushed him out the door and waited on the front porch until the taillights of his Mercedes had faded into the distance, making sure he was actually gone.

Then I went back into the house and locked the doors. As I went through the foyer on my way upstairs, I spied the package Cass had sent me. With shaking hands I unwrapped it as soon as I was in my bedroom. No letter was attached to the tied parcel of paperbacks; I had hoped there would be some greeting, some kind of message from her.

Well, I would bundle the books back up and . . .

I forgot all about my renewed irritation with Phillip as the idea took shape.

Excitedly, I pulled my suitcase out of the closet and started throwing things into it. There were charter flights from Atlanta to London. Though the strike was ended, there were sure to be cancellations from nervous travelers fearful of a reoccurrence.

The books were the last thing to be packed. I had decided to deliver them personally to my cousin.

My heart beat happily faster as I dialed for a cab to get me to the train station. I could just about make the 11:40 Floridian to Atlanta.

A note to Goody was scrawled and propped against the coffee pot, and I was on my way.

In England, in the wonderful old castle whose history we shared, I would find Cassandra again—far from the man who had caused us to lose each other.

Everything fell into place as it usually does when you're pursuing a course prescribed by pure instinct. I used the half-hour before boarding time in Atlanta to call Goody to be sure she'd found my note.

She wasn't even surprised by my impulsiveness, chuckling when I told her I'd be on my way to England in less than an hour. "I told that Mr. Phillip when he called that he'd have a hard time getting to talk to you like he wanted, with you already halfway to London."

Maybe I should have warned her not to tell anyone where I'd gone, I thought fleetingly, but, no, it was better that Phillip knew I was serious about setting things straight between Cass and myself. "What did he say?"

"Not much of anything, to tell the truth. He sounded like . . . well, he sounded tired, like. He said to tell you he was taking the horses over to Shelbyville and when you saw Mrs. Coleman to tell her he'd have the blue ribbons lined up for her when she came home."

It sounded as if Phillip had adjusted to the fact that I was determined not to let him be a destructive element in my life any longer. "I'll do that—among other things I plan to tell her. Any other calls? I was expecting to hear from Dolores; they've been at the seashore for the summer but I gave her the Alabama number."

"I was just about to tell you. My, she sounds like a nice lady."

"She is," I agreed warmly. "I guess she told you that by

the time fall rolls around, the old house won't be the quiet mausoleum it was with just you and Uncle Porter rattling around in it.''

Goody sounded like she was on the verge of tears—happy tears. ''I can't hardly wait, Miss Alix,'' she finally managed.

I can't, either, I told myself as I hung up and went to board the plane.

The nagging worry about what sort of welcome I might receive, arriving unannounced at Bloodstones, gave way to a number of more immediate concerns. Adjusting to the Vauxhall I'd rented at Gatwick, driving on the wrong side of the highway, trying to read the complex roadmap—all this provided a complex challenge. It wasn't until after I'd angled desperately with a few other wild-eyed tourists for the elusive exit from the roundabout to the Maidstone Road that I finally began to relax.

How could anyone driving through the lush Kent countryside for the first time help but be entranced? Here I was, deep in the magical forests that had once sheltered the likes of Anne Boleyn and Henry VIII. And through it all was the deep, mystical feeling of finally coming home.

Too wrapped up in dreamy enjoyment of the surrounding sights, I forgot about the hair-raising way the English think nothing of turning narrow lanes into three-car passages. The speeding Rolls-Royce that careened between my car and an oncoming MG caught me off-guard. Luckily, there was a pub just to my left and somehow my reflexes led me into its parking area. The MG roared on its way, unnerved by the near miss, as I slammed on my brakes and sat paralyzed from the close call.

I didn't hear the Rolls come to a screeching halt before it backed up to stop beside me.

''What the bloody hell were you doing, creeping along on a blind curve? You could've caused all three of us to crack up.''

I didn't raise my head from my arms until I finished

counting to ten, very slowly. Here I was getting lambasted for driving sensibly on this mad speedway, after I'd risked my neck to avoid collision. I took a deep breath and lifted my head, ready to let the arrogant bastard who was blaming me for his recklessness hear what I thought about him, his car, and the insane English road habits.

The things I planned to say died unspoken as a wave of strange *deja vu* went over me when I faced the man who was glaring at me through my car window. Where had I met this man? I opened my eyes wide, then closed them, fighting off a sense of hallucination. Maybe the face would be gone, leaving a less disturbing one in its place when I opened my eyes again.

But he was still there, the anger in his turquoise eyes changing to puzzlement as I continued to stare in disbelief. For the life of me, I still don't know what I said, but I must have said something unflattering. His look of interested curiosity turned back to anger.

"American—that explains it. You people seem to think because of that Ford fellow that you invented driving . . ."

I found my voice again and some of the uneasiness died away when I heard the English lordly arrogance. *Deja vu* I couldn't deal with; *chutzpah* was a different matter for a writer who'd run the gauntlet with New York publishers.

"Yes, thank you, I'm all right," I said pointedly.

"*Are* you?" He smiled at me, a very white smile showing that whatever my injuries might be, they weren't deemed to be of great importance.

"Yes," I said reluctantly. I wished there could have been at least a bit of blood or a broken arm that I could shove under that well-formed nose. "I'm all right."

Again, the bright gaze swept over me. "Better than that, I'd say. Actually, I saw you were quite in control of things. I just came back to warn you about driving like a snail around here. Next time, you may not be so lucky."

A woman's voice called from inside the curtained rear of the car. "Do apologize, dear, like a good fellow, and come along. We're abominably late for the services as it is."

"I'm coming. And I've already apologized."

I hissed, "Liar!"

"I wanted to save something for our next meeting. Right now I'm due at a funeral."

"It could've been mine," I said scathingly.

"That," he said softly, "would be a terrible waste. I have great hopes for . . . running into you again . . . soon."

I rolled up the window in childish fury and glared at him as he walked back to his car, but some of my fury abated when I noticed that he walked with a slight limp.

I shook out my roadmap, tracing a fine line to the approximate point where I sat in my Vauxhall. It was as I suspected; I was not more than two miles from Bloodstones. My stomach gave a lurch when I realized that almost certainly I had just had my first meeting with the current owner of the castle. The man with the turquoise eyes and the limp could be none other than the Baron Miles Geoffrey Linwood.

I stared at the mellow old pub in front of me, not really seeing it. "Well, so much for your hopes of an open arms reception, my girl." I sat there deep in thought, trying to decide whether to go back to London and try to reach Cassandra by phone or to take a chance on finding a room in Maidstone. The tapping at my window made me jump.

The sandy-haired man trying to get my attention was about as opposite to the man from the Rolls as he could be. I rolled down the glass and he peered at me anxiously. "Hey, if you're thinking about buying this place, forget it. I already did—six months ago. And if you're casing the joint, forget that, too." He waved his arm toward the empty parking area. "As you can see, the customers stay away in droves."

I grinned in delight, liking the friendly smile and lively blue eyes immediately. "You're an American!"

"Well, bless my boots!" He grinned back, recognizing my accent. "A southern gal! Second one I've seen since I got here." My ears pricked up at the mention of a second Southern gal. Could it be he'd seen Cass? Her accent was even more pronounced than mine.

"I'm Alix . . . Ames." I decided my pen name would do, for the time being. "Originally from Birmingham—or near there, anyway."

He was so delighted I thought he might be going to kiss me. "Well, I'll be a—damn! Come on inside, girl. I reckon you could use something wet and cold after that ruckus with Linwood a while ago."

We went into the inviting coolness of "The Dark Swan" where my host bellowed at the plump girl behind the bar, "Bring us a couple of pints, wench, on the double!" The girl giggled, and my host pulled out a chair for me, winking as he did so. "She thinks I'm a riot. Tells her friends about the crazy American."

"The man in the Rolls . . . you called him Linwood. I was planning to visit Bloodstones Castle. Isn't that the name of the family that lives there?"

He raised one eyebrow. "Why fool around touring Bloodstones? Hever's just a few miles away." The girl set down our frothing mugs, and he told her solemnly, "Go have one for yourself, Suzy, before the afternoon rush."

After the girl had gone off giggling afresh at the obvious reference to the pub's emptiness, he turned back to me. "Sorry, I forgot to introduce myself. Neil Willingham, at your service, ma'am. You are a very lovely lady, girl. I'm surprised Linwood didn't whisk you back to the castle. It's said around here that he's something of a lady-killer."

"It doesn't sound like you like him very much."

Neil looked down into the foam capping his mug. "Like? Linwood would never let a nobody like me get close enough to know whether I liked him or not. I'll say this much, though. In the eyes of people around Ravensbridge, which was once feudal territory for Bloodstones, Linwood is something of a hero. They don't give a damn about his moody ways or his arrogance or his women. And the creepy stories about him and his family and the castle . . . Hell, even Transylvanians would be quick to stand up for Count Dracula to an outsider."

"A hero . . . I noticed he limps."

Neil took a swig of his bitter. "With good reason. He led an escape out of a Korean P.O.W. camp that he still won't talk about to anybody."

"Korea? Why would an Englishman be fighting in a U.S. police action?"

Neil grinned. "Maybe because it was the only war he could find at the time. He ran off to Australia as some sort of rebellious adventurer. The unit he hooked up with was one of the toughest combat teams in Korea." Neil looked down at the gleaming table he was automatically polishing over and over. "I guess you may as well hear from me what is pretty common gossip around here. Linwood's wife, Rosalee, who came to live with the family at the castle while her husband was among the missing, had something going with Miles' older brother Dexter."

I knew I had no business discussing the Linwoods, but my curiosity was monstrous. "Did Miles find out about it when he got back here?" The thought of what his reaction might have been after a harrowing prison escape to return and find his wife had betrayed him with his own brother . . . well, I wouldn't have wanted to be in Rosalee's place.

"He did." Neil whispered this, cocking his head toward the clatter of cutlery that heralded the barmaid's return. "And about the baby coming that couldn't be his. Folks around here said Linwood rode like a madman day and night for the next few weeks. Poor old Dexter was so upset he lost his concentration in a polo match and fell off, breaking his neck. His death threw Rosalee into early labor, and some say she and the child might have lived if Linwood had gone after Doc Crockett earlier."

It was all fascinating. There were questions I longed to ask but dared not. "Why are you telling me all of this, Neil?"

He looked at me with puzzlement in his bright blue eyes. "Damned if I know. It's idiotic, but from the moment I saw you, I had the crazy notion that the reason I'm here is to protect you . . . don't laugh. Before you've been in this

54

crazy place long, you'll start believing in all this crap, too."

"I'm not laughing, believe me. The other southern girl—did you get this feeling with her, too? You said she was planning to visit Bloodstones."

"She said she was a long lost cousin or something. I paid attention to her, all right, but not the same way I did you. You know, it's kind of odd about her."

"Odd? What do you mean?"

"Well, I got the feeling she wanted to make sure I remembered her. I mean, like, she took her passport out to show me the picture and all, joking about being old enough to drink or something like that."

I frowned. Why would Cass want to make a lasting impression on the pub owner?

Unless she was afraid something might happen to her at Bloodstones.

"Is she there now? At the castle, I mean?"

Neil shrugged. "I wouldn't know. I've been over in London trying to set up my wholesalers' accounts. Why?"

I gave him an insincere smile. "You know how we are, we American tourists. Always eager to make contact with travelers from our home state."

The blue eyes on mine were searching. "Something tells me there's more to it than that, Mystery Lady, but I'll wait for you to tell me about it."

"I will; I promise. Not right now, but soon." I was suddenly anxious to visit the castle before the Linwoods returned. If Cass were there, we could have our first meeting alone. "How far am I from the castle road?"

"Not half a mile from the turnoff." He folded his hand over mine as I fished for currency. "Never mind that. It's on the house."

As he held my car door for me, he peered in at me and said in half-serious tones, "You could forget it, you know, going over to poke around a place that doesn't have a pretty history. You could go back to London, take in the sights and let me come up to treat you to dinner and theater."

I smiled at him and started the motor. "Thanks, Mr.

Neil Willingham, but that's not for I came for."

He stood in the parking lot of "The Dark Swan" and watched until I was out of view. As I turned into the lane marked by two very old stone posts, I remembered a question I had meant to ask and hadn't.

The Linwoods had been on their way to a funeral. Whose, I wondered.

The mellow grey stones of the castle became visible as soon as I cleared the thickets near the main road. I slowed down, suddenly aware of a heart-stopping sense of reentering the past and proceeding along a course of inevitability. To alleviate the swelling apprehension in me, I let my mind drift toward other things, like what it might have been like, traveling in England in the sixteenth century.

That was a mistake, causing me to lose concentration on the road and my driving. The blur of black crossing the lane in front of me reminded me I was in modern times with a modern car to control. I did everything I could to avoid hitting the horse and rider, eventually ending up in the shallow ditch beside the road. As I slammed into a large stone and felt the Vauxhall shudder ominously and then go dead, I decided that this was definitely not my day for driving a car.

This time I was really angry. I flung open the door and jumped out to confront the foolhardy rider who'd nearly invited disaster. "Are you crazy, dashing across the road without even looking?"

The dark-haired woman astride her still agitated black horse looked down at me with pale blue eyes. "Who the devil are you, and what do you mean speeding down a private lane? You nearly ran us down. And I suppose you're aware you're trespassing."

I sputtered, "I was going slow as a snail. It was you who nearly caused us to crash." I reached back inside the car and grabbed the guidebook I'd been using and waved it at her. "As for my 'trespassing', it says here that Bloodstones is open to the public on Friday afternoons."

"Well, I'm sure the Baron isn't aware his estate is being advertised in some cheap tourist pulp. If I were you, I'd save myself some trouble and leave before the Linwoods return."

I looked from her to the sadly misused Vauxhall and back again. "A marvelous suggestion. I tell you what—you drive my car in its present condition and I'll take your horse."

She gave a tight smile at my sarcasm. "I am the only woman Miles allows to ride his favorite horse." With that, the woman gave her mount a smart switch with her crop and galloped off in the direction from which I'd come.

I stared after her, speechless with disbelief. The nerve of her, not even offering to phone for a mechanic!

I gave the Vauxhall another try, knowing it was no use even before doing so. It wasn't far back to the pub. I got my bag and hesitated, before turning resolutely toward the castle.

No, by damn, I'd come this far and I wasn't about to turn tail after all I'd gone through.

And if Cass were on hand, as I hoped she would be, to provide a respectable introduction upon the Linwoods' return, I'd take pleasure in telling the Baron about the risks being taken with his valued horseflesh.

I was here at last, standing inside the extended gateway I knew to be the barbican. The iron gates were apparently not used now, and I walked resolutely up to the huge studded door. The massive knocker was shaped like a wolf's head. After a deep breath, I lifted the heavy ring and let it fall. The sound echoed all around me, and I waited, then knocked again. And again.

It was evident no one was home. The silence was all around me, and I had the uneasy feeling that I was being watched to see what my next move would be.

I walked out of the cool gateway into the hot sun. My throat was parched and I could feel my blouse getting damp under my suit jacket. It was frustrating; surely there must be someone around—a gardener or a housemaid.

The River Medway was perhaps 50 yards away, and I glanced over at it, thinking of its coolness.

There was a flutter of movement at the window of a cottage between me and the river. The place looked friendly and lived-in, so I set off down the path that seemed to lead there. Perhaps this was the caretaker's house or a tenant's lodging. I would ask for a drink of water at least, then find a shady spot to wait for the Linwoods' arrival.

The path was stony and uneven, the array of large stones at its crest arranged in a miniature pattern similar to Stonehenge. I stopped in the midst of them, then moved quickly on.

It was not a comfortable spot, and I wondered if these were the bloodstones which gave the castle its name.

There was again the uneasy sense of being secretly observed.

The cottage door was wide open. Trying not to appear furtive, I knocked and called out, but there was no response. I stuck my head around the door, enjoying the rush of coolness from the quiet interior. Then as my eyes moved over the small room, I forgot my timidity about trespassing. The inexplicable sensation of familiarity was much stronger and I moved trancelike into the room.

"I've been here before. God help me, I've been here before!"

The modern furnishings meant nothing. I'd never seen the chintz covers on modern chairs or the scrubbed table and painted chairs. The thick-piled rug meant nothing, nor did the bright prints on the stone walls or the baskets of dried flowers and ferns.

I closed my eyes and the words came into my head.

. . . the stone cottage near the stones.

I opened my eyes again. The modern, gaily-covered bed in the corner of the room drew my attention. It had once been a bed of straw, with a fur covering that had felt soft and warm against bare skin.

I put my hands over my eyes to shut out the sight of the bed and sank to my knees on the soft rug. My whispers were barely audible above the pounding in my head. "Crislyn . . . the girl with her falcon. She lost. Oh, God, she lost the contest!"

The pounding inside my head was eased and another sound was all around me—the bells from the castle tower. I couldn't move in the whirling strangeness of what was happening to me again.

And I couldn't keep from counting with the bells.

. . . nine . . . ten . . .

With the eleventh peal I was no longer conscious of being Alixandra Manning. I was once again Crislyn, and the only thing of which I was conscious was the fact that I had lost the battle of the falcons and must now pay the price.

4

"Isn't it about time you came out from under the cover, Crislyn? You can't stay under there forever, you know. A bargain is a bargain, after all—and you *did* lose."

I think I hated the fact that he seemed to find me amusing more than anything. How grateful I was for the darkness that disguised this unholy tryst! At least he could not see my blushes or my nakedness, I thought, as I poked my head out from beneath the fur blanket.

"Monster. You didn't win fairly, and you know it. Poor Penfeather's heart gave out in the midst of the contest; that was the only reason your bird was the victor. Penfeather was winning, and we both know it."

I put my head in my hands, in my mind's eye seeing again my wonderful Penfeather drop like a stone from the sky. But even in my despair at the consequences, I was glad the noble creature had died in the midst of fierce battle.

"I have to admit that your bird put on a fine exhibit, but fate decreed that mine would be the winner, Crislyn. Surely you can see that this was meant to be, even if it did come about in a way that seems unfair." If I hadn't known better,

I would've sworn there was sincerity in his voice. But then the arrogance returned: He shifted his naked bronze body so that it burned against mine and murmured, "The important thing to me is that I won and you're mine, all mine."

"For now," I reminded him as coldly as I could. "But it's still not fair. The winner should have been Penfeather. You saw for yourself that she was the best."

He felt for me in the dark. "The terms of the wager were clear before we started, you stubborn girl. Damn this darkness! Where are you?" He let his hand move down to the edge of the cover which I still clutched desperately. "I'm not a heartless man, Crislyn, but I'm also not a patient one." I felt the cover being firmly eased from my grip. "I want you. Now!" He kissed my bare shoulder. I was starting to shiver in spite of the heat, and he wasted no time taking his advantage. "And always," he whispered.

I closed my eyes, ashamed to discover that his langorous caresses of my throat and breasts, now free to his touch, were having their effect on me. "What *you* want . . . it's always what you want. With men like you, no one else's wishes matter."

He paused in his lovemaking. "Yes, I admit to being selfish. But I'm vulnerable, too—and maybe a little afraid where you're concerned."

"Afraid? You?" I made a sound that told him what I thought of that.

"Yes. Afraid of being overcome by feelings I've never had before about a woman. Yesterday I watched you long before I showed myself. I watched your face as it looked up to the sky, following your soaring falcon and identifying with its freedom. I saw the unconscious beauty in your body, the wildness of your spirit. I saw all those things and knew that here was a woman who could have power over me. I had to have you," he finished simply. "Neither of us had a choice."

"You can make claim to the physical part of me, my lord, but there's a part of me that will always be free, a part that belongs only to me and not to any man."

He buried his face in my stomach. I could feel the crisp dark gold of his beard scraping against my tender flesh. He lifted his head suddenly and reached up to cradle my face tightly with his hands. "We'll see about that, lovely Crislyn, we'll see. For now, though, you're all mine. Say it, Crislyn. Admit that for now you're mine. We'll deal with eternity later."

"I won't!" I shook my head wildly, suddenly frightened—of myself more than of him. "I . . . can't."

His mouth crushed mine, and I heard the tiny moans of passion that surely could not be coming from me. Could it be me responding so fervently to the bold kisses? I let out a hopeless cry and let him have his way with my aching flesh that had turned treacherous. As though a wanton stranger had possessed me, I found myself cupping my breasts for him to suckle, twisting my head from side to side with the almost unbearable intensity of feeling. His hand went to touch the flame between my thighs and explored its warmth with maddening deliberateness. I was a sensual novice, but I knew with hot anger that he was playing with me to heighten my desire.

He stretched himself slowly, carefully, fitting his body to mine, but not yet making the entry that could not be delayed much longer from what I could feel. His hands tangled in my hair, and I could swear his eyes pierced the darkness of my soul. "Say you want me, Crislyn," he whispered. "Your body has already signaled its surrender, but I want to hear it from your lips."

"No," I whispered back. "We struck a bargain, and I'm keeping my side of it—no more, no less."

He laughed at me, then moved against me, easily penetrating the barrier of my virginity. At my gasp, he paused a moment before beginning again to tantalize every part of me. "I can be stubborn, too, my precious. I promised myself I would not force myself on you, and that's how it's going to be." He traced my lips lightly with his tongue, slowly, without urgency, while his hand moved deliberately and relentlessly over my breasts. He whispered hoarsely, "I could quite happily go on like this all day and night, love, but I hate for you to leave me without enjoying the satisfaction I want us to share. Say you want me. Say it!''

The wanton spirit inside me said it for me. And it was she who made poor Crislyn's pride laughable with her shameless passion. Could it be that fiery, independent Crislyn was letting her senses conquer her reason?

Just as I had decided I would never be able to lie on a soft bed again without remembering this feeling of climbing, I reached the apex.

My lover savored it with me, holding still inside me and kissing me deeply, even after I felt the last licking flame. ''You were made for love, Crislyn,'' he murmured into my ear. ''Perhaps you really are a witch. You've certainly cast your spell on me.''

At this reference to my 'oddness,' which I understood even less than the ignorant people who'd run Nana and me out of the Cotswold, I felt the old helpless anger. I pushed away the man who was taunting me with it and leapt out of bed, feeling for the leather tunic carelessly thrown to the floor earlier. ''Please don't talk about such things as though they're laughable. They aren't. People on my . . . my level don't take witchcraft lightly.'' I pulled on my leggings, too agitated to realize that I was caught in a beam of moonlight from the one cottage window. ''You have touched a sore spot, my lord.'' I had put the unhappy events of the Cotswold behind me and never again wanted people to think of me that way again. ''Most simple folks are all too eager to point at women said to be witches. It makes their own petty wickedness less evident.''

His voice sounded disembodied in the dark room. ''You speak as if you've known these things firsthand.''

I turned my back on him, the pain still fresh from the way former friends had turned on my grandmum and me. ''Some nights I dream of a place where I no longer have to run from ignorance and jealousy. It's dangerous to be different in this world of ours. There was a woman I knew once whom the neighbors decided was in league with Satan.

They took it into their heads that her goat was her familiar."
My laugh was not a humorous one. "With all the seriousness and ceremony you might see at an execution of a
highborn at the Tower, they dressed the goat up like a
person and solemnly marched it to the gallows they'd built
and hanged the creature." I turned back to him, the same
bitter smile on my face. "Isn't that a funny story? Doesn't
that tell you a great deal about those who talk about so-
called witches?"

He wasn't laughing. After a long silence, he said in a low
voice, "The moonlight reveals just enough of you to make
me wish you would take off that outlandish get-up you're
wearing and come back to my arms."

I shook the straw from my hair, straightening the
tangles as best I could, and moved away from the window.
"I sewed these clothes myself, though Roark complained of
my burning the candles all those nights I stayed up with my
awl and thread." I tossed my head, and said defiantly, "It
seems you find everything about me laughable."

He said quietly, "There is nothing laughable about you,
Crislyn." He added abruptly, in a different tone, "This
father of yours—why do you call him by his given name?"

"Because I have never known him as a real father. He
turned my grandmum and me out when I was a tiny baby."
Not wishing his sympathy, I added proudly, "But don't
concern yourself, my lord. You won't be seeing me again."

I could sense his smile. "Would you care to make that
another wager?"

I froze with my hand on the door as his next words came
softly. "Aren't you forgetting something, my love?" I stood
stock-still as he retrieved my dagger from beneath the bed
and threw it cleanly into the door not two feet from my
head. "The fact that you didn't use use it at the moment
when I wouldn't have felt a hundred knives gives me
hope."

My humiliation at his knowing I had come prepared to
kill him and had not was too much to bear, clouding the fact
that a London fop could throw a knife so expertly in the

dark with nothing but sound to guide him. With great effort to retain some dignity, I made no move to retrieve my weapon. "Keep it. It's all of mine you'll ever possess."

The thought of seeking Nana's aid in concocting a potion that would make certain parts of a man's anatomy rot and fall off kept me occupied on my way back to the mill.

A week had passed since my encounter with the Baron's arrogant visitor. I had found myself finding reasons to stay away from the mill cottage every night till after dark, not wanting Nana's penetrating eyes to watch me too closely. She had a way of seeing through me when I had something to hide.

I prowled the forest at night on the pretense of hunting. Usually by the time I got home, the house was quiet, my grandmum and my father sound asleep. They were used to my odd hours, though Nana began looking at me worriedly in the mornings when my eyes were underscored by dark blue shadows and my movements were listless.

But one night, things were different. As I approached the house I knew there was something wrong. Ever stingy, Roark never let us keep the fire in the cottage after his supper had been heated, but I could see the glow of a fire as I quietly crept up to the back door. Some prickling apprehension set my mind to thinking of some excuse for my lateness. I picked up several sticks of wood and went in.

"Is that you, Chrissie?" Even my grandmum's voice was all wrong. "Where've you been, girl? Dawdling over those traps again that you said you'd find if it took you all night?"

She was giving me a cue, which meant that my father was still up. I gave her a grateful kiss and said loudly, "Someone's been raiding them again, Nana. I've been waiting every night this week to catch the rascal who's been robbing us, but . . ."

"Is that her, old woman?" I winced at the sound of one of my mother's last painted mugs crashing against the floor. Roark was drunk—bad drunk. "Tell the wench to get herself in here."

My grandmum mouthed, "Be careful." Her shawl slipped off her shoulders then and I saw a terrible bruise. At my look of anger, she put her finger to my mouth and said, "Shh, it's all right. He was only angry because of your lateness. There's something in the wind, Chrissie. I can see it in him and feel it in the house. Something to do with you."

I restrained my fury at the thought of my hefty father abusing this frail old woman and looked in at the shadowy hulk slumped by the fire. "I swear if he ever touches you again, I'll . . ."

"Shh, just go to him." My grandmum's eyes pleaded with me. "He's been like a bear waiting for you to get home. And when you've had your talk, I think it's time you and I had one, too."

The sound of curses and another crash made us both jump. "I'd better go, Nana," I whispered. "You and I will talk later."

I pushed her gently from me, picked up the sticks I'd gathered and entered the room where father slumped in front of the fire. His mouth hung slack from drinking cheap ale. As if it were any other night, I calmly placed the wood on the dying fire, stick by careful stick. "Have you had your supper?" He seemed to be hypnotized by my movements. I saw the glint of uncertainty that he always felt when I appeared unresponsive to his blustering and decided to move on it. "I've sent poor Nana off to her bed. She seems to have had some kind of . . ." I met his eyes steadily, ". . . accident."

His eyes slid off mine as he took a huge swallow of ale and belched, the vulgar noise restoring his confidence. "You're a fine pair, you are. I heard only a day ago how it was you two was run off from the Cotswold instead of the way the old woman told me it was."

Anything to keep his mind off me and let the ale do its work. "It's not surprising to hear ignorant accounts from ignorant fools. Poor Nana spent many a night boiling herbs and tending the sick for nothing but the risk of getting the pestilence herself. She did nothing wrong; nor did I. But why suddenly ask now? Could it be you didn't care why we left the Cotswold since it's been to your benefit ever since? The two of us cleared out your filth here and have done most of your milling, as well as the cooking and hunting." I leaned down to pick up the pieces of broken mug and threw them into the fire, my anger suddenly overwhelming my cold calmness. "You might've used something more fitting to hold your swill than the last of my mother's mugs."

"Watch your mouth, slut!" I caught my breath as his face, reeking ale, was stuck too close to mine. There was still a trace of coarse handsomeness in the ruined face, but how could gentle Amanda ever have loved this brute?

"You're the one who should watch your words, if you want me to keep on putting meat on the table with my hunting." I looked at him with cold contempt.

"I didn't see you bring in no game lately." He added slyly, "And I noticed your precious bird has been gone for some days now."

A bell of caution sounded somewhere deep inside me. Maybe he wasn't as drunk as I thought. "Penfeather flew away and would't come back. I guess I tried her before she was really ready."

He grinned. "Never mind trying to hide it from me that you've been out lately getting yourself ploughed. I know the signs."

I hardly heard his insulting words for staring at him. Had my loss of innocence brought about a new awareness of the way men looked at me? Or had Roark been hiding his contemptible lust all along?

Whatever the case, there was no doubt as to the meaning of the way he was looking at me now.

God help me, my own father desired me!

The bile that rose to my throat was kept back. Somehow, I had to pretend I didn't know he lusted for me. If he unleashed such degraded feelings . . . ! I said calmly, as one would speak to an approaching animal with eyes glazed by fever, "I'll fetch more wood. Nana doesn't need to get up to cold coals."

His voice followed me as I struck out toward the back. "You can let the old woman do that, sick or not. I want you fresh and bright-eyed in the morning."

He sounded almost cheerful. Had I let the flickering shadows deceive me about his disturbing countenance? "And what is it you have planned for me tomorrow—besides the usual chores?"

He stumbled out of his chair, stretched and yawned. "Something that ought to please you since you've lost any chance to wed one of the strong village fellows after you."

My heart lurched. "What have you done? Traded me off to some bumpkin for a horse and cart?" That awful Bart Taggert had come to Roark with just such a ridiculous proposition. "Well, if you've done something like that, you may as well know I won't be treated like a sack of grain."

He mocked me in a falsetto voice. "She won't be treated like a sack of grain, eh? Well, my girl, this is one time your high and mighty tactics won't put me off. You've been up to something this week, like getting yourself ploughed. I'm sure of it. I'm lucky to get anything for you, much less a piece of land that'll have me sitting pretty from now on." He chuckled, a low, evil sound that chilled me. "He's sending a cart for you in the morning and I'd advise you not to be wearing those britches of yours when you're unloaded at the castle."

"The castle?" I stared at him, my heart pounding. "You're crazy!" Baron Linwood didn't even know me. Surely there could be nothing to Roark's ranting. Royalty didn't come after village commoners. Unless . . . ? I suddenly felt sick at the thought that the hawk-man might have already spread jokes about the performance of the miller's daughter in bed.

"No, it's Lord Linwood himself who's crazy, to my way of thinking, for wanting wild baggage like you, but he's rich enough to stop me saying that to anyone else."

I lowered my eyes, not wanting Roark to know that my heart was sore at the thought of my first lover throwing me to the likes of the castle owner. What a fool I'd been, thinking that, in spite of the arrogance behind the forced bargain, there'd been more to our encounter than even my seducer had wanted to admit. "I can't believe any of this. Baron Linwood would never deal with you like this. Not for someone with my upbringing."

Roark's eyes lingered insinuatingly on my breasts and thighs. "You're the talk of the village with your haughty ways and such. Maybe he wants the taming of you for himself. But the fact is, he wants you, girl." He laughed coarsely. "Let's just say it probably won't be for emptying the slop jars at the castle. And that's lucky for you, girl. Not much work and no surprises. Though, if I was you, I'd be practicing up on my maidenlike screams between now and the time the Baron gets back."

Gets back? The revelation that Linwood was not at the castle was encouraging. It would give me time to think, to plan. "It's late. We'll talk about this in the morning, Roark."

He stretched and yawned again and went off to bed, but not before telling me softly, "There'll be no more talk. The papers are already drawn up. And if that hopeful look on your face I saw just now means you see yourself getting out of this, I have to disappoint you. The Baron and me made our deal. You're to be kept safe at the castle while he's away and watched the while for the slippery wench we all know you to be. Well, good-night, girl. I'll be expecting you up early in the morning."

I barely managed to get out the door and gulp the clean fresh air before nausea engulfed me.

A moment later, I cried out to the stars, "Isn't there any place in England where a woman can choose her own destiny? Is there no place I can move and think freely without some man looking at me and wanting me with nary a thought for what I want?" I beat my fists on a tree trunk and wept until there were no tears left in me. Then, cleansed and clearheaded, I made up my mind. I would leave the mill, leave Ravensbridge tonight. When Roark was snoring soundly, I would rouse Nana and we'd leave together. Perhaps we could make our way to the sea, where her bones wouldn't ache so much and my only torment would come from the gulls wanting my catch rather than men wanting me.

The image cheered me, but I didn't have much time. It was vital that we be far away by dawn. The going would be slow since grandmum couldn't walk very fast.

It was now or never. Once I was lawfully bonded to the Baron, there would be no escape.

I tiptoed back into the cottage, heartened by the loud snores from Roark's bedroom. He wouldn't awaken if the cottage were burning down around his drunken head.

That thought was tempting. There were several burning coals that could be easily scattered to insure my father wouldn't be coming after us.

No. It would draw attention to us and might be put out before we were going a mile.

I climbed up to my tiny loft and gathered up the few things I could carry on my back in the leather bag. The rabbit fur cloak could serve as a pallet and keep Nana warm at night; I rolled it up and added it to my pack. There wasn't much—a broken piece of one of my mother's mugs, a feather quill to remind me of Penfeather, a warm shawl Nana had made me, and a couple of dark dresses, plain and sturdy, in case I had to take occasional work in some inn for food.

Food. I was confident of my hunting skills, but what if game became scarce? There was salt-dried meat in the kitchen and several manchets we used for plates that would do for bread.

It was frightening, passing Roark's room to seek the dark kitchen, but his snores were loud as ever. I got back to my loft without a sound and enjoyed with grim humor the vision of Roark's face when he found I'd robbed the larder as well as his hopes for property. "If he'd been a decent father, I might be a less vengeful daughter," I said to myself without remorse.

Everything was ready. In my haste to be off, I caught

my deerskin tunic in a snag on the ladder. "Damn!" I was counting on the sturdy attire to make the hard journey through the woods.

There was nothing to do but take the time to repair it, and there was a rip in my leggings as well that needed fixing. I sat on my bed after removing both garments and went to work with my awl and thread. As the six-inch needle made the final puncture in the tough leather, I froze at a sudden noise on the ladder.

No doubt it was Nana coming up to have the talk she'd promised. She often crept up to sleep with me after Roark was asleep. Her son-in-law ridiculed her for treating me like a baby, but in this way she often defied him.

"Nana?" My whisper was tentative. It wasn't like her to climb so stealthily. "Nana, is that you?"

I reached for my chemise, not wanting to offend her with my nakedness in the moonlight.

But there was no time to put it on. The dark shape emerging from the opening to my cubicle was not my grandmum. My insides twisted when I recognized Roark. "What do you want? Why have you come up here? It's not proper for you to be here."

The words sounded silly even to me. And from Roark's evil chuckle I could tell he, too, found them humorous. His eyes devoured the part of me I couldn't hide with the chemise. "Not proper, eh? Well, ladeda, is it proper what you've been up to? I don't mean just the whoring. I'm talking about sneaking around a man's house while you think he's asleep. What's in the bag, girl?" I dove for it, but he snatched it from my grasp. He looked inside, then back at me with a slow, terrible smile. "Oh, ho. Making an escape, were you? Thinking to cheat me of the one chance I have to make something after feeding and housing you all these months?"

It was on the tip of my tongue to remind him that most fathers provided for their offspring without begrudging it, but I reconsidered. This wasn't the time to remind Roark he'd never been much of a father. "I . . . thought I ought to be ready when they come for me in the morning. I thought

72

about living in the castle and decided it won't be so bad after all. And while that isn't much of a dowry in that bag . . . well, I felt better about going into a new place with my own things."

I couldn't tell if he believed me or not—he'd fooled me with the snoring, hadn't he?—but at least he was acting like he believed me. "I figured you'd come to your senses about what's in it for you as well as me. I suppose you won't have much to do with old Roark after you're up there with his lordship."

I shrugged, feeling back on safe ground. "From the sound of it, I won't have much time for coming back here." Contemptuously I looked around the poor room and then at him. "Not that I'll miss this place or you." The last slipped out without my intending it, and I knew I'd overstepped.

He growled and lunged at me, and I fell onto the straw pallet, more afraid than I'd ever been in my life. "You little ungrateful slut. If it wasn't for you being on show tomorrow, I'd give you the beating you've been asking for ever since you came back here."

"That's right, Roark, you can't afford to mark up the goods you're trading." I didn't like the way my desperation was obvious in my voice. "You'll get your land, but not if the Baron sends me back after taking one look at the damaged goods he's bought."

I still have nightmares about that terrible smile he gave me before he said softly, "He won't send you back, not when he sees what I'm looking at. Even spoiled, as I suspect you be after the funny way you've been acting lately, you make a man lose his senses." He came closer, his hands pulling on his soiled nightshirt. "I guess it won't matter, one more ploughing, will it? Linwood won't have a way of knowing, now will he?"

I stared at him, knowing now what his real reasons for sneaking up here were and feeling sick through and through. "You're crazy, Roark." I backed up, inching away from him, but there was no place to go. He had me trapped. "You can't be thinking . . . you wouldn't! For God's sake,

Roark, think about it! You're drunk and don't know what you're doing. Your . . . own . . . daughter, Roark. Your own daughter! Do you want to burn in hell?''

I might have been the wind, for all the attention he paid me. And when he started for me with a terrible lust in his eyes, I knew I would kill myself before submitting to this unnatural passion.

He whispered, ''You're a beautiful thing, Crislyn. If you only knew how long it's been since I had anything but old women's juices.''

My insides curdled. So that's why Nana had been so afraid of him—and ashamed in a way I couldn't understand. God knows how many times she had stood between Roark and me, taking the brunt of his animal desire to spare me. I couldn't speak. My throat was dry with hate. Suddenly I didn't want to be the one to die; I wanted it to be Roark Scotney.

With boiling anger, my hands went out to find something to use against him, anything to keep him from practicing his sick lust on me.

My hand froze around the smooth handle of the awl I'd been using. Coldly, I considered the matter; a thrust against the thick back or buttocks would enrage but not kill. The steel needle had to find a mark that would bring immediate death. I wanted this animal removed from life forever.

His brain! It had to reach his brain, but without a mark that would lead to an ungrateful daughter who could be hanged for patricide.

I suddenly remembered a wrinkled drawing Nana had shown me, depicting the source of headaches, and I tensed, waiting for my chance.

Just as he groaned and lunged toward me, I thrust my deadly, long needle up through his right nostril to the hilt, with the palm of my hand driving the weapon home with an impetus that made the thin membrane to the brain offer little protection.

Without a sound, he slumped and fell against me, bearing us both to the rough floor. Roark was dead!

''Chrissie? Chrissie, I thought I heard him com—oh,

dear God in heaven, what's the monster done to you, then?''
Nana stumbled at the opening to the loft, staring.

"Dear God, help me get him off me. Get him off me!"
My hysteria was short-lived. Once his eyes were no longer
staring into mine not an inch away, with the handle of my
awl still ludicrously sticking out from his face, I was once
more in control. "You know about these things better than I
do. Check to see if he's really dead. I think he is." I knew it,
but I wanted to hear it from Nana.

My grandmother put her hand to his throat and after a
brief time looked up and nodded. "He is. But I'll say no
religious rites over him, him already being in hell by now if
there's any justice in life or death."

I started shaking with the thought of what had nearly
happened. "May his soul burn in torment for what he came
close to doing to his own flesh and blood."

Nana looked at me with a grim smile. "It will, but
maybe 'twill bring you comfort to know he wasn't your
father, Chrissie. He was your mother's husband right
enough—in name only—but he wasn't the man who
fathered you."

The joy and relief that crept up my body was cleansing
and wonderful. "Not my father? Oh, Nana, I always knew
that in my heart but I kept thinking . . . not my father! Oh,
thank God!" I looked at the dead man and back at my grandmother. "Did he . . . did Roark know he wasn't?"

"Yes. But, like me, he was sworn to secrecy. You were
to be told on your eighteenth birthday or on Roark's death.
I'd already decided to breach my oath, but thinking of your
mother, it was mortally hard to do."

"You can't imagine how much it means to know the
truth," I said gratefully. "It makes this more bearable somehow." I had killed a man, but not my father. The relief
made my knees buckle in weakness. "That's why he sent
me away, then, and couldn't feel love for me."

"If you'd been born a boy, you'd have stayed here and
then been made an apprentice to Roark for several years.
But since you were a girl and no good to a man like
him—and your mother was gone—Roark sent us away."

I was starting to realize that being born a female meant that you had to fight for your rights to exist, much less govern your own person and life. "Who was my real father?"

Nana shook her head. "I never knew. All your mother would confess to was that he was highborn, likely a visitor to our castle near Hastings."

"Why did she marry Roark and come here?"

"My son's wife was already jealous. She convinced everyone it was the best solution, having my daughter and her disgrace far removed from the family."

Her disgrace. Me. "And you went with her," I said, softening.

"It didn't seem fair to me," my grandmother said simply. "My son had whored everywhere he could since his youth, but poor Amanda was punished for erring once." She looked sadder than I'd ever seen her. "She was so much in love, Chrissie—never forget that—and when he never came back for her, her heart was broken. But still she never disclosed his name, though her brother threatened to beat it out of her."

"But to marry this poor substitute of a man . . ." I looked at the dead miller and then quickly away. He was a horrid sight, staring up at the ceiling with the awl sticking out of his nose. "How could she bear to . . . to . . ." I shuddered.

"He never touched her," Nana said in a hard voice. "It was part of the bargain and I came to see he kept it."

"I'm going back there with you, and together we'll find out who my father was," I said determinedly. The thought of being daughter to some fine nobleman robbed the past hour of its horror.

"No, we can't do that." My grandmother looked terrified, and I wondered if she had told me everything about the banishment of the two women.

"Why not? We can't stay here, you realize."

"*You* can't, not with the castle lord after you, but I can. In fact, I must. If we both fled, we'd be hunted to ground."

"Nana!" But I knew she was right. If both of us vanished, leaving the miller dead of mysterious causes, there would be no question that we'd been involved in his death. "I can't leave you here to face things alone."

My grandmother smiled slightly and looked over at the dead Roark. "What's there to face? Questions about my son-in-law dying in his sleep, no doubt from his publicly known excesses? Look at him; there will be no sign of a struggle, once we straighten things up."

"But how will you explain my being gone?"

Nana shrugged. "Everyone knows you have odd habits, girl. This time it's in your favor. I'll just say you found Ravensbridge too confining for your restlessness. And the Baron will think you were running away from something you never wanted in the first place." She smiled. "Most folks will just nod their heads, saying they knew you were a wild one, not natural to this small village. Can you not imagine what your rival, Meuriel, will say?"

She was right. Most of the villagers would be relieved to see the last of me, who kept their men stirred up and their daughters jealous. As for Meuriel, the town midwife's daughter who had hated me on first sight for "stealing" her place as the belle of Ravensbridge . . . Well, Meuriel could spread all the nasty stories about me she liked. I had no plans to return to this horrible village. "I'll send for you when I reach our family's castle." Family . . . castle . . . I still couldn't believe it. Roark not my father!

"Crislyn, it is no longer our castle."

"Nana, why shouldn't I return to my own mother's home?"

"Because you might not be welcome." She brushed the hair softly back from my forehead. "You're so very much like her, love." She looked sad. "Unfortunately, that would be to your disadvantage. Your mother was never loved by her brother. He was eager to take the opportunity of turning her out and taking her inheritance for his own, when she refused to reveal the father of her newborn child. And by then he had married Madelina, who was jealous of both your mother and of me and easily turned Cecil's heart against us.''

I refused to believe that blood kin would turn away its own, especially refugees in such need of protection. Part of the stubborness came from my newly born fantasy of being restored to a highborn family that would put me on equal footing with the hawk-man. Somehow that had become important to me. ''Nana, he is your own son. He could never turn you away.''

Nana's eyes flashed. ''You don't know Lord Cecil and what a weakling he became after Madelina assumed control of the household—and of him.''

''I'm beginning to think it's the women of our family who have the strength and character.'' I walked over to look at the stiffening miller, feeling only revulsion that his body still stank of bad ale. ''But right now there are more pressing matters at hand than planning a reunion with my uncle and demanding our rights as kin. We must do what we can to cover up my crime. Perhaps the first step would be to remove my awl.''

Grandmum looked away, but I no longer had any twinges of conscience over what I had done or was doing. Pulling out my weapon, I thought only that Roark had died more painlessly and quickly then he deserved. I wiped the slender iron needle clean and put it back in my sewing box. ''There. Very little blood to speak of, you'll notice.''

''I don't like seeing you so hard, Crislyn.''

''Would you rather see me on the gallows?''

She winced. ''He's so heavy. How can we get him down the ladder?''

''I've been thinking about that. Do you think you could drag your pallet down there?''

Grandmum looked at me in horror. ''You plan to drop him through the opening like a sack of grain?''

I smiled grimly. ''Are you worried about hurting him? The only reason we need the pallet is to prevent any obvious bruises or broken limbs.''

Shuddering, Nana went down the ladder to follow my instructions.

After completing the macabre arrangement of the miller in his own bed, I decided that I would seek out the first cleansing stream at a safe distance and wash the last trace of him from my life.

We said our tearful good-byes, my grandmother and I, and I was on my way. I confess to a heightening sense of adventure as the distance between me and the mill cottage increased. I no longer was bound to any man. My life, my survival, rested solely on my own resourcefulness.

Hours later, I stopped to rest in a thick copse. As I drifted off to sleep, I held the soft rabbit fur cloak against my exhausted body and thought about the man who had first loved me—and betrayed me.

5

It had happened to me again, the strange entry into another world that seemed too real to be part of a dream. My cheek against the fur rug was warm, and I felt my sleek blouse and skirt, expecting the rougher feel of leather. But, no, I was Alix, lying in somebody's living room during the twentieth century, not sleeping under a hedge in the sixteenth.

"My God, what's happening to me?" I sat up, still dazed from the tumultuous events that had taken place apparently only inside my head. A glance at my watch told me once again only minutes had passed, though it had seemed like hours, days, even weeks.

There was the sound of a powerful motor. No doubt it was the Linwoods returning. By now, they'd be wondering whose car was stalled alongside their private property, or, recognizing my Vauxhall, they'd be wondering if its driver was wandering around injured or dazed. I scrambled to my feet. "Get ahold of yourself, Alix. You can't be caught trespassing here." I caught sight of myself in the mirror. Except for flushed cheeks and rather wild-looking eyes, I appeared sane enough to walk back up to that castle door and ask for help.

The scar on the cottage door looked like one that a knife might have made and gave me pause. "Don't be ridiculous, Alix. It couldn't be Crislyn's."

It took even more convincing to quiet myself and force my hand to lift the leering wolf's head knocker. "Now you really are being ridiculous, my girl."

I knocked and listened, then knocked again. As I waited, I looked at the big car sitting in the graveled parking area. It suited the arrogance of the man who'd been driving it better than the sleek Ferrari parked alongside it.

I was so busy looking at the Linwood auto fleet that I didn't notice the door had opened under my upraised hand.

"Just as I thought." I jumped as the amused voice spoke in my ear and turned to meet the eyes of Baron Miles Linwood. "I told Lilah it had to be you, since I could think of no one else who could have an accident on a deserted country lane."

"It was not deserted. A woman in black on a beautiful stallion popped out in front of me. I nearly . . ." I put my hand on my forehead and said pitifully, "would you mind very much if I got a drink of water?" It was all too much.

"I'll make it a brandy if you'll tell me why you keep staring at me like that."

"I'm sorry." I looked at the hall behind the tall figure, at my dusty shoes, at the handsome tie the Baron was wearing—anywhere but at the face that was doing strange things to my insides. "It's just that no one answered when I knocked before, and I guess I was just startled when you came to the door."

"Since this is my home that shouldn't be such a shock. Now if Count Dracula had appeared . . ." He gave an exaggerated bow. "Miles Geoffrey Linwood at your service, Miss . . . ?"

"Ames. Alix Ames." My pen name sprang to my lips quite naturally, and I decided to leave complicated explanations about who I really was until Cassandra appeared.

"Miss Ames. As you'll recall, we were on our way to a

funeral when we . . . ah, met before. Which is the reason," he added reasonably, "no one was here to come to the door when you knocked previously."

"A funeral?" I asked weakly, thinking of Cassandra for no good reason.

"Didn't you hear the bells? Jocko came home early to ring them. It's an old family tradition."

"Then someone died," I offered brilliantly.

The sensual lips twitched. "Let's hope so, since we buried poor old Cousin Belinda an hour ago." He held up his hand. "Please, no murmurs of sympathy. Cousin Bee overstayed on Earth the way she overstayed here when Lilah once unfortunately let it drop that her illness made a companion necessary." He grinned. "Lilah keeps outliving all of her companions. Nine, I think now, with Cousin Bee."

"I'm sorry. It's really too bad about your cousin." As I mentioned, we southerners take our funerals seriously, and I wasn't sure I approved of this man's mockery.

He seemed aware of the fact. "Not really. Cousin Bee depressed all of us, herself included. Dowdy taste and terrible legs. Lumps everywhere." He looked at my legs and then at my tailored suit. "I don't suppose you'd take Lilah on?"

I said testily, "I expect your mother would be interested in selecting her companion herself. And I'd bet she'd want to look at references other than legs."

He laughed. "You don't know my mother. She'll adore you on sight, though I find you a bit prickly myself."

Between gritted teeth, I said, "That might be because you've kept me standing out here for a good quarter-hour while we carried on a perfectly ridiculous conversation. If you don't intend to give me a glass of water, perhaps I could talk you into letting me use the phone."

He raised his eyebrows. "You're going to telephone for a glass of water?" His laughter was rippling just under the surface.

I counted to ten very slowly. "I thought," I said softly, "I might phone a mechanic about getting my car going."

''Ah, very sensible, but I'm afraid you'd be wasting your time. Our one local mechanic goes off to London on Fridays.'' His laughter had faded and he was staring at me much as I'd stared at him. ''It's the strangest thing, but I have the strongest sense of having known you before.'' He tried but couldn't quite carry off the old mockery. ''Are you sure we haven't crashed into each other before today?''

''This is my first trip to England.''

At his gesture, I stepped past him into Bloodstones Castle, almost afraid to look around me, but the overwhelming sense of familiarity didn't turn into any whirling strangeness. I looked at the courtyard—wasn't it called the bailey long ago?—and at the spray of rose bushes near some outer steps and felt dizzy with memories.

But I remained Alix, staying in my own time.

''Are you all right?'' The Baron took my arm, and I felt the high voltage of our touching and knew he felt it, too. ''I'll send for that brandy. And maybe you should lie down somewhere.''

''I'm all right,'' I said sharply, pulling my arm away almost rudely.

He reached out and touched the white blaze of hair at my brow. ''Striking, that.'' We stood there looking at each other as if frozen in time. When a tall figure materialized at my side, I screamed, effectively breaking the spell.

''I'm sorry, Miss, if I startled you.'' The newcomer lowered half his gauntness in a creaky bow. How my fingers itched for a pencil and paper to describe this marvelous character straight out of a Bram Stoker novel.

''Your brandy, Miss.''

I swallowed the small draught he held out to me in one quick gulp. ''Thank you,'' I whispered.

''This is Jocko, our steward, Miss Ames. Jocko, Miss Ames will be staying over until we manage to get something done about her car.'' I protested feebly, but he said with formal politeness, ''Nonsense. Even if there were rooms to let close by, I'd feel badly. It was my horse Samantha was riding, and she's my tenant, so I feel responsible for all this.''

Samantha? She must have been the woman who'd caused my crash. And my guess was the little cottage was hers. Thank God she hadn't walked in to find me trespassing. The thought of those pale blue eyes fixed on me in another unpleasant encounter was unsettling. "It's very kind of you." Why had no one mentioned Cassandra? I kept expecting to see her at any moment, amazed at my being here. "I expect you're not used to taking in stray tourists, especially Americans."

Jocko and the Baron exchanged glances before the latter said smoothly, "As a matter of fact, we just lost a guest from the States. A relative of sorts." *Lost?* "You'll be using her room, in the far tower. It is in order, isn't it, Jocko?" At the butler's nod, he smiled at me. "Then see that Miss Ames' bags are taken to the sealed room, Jocko. I think our guest will enjoy staying in the castle's most famous suite. Mrs. Coleman seemed excited by it."

The sealed room was also called the King's Tower. My host didn't know it, but a lot of Cass' and my childhood had been spent listening to Uncle Porter's stories about Bloodstones. The tale about the tower where King Henry VIII had allegedly slept while courting Anne Boleyn at nearby Hever had been our favorite. "So long as the ghosts don't snore," I said lightly.

The Baron laughed. "I forget how you Americans make fun of our English phantasma. So if you see our famous ghost walking about tonight, be sure to remind her she doesn't exist."

"Was Mrs. Coleman frightened of the castle ghosts?"

"Mrs. Coleman wasn't, I suspect, one to be easily frightened off by anything," the baron told me coolly. Unexpectedly, he added, "You're really not married? That astounds me."

I gave an uncomfortable laugh. "As your question astounds me. I'd always heard the English were stiff and reserved and never asked intimate questions of strangers."

"Strangers?" The look the Baron gave me challenged me to deny the currents that flowed between us. Then, he said softly, "You and I aren't strangers, Alix Ames, and you damn well know it." He added more lightly, "From the moment you ran me off the road and came back to knock at my door, I knew we were destined to know each other better."

What was keeping me from asking outright about Cass? I kept trying to force out the question, but it wouldn't come. "When will I meet your mother?"

"Soon. She's resting now but has already sent word that you're to be sent to her the moment she arises." He smiled at me. "My mother's quite demanding. I wasn't joking about the companion business, actually. You'd be perfect. She has her way with most people. Besides, we've run out of cousins, since Cousin Bee was the last. Our last resort is the service agencies. Can't you just see all the little grey and brown wrens perched on our doorstep to interview for the post?" He shuddered and I had to smile at the picture he drew.

"I'm not any Mary Poppins, Baron."

"Still, you more or less did drop in most providentially. What did you come to England for? To sightsee? Visit castles? Well, what would be better than staying right here and doing your touring from here?"

Where was Cass? What had happened? "Some companion I'd be, flitting around and visiting places."

"You force me to tell the truth. There's no work to the job, just being around the odd times my mother needs company—talking, reading, that sort of thing."

Looking around the beautiful place, I asked, "How much will you charge me to take the job?"

He let out his breath, and I realized he hadn't expected me to consider the offer seriously. Neither had I, but some powerful inner process seemed to be directing my every move since I'd thought about coming to England. And I was letting it have free rein, without making conscious decisions. "Thank God. I was afraid I might have to resort to something more desperate, like having you arrested for trespassing."

I laughed. "I'm thankful you didn't do that. I think I'm

already in enough trouble with this family." I would have liked to stop and admire some of the sights, like a charming tilting yard I glimpsed from the narrow windows in the long arched passageway leading to the farthest tower, but by the time we reached the foot of the curving stairs that I knew led to the famous sealed room, I'd lost interest in everything else. I caught my breath at the ragged edge of stones at the base of the steps. "It's true. It's really true."

The Baron looked at me from several stairs above. "Are you all right?"

I let out my breath and started up behind him. "I'm fine. It's just that I can't believe I'm really here, walking up steps that a king walked up. And seeing the signs of the wall he had built every night." I shook my head slowly, wondering if this were a dream, too.

The Baron's face was in the shadows as he waited for me at the top of the flight. "Some say they can hear the sounds of the wall being built at night and the sounds of Henry's men tearing it down each morning before he came down." He said more softly, "You sound like you know a lot about the history of Bloodstones."

"I . . . read about it in the guidebook. I guess every one with an ounce of romance loves castles."

"It's not well-known, our little castle. Compared to the real tourist attractions like Hever or Dover, Bloodstones is a tiny castle, of no significance whatever."

"I guess that's why it's marked so poorly." I laughed. "I was busy looking for signs when you and I had our first meeting."

"Most tourists don't bother to look for us, with so many other splendid places to visit." I was near him now in the shadows, and he still hadn't made a move to open the heavy carved door that was the only one to the tower chamber. My heart started thumping like mad.

"I'm not really much of a tourist, and crowds make me miserable." His closeness was making the perspiration under my blouse prickle. "No matter what you say, I think Bloodstones is lovely. I'm glad I found it."

"So am I." His arm grazed my breast as it reached out suddenly, and I jumped back like a fool.

He was merely opening the door.

I walked past him stiffly and forgot my mortification at acting like a schoolgirl when I stood inside the ancient, round chamber. My familiarity with this room could not have come only from guidebooks or my uncle's stories.

It came from having been here.

"The bed . . ." I nodded toward the huge fixture dominating the room with its massive posters and dramatic linen hangings, finding it hard to speak. "It's . . . it's been there forever, hasn't it?"

He was watching my face intently, puzzled, I knew, by my almost dazed state. "Basically. We've had to restore the leather springs, the draperies, bedcovers, that sort of thing."

With great effort, I dragged my eyes away from the room's main furnishings. "I can't believe nothing has changed." As soon as the words were out, I realized how odd they sounded, even to me. "I mean, with you and your family living modern lives here, it's amazing you've kept everything authentic."

The Baron didn't take his eyes off my face. "The feudal lords were pretty civilized, actually. They had all the conveniences, even back then." He nodded toward a curtained stone nook. "The W.C.'s over there, even a small tub."

I was finding it hard to breathe naturally, much less respond to natural conversation. "It's all . . . quite wonderful. Very comfortable."

"Then you'll stay?"

There was a soft wind from the lone archer's slit that felt like a sigh from the room itself, and I heard myself saying, in that same semiconscious state, "Yes. At least until you find someone suitable for your mother. If she's agreeable, that is."

The soft breeze became stronger, rippling the linen bed hangings and making some subtle change in the air between the Baron and myself, standing in the middle of the room looking at each other.

Finally I broke the silence, whispering, "Why is this happening? Why am I here, like this? It doesn't make sense, none of it does—your bringing me up here and talking about my staying. You never laid eyes on me before. I could be a thief, a con artist, a front for one of those dreadful terrorist rings . . ."

He lifted my chin and looked deep into my eyes. "You have to ask me what's happening? You who are the cause of it all?" With that he kissed me, a kiss that lasted several centuries. A thousand visions sped around me—of burning lips at my throat and breasts, of hands and hotter flesh readying my body for the impatient spear of conquest.

It was hard to breathe; I fought for air and freedom. "Let me go! Damn you, let me go!"

The Baron's breath was hoarse and ragged, his face struggling between desire and puzzlement. In a voice I could hardly recognize, he said, "You'd better lock your door tonight, Alix. I don't know what in hell is going on or why, but I know I came damn close to losing control just now."

"Lock my door?" I cried, trembling all over. "How can I stay here now?"

The Baron was almost himself again. "Don't be melodramatic. I assure you it won't happen again. This room sometimes has . . . peculiar effects on people. You're safe now, I assure you."

I could sense that the sexual tension had eased between us. "Maybe some of those peculiar effects made Cassandra decide to leave."

He froze midway to the door. "How did you know her first name? I only spoke of Mrs. Coleman."

The lie came easily. "The bartender at The Dark Swan. I guess since he's American, too, he remembered her."

"Oh, yes. Well, as for her leaving because she might have been disturbed by something here, I really couldn't say." He shrugged. "She was here to learn all about her roots or whatever it is all you colonists call it. Maybe she stumbled on a rotten one and decided to leave well enough alone. Or maybe she sensed her welcome here was at an end as, frankly, it was."

I overcame my shock at that enough to ask, "Where did she go?"

The Baron stopped with his hand on the doorknob, without looking around at me. "How the hell should I know? She was rich enough to go wherever she pleased. What's all your interest in this?"

"Just curious."

"I'll send Jocko up to fetch you when Lilah's awake for tea. I'm sure you'll want a bit of rest." He said more softly, "Are you angry with me?"

He knew the answer to that. I waited until the door had closed and his footsteps had died down along the reverberating corridor before dragging out my suitcase and fishing for my good walking shoes. There was no point in my staying here, no point at all. Cass was gone. Apparently something had happened between her and the Linwoods, but none of that concerned me. I looked around the room as I shed my Italian pumps for the sturdy hushpuppies that would serve for a walk back to the pub. "Sorry, my friends. I came here to make things up with Cass, not to get involved with some ancient romantic puzzle." The fact that I was talking aloud to an empty room as if it were full of spirits was a sign that I needed to get out of here—fast.

Still, I turned back at the door, bag in hand, to take a last look at the chamber that might very well hold the key to a lot of mysteries, including that of Crislyn and what had happened to her and why I was reliving her life.

"Good-bye," I said softly. "I'm sorry."

The corner of something protruding from the flowing bed coverlet caught my eye. Stooping to see what it was, I had a sense of vague recognition.

The scrap of faded, fuzzy orange turned into a felt ear, which when fully retrieved from under the bed turned out to be part of a stuffed animal—an elephant, missing one eye and worn off in spots and sporting a silly, limp snout. It wasn't just any stuffed animal, I realized with a sinking feeling; it was a very special one.

Cassandra's Punkin.

She had never gone anywhere, if it meant being parted from Punkin for overnight. It was her good luck charm, her best friend. I could remember Uncle Porter and Aunt May driving back 42 miles to get Punkin so Cass wouldn't cry at a friend's overnight.

She had brought it with her to Bloodstones. She wouldn't have left without it, unless she intended to come back.

I slowly took my shoes off and replaced them with the dressier pumps. Cassandra would either come back or she was in some kind of trouble and couldn't get back. Either way, I couldn't leave.

The other alternative was too chilling to contemplate. Punkin's abandonment could mean that my cousin had never left Bloodstones at all.

I was in my robe and about to change into something fresh when Jocko came to check on me. "I'm sorry, Miss. I have a message from the Baron about a change in plans."

I opened the door, still finding it hard not to gape at the living, walking epitome of the classic "B" horror film butler. It was all I could do to fight the tempting "Yass-s, Igor?"

"What change, Jocko?"

"Madame's having tea in her room. She'd like you to stop in on your way."

"On my way to what?"

The butler held out a moss green riding ensemble. "For the ride with the Baron that he thought might help you relax from the day's rigors. These should fit nicely, Miss." He held out boots as well.

"I'm surprised you could provide my size."

"The Baroness was much your same fit, Miss." Jocko blushed. "The Baron commented on it, saying there was only one, er . . . slight difference between the two of you."

I didn't laugh outright at the provision of a shirt that had apparently come from the Baron's own wardrobe.

Jocko, no doubt, considered my rather full bosom more

unaristocratic than inconvenient.

He waited for me outside the tower door. When I stepped out, fully attired, he said, "Quite nice, Miss, that outfit, if you'll allow me to say so."

"I always allow compliments, Jocko. Thank you for yours. Shall we go down, now?"

As we passed the occasional mirrors on our way along the long hall, past the refectory and inner courtyard to the great hall, I had to confess I did look rather smashing in the tight fawn-colored breeches and silk shirt topped by a handsome leather jacket. Tapping my riding crop against soft kid boots, I smiled to think how easily I could fit into this kind of life.

"This was once the lower solar room that Madame now occupies," Jocko whispered as we echoed through the Great Hall with its massive if sparse furnishings and ghostly suits of armor. "When her infirmity became greater, we adapted it to her use as a bedroom."

If I'd thought to find a sickly creature awaiting me amid the silver and lavender bedroom furnishings, I was in for a shock.

Madame Lilah Linwood was a most remarkable looking lady. I wished I knew more about curtsying before such splendid queenliness.

What presence the lady had! Added to lavender hair piled high, a la Marie Antoinette, were the snapping turquoise Linwood eyes and alabaster skin set off by mauve chiffon and grape-sized pearls. Top it all off with an aura of crackling energy, set in a room of silver and flattering violet shades, and that was Madame Lilah.

We looked at each other for a long, appraising moment. "So. You're Alix."

"Yes. There's some talk of my taking care of you for a few days. Shall I pour you some tea?" Unnerved by her steady scrutiny, I started toward the tea cart, all laid out quite elaborately.

Madame's blue-veined hand waved me to stop. "Good God, no. We may as well start off on an honest basis. That's only window dressing for my son's peace of mind. There's a bottle of sherry underneath. Jocko understands a poor old woman's weakness, even if my son doesn't. Ah, that's my girl. A glass for you, too; there's a dear." She sipped the sherry I handed her and eyed me benignly.

"Strictly forbidden, I suppose," I murmured as I settled back with my own glass. "But you seem old enough to decide what's good for you."

Madame grinned impishly. "I knew I'd like you, the moment I heard you standing up to Miles. I told him he acted like a total jackass." She took a deep swallow and held out her glass. "More, please, Alix dear. And there's a lacquered case on my dresser. Ah, that's the one. Lift out the little shelf with the pearls. There, that's a bright girl. Matches are in the drawer beneath."

I lit a Player for her and shook my head. "You really are wicked, aren't you? I suppose these are forbidden, too?" I lit myself a cigarette as well.

"Wonderful. Splendid. How I dearly love vice in its minor, pleasurable stages." Madame leaned back with contentment, eyeing me with approval. "You're an extraordinary young woman, of course. I knew it at once."

I adored her. We understood each other at once, and what can be better between two women, whatever the age gap? "If I'm lucky, I'll grow up to be like you."

She let happiness flutter for a moment across the incredible face, then said, "I knew someday you'd come to us. For a while, I thought it was the other one . . ." She coughed and waved her hand frantically to clear the curling smoke. "Quick! Half the tea down the lav . . . hide the sherry . . . and do light a cigarette to cover, will you?"

I barely managed all this before a cool voice spoke behind me. "I thought, from the clouds of pollution in the hall, that I should call the fire constable."

Lilah's delicate cough was heartrending. "Miles, darling, I hope you've made arrangements for this poor child to rest up from her harrowing experiences. First, you ran her down, then Samantha, and I think it's time we made retribution.''

The turquoise eyes were affectionate, but mocking. ''This 'poor child' is an accident on its way to happen.'' Miles' lazy gaze rested on me and my unhappy efforts at handling a stronger cigarette than I'm used to. ''I do hope you're better at riding than you are at smoking or driving, Miss Ames.''

He had me on two out of three, I conceded, but as for riding . . .! ''It's not really all that difficult, is it?'' I looked at him innocently. ''I mean, one climbs up on the left side and gives a nudge and off the beast goes—right?''

I caught a gleam in Lilah's eyes as she looked from me to her son and back again. ''You will be careful, won't you, • Alix? Miles is a devil with either a powerful horse or a motor under him. Don't let him goad you into anything you can't manage.''

I put my glass of sherry down with a smile. ''I have no intention of doing so, Madame Lilah.''

''Lilah, please—no more 'Madame.' '' To Miles, more sharply, she said, ''Don't you dare do anything outrageous, like dashing pell-mell through the brambles or jumping fences or the like. I want to keep Alix here with us as long as we can.'' I realized she'd had a sedative, since there was a droopiness to the painted lids and a sluggishness about the words. ''I just wish you'd come a little sooner, dear,'' she whispered drowsily as I bent on sudden impulse to kiss the smooth cheek. ''Not . . . much . . . time. So . . . little . . . time . . .''

Miles was watching us, then he bent over to drop a crisp kiss on his mother's forehead. ''Don't worry, love. We'll think of some way to keep her here as long as you like.'' The eyelids fluttered and Lilah dropped off with a soft smile.

On our way out of the castle to where Jocko was holding our horses in the tilting yard, I said, ''Your mother said something rather odd, about expecting me. She said she'd thought it might be 'the other one.' What did she mean?''

The Baron hesitated. ''My mother always wanted a daughter. There was only Dex and myself, she didn't care for my wife, so she's always maintained someone 'right' would come along to fill the void. She had high hopes about the American, Cassandra Coleman, but . . . that was a disappointment. My mother's rather fey, as you might have noticed." I could feel his eyes on me as he took the reins of his stallion, Shadow. "She seems to feel you belong at Bloodstones for some reason. I've never seen her react to any other woman as she did to you."

The small chestnut mare Jocko was holding for me looked gentle enough for a child to ride, but I liked the secret gleam in her eye. I had my own secret gleam as I mounted. Let the Baron find out for himself that I was no stranger to riding. I leaned over and patted the quivering neck of my horse. "What's her name?"

"Pandora. Don't be frightened of her running away with you or anything. She's quite gentle."

I hid a smile, having already communicated to Pandora that this would not be one of the dull rides she'd apparently been subjected to up till now. And the excited quiver in her sleek haunches sent back the message that she was ready for anything I was. "I can see that." If I stayed in England for a while, I might teach Pandora some of the rodeo tricks Cass and I had practiced for hours on Uncle Porter's horses. I could see the two of us now in our swimsuits, galloping madly around the huge fish pond, sometimes changing horses in a furious neck-to-neck race, other times diving from our horses into the cool water. "Oh, thanks, Jocko." I grinned at the butler when he handed me the trailing reins. "Be sure you have the ambulance number ready."

He shuddered. "Please, Miss, don't joke about such things."

We took a path that led off toward the river. The Baron waited for me to catch up. "There's a very old bridle trail that I thought you might enjoy. The castle hunters often came this way to spot game."

"It's beautiful," I said, delighted to think I was riding on a path that might have led the hawk-man to Crislyn that first time in the woods.

95

The path was wide enough to ride side by side. The Baron had to keep his larger horse in tight rein, the powerful creature being used to more action. Pandora, on the other hand, ambled along peacefully without guidance from me. Like any fine piece of horseflesh, she sensed her rider's mood in that special way horses have. "I'm glad you decided not to leave," the Baron said suddenly. "You were so angry with me, I was afraid you might."

"Is this an apology for what happened in the tower room?"

"I suppose, though I enjoyed kissing you very much." He put his hand over on Pandora's bridle and stopped his own horse. His knee pressed against mine. "What are you, Alix?" he asked softly. "A witch? Look at what's happened to the people here since you came. Jocko's like a schoolboy with a new little princess to pamper. That blasted pub keeper called twice while you slept to be sure you made it to the castle. Lilah . . . well, you know her reaction." He gave a little laugh. "I won't say Samantha is a fan of yours, but she's like most mannequins and hates competition."

I looked at him without embarrassment. "Are you trying to say I somehow bewitched you into making that pass at me a while ago?" I lifted his hand gently from Pandora's bridle. "Well, do you know what I think, Baron? I think you're a man who hates losing control for any reason. Wanting to make love to a woman you met fifteen minutes earlier doesn't fit into your superior little box and having her push you away doesn't compute, either. So, I'm a witch, if it makes you happy." I shot Pandora the signal she'd been waiting for. "And this horse is my familiar, so watch us fly to the moon."

We were off like the wind, and, God, it was glorious! I hadn't ridden for years and had forgotten what an exhilarating experience it could be. Pandora and I were one, with the forest an autumnal backdrop and the river dead still compared to our mercurial speed. I let my laughter spill into the wind to taunt the man we'd left behind in surprise and spurred Pandora to a faster pace when I saw the Baron pounding in pursuit on a fiery-eyed Shadow.

My slender steed was taking great joy in outrunning Shadow as well. Her mane streamed as wildly as my hair, and the delicate nostrils flared and snorted at the smell of victory in this race that we weren't supposed to win.

I expect I looked like a madwoman and sounded even crazier as I shouted back, "You'll never catch us." But as I looked back, taunting and laughing, I couldn't help admiring the sight of the Baron and Shadow. Strong and silent and determined, they blended with each other and were a beautiful pair.

But the look on the Baron's face made me return my concentration to the trail. This wasn't the game it started out to be, I thought uneasily. It was one I had to win.

He was shouting at me but I just galloped on even faster. Pandora was just getting into her stride, the darling, and I knew we could run forever.

I turned in my saddle to shout another challenge, but the taunt froze on my lips. For the Baron was closer now and I could hear what he was shouting.

"For God's sake, Alix, be careful of the fence! Pandora's never jumped before!"

Oh, lord! The stone fence loomed in front of us and there was no way on earth to veer my speeding mount, no chance of stopping in time. I bunched my nerves and willed the straining flesh beneath me to soar, to be unafraid.

There may be no blue ribbons or trophies in Pandora's stall, but that horse will always hold the Purple Heart for courage in my book. I'll never forget that sailing, soaring jump which seemed to last forever. I can still feel the shared triumph as we cleared the stones in a graceful, stretching leap.

I still remember the echo of my laughter. "We did it, Pandora! We did it, you wonderful creature!"

But the boast was premature. Pandora had jumped magnificently and what then happened wasn't her fault. There were some stones scattered from a recent wall-mending, and there was no way the surest footed horse in the world could have kept from stumbling.

When Pandora fell, I was flung through the air, through space and time.

As I rolled to a stop against a stone, I felt the blow with an inner cry of remembered pain. This wasn't the first time I'd fallen against a rock in a lonely forest.

6

The security of my bed in the copse had been sharply shattered by the sound of voices alarmingly close to my hiding place. It had been foolish to panic when I thought I heard the Baron's hunters after me. My wild, crashing flight could only end in capture since I was a novice as to survival in the wilds.

Ironically I had evaded, skulked and survived all these days only to stumble on a root and fall against a stone, knocking myself unconscious.

Glimpsing a circle of strange faces made me close my eyes quickly after I came to. My freedom was surely lost. In a few minutes I would be dragged back to Bloodstones and thrown to the Baron's snarling hunger like a bone to a dog.

And God knows what they'd do to me when it was learned I'd killed Roark.

A gentle touch with a cold cloth against my bruise made me brave enough to peek once more. This could be no servant of Linwood's perverseness, not this gentle-fingered elf whose grime couldn't hide a thousand freckles and an upturned nose. I wondered about the soothing hands having black stains on them, but decided that was part of my waking dream. I groaned and, I think, produced a grotesque smile to indicate my harmlessness as well as my gratitude for the ministrations.

Uncertain as I was of my circumstances or the degree of danger I might be in, I felt a warm instant liking for the girl peering at me so anxiously and smiling in obvious relief.

"Lord love us, Perk, she's not dead after all. A bump on the head is the worst of it, thank the saints. Lian will be surprised when he sees her, he will. Won't he have a laugh to know it's a lady leaving all those hunting signs after worrying that we've been followed?"

The short, balding man kneeling next to the girl fingered the fringe of my deerskins and looked at the matted curls on my neck. "Lady? Not this'un. These clothes look like something you might fancy, Meg, but no lady'd be out in the woods dressed like this." He moved my hair off my face with fingers nearly as gentle as the girl's, though dirtier. "Mother of God, would you look at 'er, Meg. A beauty, even under all the mud and brambles. I just hope that new man, that Rolling John, doesn't see her. He's got a twist in 'im about women, that one does, and . . ."

"Shh, I saw her eyelids flutter. She'll hear you—and such talk! Rolling John went in the other direction, so he'll not be taking out his strange needs to be hurting someone on this helpless lass."

"Did I hear my name?" I didn't like the sound of that third voice, and something told me to continue playing dead. "Ho, ho, what's this? A girl posing as a woodsman? Is she dead?"

"No, she's not. Only bumped her head a bit. Perk and I found her," the girl said sharply, "and we'll be the ones to see that Lord Blackheart decides about her without any other 'un harming her."

Lord Blackheart! I felt my heart go to my toes. The notorious highwayman's real identity was a secret, but everyone had heard he had once been a rich, titled landowner. He robbed only the carts returning from the seaports where sheepskins were traded high with Calais merchants. To poor people in and about the Weald and even more distant sheep country and forests, the robber lord was a hero.

But Henry himself had offered a huge ruby in reward for the highwayman's capture. It was many of the king's richest patrons who were being victimized.

"I'll watch her," the hateful, new voice said. "Lord Blackheart sent me to tell you, Meg, to forget the search and gather firewood for breakfast. And you, Perk, he said to sneak a sack of hay from the field that's been feeding our horses without anyone the wiser."

Don't go, I begged them silently. Don't leave me with him.

Meg, as if hearing my mute plea, stood up and said with spirit, "I'll not take orders from the likes of you, Rolling John, and neither will Perk. So go on with whatever slimy business you're up to. I still don't know what made Lord Blackheart take you in with us. I'd sooner trust a snake."

The man's arms shot out, and I opened my eyes to see Meg held high, squealing like a stuck pig, Rolling John's huge hands biting into the bony flesh. "Someday," he told her in a soft, menacing voice, "I'm going to teach you some manners that your precious lord doesn't see fit to teach you."

Perk was upset by the other man's mistreatment of the girl and shook in his tattered clothes as he stood up to the other, but I could see he wasn't without courage. "Put her down, Rolling John. She's right, about our taking our orders from Lord B. himself, not you. And the girl isn't for you to play with."

The man set the girl down roughly and reached for the bag lying near me. "What's in here?" He threw everything out without regard. "Bah. Stale manchets and moldy bits of cheese. There's no hope for any reward to be offered on the likes of her." He looked at me then, and I could feel the hateful eyes stripping the clothing from my still body. "Or there might be," he said softly. "There was talk about a girl the likes of this 'un having the richest, lustiest man in the county standing on his ear to get her back after he'd already traded for 'er.''

I held my breath. There'd be no ruby offered for my head, but the terrible Baron would pay this filth for news of me, of that I was sure. "Would one poor as I turn down a lord?''

Being a greedy man himself, Rolling John could understand the logic of that. "Well, it's said the girl's strange, has witch-like ways, and turns her eyes down and acts humble to no man."

One blast of a mournful horn cut through the misty morning. "That's me," Meg whispered, looking nervously from me, to Rolling John and back to Perk. "Lord Blackheart's call for me. I must go. He's a devil when it comes to keeping order in the camp."

She hadn't been gone a moment when the horn sounded two times. Rolling John grinned malevolently at Perk. "It's your call, Perk. And you know how impatient Lord Blackheart can be."

I was left alone with the man called Rolling John, and I had no doubt as to what he had in mind for me now that there was no one to call him down. My hands curled around a stone on each side of me, and I tensed to spring and escape. "You'd be foolish to do what you're thinking," I said coldly. "This Lord Blackheart may be a ruffian, but I have the feeling he wouldn't like one of his men attacking a lone girl while everyone else is off doing his work."

Rolling John grinned at me, the long, yellowish teeth those of a predator. "You might say I'm not completely bound to the highwayman like the others." He untied his soiled breeches and let them drop, and as he moved toward me, he said, "No noise, girl, or I'll have to hurt you. But I doubt you'll do anything but enjoy what's coming. I've not had a woman in a long time, and there'll be pleasure for both of us if you're sensible." He was on me then and had my head captured so he could fasten his wet mouth on mine. I lay stiff and still, my hand grasping the larger rock in a painful grip.

"You seem to want a man as much as any ripe wench," he whispered. "I thought from the looks of you I'd have more of a fight."

His voice held a disappointment that chilled me. He was a man who apparently enjoyed watching his victims thrash and squirm. I accommodated him by turning my head away from the searching mouth and crying out and trying to protect myself when he yanked my tunic up to my neck. The cries were sincere. His hands kneading my tender flesh were harsh and relentless; the beastly sounds of his mouth at my breasts and the clawing at my leggings finally drove me to desperate action.

The jagged stone seemed to sink into his temple as if it wer a soft, rotten apple. I didn't know I was so strong.

As with Roark, there was no sound, just a shocked, glazed look before the body went limp, but this time there was blood aplenty. I rolled away from him quickly before the spouting redness could cover me, and ran as fast as I could from the scene of my second terrible crime within an incredibly short period.

I carried with me another bit of survival knowledge that I was learning most dearly: surprise was my best means of protection.

My breath was as ragged as my gait, and I was leaving a trail that a child could follow. I stopped to listen for sounds of pursuit.

The forest kept its peace. There were no shouts or crashing footsteps or pounding hooves. I might be safe for the moment, but I was no better off. I'd totally lost my bearings and would have to find the stream I'd heard trickling off and on if I were to make it to the sea. What if I were turned around toward Ravensbridge even now?

The stream found, I felt hope. I tied my bag to my back, with the fur cloak secured under the straps, rolled up my breeches and started wading, cursing the stones that bruised my feet. Cold though the water was, I held my treasured boots aloft. They were essential for future travel and couldn't be ruined.

There was a rustle in a low-hanging tree ahead of me. I

stopped and stood still, listening. When a brace of birds flew out of the treetop, I let out my breath and continued on my way.

Relieved, I stopped under the branches stretching halfway across the stream to rest. At the unexpected, undeniable whinnying of a horse nearby, I froze, suddenly aware of danger. The stirring above me made me look up just in time to see a circle of rope descending, and I bit my lips against the cruel tightening that held me fast.

A voice filtered down from the leafy fort that had barred my escape. "It's not my usual sport, fishing with rope, but after seeing what happened to Rolling John, I decided not to be sporting."

I tried to see his face but could only make out a massive dark shape in the foliage. I knew that it had to be Lord Blackheart, the legend of the Weald, and I was trapped by him. "Let me go. Please. I won't tell anyone I saw you. I only want to get to the sea." I felt like crying, standing in the cold stream like a captured animal. "I'm no good to you, alive or dead. Please!"

He leaped down from the tree to the bank, graceful as a cat. A horse came out of the brush at his signal, and he tied the end of the rope that held me tight onto the saddle. "That's probably how you disarmed Rolling John, acting like an ordinary, sweet little wench. It's a wonder he's still alive, with all the blood he lost."

"Still alive? Oh, my God. Then you have to let me go. He'll kill me."

"Not likely, the state's he's in." He mounted his horse and, without looking back to see if I were keeping up or being dragged over the rough ground, started off. "Meg and Perk said you were both odd and sly. I think I can add a thing or two to that description. Unfeeling, for instance. You acted disappointed when I told you Rolling John might live."

I was half-trotting, half-dragged. "Damn it, talk about someone who's unfeeling! All right, I hit the man, but only to protect myself. Ask Meg. Ask Perk. They'll tell you that

they knew even before I did that the man would try to . . ."
I felt tears of rage mixed with self-pity streaming down my
face. "Damn you, can't you stop for a moment and listen?
I'm no cow to be led by a rope."

He pulled up so suddenly I nearly ran into the smooth
rump of his horse. Still he wouldn't turn so I could see his
face. I almost forget my chafed arms, rubbed raw even
through my deerskin, in my curiosity about the man on the
horse. "No?" His voice was that of a man who hadn't grown
up in a forest among thieves. "Then perhaps you'd rather
have it around your neck. Our camp can mete out its own
justice, and I wouldn't give you much chance of winning
over the men who might judge you. Rolling John was no
prince, but he had a strong back and a spectacular shooting
eye. You put him out of action. If there were a vote tonight,
you'd be hanged in the morning."

I said scornfully, "The heroic Lord Blackheart hang a
woman? Ha! He might pass me amongst his men, letting
them have a taste of what caused John to lose a goodly part
of his skull, but he wouldn't have me hanged. Even a filthy
robber couldn't stoop so low."

He turned slowly on his horse, and I moved back a step
or two when I saw the face of Lord Blackheart. I gasped at
the black patch covering one eye. But never had I seen such
a man, nor experienced such a feeling of knowing him,
though I'd never before set eyes on such wood-hewn
features, nor such jet black hair and beard. Dressed all in
black on his black horse, he had to come straight from Hell,
with his covered eye that spoke of dark violence and his stiff
backbone that made his black horse part of his grim sil-
houette.

"Low?" he asked with a chuckle. "You say a highwayman living off the fat of robber barons would be stooping
low to pluck a marauding fox off the entry to its hard-won
rabbit warrens?" He glared down at me. "Look at this place
covering a dark hole in my face and tell me if I should take a
chance on you bringing hanging down on all of us,
deserving or not."

How could I answer? Lord Blackheart's questions weren't really questions. "I . . . I'm sorry about your eye." It was strange. Here I stood tied like a ewe bound for market, with God knows what kind of fate in store for me, expressing pity for my captor. But the surge of sympathy wasn't just for the highwayman's missing eye. I felt an odd kindship with this man who fought for survival in his way as I fought in mine. "I can't blame you for sounding bitter."

I'd said the wrong thing. Too late I realized that pity would be the final insult to a man like this one. I cried out when Lord Blackheart caught up the rope slack and pulled me in sharply, till I was pressed against his boot. "Never," he said between clenched teeth, "say to me again, by any look or words, that you're sorry for me." He held the rope painfully tight for a long time, then released the grip so suddenly I almost fell backward. "Why were you following us this morning? Are you, like everyone else, after the reward Bluff Hal's put on my head?"

I shook my head, keeping my eye glued to his one good one. "No, sir. Truly, I've no desire whatever to see you captured or collect any record. I have good reason to stay out of any constable's way, having run away from . . . from a . . . position of servitude. As for following you, I fancied myself trailing a rabbit."

He stared at me in disbelief, then threw back his head in laughter. Thinking of what I'd just said, I almost joined in. "A . . . rabbit? I look forward to telling my men how quiet their skulking through the woods has become." He leaned forward, his face stern and suspicious once more. "And tell me, wench of the weald, if you'd found your rabbit, how would you have caught him? There were no weapons, according to my cohorts who found you. You could pass for a forest denison yourself in that deer hide, which I must say I find totally fascinating. Do you walk up to the rabbit and invite him to join you in a pot of stew?"

I'd never mentioned my special talent, my way of hunting, to anyone before. But without thinking what light my explanation might cast on me, I said to this man,

"There's a way I have that brings the woods creatures to me, and my knife is quick and merciful. No creature ever suffers more than the blink of an eye. I kill only for food, unlike some."

Surprisingly, Lord Blackheart didn't laugh or sneer. "Interesting. A half-wild girl dressed like a deer who can 'think' small game into her supper pot. I'd like to see you work your magic." He reached down suddenly and untied the rope. I flexed and rubbed my arms, looking at him without knowing quite what he expected. "I'll make it easy," he told me with a thin smile. "Meg's responded to my complaints about mutton every meal by serving up a scrawny squirrel every other morning. I haven't the heart to tell her I'm sick of that, too. Eggs." He took a deep breath. "That's what I've been dreaming of—soft, fluffy, delicious eggs."

"You act like I'm a magician," I said. "I've never done it like this."

"Ah well, we'll forget it then and take you back to camp and try to be happy with Meg's gamey cooking fare."

He held out the rope, and I said quickly, "Wait! I'll . . . I'll try." I closed my eyes and shut out everything around me that had to do with man, letting the soft purity of nature, the fresh forest smells, the hidden sounds of life come into my mind.

There was a sound that separated itself from the others. I could sense the billing and cooing and fluttering of a nesting pheasant in some part of my consciousness as I moved toward the commotion in the underbrush. A short foray into the woods brought me to the place I had seen in my mind's eye. I sensed Lord Blackheart behind me as I knelt.

He was silent when I held out the eggs in my cupped hands. Then his eye went slowly upward to my face. "This talent of yours enables you to enter the minds of men, as well as animals, giving you control of them?"

"No, my lord." I thought of Roark and the Baron and said honestly, "If I could do that, would I be sleeping under a hedge, hiding from robbers and chasing skinny rabbits?"

He laughed. "You have a point. Come. I've got a hunger that won't wait any longer." He chuckled at the look on my face. "For eggs, wench! I never attack stray witches on an empty stomach. Come on. I have to tie you again; you're too slippery to trust."

I dug in my heels and shook my head slowly, feeling the warm tears of anger and humiliation at the thought of being led into the midst of Lord Blackheart's sorry band, roped like a dumb animal. "No." I looked at him with all my fierce pride there to see. "I won't be treated like that. You can leave me untied like a human being or you can kill me. And if you don't kill me, I feel bound to tell you I won't be kept prisoner by you for any longer than it takes to plan an escape."

He looked at me with that unfathomable good eye. "Then tell me what I must do to keep you, wench of the weald," he said softly.

I felt my cheeks redden. "I . . . I don't . . . why would you want to keep me? I'm trouble, first and last."

He laughed, and I saw the strong white teeth and one flashing bright eye and thought again that, except for his infirmity, Lord Blackheart was quite the handsomest man I'd ever seen. "I can see that, girl." Without warning, he tossed the rope over his shoulder and reached down to gather me up. Suddenly I was sitting stiffly, wedged in front of him, my bag of eggs close to my chest. "Unless you slow down," I said with some asperity, "you'll have to settle for scrambled eggs."

He laughed, but slowed the huge stallion to a walk.

The camp had been cleverly sited; it was set in a deep hollow with rough rocks on two sides and a brambly, impassable thicket on the third. We came in through the camp's thoroughly shielded entrance. As we burst through the thick foliage into the clearing, a dozen pairs of eyes were on me. Meg and Perk, bent near an unconscious Rolling John who lay next to the fire, smiled at me timidly, but theirs were the only remotely friendly faces.

What a raggle-taggle crew, I thought. I was glad to see that none seemed openly evil like John, but I didn't like the blatant stares at the curves I hadn't lost even with my lean meals of late. Lord Blackheart handed the bag to Meg. "Be careful with the breakfast she's found me, sprout. And, Perk, I want her kept inside the hut, watched every minute so she gets no chance to play any tricks." He swung me down with about as much regard as he might have for a sack of potatoes.

Meg put her hands on her hips. "I'll see to your breakfast, Lord B., but first I'd like a chance to see that the poor girl gets over all the horror she's been through here." She handed the bag to Perk and moved over to put her arm around me. "Poor thing—trembling and scared out of her senses, not to mention starving to death." She looked Lord Blackheart squarely in the eye. "I'll take 'er in and calm her fears while you settle things out here," she said meaningfully. "The girl's a beauty, not like me who can lie near Perk at night and not be bothered by him nor any man. If you don't let them know . . ." jerking her head toward the men who still stared at me, ". . . it'll be Rolling John four times more."

Lord Blackheart laughed softly, then put his hand on Meg's curly head. "All right, sprout. I'll let them know, but at the right time. In the meantime . . . well, I hadn't planned to give up my dry bed out of the rain."

I heard a groan from the man I'd injured and looked fearfully over at John in his bloodstained, dirty bandages. When he regained consciousness, my life would be in worse danger than it already was.

Meg was my only hope.

She squeezed my arm as she led me into the little hut where apparently I was meant to stay—with the camp leader, I feared, from his conversation with Meg. "Be glad the fellow didn't die, girl. He's new, but the men have taken him in as one of us."

"Are you sure he'll get well with such a wound?" I decided I'd rather take my chances against the four men who'd stared at me than Rolling John when he'd recovered from his terrible blow at my hand.

"We had a sheep doctor sneak in for a look who said he's got a head harder than the stone you bashed him with." Meg handed me a mug of warmish ale. "Here. You look done in and could probably do with a swig."

I drained the mug thirstily. "What did Lord Blackheart mean about not giving up his place?" The straw bedding in the corner didn't look like a bed a man would become attached to. "Meg, he's not planning to . . . I mean, you don't think he's . . ."

Meg giggled. "There's just no proper name for it, is there, lass? Well, when you think of how Lord B. set Perk as my protector, so to speak, and then look at me and see how far from tempting I am . . . and when you look at *you* . . ." She grinned. "Love, Lord B.'s doing you a favor, keeping you safe with him at night. Them men see their women once a fortnight, if they're lucky. I even see 'em eyeing me on long nights, straight piece of meat that I am." She giggled again. "Would you believe it? I'm still a virgin, love. Living out in the woods with seven lusty men, and I'm still pure. I'm saving myself, you might say, for a sweet, serious fellow with blond curls and soft eyes and . . ." She cocked her head at me. "Why're you looking at me like that?"

"I was just thinking how much I like you, and that I've never had a friend before—not a woman friend, I mean. Well, except for Nana."

Meg's dancing eyes got serious. "It's funny, but I haven't either, and the first minute I saw you, I said to myself how I'd like someone like you for a sister."

We looked at each other for a long moment, letting the warmth between us chase some of the loneliness away. Then I had to say, "Even so, Meg, I don't like being cooped up and won't stand for it any longer than I have to. I'll try to get away from him. Know that before you trust me too much."

She said softly, "I know. But try not to hurt 'im, lass. He's been hurt enough."

I hurt Lord Blackheart? It seemed like an odd inversion of the situation. "Meg, I haven't told you my name. I'm Crislyn."

She smiled. "Pretty as Meg is homely. Don't bash Perk's head in when I send him back with breakfast for you. The men'll be screaming at me if I don't dish up their vittles."

She was gone, and I had the opportunity to examine my prison. It might as well have been the famous Tower of London. Primitive and meager as the room was, the place offered no ready escape route, and I saw nothing that might serve as makeshift protection should I need it come nightfall. The rough, three-legged stool with its greenish candle next to the straw bed wouldn't be much of a weapon, I decided, nor the . . .

"Meg sent you this, Missy." Perk came in and handed me a wooden bowl with eggs and a chunk of bread stuffed with white cheese. I thought I might faint from the delicious aroma. He whispered, "Lord B. said you was to have the bread and cheese, but Meg's taken a liking to you and slipped you some of the rest."

"Umm! Perk, I may just die here on the spot, this is so delicious." I stuffed myself for a moment, then glanced at the curious, watching face. "You don't have to worry about watching me every minute, Perk. If it's the spoon you're worried about, the floor's too hard to dig out of here."

He shook his head. "Don't joke like that, Missy. Meg says you're stubborn, and I can see you need more understanding about the man holding you. He's stubborn, too. The more you try to cross him, the more he quietly decides he'll have his way about things. Make friends with him; use your woman's sweetness to talk him into letting you go."

"No." I set the bowl down and shook my head. "I don't feel sweet toward your robber lord, Perk. And if I can escape, I will."

Perk's face fell. "He says he's holding me and Meg responsible. If you get away, it'll be us that pays." He said more entreatingly, "Stay, Missy. We're not a bad bunch, not a bit of it."

''Oh, you're a fine lot, all right. I heard how you rob without reason and murder without mercy.''

Perk shook his head sadly. ''The bad stories about us have gone around, right enough, but there's not one of us here started out as thieves. Except for the man Rolling John who just joined us, we're all men who once worked our little farms and led respectable lives. There weren't no luxuries nor fine homes nor much to brag about, but we worked hard, like our families before us and those before them, and took care of our own. Then *they* came along with the inclosures. It drove out many a poor farmer; we're only a small number of the poor who were made homeless by the inclosures.''

''Perk, I don't know what you're talking about. Who are 'they'? And what are inclosures? Why would you lose your homes because of either?''

The man shook his head sadly. ''See how no one is aware of things happening to his neighbor. With all the handsome prices being offered for English wool, a lot of greedy men have started looking at sheep farming for great profits. But the fields have to be closed off with fence hedges to keep the sheep in, and the fields we've farmed for years can bring handsome rents.'' He shook his head. ''When these rich men, most of them close to influential peerage, even the king himself, offer large bribes to have us evicted and our fields rented to the new sheep farmers for their use, they forget how long we and our families have lived on the land, turning back some of everything we produced.''

''But Lord Blackheart was not one of you.''

Perk shook his head. ''If you mean he's one of the gentry as none of us is, you're right. He owned a fine castle before he was cheated of it. Unlike some others, he fought the inclosures and the profiteering that was making good families homeless. But due to a bit of trickery, he lost his property to one of the sheep barons.'' He added sadly. ''That ain't all he lost. He's a bitter man, missy, but he has a right to be. The rest of us have our families, scattered and living hand-to-mouth though they might be. And we've still got our two eyes, all of us.''

"Lord Blackheart lost his eye when all this happened?"

"Missy, it's not proper I should be talking to you about Lord B. You'll be making your own judgments about 'im same as us, once you've gotten to know 'im. Let's just say without Lord B. them robber barons would still be taking everything they could from the likes of us, 'stead of looking to it that their own carts ain't stole."

"He raids the carts bound for the seaport?"

"No, we have no use for the wool. We do our robbing after they've done their trading to the French, who love the English wool. They come back loaded with better goods for our purposes—mostly gold."

I laughed. "Perk, you're all pirates. Has it ever occurred to you what they'll do to you if you're caught?"

He bristled. "It was piracy when they stole our lands, too, Missy. And if folks knew the truth of it all, we'd be heroes instead of having bounties on our heads."

I sighed. "I don't think anyone after the reward will stop to ask if you had a good reason to turn highwayman." Perk shifted uneasily. I was sure he and Meg were about as unlikely a pair of robbers as any could be. "Look at this room. Look at the clothes you're wearing—and Meg, too. All of you look like walking beggars. And the food. Mutton stew. Mutton chops. Mutton roast, cold, hot, sliced, breaded . . . " I stopped for breath. "On the other hand, Lord Blackheart wears a silk shirt, I notice. And the horse he rides has fancy gear that is worth more than all of yours put together." I looked at the little man and said softly, "The gold, Perk, the fine booty all of you have risked your life for . . . where is it?"

The answer came not from Perk, but from directly behind me. "In the safekeeping of my London contact who is quietly and efficiently arranging for land purchases for each of my followers. Perk and the others, with their families, will soon be landowners themselves in provinces far away enough to escape recognition and reprisal."

I blushed. "And, you, of course, are using none of the stolen money for yourself. They should rename you Lord Goodheart."

"I'm using my share in a gamble that you'll know more about later. But at the moment, if you have no other questions for Perk, he's needed to prepare the horses." He turned to Perk. "There's a return shipment expected from Welchelsea late tonight. Tell the others I'll be out shortly."

After Perk had left, his eyes downcast at the rebuke in his master's voice, I said sharply, "Don't blame him for anything. I browbeat him into talking."

"I know what you've been doing with Perk and with Meg, wench of the weald, but you're wasting your time trying to turn them against me or anyone else. Oh, except Rolling John, who hasn't the same loyalty to me the others do. But somehow I think you missed your chance at charming that fellow into helping you escape."

Perk stuck his head back in. "Begging pardon, Lord B., but the three you want waiting near the turnoff to Guilford—should they go on ahead of you and the others? And Darby wants to know why we're splitting up, with us being a man short on this raid."

"The three of them should set out now, Perk. Their job's to lead astray the two guards who ride a mile ahead of the wagons. The deep wood next to the turnoff should offer a good place to lose them. Then Darby and I'll be coming up behind the carts to join with the front three."

After Perk left, I said with some honesty, "You seem to be very careful about these raids of yours."

"I have to. They're getting smarter and more anxious to put my head on a spike."

"Eventually you'll be caught."

"Quite right. That's exactly why I intend to disappear as suddenly as I appeared, just as soon as my goal is attained. And that's not far off." He smiled the cynical smile that cut through his face like steel. "I have several identities, you see. I'm a wealthy investor who often visits provincial relatives to the people in London who know me as Lord Carnton, with a respectable house on Chancery Lane."

I stared at him. "Lord Blackheart. Lord Carnton. What's your real name? Or do you have one?"

"I have one, but only Meg and Perk know it. No one else ever will, since that part of my life is over. The man I was before I became Lord Blackheart no longer exists or matters."

"Relatives . . . Surely you . . . the man you were had kin who'd want to help you, or at least to know you're alive."

"Who'd want to claim me now?" His face hardened. "Even if there were someone, and there isn't, I like things the way they are. I owe no one, am dependent on no other—nor they on me."

"Meg and Perk look to you for leadership, as do your men."

"Don't mistake loyalty for dependence, Crislyn. And when Meg and Perk start their new lives, there'll be no one tying me to my past."

"It sounds very lonely. But as Lord Carnton I suppose you'll make friends and perhaps . . . perhaps even marry again."

The handsome face looked murderous. "The friends I have will be those I can use to obtain my wealth and power. I intend to devote my life to turning the greed and corruption of England's hierarchy toward my own advantage. As for marriage . . ." the word was practically spat out ". . . I'll have no woman in my life on a permanent basis. Those who can help me achieve my goal can expect to be treated as my equal, as long as it doesn't involve trust, love or any binding agreement."

"I see." I was silent for a moment, trying to think how to phrase my question. "You say Meg and Perk won't stay with you indefinitely. Dare I hope this means you'll let me go, too, since I don't suffer from a compulsion to love or trust you or expect the same? And also I can't be any use to you in building this empire of yours."

He looked thoughtful. "Actually, it's been in my mind that you can be useful to me. Not only useful but vital." His eyes stirred as he looked me up and down as if he'd never seen me before. "Yes, come to think of it, you'd be the perfect woman for the project I have in mind.''

I stepped back, not liking the look in his one good eye. ''Project? What kind of project?''

He seemed to be thinking out loud. ''You could be my pampered little sister from the provinces, innocent to the ways of the city and men like Hammond.''

''What do you mean 'men like Hammond'?'' I didn't like the sound of this at all.

He ignored me, his face showing that the idea was becoming more and more appealing, whatever it was. ''Yes, it would be perfect. My pampered, beautiful little sister, coming to stay with big brother and leaving her rich, dull husband behind in the country while she lets herself be seduced by Wolsey's handsome, influential Advisor on Royal Charters.''

I said coldly, ''I did not run away from Baron Linwood to be thrown to some other man.''

''Linwood?'' Lord Blackheart was momentarily distracted from his plan. ''Linwood of Bloodstones at Ravensbridge? He's the man after you? That certainly surprises me.''

''You know him?'' I hadn't meant to let slip the identity of my pursuer.

''Know of him, more accurately.'' He laughed, looking at my dirty face and knotted hair above the soiled deerskins. ''It's Linwood who's scouring the countryside for you?''

I reddened. ''I'm glad you find it amusing. I don't happen to think it's very funny.''

''It's not as funny as it is unbelievable. Linwood, a rich Baron—and quite handsome, I've heard—after you, and you choose a fugitive's life over the soft one in his castle. Why, girl, if the man likes you, you could have been sipping wine in your beautiful gown in a fine castle instead of scratching your way through the woods.''

I saw no reason to tell him I'd never met Baron Linwood. And how could I explain my deep, stubborn pride that wouldn't allow me to be bartered to another? ''There's another reason I can't go back to Ravensbridge, but I can't tell you about it." If he knew about Roark, he'd hold a weapon over me that could be used any time to make me do as he wished.

Besides, I never wanted anyone to hear about the debasing use Roark had tried to make of me. It was still too shameful to admit.

"So you're trying to lose your own past." Lord Blackheart looked at me thoughtfully. "I wonder . . . ? Perhaps we have more in common than we both realize." He stepped closer, and my heart started thumping erratically. Softly, he said, "Meg told me you hated being put in my hut. I know you're no virgin, Crislyn. And you're sensual—I know that, too. It would be to your advantage to be seductive, using your body to gain power over your fate, and yet you fight me at every turn."

He put his mouth on mine. I endured the kiss without the slightest response, even when I felt a rising anger. His mouth was cruel, his hands biting into my flesh, but I stayed as stiff and unyielding as a stone.

He pushed me from him and turned his back on me. "At least you make no pretense of enjoyment. No doubt you find it repulsive, kissing a man with one eye."

It wasn't couched as a question but I knew that's what it was. I answered truthfully. "You've shown me neither kindness nor consideration; I'm your prisoner. How could I be drawn to you? As for being repulsed . . . no, Lord Blackheart, I'm not repulsed by your infirmity. I find myself wistfully longing for a man, one-eyed or two-eyed, to allow me a choice in what happens to my person."

He turned around, his face shadowed. "I won't force myself on you again. You'll stay with me at night, for your own protection, but I won't try to make love to you." He gave his bitter smile. "You may not think so, but I *am* human. I want to be loved by a woman for myself alone, not for my outer appearance or what I can give her."

He reached into his pocket and brought out a black silk scraf that fitted over his whole head, like a hood with two eyes and a hole for breathing. "Clever, the two eye slits, eh?'' He laughed. ''In London, my patch is considered debonair, but on the highways I plunder, it might give me away. Besides, the hoods we wear add a touch of horror to the whole operation.''

''It does look macabre, Lord Blackheart.''

He pulled an elaborate velvet case from under the pallet I'd be using. I couldn't help watching curiously as he lovingly removed a beautiful tooled weapon with a silver, engraved handle. ''A gun!'' I gasped. ''I've heard it said that someday it will be in the hands of even the most common Englishman.''

''Not likely for a long time, which gives me an advantage over the men I rob.'' He stuck the pistol in the belt of his breeches. ''It's called a wheel lock. I'm sure the German prince who presented it to me when he was a guest at my castle would be appalled at my use of it. Meg, bless her, knew how I treasured the gift and bribed a servant to retrieve it for me.''

With enthusiasm, I said, ''Could I see you shoot it sometime? I've always thought that . . .'' He was looking at me oddly, and I stammered. ''Oh course, you'd never do such a foolish thing. I don't know what got into me.''

There was a shout from outside. Lord Blackheart got his cloak and paused at the door to look back at me. ''What an odd little thing you are. I'll do even better than letting you see me shoot the wheel lock. I'll teach you how to use it . . . if, that is, you'll promise to be here when I get back.'' He waited, but I didn't say anything. ''You can promise not to try to escape, can you?'' He sighed. ''Well, I have to tell you that I'm holding Meg responsible if you run off before I'm back from the raid. I told her—and meant it—and I'm telling you now that she gets a thrashing if she lets you get away.''

''That's unfair.'' But I was crying my protest to empty air. ''Bloody unfair,'' I said to myself, knowing I couldn't bring punishment to the young girl I'd begun to care for. And then I forgot about escape or Meg as I went over and examined the gun case. As I rubbed my hand over the soft covering and fingered the elaborate, scrolled mark that matched that on the gun, I thought of the irony of Lord Blackheart going from the company of royalty to a company of ex-villeins—and me.

And I thought of shooting the wheel lock and decided on the spot that I would someday have my own gun.

Just think of being able to protect myself from the likes of Rolling John!

After we'd gathered wood for the campfire and put the mutton on to boil for the men's late supper, Meg asked if I'd like to bathe in the nearby stream. "There's a little pool with a bit of a waterfall," she told me. "And with Perk to look out for us back here in the camp, we could have such fun."

Who cared about fun? I was thinking of getting clean for the first time in ages.

Perk said he'd look after the cookpot and see that Rolling John, still too weak to do more than sleep, got the water he craved fitfully.

Meg led the way to the shallow pool and shyly turned her back while we each stripped down. When she found out I had no underthings, she was shocked and made me wear her shift which she had on over modest cotton drawers and thick underblouse. I giggled at the way her small shift stuck to me as soon as I got wet, looking like a second skin. And then we forgot everything in the joy of getting clean again. After we'd scrubbed and rinsed from toe to top, we had water fights and played like two little girls. I don't think Meg had ever acted so silly; I know I hadn't.

"Thanks for not doing what you were thinking of when I had soap in my eyes and the way was clear for you to run away." Meg said this so quietly that I stopped splashing and sat down in the shallow water, facing her. "It made me feel warm inside to think you might care a little about what happens to me."

I said softly, "I do care, Meg. Lord Blackheart isn't my idol, like he is yours and Perk's, but when I first saw you, I felt we'd be friends somehow. And though I've known you such a short time, I feel like it's been for years." I put my hand on hers. "I have a feeling you've had some pretty hard times."

She turned her head away and said gruffly. "Things are hard for folks like me, all right, but I keep laughing a lot and thinking how lucky I am to have Perk and the others, kind of looking after me like a family. Lord B., though he fought for us and saved me and will see I'm cared for, wants to be rid of us all. I can see 'im wanting to be by 'imself again, and that's how it'll be soon."

"Do you have any sisters?"

Meg shook her head. "Nor brothers. Do you?"

"No. Not anybody, really, except my grandmum and I had to leave her." I turned my head away. If Meg could keep from crying over her life, then I could keep from crying over leaving Nana.

"Crislyn, there's some terrible thing inside you that I wish you'd let out. I can feel it eating at you. Would you tell me? I promise I'll keep it to myself."

I looked at that plain, good face and felt the clean water and thought about Roark and the ugliness he'd made me feel, and before I knew it, I was telling her the whole sordid story. She held me close and rocked me as I wept like a child.

"That's a terrible thing to carry inside you," she said simply. "I'm glad it's out now."

My tears dried, and I felt my guilt over Roark finally wash away. Almost cheerful, I changed the subject. "Meg, I know Lord Blackheart is thinking of a scheme that involves me. He couldn't possibly be thinking of keeping me with him even after he goes back to London, could he?"

Meg said brightly, "Lord Blackheart doesn't often tell the rest of us what he's thinking, so you'll just have to wait and find out what he plans for you."

I said darkly, " 'Wait and find out,' my foot! I've no intentions of going to London with a one-eyed highwayman. He has some notion of my seducing, or letting myself be seduced by, some high and mighty nobleman." I stood up in my agitation. "He's even talking about passing me off as his sister." I pulled the girl to her feet. "I ask you, Meg, do I look like a lady? Look at me and tell me truthfully if I could pass for the sister of a princely lord."

She didn't laugh as I expected. After a long time of looking me over seriously, she told me, "You're so beautiful, Crislyn. It takes away my breath just to look at you."

I said impatiently, "I'm not talking about just how I look, Meg."

"Well, I've noticed that it's more than clothes and such with you. I knew from the first time I saw you, Crislyn, that you were meant to be a lady. You have a way about you, something I'm too dumb to put in words." Meg shook her head. "Lord B. knows what he's about, all right."

We didn't have any further chance to discuss the matter for Meg heard the sound of the returning men and went scrambling for her clothes. "Oh, lord, if he catches me gone, there'll be the devil to pay."

Perk called from the bank, keeping his plump hand over his eyes at the sight of us. "You'd best come quick, Meg. John's stirring and asking for food, and I'm not much good at it. I nearly choked 'im with the first spoonful."

I wished he had. "Let me do it, Meg," I told her.

She grinned at me and hurried off. "Stay with her, Perk, and be sure nobody comes up sudden-like before Crislyn has her clothes back on."

I laughed quietly at the blushing Perk. "Why don't you come in for a bit, Perk? I won't peek."

He shut his eyes when I sat in the water and slowly dribbled it over my arms and half-exposed breasts. "Please, Missy, come in now. Lord Blackheart'll take the hide off both of us."

No, he won't, I thought suddenly. I promised him I wouldn't try to escape until after he got back from the raid. And he was back. I had to move fast, though. I took one more tiny swim, with my shift up over my buttocks enough for Perk to catch sight of my dimples. He was red as a beet.

''Missy, please . . .''

I laughed and stood up, throwing my hair back and letting every motion make my breasts jiggle.

Perk hid his eyes as I walked toward him, and I realized why Meg was safe with him. The poor man was terrified of women.

''I can see what a gentleman you are, Perk. If you'll keep your eyes shut, I'll get my clothes from behind that bush over there and be dressed in a few moments. When I'm all covered up, I'll give a little whistle.'' I knew he would stand there like that half the night, if I didn't whistle.

No time to dress! My deerskins over my arm, I moved at a soft trot till I was out of sight of Perk. Quickly! Quickly! If I were going to get far enough away, I had to chance his hearing me run.

''No, they'll catch you. They're on horses, remember. It'll be a simple matter to close off this part of the weald and trap you.''

There was a well-used animal path which was the obvious way to cut through the thicket back to the main road. I jerked off a bit of my deerskin fringe, stuck it on a bramble, then snapped a few twigs here and there. Then I went back to the stream and found what I wanted—an over-hang of roots and turf with a heavy growth of bushy reeds. It was a tight little cave, but I could stay there without detection till morning, when the search would have been abandoned.

It was my best chance. No one would expect me to stay this close to the camp.

It would be wet in the hole, so I looked around and found a tree hollow to hide my clothes. They'd be dry when I made my real escape the next day after the hue and cry had ended.

It made me feel guilty to hear Perk's shamefaced explanation when someone finally came to fetch the poor fellow and see what had happened, but freedom was more important than his feelings. And I couldn't help feeling smug when the search party galloped right past me and one of them exclaimed at the sight of my torn fringe, "This way, Lord B. The girl fooled the poor fellow into giving her enough time to be halfway back to the main road by now."

Their voices faded, and I had to grin when I heard them return a half-hour later and heard Lord Blackheart say without much regret, "She's gone for good, all right, and good riddance. Let's go back and have Meg dish up the supper, and afterwards we'll take a look at the best haul we've made in a month."

That put them all into a good humor, and I relaxed. I wouldn't even have to stay here till morning.

But I'd better give them plenty of time to get into their ale, celebrating the rich booty. Realizing suddenly how exhausted I was, I stretched out the best I could and dozed off.

A very large frog croaking in my ear woke me perhaps a half-hour later. Refreshed though cramped by my nap and elated by the successful outmaneuvering of my captors, I whispered to the frog. " 'Nedeep' to you, too, frog. And don't worry; I'm leaving and you can have your house back."

Sore in every muscle, I crept over to the tree and reached in the hollow for my deerskins and boots. Damn! The hole must have been deeper than I thought. My hand touched bottom, but they weren't there. Suddenly frightened, I bent and felt around the base of the tree. Maybe an animal had somehow pawed them out and . . .

"Are you looking for these, by any chance?"

A full view of the dimples that had sent Perk into shock was available to Lord Blackheart. I straightened up slowly and turned around to face the mocking eye, ignoring the clothes he held out to me. "I should have known you wouldn't give up. Did you know I was here all the time, or was it a lucky guess?" Twice now he'd outwitted me. It was beginning to get discouraging.

"You're too skilled in the woods to leave such a clumsy trail. So I asked myself what I would have done in your case." He smiled at me. I was quite surprised he wasn't angry, but then realized he'd enjoyed outwitting me again. "Apparently we're alike in other ways than I mentioned earlier."

"You're a better hunter than I gave you credit for," I conceded grudgingly. I hugged my breasts.

A breeze had sprung up and Meg's shift was thin and still damp. "Let me have my clothes. I'm no good to you dead of croup."

He looked at me and then back at the deerskins as if making up his mind about something. "So far you haven't been any good to me alive." With a sudden movement, he threw the bundle into the stream and said unfeelingly, "They were developing an awful smell."

Something snapped in me as I watched my clothes floating off, lost to me forever. The deerskins had been a sort of symbol for me, a flag of independence, a display of self-reliance.

"You devil," I cried. "You one-eyed savage from hell!" I lit into him then, biting and pummeling and scratching like a crazed forest creature. Lord Blackheart didn't laugh out loud, but I could feel the amusement as he held me at bay, nimbly dodging my blows. I stopped as suddenly as I'd started and burst into helpless, gulping, ugly tears.

"Now are you ready to hear my proposition to you?" he asked after I'd calmed down. "I told you it would be an equal exchange—and it will."

I hiccupped and wished I had something besides my shift to blow my nose. "What will you do with me if I flatly refuse, bargain or no bargain? Anyway, what will you do for me if I let this randy lord of yours have his way with me to get you what you want? And what do you want anyway?"

"If you'll shut up for one minute and not ask so many damn questions at once, I'll tell you." He looked at my clinging shift and smiled. "It's difficult discussing business with you dressed—or undressed—like that."

I glared at him. "It's not easy for me, either, but then I wasn't the one who threw my clothes in the water."

"Listen to me, Crislyn. All I ask is that you accompany

me to London—it won't be long now, after tonight's haul—and stay with me, oh, I'd think a month would do. Except it'll be better for you to pose as my wife instead of my sister . . ."

"Your wife?"

"Yes," he said calmly. "I did some thinking after we talked. Hammond might wonder if I let my sweet little sister fall into his clutches without a protest. A wife is different matter, especially one I've hidden away while I pleased myself in London." He saw my questioning look. "Yes, I do have something of a . . . ah, reputation as Lord Carnton, and everyone's assumed there's a Lady Carnton around. I allowed the myth to continue since it kept the mamas with plain daughters off my neck."

"That's the most ridiculous idea I ever heard. Me posing as your wife. Anyway, you haven't said what I'd have to do. Become this man's mistress?"

Lord Blackheart held up a finger. "One night in his arms—that's the bargain that will be made and kept. He's handsome and popular with the court ladies, I've heard. I've not met him but my sources tell me he's totally corruptible but only when a beautiful woman is part of the trade. The money's the easy part of the bribe, but I had no idea about the beautiful woman—until now." He added softly, "You are very beautiful, Crislyn."

"Ah, the great lady in her beautiful gown thanks the gentleman," I said, curtsying in a mocking fashion. I did a couple of dance steps Nana had taught me, holding out the sides of my shift. "Such a lovely lady, Mrs. Blackheart, whose style and elegance has set all of London on its backsides." I stopped, serious again. "You didn't say what you'll do if I refuse."

"I have no choice. I can't trust you not to talk. I'll have to have one of the men take you to Calais. There's a man there who deals in . . . shall we say human merchandise?"

I gasped. "You wouldn't!" But he would, and we both knew it. "All right, say I agree. What do I get out of it? Besides my wonderful night in the arms of the Prince of

Philanderers, that is.''

Lord Blackheart shrugged. "What do you want? I rather thought a thousand pounds in gold. Or jewels."

"Or its value in something else?"

"Yes, that's reasonable. Anything up to a thousand pounds."

He didn't even suspect where I was leading. "Will you swear it? Anything I want that's worth that much or less?"

"I said it, didn't I?" Lord Blackheart said irritably. "Unlike you, I keep my promises."

"I haven't broken any to you. Swear it, Lord Blackheart, and we have a deal. And if you'll promise to help me get back to my mother's people after all this is over, you can be sure I'll never breathe a word to anyone about you."

Lord Blackheart sighed. "I promise to help if I can. And you can have whatever your odd little mind decides it wants, up to a thousand pounds. I swear it."

"Cross your heart and hope to die?" The odd phrase startled me as much as it did him. The fleeting image of two little girls with their arms solemnly crossed over their ruffled fronts came and went, confusing me as much as the strange phrase.

"Is that a blood oath?" But he repeated the words and gesture, and then we looked at each other warily. "Is it premature to ask what you want?"

"No. I'd like it the day we leave for London. Your wheel lock."

He stared at me, his face assuming its grim bitterness when he realized I was being serious. "Very well," he said coldly. "I should have anticipated that, should have known you wouldn't make it something easy, like jewels or a coach of your own or anything an ordinary woman might choose."

I smiled, feeling I'd paid him back for throwing away my deerskins. "There's one other item that should be cleared up ahead of time, Lord Blackheart."

"I shudder in advance, but go ahead."

My eyes went to his face and stayed there for a long, appraising time. "I'll be acting as your wife. Does that mean we'll share a room in your London house?"

"I told you . . . I won't force myself on you."

It wasn't really a straight answer, and as Lord Blackheart and I stood there looking at each other, the unspoken things between us took on more shape and substance.

I knew he wanted me. I knew, too, that he was too proud to take me when we went to the hut together, but that wasn't what bothered me. I was beginning to feel something that I hadn't expected to feel.

The sound on the path made us both jump. Lord Blackheart whirled, his wheel lock drawn and at the ready.

Meg gave a little scream with she rounded the bend and faced the evil-looking pistol. "Lordee, Lord Blackheart, don't shoot me." She saw me and shook her head as she looked at my seminude state. "Lord love us, you've ruined poor Perk for life, you have. Aren't you ashamed of yourself?" But her mouth was twitching at the corners, and I could tell she'd found the whole episode hilarious. I knew we'd giggle about it together later.

"Don't let the dress drag the ground, pebblebrain." When Lord Blackheart chided the girl I saw that she had a dress of blazing dark red silk over one arm. My gasp was already out before I could pretend indifference to the most beautiful dress I'd ever seen in my life.

Meg was shaking out the gown, filling the whole place with color, even with just the moonlight to highlight the rich fabric. My hands itched to smooth out the folds as she was doing so lovingly. My body longed for the feel of the sensuous silk against my body. I could hear the whispering rustle as I walked across a room.

"It's not appropriate, Meg. Too dressy and fine for my purposes. See if the trunk holds something sturdier, perhaps in fawn or hunting green velvet."

My mind shouted, "Oh, no!" as Meg started back to camp with the gown. Lord Blackheart turned at my silent plea, saw my face and said softly, "Leave the dress, Meg. We'll look through the other things tomorrow."

As soon as she was out of hearing, he said triumphantly, "And I'd begun to think you weren't like every other woman—wanting beautiful clothes, enjoying luxurious trappings . . ." He moved toward me as he spoke and I was mesmerized by the silk rippling from his hands. "Drop that dreadful shift, Crislyn. Let me have the pleasure of putting your first real dress on that lovely body. Come here, Crislyn. You can't run away, Crislyn. We made our bargain. Come back . . ."

I felt the shift shiver to the ground, not knowing if I took it off or he did. There was a peculiar dizziness and a confusing buzzing that was like a humming of voices that spoke a jumble of incomprehensible words.

Come back, Alix. Alix, I'm just trying to help with your gown! There was the strange name again.

"Don't! I can put it on myself. Let me do it. Please let me do it."

I breathed rapidly, trying to keep the soft curtain from covering me up, fighting the red softness as it slithered over my head, obliterating Lord Blackheart's face and everything else but the brilliant darkness all around me.

7

I fought and kicked against the soft garment being pulled over my head, but as my reeling senses focused and my eyes opened, I saw it was not Lord Blackheart with whom I struggled, but Madame Lilah.

Her voice was soothing. "Your poor thing, the fall must have been so frightening. Such raving and thrashing about!" She smoothed the soft gown around me and sat down on the edge of the bed, smiling at me sympathetically. "I'm sorry I added to your fright, but Victor said you would be more comfortable in your nightgown instead of those snug riding breeches."

I looked around me, realizing I was lying on Lilah's bed, back in the modern world. It wasn't easy, struggling back to the present after my experiences in the past, but I could see Lilah's worry and had to no wish to add to it.

"Who's Victor?"

"Doctor Crockett. He was just coming in to check on me when Miles brought you in. I had them put you down here momentarily so I could make you comfortable." She smiled more broadly. "Miles would have gladly carried you up to your room, but I wouldn't hear of it, and since I'm not able to climb those dreadful tower stairs . . . well, it seemed best to see to you down here. I'll have my son take you up to your room later.''

I sat up, gingerly feeling the lump on the back of my head. "I've gotten worse bumps than this, believe me. I'll go up myself and leave your bed to you. God knows I've already caused you enough inconvenience as it is.''

Madame Lilah leaned forward, her face concerned. "Dear, you mustn't move that much. Victor says it's only a sprain, but you definitely could do yourself harm putting sudden weight on that foot.''

I settled back against the pillows and let out a little groan. The throbbing in my ankle suddenly was making itself known. "Oh, Lord." I squeezed my eyes shut, more embarrassed than anything. What a klutz the Linwoods must take me for. "First, I nearly have a crash with you and your son, then I pile up my car in your ditch—and now this. I should have read my morning horoscope more carefully.''

Madame Lilah said cheerfully, "Well, it's said these things come in threes, so perhaps you're safe for a while.''

I grinned a bit lopsidedly. The knot on my head may not have been fatal, but it didn't feel much better than my ankle. "Imagine, the Baron was talking about my staying on for a while to look after you. Things seem to have gotten turned around, didn't they?''

She patted me maternally. "I couldn't be more delighted." She looked abashed. "I mean . . . not that I'm delighted about your fall, dear. It's just that now you'll be staying on at least long enough to find out we're not a dreary bunch of old folks as I was afraid you were thinking.''

"Dreary? Madame Lilah, I've gone for a year without having as much activity as I've had in a few hours at Bloodstones.''

"Good." Madame Lilah carefully raised my bandaged foot to its former position on the pillow. "I just hope future recreations don't have as painful results for you.''

Her cheerful kindness was making my guilt at being dishonest with the Linwoods even worse. "You haven't even asked me why I came here.''

The remarkable eyes looked innocently on mine. "Why, to be my companion, of course. Fate has a lovely way of making my life comfortable. Poor Bee is buried, may her soul rest in peace, and then, pouf, up you pop on our doorstep, so to speak."

"Madame Lilah, I didn't just pop up. As a matter of fact, I'm . . ."

" . . . and accident on its way to happen." The voice from the door had its usual startling effect on my insides. I hastily tugged my nightgown back down over my bare leg. "That's what I told Lilah about you earlier before we went on that madcap ride." Miles folded his arms and contemplated me from the doorway. "Victor seemed amazed that you'd come through such a nasty fall with so little damage, but I assured him you were quite good at bashing yourself into things without apparent injury."

I suddenly remembered that I wasn't the only one involved in my latest bash. "Oh, my God . . . Pandora! I forgot to ask—is she all right?" If anything had happened to that beautiful horse, I would never have forgiven myself.

"She'll never be the same."

"Oh, no." I covered my face in shame.

Madame Lilah gave her son a withering look. "Miles, even if you are my son, you're a monster." She added comfortingly, "Don't listen to Miles' cruel teasing, dear. Pandora is fine. She wasn't hurt at all."

"But she'll never be the same, as I said. She's really feeling her oats now, after beating Shadow. I'm thinking of entering her in the Ascot." He said casually, "You're not such a bad rider, either. I'll admit to being sandbagged by all those innocent questions about which foot to put in which stirrup. Perhaps we could have a rematch when you're up to it. Shadow didn't like being beaten." And neither did I, his mind telegraphed to mine.

Rather than flinching at the challenge, a familiar excitement churned inside me. "If I'm still around, I'll be happy to a new race—if Pandora's game."

Madame Lilah was looking at her son and back to me,

obviously bewildered by the unspoken level of tension. "That's the most ridiculous thing I've ever heard. Miles, I do believe you've had your own brains shaken up today, more than poor Alix." She looked at me apologetically. "My son is not usually so outrageous, Alix."

I said truthfully, "I must admit it's I who have been guilty of outrageous behavior. Riding your horse like a crazy woman over a strange bridle path like that . . . ! Baron, you and Pandora both have my humblest apologies."

He bowed. "Accepted, though I can't imagine your giving anything humbly, Miss Ames. At least, now, you can be more understanding of Samantha's recklessness earlier today."

Madame Lilah said sharply, "I see no comparison in the two incidents, Miles. And I haven't noticed dear Samantha rushing over to apologize for her thoughtlessness."

It was obvious that Madame Lilah had about as much admiration for the dark-haired model as I did. I began to think that the elder woman's eagerness to keep me around might have something to do with her son's association with the arrogant Samantha Hightower. "It's quite all right," I lied, noticing that Madame Lilah was looking weary once more, and all because of me. "Baron, if you'll ask your butler to give me a hand, I really think I can hobble off to my room now."

"Nonsense. Don't let Miles' limp fool you. He's strong as an ox, used to carry me upstairs every night before we converted this room to my use."

The thought of those strong arms bearing me up the dark stairs to the sealed room brought back a lurching feeling in my stomach. "Really, I don't need . . ."

Miles was gathering me up in his arms, and I was glad I'd brought one of my sturdier nightgowns like the one I was wearing. Even so, I was conscious of his flesh as I was sure he was of mine through the soft cotton. "If you'd relax a bit, and put your arms around my neck . . . there, that's much easier for both of us."

Madame and I said our good-nights, I feeling silly doing

so elevated in her son's arms, and Miles bore me off to the King's Tower.

It was a strange, silent passage, through those dark halls. At the foot of the stairs to my room, I said stiffly, "I'm very sorry for all this. With your leg . . ." We were starting up the steps and I could hear Miles' breath become more ragged. "Jocko could have helped me, or . . ."

"Jocko has a bad back," Miles said sharply. "Don't worry, I'm not going to drop you. The plate in my leg just makes it stronger. I'm not an invalid."

"I didn't mean to imply you were."

We were at the door. I pushed it open and, as before, entering the room brought forth peculiar sensations of *deja vu*. Miles laid me carefully on the bed, but rather than moving away, he stared down at me, his face in the shadows. "You and I aren't the only ones who noticed it," he said unexpectedly. "My mother, even old Jocko, noticed it, too." He continued, answering my unspoken question. "They saw there was an immediate bond between us, just as you and I felt it from the start."

"I don't know what you're talking about," I lied.

"The hell you don't. It's like something coming full circle, your being here. I'm not sure exactly what, but the whole castle seemed to start vibrating the moment you arrived." He looked around the room, saying softly, "It's as if all the old, unanswered questions, all the old mysteries have come to life, waiting for the answers to be given at last."

I felt suddenly weary. The castle wanted too much from me. I had only come to find Cassandra, not to find myself involved with these people and their castle. "Places this old are always haunted. My coming in and making all this stir just upset the normal routine. It's as simple as that."

He laughed. "Nothing is simple where you're concerned. I've already discovered that, even in our short acquaintance."

I was incredibly sleepy. "I'll try very hard not to complicate your life further, Baron." I yawned. "At least you know I won't be doing any poking around tonight."

"If I thought you might, I'd seal up the tower like in the old days."

My drowsiness was temporarily vanquished. "Did that really happen, or is it just another yarn for the tourists?"

"You saw the evidence for yourself. Bluff King Hal didn't like the idea of being murdered in his sleep."

"Who does? But it still seems incredible that he'd go to all the trouble of building that wall every night, and then tearing it down every morning." My eyes widened. "What did you call him? Henry VIII, I mean."

"Bluff King Hal. All the colorful monarchs had nicknames. Why?"

"I just never heard him called that except in . . ." I stopped. If I hinted that I'd been having strange fantasies about living in Bluff King Hal's world, one in which Miles Linwood would fit in with the hawk-man and Lord Blackheart . . . !

I just wasn't ready to tell this man anything that might substantiate his claim of a sexual bond that I already was feeling too strongly.

"I guess there are lots of history tidbits I haven't read about." I closed my eyes and turned over, away from him. "Good-night, Baron, and thank you for bringing me up," I said with a note of finality.

The exhausting events of the day took their toll. I hardly heard the door close as Miles took his leave. There would be no more strange dreams, I told myself sleepily, at least not tonight. And as soon as I could hobble about again, I'd find Cassandra and . . .

Cassandra! How could I be involved with myself? How long since I'd even thought of my real purpose in coming here? I'd become infatuated with Lilah and let myself get distracted by Miles Linwood. How could I?

I felt around under the bed and found Punkin. Putting him in the curve of my arm, I promised the glassy-eyed, fuzzy creature, "Don't worry, Punkin. I haven't forgotten. We'll find her, if I have to dismantle this damned castle stone by stone."

LOVESPELL

I fell asleep clasping the warm stuffed animal in my arms. Somehow, it made me feel closer to Cassandra than I'd been in years.

The next few days passed in a pleasant blur, as everyone in the castle tried to make my confinement as sociable as possible. Victor Crockett (whom I soon learned to call 'Crock' along with everyone else but Madame Lilah) turned out to be the charming village doctor I'd expected. His visits in the morning graduated from mere medical examinations to being something we both enjoyed.

He was a white-haired, cherubic man of about 65, who made no bones about the fact that Madame Lilah was the love of his life. Before the week was out, I was teasing him about his crush on the castle matriarch.

We were working the morning crossword puzzle together, having discovered a mutual addiction to obscure words. "Have you ever asked her to marry you, Crock? I mean, really come right out and asked her?"

Crock settled his half-glasses further down on his nose as he filled in a word we'd both been struggling for. "Young lady, if I had a shilling for every time I'd asked—and been turned down—I'd have enough money to pay for that new scanner I'd love for my clinic."

I looked at the finely drawn features and splendid white mane and crisp mustache, thinking what a lovely pair the two would make. "Why won't she marry you? Every time Lilah and I chat on the house phone, she mentions you, and always so fondly."

The intelligent blue eyes lost their twinkle. "If I weren't already fond of you, young lady, I'd say that's none of your business. But since I'm already used to your incredible curiosity about everything here, I'll tell you why Lilah won't marry me. It's because she knows I'd be after her to make this a rest home for abandoned old folks or crippled children or some such charity. Lilah loves her grande dame role and all the luxury; I love nothing better than giving money away, when I have it. I'm not making myself a saint and her a sinner, mind you. I love her the way she is, but the two of us disagree in every conceivable way—on politics, religion, economics, society . . .'' He grinned at me, out of breath. "Probably even making love.''

I was silent, unable to visualize elegant Madame Lilah pinching pennies in a cozy doctor's cottage—or, for that matter, being anywhere but Bloodstones. And after she was gone—well, I didn't want to think about it. "Not putting down your socialistic generosity, Crock, I have to say I can't imagine Bloodstones without a Linwood or two. And I can't see Miles ever giving up this place and all the history that goes with it.''

Crock filled out a word in our puzzle, apparently not at all unhappy that I'd given up on helping him. "Hmm, thought so.'' He looked up at me in an oddly appraising way. "Can't you now? Well, he won't have to in his lifetime, but if he dies without a male heir bearing the Linwood mark, Bloodstones will go out of the family and belong to the village itself.''

I hoped he wasn't aware of the lurch my heart gave. "The Linwood mark?'' My smile took a lot of effort, as did my joking, "Surely Linwood babies don't come with the family crest embossed on their bottoms.''

Crock chuckled. "Where's your respect, girl? No, the Linwood baby boys aren't marked in quite that fancy a way, but just as distinctively. Ask Miles to show you his scar when he comes to visit today. Like his father and his father before him, and on back through the ages, he was born with the Linwood inheritance—an extra finger on the right hand.''

I couldn't maintain the joking attitude in my next question. "He . . . he didn't have it removed in a ceremony at the blood stones? But of course, surely today such a barbaric act couldn't happen.''

Crock's hand froze over the puzzle. "How did you know about the ceremony of the stones?''

Had Uncle Porter told Cass and me about it? It was getting harder and harder to separate what I was learning from Crislyn and her strange invasion of my mind from what I already knew. "I'm . . . I'm not sure." Changing the subject back to one I knew Crock loved, I said quickly, "It would benefit Ravensbridge a great deal, wouldn't it, to own the castle and its lands."

Crock's eyes got a little dreamy. "That it would, Alix. Think of the benefits to the people, to all of them, think of the pride at having their own landmark. Think of the economic benefits from the land and tourist trade profits. Think of the . . ."

". . . new scanners and other wonderfully modern and expensive equipment for the clinic," I filled in softly.

He turned the tiniest shade pinker and looked back at his puzzle. "I'm not likely to be around," he told me tersely. "Maybe the clinic will be, and, yes, I should think the future village fathers will see to it Ravensbridge improves its medical benefits, including the clinic."

He still hadn't told me if Miles had endured the public amputation of his sixth finger, but I wasn't about to have those probing blue eyes questioning me further. I poured us both more tea from the tray Crock had brought up with him for our midmorning chat. "I'm really getting spoiled, you know, but like it or not, I'm hobbling around the room pretty well now. All this special service will have to stop, I suppose."

Crock folded up the *Telegraph*. "You'll forgive my saying it, but your accident has had some happy side effects. Lilah . . . well, I haven't seen her look so young and happy in years." He grinned. "How that woman loves to order people around. You should hear her, telling this one to see to that for her Alix. Even though she can't get up here herself, she's enjoying your being her charge." He said more seriously, "The whole mausoleum seems to have sprung back to life with you here. The other young lady was more of a strain to them all, I suspect, but . . ."

My cup froze on the way to my lips. "You met Cass—Mrs. Coleman while she was here. Tell me . . ." I was very careful that my cup didn't clatter when I set it carefully back on its saucer. "Wasn't it very strange, her leaving so suddenly? And the way everyone seems so nonchalant, as though she were never really here?"

"I wouldn't know about that," Crock said bruskly. "All I know is the young woman upset the household and no one was sorry to see her go."

"But why would she just . . ."

Crock interrupted with a tone that told me I would learn no more about Cassandra from him, "It's not my place to be talking about someone the Linwoods don't seem to want discussed. Now, about you, young lady, and that bump on your head the other day . . ."

I looked at him, puzzled. "It's not even tender any more, Crock. You said yourself I didn't even suffer a mild concussion, and that . . ."

"I know what I said." The blue eyes were probing on mine. "When I was checking you over after your fall, I realized you weren't really unconscious; your lips were moving, your eyes were open. Only you weren't really here, Alix! I don't know where you were during the few moments you were gone, but I know from what I heard that it was some very real place—and not in the present."

The wave of relief that washed over me came from knowing that here was someone whom I could tell about the disturbing "dreams." And I knew the doctor wouldn't think I was going insane as I sometimes feared. I took a deep breath. "You're right, Crock. I was in another very real place, only I wasn't exactly myself. I was . . ." I took another deeper breath. "Maybe it would be better if I just told you about it, starting with the first time."

An earthquake could have occurred during the next hour, but I don't think it would have caused Crock to lose his intense concentration on what I told him.

The doctor sat like a stone, his bright eyes still glued to my face as I finished the remarkable narrative. Finally, he let out a long breath and uttered his first word since I'd begun. "Remarkable. Completely incredible. I don't know what to think, what to say. I've never heard anything like this, and I've encountered a lot of unusual mental illusions in my time."

I gave him a shaky smile. "I'm a writer, you know. Could it be my imagination has just gone over the deep end? I mean, coming over here—and before that, having the old stories about Bloodstones on my mind?" I wanted more from him. "Come on, Crock, you're a flesh and bones doctor. Give me a medical opinion."

He didn't smile. "I'm not that big a fool, Alix, or that presumptuous. I learned a long time ago that life and people don't fit entirely in the box of facts and suppositions we're strapped with in medical school."

"Damn it, what kind of medical man are you? You haven't even suggested a psychiatrist or so much as a valium."

Not paying any attention to my outburst, he said thoughtfully, "I've studied more orthodox regression case histories, but yours doesn't fit any of the circumstances, Alix. And that worries me. There's not the control of the ordinary hypnotic session. This whole thing could be . . . well, dangerous."

"Dangerous? You mean, because there's no one to snap his fingers and bring me out, I might never leave Crislyn's world?"

"More than that," Crock said quietly. "As intensely as you're living this girl Crislyn's life and feeling what happens to her, you could go one step further."

I was no fool, either, and was quite conscious of the violence in Crislyn's existence. "You mean . . . if she were killed or died, I might . . ." I stared at him, then whispered, "Crock, that scares the hell out of me." Crislyn's death could be as real as the sexual experiences I'd relived somehow. The prospect of also reliving someone's death was a chilling idea. "What am I going to do?" I whispered. "I never know when I'm going into one of these reveries, or how to stop it."

He looked at me with the same thoughtful gaze. I knew he was sympathetic, but at the same time, I was somewhat like a patient with a rare, fascinating aberration. "The trained, medical side of me insists we employ modern protection for you, and yet . . . I admit that my fascination has nothing to do with science or treatment along orthodox lines. Instinctively, I feel you're the vehicle for some mysterious unfolding that needs to be carried out in some equally mysterious, logical sequence. To tamper with that, well . . ."

I knew my laugh was nervous and false. "What you're saying is that you don't think there's anything scientific we can do about this, is that it? I guess I should see about getting myself a wolfsbane necklace, or perhaps the old silver cross and holy water trick might work." His face looked glummer than ever at my faltering humor. "Sorry. What do you think about my getting a trained hypnotist to help me?"

"The thought occurred to me a moment go. As a matter of fact, I do a little hypnotizing myself, for medical purposes. It's helpful with patients undergoing painful treatments, like badly burned children whose raw flesh has to be scrubbed."

I shuddered. "Never mind, please. Could you hypnotize me and take me through this thing on a more controlled basis?"

"I don't know." He swallowed the rest of his cold tea, obviously not tasting it. "It's not my line, but I have a stronger reason for hesitating. There's something here that doesn't fit with the medical approach. I have the feeling we have no right to tamper with the natural course of what's happening to you." He sighed. "I want to help you, Alix, but I don't know exactly how. Just be assured that I'll be here to help however I can. I just wish I could be there, too, when you need me."

"Does your beeper have a line to the sixteenth Century? If Crislyn gets tied to a stake and somebody lights a fire under her, I may holler for help." I gave a weak grin. "Sorry. I guess I'm reaching for the humor in all this. Crock, she was a witch, wasn't she? A wicca witch, maybe, but still a witch?"

He smiled for the first time since we'd begun this strange discussion. "You know her better than I do. Was she?"

"All that business about charming game out of the woods. Of course she was a witch."

"I think we could safely say she had some sort of developed extra sense. How about you?"

I stared at him. "Are you asking me if I'm a witch? Are you honestly asking me that?" I felt a little trickle of perspiration roll down my back. "No."

He persisted mildly, "Think about it, Alix. This wouldn't be happening if there weren't something, even an unconscious something, unusual about you."

I said tightly, "Everyone has one or two psychic experiences, Crock. Damn it, you know that." I flounced around on the bed under his steady gaze and finally burst out, "All right. I saw my parents' crash in a dream the night before it happened. Just like it happened. Are you satisfied?"

He wasn't. "This prescience—did it occur again?"

I said sulkily, "I once read a newspaper account of a schoolmate who was killed. Only she wasn't—until a year later."

"You repressed this power of yours, then. Why?"

"Because I was already a weird little kid and didn't want people thinking I was any weirder. Crock, I swear those are the only two incidents like that in my life." I was being truthful; no one in her life ever had worked harder at being an ordinary little girl than I had.

"I believe you." Crock looked down at his watch. "My God, Mrs. Traester's gallbladder! It can't wait any longer." He came over and put his hands on my shoulders. "You're a strong woman, Alix. And, obviously, a very special woman."

"And weird," I muttered, hugging him around his chunky waist. "Tell me, if Lilah won't have you, would you mind marrying a slightly wack-o American instead?"

He chuckled. "You'll keep me posted—any time, any hour—and don't worry. Together we'll see you through this thing, whatever it is."

I brushed off a smudge of powder from his handsome tweed coat. "Thank you, Crock, I feel better already—about everything—even if I probably sent you into shock with all those raunchy details about Crislyn's love life."

He grinned at me, again the endearing cherub. "I enjoyed that part best. No doubt it's the only X-rated regression I'll ever be privy to!"

I was still chuckling to myself when Jocko came in with my lunch tray and told me Miles was on his way up. That put a quick end to my feeling of relief. Miles' several visits during the past few days had not been successful. His politeness had been tinged with an uncomfortable coldness that brought out my own sandpaper edges. I found it hard to believe that this was the same man who had kissed me passionately within the first few hours of our initial encounter. Apparently, the current lord of Bloodstones Castle was a man of many moods.

I'd just managed to finish thanking Jocko for my lovely luncheon tray (adorned as always with a fresh-cut, perfect rose which he said came from the garden next to the tilting yard) when Miles strode in without so much as a knock.

"I passed Crock on my way up. The King's Tower hasn't had so many visitors since the old days." Miles looked at my tray, on which a perfect slice of quiche was untouched. "Don't tell me our cuisine doesn't compare to that of The Dark Swan. You're not eating."

I blushed, wondering how he'd found out about Neil Willingham's visit the evening before. The dish of fresh partridge he'd brought had been delicious. It had been a pleasant change, too, having a laugh or two with the easygoing pubkeeper. No doubt the Baron wasn't pleased about his guest entertaining a lowly tavern owner within the exalted confines of his royal tower. "I didn't have the heart to tell Jocko but I'm not very hungry. He's been so sweet about preparing special dishes for me."

Miles folded his arms and looked at me without smiling. No doubt he disapproved of my frilly bedjacket and the way my hair was carelessly tied up and uncombed. "Like everyone else around here, he seems to be quite taken in by you."

I set my tray aside with a clatter. "Taken in? Baron Linwood, it was you who insisted I stay here, giving me that crazy story about your mother needing a companion and not wanting another brown wren around and . . ." I stopped for breath and just glared, shaking my damaged foot at him, "It's all your fault if I'm giving everybody trouble. It was *your* horse that ran my car into a ditch, *your* goading that made me lose my senses in that crazy race . . ."

"Will you shut up for a moment? Just one?"

I plopped back against the pillows, knowing I was acting like a spoiled little girl and unable to stop it. "I don't know how I like you best—polite and uncommunicative like you've been lately, or rude and bossy like you are now."

"I haven't found you to be exactly the picture of sweet southern femininity I've always heard about. Maybe after a while we'll grow on each other."

"I certainly wouldn't count on it. Now that my ankle is almost usable, and surely by now my car must be fixed . . ." I saw his look of bland innocence and narrowed my eyes. "It is repaired by now, of course."

Miles picked up a sliver of cheese from my luncheon tray and calmly chewed it before answering. "Oh, yes. The rental agency, a branch of the London one you used, took care of all that. With a few comments about American drivers, I might add."

"I can't believe you turned in my car without even consulting me."

"You weren't in much of a position to be using it." Miles shrugged. "You know how we British are about waste."

"I know how *you* are. And maybe I should remind you that I'm not one of your little brown wrens."

"I'm acutely aware of what you are, Alix, if not exactly who—and perhaps it's time we discussed that. It was amusing watching you charm your way into the household to carry out whatever scheme you had, and I was enthralled by the lengths to which you went in order to make sure you had our sympathy." He eyed my ankle significantly.

I know my mouth was hanging wide open. Then I

slowly said, "Are you accusing me of flinging myself from Pandora and doing this?" I pointed at my damaged foot, my finger shaking. "On purpose?" My voice was shaking, too.

"It wouldn't be the first time we've had some adventuress or other attracted by the old legend of buried wealth."

I forgot I wasn't supposed to know about the Linwood family history. "Do you really think I'd risk my neck just to worm my way into a damned old castle? Why, even if I were sure there was any truth to the story about that ruby old James Gerald was given by the king, I . . ." I stopped, realizing what I'd just given away. "Uh, oh." I sighed. "All right, so I've been a little . . . uh, less than honest about a couple of things."

"Scheming."

"All right," I said angrily, "but I had my reasons. So, what do you plan to do? Throw me in the dungeon?"

"I would, if the tiny one we have weren't used for Friar Gene's living quarters. By the way, if no one's told you, I will. Don't be frightened by our little monk. He's rather simple-minded, but harmless. I'm not getting off the subject. Back to dungeons. I'm reduced to the more civilized means of interrogation." The brilliant eyes drilled into mine with a cold fury that made me thankful there wasn't a dungeon handy at the moment. "Who the hell are you? And how the devil do you know so much about us? About the Devil's Eye Ruby? You're in league with the Coleman woman, aren't you? She was more clever, though, talking about our kinship and pretending to be fascinated with her so-called roots and tracing the Linwood geneology."

I shrank back on the bed as he towered over me, suddenly conscious of how flimsy the truth would sound now, but I'd waited too long already. "Cassandra Coleman was . . . is my cousin. We quarreled a long time ago. I came here to find her again, to make things up between us. I know it sounds crazy, but it's the truth. We'd always talked about visiting Bloodstones together, and she was already here. I just had this impulse to follow her over here, and then she wasn't here anymore and everything was so strange and everyone was so odd about her. Why are you looking at me like that?"

The murderous rage on Miles' face subsided to icy control. "I'm thinking about what a terrible liar you are. And thinking about my mother."

I felt a heavy sinking guilt. "You won't believe this, but I hate the thought of that wonderful old lady thinking ill of me."

Miles' lips curled. "That's why you won't mention one word of what you've told me, not until I've prepared Lilah in my own way. As I told you, Alix, she's decided you're the daughter she's never had. All she can talk about is how much she likes you, how you seem to fit in as though you'd always been part of us." He took a deep breath. "Crock told me this morning that, with you around, she doesn't seem to be as aware of the pain she's in or the short time left to her."

I forgot about our quarrel, as the significance of his words sank in. "Oh, no! Madame Lilah dying? Miles, no!" I turned my head so he wouldn't see the tears that were starting. He'd only think I was trying to regain his sympathy. In control again, I turned back to him. "I'm truly sorry. Truly, truly sorry. How long?" I asked, the last with a lump in my throat. Never had I felt such immediate affection for anyone. I almost couldn't bear the thought of losing that wonderful old lady so soon after I'd found her.

"Probably six months. Maybe less. Crock seems to think we'll be lucky if we have her with us in the real sense as long as six weeks."

The lump was hard to get my words around. "Then you weren't altogether playing games with me about the companion business."

"I was never more serious about anything in my life. Another senile, cheerless wren is the last thing Lilah needs around her these days."

I looked at him, my eyes bright with the unshed tears I was determined he wouldn't see fall. "You're full of contradictions, Miles. One moment you're accusing me of planning to steal the family's famous treasure . . .''

His lips curled upward. "You have to find it first; that's the hardest part. Your cousin failed, and you're no more clever."

I ignored that, feeling it beneath my dignity to acknowledge such an outlandish remark. ''. . . and the next you're hinting I might stay around to make Madame Lilah's final days more pleasant.''

"I told you—she dotes on you. My mother's happiness is well worth the inconvenience of having to keep my eye on you."

I fought the urge to slap his arrogant face. "I like the job itself, but can't say much for the benefits." Even as I spoke, I felt a tiny triumph. Despite all my bungling, here I was being invited to stay within the gates.

Miles' insults and accusations might rankle, but they didn't matter nearly so much as a dying old woman whom I already loved, or the cousin I'd come to find.

I looked down at my foot and back at him with a mocking smile. "That shouldn't be too difficult. Without my car, I can't walk very far."

His smile was just as humorless. "I'll admit that fact has occurred to me."

"When I'm up and about I'd like the use of a car. For sightseeing and such." And for continuing my search for Cass. Surely someone had seen her leave the castle, if indeed she had left. There was also the chance of her returning, though I had little faith in that, considering the cloud under which she'd left.

He bowed deeply. "Say the word, my lady, and any vehicle on the premises is yours." He stayed bent over, looking up at me. "Except for the Ferrari, which is not touched by anyone but myself and its mechanic."

I told him coldly, "I haven't the slightest desire to play with his lordship's expensive toy."

"You'll have to be careful about the tart comments, Alix, my love. My mother thinks the two of us are cozy as teacakes."

"And you," I told him coolly, "will have to be careful about addressing me as 'my love' in Madame Lilah's presence. I'd hate for her to discover, as you think you have, that I'm no lady."

He saluted, and I saw the white scar on his right hand. He caught my look and smiled. "Ah, you know that old legend, too, about the ceremony of the bloodstones. Well, don't look so pitying; that ancestral encumberance was surgically removed at Charing Cross when I was fifteen."

"Believe me, I wasn't being pitying." I smiled at him. "I was just thinking that if they sacrificed a limb of yours in some bloody rites of hell, the Devil would still be suffering from indigestion."

He laughed and, with another mocking salute, left. I could hear him chuckling halfway down the stairs.

With grim determination that I would stay helpless no longer, I threw my bad foot to the floor, gritting my teeth until the pain from the rush of blood stopped. By the time Lilah called for her afternoon chat, I was walking the length of the room and back with little discomfort and a barely noticeable limp. At the end of our inconsequential tete-a-tete, I told her, "I have a surprise for you at cocktail time, darling. No, I won't tell you—then what kind of surprise would it be?"

"Wonderful. Samantha's joining us, and it always depresses me to look at that emaciated body. Thinking about my surprise will cheer me up."

I hung up, thinking my first night downstairs after my accident might not be as pleasant as I'd hoped. Samantha and I, mildly speaking, had gotten off to a very bad start.

It was good to be up and about. I put the unpleasantness with Miles out of my mind and enjoyed the scene from the arrow-slit. There was a perfect view of the bloodstones and the river beyond, but I averted my eyes from the stone cottage, not liking to remember my wanton behavior there as Crislyn.

A movement in the bloodstones below caught my eye. I watched with interest a chubby little brown figure walking slowly, his head bobbing, his hands clasping and unclasping, as he seemed to be chanting to himself. My mind flipped through the bits and pieces of data a writer's mind is trained to file away for possible use at some time.

"Carmelite. Order of the Carmelites." The little man must be Friar Gene, then, who lived in the old dungeon. Miles had warned me that he was simple-minded, and Jocko had made a few cryptic references about the little fellow's peculiar habits of popping in and out at unexpected times. Nobody, it seemed, paid much attention to the little monk or to (as Jocko described it) 'his babbling nonsense about ghosts and such.'

I resolved to talk to the friar at the first opportunity. Feeble-minded he might be, but perhaps that would make him disarmingly truthful when we held our little conversation. I would bet my Halston original, which I planned to wear down to dinner, that the little brown man could tell me something about where Cassandra had gone.

There was a delighted gasp from Madame Lilah when I entered the great room just as Jocko was wheeling in the cocktail cart.

"Alix, my dear, it *is* a wonderful surprise as you'd promised." Her concerned gaze went to the flat shoes I was wearing. "But should you be up on that foot? Victor, did you say it was all right for Alix to come down tonight?"

The doctor moved over to peck my cheek. "Alix isn't one to wait for permission, Lilah." The blue eyes searched mine. "Are you feeling better, my dear?"

I knew he wasn't just referring to my ankle. "Much, thank you, Crock. No more of that dizziness I told you about."

His face relaxed. "Then let me prescribe one of Jocko's martinis. They're less lethal than Miles', who usually makes them."

I had already sensed from my moment of entry that the Baron was absent. I wasn't sure if I were relieved or disappointed. Maybe I was getting inured to electrical shocks.

The throaty voice from a highbacked chair caught me unawares. I felt the sharp eyes taking in every detail of my appearance, but waited for my drink before taking on Samantha again. "That's a lovely dress, Alix—you don't mind my calling you that?—and so daring of you to wear the flat shoes, so American, like ice in one's drink."

I decided there wasn't much point in trying to be friendly with someone as hostile as Samantha. Being civil would be my limit. "You have your customs; we have ours." I held out my hand which she took with about as much enthusiasm as she might have handled a proffered tarantula. "Since we do keep running into each other, perhaps I should offer a formal introduction."

Madame Lilah said contritely, "Oh, I'm so sorry." She introduced us though Samantha and I were only too aware of each other's identity. Her glance at Samantha was icily disapproving. "I naturally assumed Samantha had paid her respects to my guest by now, especially under the circumstances of your first meeting."

Samantha shrugged and gave her attention to Crock while Lilah and I continued our mutual admiration of each other. After I'd admired her mauve chiffon and ostrich feather boa, she confided, "I wish Miles were here to see how beautiful you look tonight. You must dress my hair in a chignon like that sometime, my dear. So much more elegant having long hair, instead of these dreadful bobbed styles."

I carefully avoided following her critical glance at Samantha's gleaming boyish coiffure. "Where is Miles, by the way?"

Lilah's lovely eyes lost their glitter. "I may as well prepare you for something that's bound to occur while you're with us, Alix. My son . . . well, he suffers from terrible depressions that sometimes last for days. I knew he was in one of his moods right after lunch, when I heard him tear off in his car after being rude to Jocko and anyone else unlucky enough to get in his way."

Her distress was obvious enough to make me feel guilty

that I, no doubt, was the cause of Miles' fit of bad temper. "I hope it wasn't anything I said to him, Madame Lilah. He was visiting me just before . . ."

"Nonsense! Of course it wasn't anything you said, dear Alix. Actually, it's not at all unusual for my son to dash off to hole up in his London flat, sparing the rest of us the gloominess of his awful attacks, but I can't help but worry while he's gone. He drinks like a fiend, Crock says, to dull his memories of that horrid prison camp and . . . other unpleasant things . . . and inevitably winds up in the company of dreadful unsavory people. It's perfectly awful, worrying if he's in jail or crashed in a ditch somewhere." She shuddered, and I privately resolved to tell Miles what I thought of his indulgent behavior so obviously worrisome to his ailing mother.

There was a blur of movement above us as we talked, and my eyes went to the window that opened onto the great room. "What an odd place for a window. What is that place up there, Madame Lilah?"

She was glad to leave the subject of her son's moods and laughed. "Oh, that! It's the solar gallery, dear, with its original spying window. In the old days, even before the Tudor-influenced changes to the castle, that was where the ladies of the house sat and sewed and kept an eye on revelers down here. The men, I suppose, kept their manners in line, knowing their wives were watching their behavior."

I didn't mention the fact that apparently the spying window was still serving its original function. Madame Lilah was enjoying an anecdote Crock was telling her after coming over to refreshen our drinks, and I didn't want to destroy her light-hearted mood.

Besides, whoever had been furtively watching us was apparently gone. And Jocko was calling us to dinner.

As we sat at the long table in the refectory with its gleaming silver and fine old china, I found it hard to concentrate either on the pleasant conversation of my dinner companions or Jocko's delicious offerings of roast beef and Yorkshire pudding.

LOVESPELL

The portrait of James Gerald Linwood I, its turquoise gaze as mocking as Miles', seemed to be the compelling focus of my evening. I could swear those lifelike eyes followed my every move, and no one else's.

To tell the truth, I was glad when Madame Lilah suggested the two of us retire to our respective beds without joining the others for brandy in the great room. Between Samantha's cold glances and the portrait's unsettling stare, I was happy to escape.

As I dressed for bed in my tower room, I watched the moonlight doing interesting things to the landscape outside my arrow slit. Lilah had told me at dinner that some of the Saracen rocks in the circle of stones were thought to have been imported from the Stonehenge terrain. Certainly, the ghostliness of the place, even from my safe loft, was one to cause prickles along the spine.

As I watched, I saw a dim light. There was someone, or something, moving purposely about the shrine. Perhaps Crock was seeing Samantha home to her cottage.

But no, this was not movement of that sort. It was more of a steady, searching kind of light.

Hastily, I moved away from my window. If what I was seeing had something to do with Friar Gene's presumed ghost, it was better for me to pretend I hadn't seen it.

There were already enough mysteries crowding my brain in this incredible place.

That night my dream was not like the others. This time I was Alix, and the man who was passionately making love to my willing body was not the arrogant hawk-man or Miles Linwood or even Lord Blackheart, but a combination of them all. Since Phillip my life had not been devoid of sex, but there had been none of the earthshaking encounters such as my dream world was creating for me these days.

I awakened, trembling and damp and longing for a real man's arms around me.

It shamed me, feeling this way, but I was helpless to control it. I'd flung off my gown in the writhing dream and felt the cool sheets against my nakedness, aching for a flesh

151

and blood lover.

The heavy footsteps on the stairs made my tingling body freeze. What had I done, with my wanton crying-out from the depths of passion? Had I summoned a demon lover?

The door was flung open wide without pretense of furtiveness. Miles stood there, staring at me. I could hear his ragged breathing (or was it my own?) and see his disheveled state.

The shirt he wore was soiled and crumpled, and as he approached me, I could smell brandy and some other pungent smell I suspected was a seductive cologne.

I made no attempt to cover myself from his raking gaze. There was a throbbing ache in my loins that told me how this night would end. There was also a tiny sense of triumph that I'd willed this to happen somehow, and he'd submitted to that call.

"What are you doing here?"

He bowed, nearly falling. "I've come . . . to be sure my guest is being handled . . . properly." He looked at my discarded gown and then at my breasts, milky-white in the gleam of moonlight. "Am I too late?"

I looked at the smudge of lipstick on his collar and smiled. "Apparently, it's a bit late for both of us."

He looked down at the smudge with a harsh little laugh. "It always worked for me before. Before you, devil-woman. But tonight it didn't work. Not since my wife betrayed me, not since she died and left me hating the thought of ever needing another woman, have I wanted anyone like this."

I wasn't sure if I were Crislyn or Alix; "But you've been with another woman tonight. What makes you think I'd have you now?"

He reached out and pulled me up roughly, till my knees were bent and my face close to his. "This." He put his mouth against mine, and the fires between us leapt into full flame until I felt it had consumed all the air in the room, leaving me unable to breathe.

I felt the arousal of his body against mine and made a sound that could not be that of the controlled, sophisticated

Alix. His lips moved to bury themselves in my throat as he voiced his own wonderment at what was happening to us. "God help me, I don't know what's going on. What I do know is I've never wanted any woman like this." He lowered me back on the bed and lay half across me, looking down into my eyes. "You are right. I was with another woman, but I hardly touched her. All I could think about was you. I could see you lying here, like this, wanting me like I've wanted you from the first moment."

My face burned at the knowledge that he'd felt my own desire as well as his own. "We're not even friends," I cried, trying to tear my eyes away from the beauty of his bronzed body with its terrifying familiarity. "We're more like enemies than lovers, neither of us trusting the other or feeling tenderness."

Even as I protested this unloving coupling to which our first encounter had led, I was savoring the licking warmth his lovemaking was causing throughout my body. Never before had I felt such flames of wanting and hating and needing and aching. Every part of me responded to every part of him. I felt my breasts swell in answer to his seeking lips and my hips burrowing against him, unshyly searching for the joining we both craved but cruelly denied each other.

The room was full of cries and hoarse whispers and the air thick with sensual smells and tastes. I felt my body open to the fullness of his and for a moment could not move or breathe.

How I hated him for knowing so well when I was close to ecstasy and how to withhold it so cruelly, even though his need was equally strong. He stopped us at the crest, time after time, till we were both bathed in dampness and the hate between us was as palpable as our passion.

I knew, then, that he wanted mastery over me more than he wanted fulfillment. He held me brutally tight, savoring the throbbing waves inside me as they crashed to an end.

When I could finally speak, I turned my head away so

he wouldn't see my tears of humiliation, and said softly, "You son of a bitch."

My anger didn't keep me from knowing that what had happened dismayed him as well as me." I don't like being manipulated by any woman, Alix—even one as beautiful as you." He turned back to me. "It occurred to me this morning, after we had our talk, that it might be interesting to see how far you'd go."

With sudden clarity, in the midst of my anger, I saw that he was lying. He knew as I did that his compulsion to come here had been as uncontrollable and inexplicable as my response to him. My anger died. Miles Linwood was as much a captive of some unfathomable circle of events as I; only I accepted it, while he insisted on his damned self-control.

I smiled, thinking that the next time we were sucked into the vortex of passion, the outcome would be quite different. And I would look forward to the rematch.

"What are you smiling about?" Miles' look of male satisfaction held less confidence now that I'd apparently dismissed his unkind lovemaking as cavalier tactics to get the upper hand. "Were you thinking about asking me to stay?"

I ignored that. "I was thinking that, if you hurry, you might be able to catch Samantha still awake." I smiled at him. "Your lovemaking techniques aren't bad, but could do with a few refinements."

He gave me a sharp look of surprise. "Who's been gossiping to you about me and Samantha?" He went back to adjusting his tie. "I broke that off sometime ago. Sam is one of those women who, once they get their sharp little teeth into you, won't turn you loose."

I bared my own sharp little teeth, wishing they were at that moment sinking into that muscled, self-satisfied neck. "I can hardly wait to hear how you describe me to Samantha."

He smiled, looking me up and down, and said softly, "As you are at this moment? I don't think she'd like that."

He stepped outside the door and then came back immediately, carrying a large box. "Oh, that reminds me—I brought you a present. It would please me if you'd wear it to Lilah's birthday party next Wednesday night." He saw my scathing look and smiled thinly. "More importantly, it would please my mother. She adores fancy clothes parties and likes her guests to indulge her for this particular occasion."

I made no move to open the box. "Rest assured the only reason I'd consider wearing something you gave me would be to please Lilah."

"For whatever reason." Miles shrugged. "The dress is pretty old, but I think it'll suit you." When I still made no move to open the box, he added, "I happened to be wandering around in Chelsea and saw it in a window. The shop where I bought it specializes in Tudor fashions, even has some originals."

My indifference faded sharply. Something icy started forming in the pit of my stomach. "Tudor? What color is it?"

"And here I thought you weren't even mildly curious. Dark red." He cocked his head. "Just your color, I'd say."

"Is it . . . is it a kind of silk?"

"It *is* silk. I never compromise on quality when buying for a beautiful woman." He looked at me, the mocking light gone suddenly from his eyes. "I saw it in the shop window and for some reason thought of you." He shrugged. "God help me, I even left my friends at my favorite pub to go back and buy the damn thing."

I didn't really need to open the box. I knew Miles had bought me the red silk dress that Lord Blackheart had forced me to wear.

"What?" Miles had said something, but I hadn't heard it for my whirling thoughts.

"I just said, the next time I'll bring you a nightgown since you seem to be in short supply." He managed to get out the door before the anger exploded and I hurled the box at the heavy door.

As in a dream, I walked over and picked up the spilling

red silk from the floor. Holding it against me, shivering at the feel of it against my body, I walked over and looked in the mirror. The dim light from the washstand highlighted the shimmering dress, turning it into a candle and illuminating the mirror.

For me, the looking-glass had become, in the odd sequence of occurrences that were becoming familiar to me, a door to the past. But unlike the fabled Alice, I knew what lay on the other side.

I walked through, with fearful excitement, into Crislyn's life, wearing the same red silk dress she had worn.

8

As I followed Lord Blackheart into camp where Meg was serving up mutton stew to the men, I was aware of the bizarre spectacle I must present. My hair was loose and wild above the lowcut gown, its red silk whispering around my boots, my eyes wide from the night's experience. No wonder they all stared.

My heart gave a leap when I saw that Rolling John, his head still bandaged, his dark face gaunt and evil, was sitting up with the rest. When he saw me, his bowl clattered to the ground and he started to rise to his feet.

My companion told him sharply, "Stay where you are, John, or I'll give you another broken bone or two to go with the cracked skull she gave you."

The man sank back in his place, his lips moving in silent curses that I knew had my name foremost. "The men don't like it no more than me, Lord B. The girl's trouble and nothing but, and you know that as well as us."

Lord Blackheart gave the man a grim smile. "That she is, but as you know, I was born to deal with trouble." His good eye went from John's face slowly around the group seated around the fire. "I'll say this once and no more, to all of you." His hand bit into my bare shoulder. "This girl suits me for more reasons than you need to know, and I won't have any man after her, whether I'm here or not."

There was a long silence during which all but Rolling John averted their eyes from my generous show of bosom above the red silk. Then a scrawny fellow with snaggled teeth grinned. "Can't say we blame you, sire, for keeping her close to your own side. Pretty girl like that warming your bed might improve that hornet's temper of yours."

Everyone laughed and threw in a good-natured jibe or two. I felt myself blushing at the raw jokes about my function in the camp, but kept my head high and my mouth shut.

Meg brought up a steaming bowl of stew, her pert face showing disapproval of her beloved master's silence in the face of such rude treatment of me. "The poor thing's half-dead from weariness and hunger, Lord B. Can't you see she's near to fainting?"

The smell of hot food, plain though it was, did indeed make me feel dizzy with hunger. But when I reached for the dish, Lord Blackheart caught my arm. "Not now. Meg, I'll have our dinner served like I told you earlier—in the hut."

Meg's thin face looked pinched. "It's all laid out like you said, sire, though it's crazy, like I said when you told me, to be eating inside like a couple of—"

"Bring it in five minutes," he told her firmly as he led me to the hut.

I'm not sure quite what I expected, but certainly not what I saw inside the meager shelter. A makeshift table had been built and was covered by a gleaming, gold-threaded tapestry. Never in my life had I seen such things—gold plates with matching goblets and forks, an ornate candlestick in the center with a flickering candle completed the picture. "God in heaven," I breathed, wondering if my fatigue made me see things that weren't real. "What's all this? Another trick?"

"No trick." With mocking deference, Lord Blackheart pulled out the rough stool and motioned for me to sit there. "I thought it wise to let you practice manners before I fobbed you off as a lady. It would be better at a real table, but . . .''

I had no intention of telling him that Nana had taught me manners from the time I'd been tall enough to sit at a table. With evil glee I snatched the exquisitely embroidered napkin from its initialed gold ring and stuffed it in the top of my gown. Before Lord Blackheart could correct me as to the proper way of using that, Meg came in and placed bowls of clear soup before us.

With sincere hunger and great satisfaction, I slurped my soup up in a moment, ignoring the spoon I knew to be designed for it, and sopped up the remains with dainty rolls of bread.

I downed the wine in one great, gulping swallow while Lord Blackheart gaped in awe, his own goblet halfway to his lips.

When I stabbed the cold mutton with my fork and nearly choked on swallowing it practically whole, he looked at me with evident distaste. ''I can see you have a lot to learn, Crislyn.'' My belch was rather dainty but still made him cringe. ''Now suppose we have Meg replenish your food and we'll start from the beginning, with the soup.''

It suited me fine to have a second helping since I hadn't had such a wonderful meal in weeks, but my table manners showed no obvious improvement, much to Lord Blackheart's disgust. It was hard to keep a straight face when he kept trying to correct me; I was enjoying myself for the first time in weeks.

''Crislyn, be careful with the wine. I don't want your gown spoiled,'' he told me with exploding impatience as I drained my glass carelessly again and again. What he meant was that I was getting drunk. I reached across the table unexpectedly with my fork and tried to spear his untouched slab of meat to repay him for the slur, but he caught my wrist and glared at me. ''You've had enough, Crislyn. If you get fat, you won't serve my purposes in London.''

I flounced back and picked up my wine, though I didn't want it any more than I'd wanted his old mutton. ''A bargain's a bargain, Lord B.'' I giggled and hiccupped.

"Maybe this Hamilton . . . Hammett . . ."

"Lord Hammond," he said coolly.

"Maybe he likes his women with a bit of flesh to 'em." I set my wine down, suddenly sober with the thought that I'd agreed to give myself to a man I'd never laid eyes on in my life. What had gotten into me? The threat of being sold to a slaver was no worse. "Lord B., I've given this matter a lot of thought. You can have your wheel lock back."

"A bargain's a bargain," he reminded me. "Frankly, after observing your social graces tonight, I look forward to the challenge of civilizing you."

"Then at least throw in a bit of gold with the pistol, so I won't leave London penniless as well as disgraced."

"I'd already planned to do that." He put our soiled china and utensils on a tray and set them outside for Meg to find. He poured himself more wine, leaving my half-full goblet as it was. "I apologize for the raw language from the men about our . . . ah, arrangement. The men were feeling salty from the success of tonight's work."

He was treating me as a lady in spite of my spectacle at the dining table. I dropped my eyes, not wanting him to see my surprise at the unexpected courtesy. "What else would they do in the face of your public announcement that you and I would be sleeping together?"

"I said I was sorry, but that's the end of it. If you were a simpering virgin, I might have made different arrangements."

"That's another thing," I said. "What makes you so sure I'm not?"

He leaned across, his one eye full of malevolent humor. "Are you, Crislyn?" The answer was plain on my face, but then he already knew. "Our agreement would have been impossible if you had been. I'm not entirely a fiend."

"It's beginning to seem to me that most men are fiends." For some reason, I could not include the hawk-man in that category. Though he had taken my innocence, I found I could not hate him. But I had no such qualms when it came to Roark's despicable memory. "My so-called father, for instance, who turned out not to be my father after all, was certainly in that class." Then I told him about Roark, about what he had tried to do to me and what I had done to protect myself.

The silence was so long I finally looked back at Lord Blackheart. His face was full of pity, not shock as I'd expected. "My God." That was all he said.

He turned his back while I undressed for bed, exchanging the carefully folded red silk dress for the warm, chaste gown Meg had put out for me. I snuggled down on the straw pallet and pulled its cover to my chin before calling out softly, "You can turn around now."

Lord Blackheart didn't undress but lay down on the sheepskins he unrolled in the other corner of the room. I blew out the candle, knowing both of us were lying wide awake. "Crislyn." I turned at the different tone in his voice, one I hadn't heard before. "Has it occurred to you that there's another way we're so much alike?"

"I'm not sure I know what you mean."

"We both carry terrible scars—you from a man, I from a woman. You see, I was married once. My wife ran off with another man when I lost my fortune. Maybe, just maybe, we can heal each other's hurts."

"How?" I held my breath; if only he'd say the right thing.

He did. "I thought we might give a try at becoming friends. Love is out of the question for me ever again, but it's awful not to like anyone either."

I let out my breath. "We could start with your teaching me to use the wheel lock. You were serious about that, weren't you?"

There was a low chuckle from the corner. "I have a feeling I might be creating a new menace to society."

"Not to society; just to scum like Rolling John." I leaned up on my elbow, excited about learning to shoot. "Lord B., there's something else I've always wanted to learn." At his groan, I said quickly, "One of your other men could teach me; they're all very good at it. I want to be able to ride like the wind. Except for the falcon, I've never seen a creature any more beautiful in movement than a horse."

He was silent so long I decided he'd decided to go to sleep in case I came up with any more skills I insisted on being taught. But then he said, "I'll have Perk bring up Cara for you in the morning. She's small; I got her for Meg to ride, but the girl is scared to death of horses."

"You're sure she won't mind?"

"On the contrary, she'll be relieved. As a matter of fact, if you turn out to be a good horsewoman, you may consider her yours." I was speechless. My own horse! I tried to stammer my thanks, but Lord B. just ignored it for the gibberish it was. "Never mind that. I don't want your gratitude, just your promise."

I repeated cautiously, "Promise?"

"That you won't shoot anybody here or try to run off again."

"I promise."

"I'm not sure that's enough. What was that expression you made me use when you foxed me out of my wheel lock?"

I smiled into the dark. "Cross my heart and hope to die."

He sighed and murmured a soft curse. "Witches and blood oaths! Good-night, wench of the weald. I hope you don't snore."

He wouldn't know if I did that night or not, because I couldn't close my eyes for thinking about all that was happening to me.

Cara was really the nicest part, but I was beginning to get that strange nervous quiver in my stomach at the prospects of living as a lady in a house in London.

As for my future business with Lord Hamilton, I tried to put that as far back in my mind as possible. There was no point in borrowing trouble.

I suppose the next few weeks were the most carefree I'd

ever spent. Certainly my childhood with Nana had been more restricted, my grandmum being determined to maintain the breeding I was apt to lose in the Cotswold. And life in Ravensbridge with Roark had been sheer drudgery.

But living in the weald, with the highwaymen's camp as my base, I felt freer than I had ever been. Even the men whom I'd feared at first learned to look on me as more than a piece of desirous flesh. One by one (except for Rolling John who still kept a furtive distance), they shared with me their special if minor skills and marveled at a girl who laughed at the discomforts of the forest.

Meg and I were like sisters, giggling over feminine jokes together and poking gentle fun at the men who seemed to place us on some special plane that had nothing to do with ordinary women.

Lord B. kept an eye on us and was an unsmiling older brother, who chided us for frivolity and took his teaching of his "wench of the weald" with dead seriousness.

Our evenings over candlelight and special meals, with me in my red silk and him watching every move I made, became enjoyable sessions. If he suspected my transition from slovenly table manners and hoydenish behavior was too swift to be sincere, he said nothing.

I loved shooting the wheel lock. Such a feeling of power it gave me! Though Lord B. patiently explained how the lump of iron was held tense against a wheel wound by a key operated to cause the burst of exciting fire, I simply thrilled to the power of shooting such a frightening weapon.

I was a natural horsewoman. Darby, the best rider, taught me on the mare, Cara, how to elude pursuers. Off we would gallop, with him far behind me, while I practiced the elusive tactics of a nimble highwayman. A low-lying limb would be my temporary perch, caught mid-gallop, while Cara pounded on off at full speed to distract would-be captors. With the special closeness that I possessed with all animals, I soon taught my horse how to double back to retrieve her mistress. We would then gallop away in the opposite direction from the enemy.

Lord B. just hated it when I outmaneuvered him, but I would soon coax him back into reasonable spirits with some of my tricks.

He didn't bring up the subject again about my talent allowing me to communicate with nature through my mind somehow, as though he knew how much it disturbed me that I had such an odd gift. Nor did he seem amazed when I spoke of strange things that belonged to the future.

I don't know how to explain what Lord Blackheart's and my relationship was turning into. I only know I'd never known anything like it with another man in my entire life. The simplest explanation is, I suppose, that we left each other's scars alone. There was no probing. We accepted each other as we were from day to day.

Maybe we knew that there could never be any kind of normal relationship between us, things being as they were. Or maybe we were mutually aware of the great pride each of us wore like great chips on our shoulders. Occasionally, I caught a certain look on his face that I'd never seen before when I undressed for bed. And when I snuggled beneath the covers, I had disturbing longings that often kept me from sleeping. Many times, I heard him awake in the corner, too.

. I'd just fallen asleep after one such night when Meg burst into the hut, something she would never dream of doing unless she were beside herself with exciting news for me. "Crislyn, guess what! Oh, dear sister, the camp's fairly buzzing with the talk of what Lord B.'s told us."

I looked over at the corner pallet, which was empty. "He's up, with it just a bit past dawn?

"He said you were to be left quiet, since you didn't sleep much last night." Her eyes teased me. "So, both of you awake all night and you looking pretty and rosy as a ripe plum."

I blushed, but not because of any truth in Meg's teasing. "Well, now that you've awakened me, you can at least tell me what's going on, since it seems no one else has bothered to tell me."

"Don't be such a grump." Meg bounced down on my

pallet and burrowed under the covers playfully. "We're going to London tomorrow, love. The four of us. Lord B. will be riding on far ahead, so's to get ready for us, and you and Perk and me, we'll be bringing things on the cart and rent us a coach and—"

I broke in, laughing with her infectious merriment. "Slow down, little sister. What about the others? And I thought you and Perk were going to new homes and starting your own lives over." The thought had saddened me, but I just hadn't let the idea of actually losing these new, dear friends linger.

"Well, we talked Lord B. into letting us stay with him and his 'lady,' to help take care of both of you, and after that, well . . ." Her impish face lengthened for a moment. "I expect ol' Perk will be going on to his family, but I don't know yet about me." She said shyly, "I don't like to think of being so far from you, Crislyn. I kind of hoped we'd stay together from now on."

.I hugged her. "Maybe we can, Meg. Anyway, you're going to London and that makes me happier than anything at the moment."

"Me, too." She turned mischievous again and, poking me in the ribs, asked slyly, "Tell me the truth, Crislyn—ain't you two even done it once?"

"Meg!"

"Well, I know he's been sleeping over there, with you over here, and there's still kind of a stiffness between you two that wouldn't be there if he was poking you every night . . ."

"Meg! What language!"

"Sorry. But, Crislyn, it's hard to believe a man like him could sleep in here night after night and not want . . . well, you know!"

I pretended indifference, though I, too, had begun to wonder if the invincible Lord Blackheart had something lacking that other men possessed. Not once had he approached me, though Meg had once confided to me that his men often swapped bets on when I would show up swollen in the belly from my nightly pokings.

She turned more serious at my morose face. "I suppose you know they've all thought he spilled his seed in you every night you've lain in here. Only I knew the truth of it, and I wasn't telling, since I guess you both have your own, crazy reasons."

I longed to ask her what they might be, but didn't. This chit of a child had no cause to know her 'sister' was beginning to wonder if life in the forest had stripped her of every ounce of beauty.

It worried me, even as I wandered around, teasing the men in camp about returning to wives and soft beds, and realizing I would never see some of them again. Was I no longer desirable?

Even Rolling John averted his eyes whenever I came into view. I'd been so intent on learning my lessons, I hadn't paid much attention to my appearance, except for the nightly ritual of the red silk dress.

There was a farewell party that night that made me realize how sad I might be at seeing the last of these people. Someone brought out wine jugs presumably mislaid from a shipment to Calais, and Perk displayed a hidden talent for playing a flute to Meg's high, sweet ballads.

Lord Blackheart joined the merrymaking, but without enthusiasm. I suspected he felt as I did that this might be the final disbanding of the motley crew that had served him so faithfully. He drank steadily, though there was no heightening sign of it in his eyes or speech as with the others.

At last the party was over, with men snoring haphazardly around the fire and the sound of the night insects competing. The stream was full and gurgling. Above us, the moon was adding its romantic light to the sentimental gathering, though few were awake to appreciate it.

"Crislyn?"

I turned from my dreamy stance by the dying fire. I had felt warm all evening and thought of the coolness of the stream with intemperate longing. "Meg? I thought you'd gone to bed. Is Perk all right?''

The girl grinned. "Aw, he's just full of that wine that's too good for him and all these other blokes. Give 'em rotten ale, their stomachs thrive, but French spirits . . .'' She pantomimed the act of regurgitating, and I had to laugh at her.

"Lord B. must not have fared much better. He's not around."

"He's sad, I suppose. Maybe being a robber is more fun than being a rich, fine lord like he hopes to be again.''

I had to agree to that. "You'd better get your sleep. Perk'll be rousing you early come morning."

"That's for sure. And you better do the same."

I took a deep breath. "I'd like to sit for a while, Meg. It's been a while since I was by myself."

She understood. I suppose we initially became so close because she knew how I felt without words. "Well, good-night, Crislyn. And watch out for Rolling John. He was drunk and mean as a snake. I saw him when you were dancing that reel with Perk, and he looked mad enough to kill.''

"Good-night, Meg." I didn't want to ruin this magical night with talk of Rolling John.

It was the first night I hadn't been obliged to wear my finery. I reveled in the freedom of my loose shirt and trousers Lord B. had dug up for me from some treasure chest of clothes. And I reveled in the quiet of the weald, enjoying the answering calls of the owls and night insects when I playfully summoned their attention.

After all that wine, the thought of the crystal water was too tempting. Quietly I made my way from the camp, loving the outlines of the trees against the dark sky as I walked toward the small pool at the little cascade of water feeding the stream. Meg and I had washed clothes here many times, but this time I would take advantage of my solitude to have a refreshing swim.

The water against my naked body made me laugh softly with pleasure. How wonderful the cold water was! I felt at one with the small fish in the pool, playfully imitating their body motion by pretending I was one of them. I laughed at a turtle craning his neck at me from over a large stone and lay on my back, paddling awkwardly in imitation of his ungainliness.

The moonlight was so bright I knew my white belly and breasts were as clearly visible as the marble statues I'd once glimpsed in Bloodstones' garden.

My hands went to my cheeks, no longer thin from my scanty meals before joining Lord Blackheart's band. But was I still beautiful? The pool was too dark to see my image. I lifted my hair, dripping wet, and asked the question aloud, thinking of the man who'd seemed to see me without desiring me like other men.

"Yes, you are beautiful, Crislyn. More beautiful now than the first time I saw you."

My head swiveled to see the dark shape on the bank, and my heart pounded crazily. I was aware of how vulnerable I was in the moonlight, the water still glistening on my naked body. And the thought of Lord Blackheart seeing me like this brought a tingling to my loins that made me unashamedly aware of how much I wanted him to make love to me.

"How long have you been watching me?" My voice was soft and inviting as I said, "The water is wonderful." I wondered if I'd sensed his presence all along and my antics were unconsciously staged to entice the man who'd pretended to be oblivious to me. I didn't wait for him to reply, but said softly, "Perhaps it's too cold for you. My grandmum said I always flung off my covers on the coldest nights when I was little."

He didn't take his eyes off me, but deliberately began unbuttoning the black shirt and trousers, saying only, "It's not too cold for me." He stood there, then, poised on the bank, and I took a deep breath, feeling the anticipation of what was to come.

"You're beautiful, too," I breathed softly. And he was beautiful, with his lean muscled strength emphasized by the curling gold hair at his chest and loins. He was ready for me; I could tell that at a shy glance. I stood still as he approached me though the shallows where I stood.

Without words, we sank together into the rippling stream, our mouths locked together and our bodies tightly clasped. I felt the cool water entering my secret parts as he moved my legs apart and positioned me with his strong hands at my buttocks to keep me close against him. His lips gave up the hot wetness of mine and found the pert tips of my breasts. I heard him give a low groan when I arched backward to give him more freedom with the delicious maneuverings.

My eyes closed, my hair trailing the water as my robber lover caused one exquisite feeling after another to run from my breasts to my loins. I gasped to feel him slide inside me. Never had I imagined the act of passion could be so graceful, so beautiful.

Our rhythm was at one with the night, the stream, and the universe, our bodies seeking together the crashing ecstasy of mutual surrender. In the midst of my pounding senses, I felt a soft tenderness toward the man who held me tight. He was a robber, but he had not robbed me; rather, he had given me back a sense of my womanhood.

He had allowed me the gift of giving myself freely, which no man had done before. For that gift, I would be eternally grateful.

The chill of the night air made me grateful, too, for the warm cloak he'd brought. Snugly wrapped in it, I felt happy and serene as we sneaked quietly back to our little hut. I giggled at the sight of Perk lying open-mouthed on his rug by the fire, his snores rippling Meg's bright curls on his shoulder.

This time, Lord Blackheart made no bones about where he would sleep. The moment I'd tucked myself in my usually pristine pallet, he crawled in beside me, his mouth finding mine almost at once and his hands telling me the encounter in the stream was only the first of many before the night was out.

His warm weapon, ready for action once more, found its sheath, and he whispered as he moved inside me, "You're so beautiful, so responsive, Crislyn. Do you really not find me repelling?"

I gently outlined the black patch over his eye. "What do you think?"

"I think I like making love to a woman who doesn't seem afraid of anything life throws at her." He lifted his head and looked down at me. "I think, too, that it's exciting having a lover who's part woman, part sorceress—both parts equally delicious—who doesn't find a one-eyed man repugnant."

I pulled his head down to mine and whispered, "I find everything about you exciting, including this." My lips found the spot in question and lingered, truly, without repugnance. "Let me remove the patch," I requested softly, wanting to remove the last doubts from his mind that I found him anything but attractive. "I would like to kiss the wound that makes you so unhappy. And I would like a name to use with my lover."

"No," he said sharply, pulling my seeking hand away from the patch. "None of my robber friends, nor anyone else has seen me without the patch." He kissed me gently. "Call me Lian," he whispered. "It's not my real name, but it will do."

Meg's bright eyes didn't miss the rumpled pallet nor my bareness under the cover when she brought me tea the next morning. "Ah, you're lazy this morning. The others have all left, except for the three of us." She handed me a mug of tea as I struggled to sit up and keep the covers over my nakedness.

"Rolling John? Has he gone?" Meg nodded, and I relaxed. "Thank goodness. I always thought he would go to any extreme to cause me trouble."

"I think Lord B. knew that, which is why he waited till the man was on his way before leaving himself."

"That really surprises me," I said with some sulkiness.

"The least my so-called husband could do was wait and say farewell in person."

Meg grinned, those dancing eyes missing nothing. "He left two messages for you. One, he didn't dare wait till you awoke because you might never get to London where he had business to see to." I blushed and Meg's grin got wider. The imp knew we'd spent the night in each other's arms. "The second was that he left you something special under your pallet."

I smiled as I drew out the case with the pistol, then laid it down as I felt a heavy cloth bag behind it. "What's this?"

The spill of gold coins made me catch my breath, and Meg gasped audibly. "He's left you a fortune," she finally said. "Sweet Heaven, I can't believe he'd leave all that for you."

"I can't, either. I only asked for a little . . ." I looked at Meg, my eyes full of disbelief. "He trusts me so much, Meg, that it scares me. With everyone gone and the gun and this money, there's nothing to stop me from going in the other direction."

She said softly, "Like you said, Crislyn, he trusts you. We both know you can't run away now."

She left me to dress and I hurried to don the hunter's green travel suit she'd laid out for me. With my hair twisted into soft whirls under a smart hat, I felt elegant and beautiful. It was a shame there was no mirror.

I heard someone just outside and called, "Meg, come see the fine lady you'll be attending. Have you ever seen such . . ." I pirouetted gaily and pulled the long feather from my hat playfully over one eye as the door opened.

Rolling John's drawling voice answered, chilling my bones. "Can't say that I have seen a finer looking sight." His burning eyes went from my face to my breasts in the snug, puffed jacket.

I drew myself up, like the fine lady I was pretending to be. "I'm sorry I can't say the same for you." I looked at his rough-bearded face and red-rimmed eyes and said coldly, "You hardly look fit to stand, much less able to travel back to your kin. I might have known you didn't really leave."

He let his lips curl in a grin that was more of a snarl. I saw the flicks of saliva at the corners of his mouth and edged my way to the bag hanging on the wall where I'd stored my weapon.

"That's thanks to you, like a lot of other things, wench." He licked his lips and moved closer. "I saw you and your lover come in last night and brought my pallet close so I could find out for myself if it was true what I overheard Meg saying—that he hadn't been poking you every night like we thought." His tongue lingered at his lips as he looked boldly at the bed and back at me. "I heard 'im, heard the two of you, going at it the whole night. Him spilling his seed into you and having you all the ways that I could only dream about. And I had to lay out there hearing you loving it. That's worst of it." He took another step closer, and I didn't move this time. I had a firm grip on the handle of my wheel lock. "Tell me, will it be like that when it's you and me, wench? Will you love having me at you like he was?"

I said calmly, "I think the scar over your filthy ear should give you the answer to that, Rolling John. And if that's not enough . . ." I pulled the gun out with a swift motion and held it dead-level at his belly. ". . . then maybe I can provide a stronger reply."

His eyes widened when he saw the pistol. He knew, as I knew, that I would kill him without a moment's hesitation.

"So you win again, wench. I'm getting tired of you winning out over me." He backed out slowly, with me following, my eyes as cold as my hand was steady. "I'm going now, but there'll come a time when I'll get even. Mark my words."

"Don't come back again, Rolling John." I smiled almost pleasantly. "I haven't had any human targets to practice on. It might be fun."

I watched him mount his horse, as scrawny and mean-eyed as its master. He shot me one last vengeful look. "We'll meet again, slut." He moved off at my threatening gesture with the pistol. "There's more than one way to get you back for what you've done to Rolling John." He looked at Meg who was bringing over bags to load into the cart. As clearly as if he'd spoken the words aloud, I knew what Rolling John was thinking.

He was planning to do harm to Meg, whom he knew to be like a sister to me. I pulled the girl to me and said to the man over her puzzled head, "If you ever, if you *ever* touch one hair of her head, I'll shoot you half-dead and carve what's left for dog meat!"

His eyes showed fleeting fear, at my divining his thoughts so well. He knew the talk around camp about my being a sort of quiet witch. But then he smiled, seeing he'd found my weakness. "We'll see, witch," he told me softly. "We'll see who turns up dog meat."

Meg looked up into my face, her eyes puzzled. "What did he mean, Crislyn? Rolling John would never dare hurt me if that's what you're worried about."

I hugged her, watching till there was no further movement in the woods. "Of course, he wouldn't, Meg. He'd have to fight Lord B. and then me, and even old Perk." I patted her, wishing I'd gone ahead and shot Rolling John like he deserved. Then I wouldn't have this nagging worry about the scoundrel turning up again to plague me—and possibly do harm to little Meg. "Now get on with your work so you can get into your finery. Lian said you'd taken your new clothes out of their box so many times yesterday that they already needed patching up."

She skipped off, happy as a carefree young girl (instead of a member of a gang of highwaymen) who'd just been reminded she had a pretty new dress.

I didn't feel quite so spirited as I walked back to the little hut to gather up my meager mementos of my life back at Ravensbridge. But seeing the pallet that had been the scene of a delectable night of lovemaking, I felt better and eager to get on to London. There would be a real bed there, I knew, and tubs and real tables. . . .

It would be exciting to be in the glamorous city with Lord Blackheart. And the nights in each other's arms . . . I looked at my reflection in the pan of water Meg had brought for my wash. "You, my girl, are a shameless hussy. Think about Nana and what she'd say if she knew that you were mooning over being with a man."

But I couldn't do more than conjure up a fleeting picture of my beloved grandmum. And then it was replaced by the image of Lian as he'd been last night, that strong, dark bronzed body crushing mine, his mouth drawing the breath from me while his love shaft held me firm, till it had burst deep within me.

The warmness at my center made me blush at the sight of Perk when he came in to help with the last of the packing. "It's awfully hot today, Perk. Since we won't be renting a coach till a day's ride from here, maybe we should wear our work clothes."

Perk didn't look at all like the hardworking shepherd he really was in the fancy outfit that could make him pass first for a footman and then a butler when we reached London. He looked horrified. "Oh, no, Lady Carnton, it wouldn't do for someone to see us like that."

He seemed to have his role down pat, and I let the pleasure of the "Lady Carnton" roll around for a bit before arguing. "But we'll look peculiar riding in a cart like this."

Perk said patiently, "Lord Carnton worked all that out. We're to hide the cart not far from the inn, then I'll go on foot to hire a coach and come back for you and Meg."

"But what about Cara?"

Perk was patient with me. "We'll tie her onto the back, Lady Carnton. Please, leave everything to me."

I still wished Lian hadn't gone on ahead of us. Even with my pistol and Perk's newfound confidence, we weren't much of a band to ward off any would-be predators.

I suddenly had a distressing thought as we made our bumpy way over the back road that would get us up to the inn just outside Tunbridge Wells by nightfall. I stood up and called to Perk over the deafening noise of our ill-made sheepcart. "Oh, my God, Perk, I almost forgot. The people in Ravensbridge used to talk about all the footpads around here."

I realized then what I'd said and clapped my hands over my mouth, laughing with Meg and Perk over the ludicrousness of Lord Blackheart's mistress worrying about being attacked by highwaymen.

9

Lord Carnton seemed as pleased to be reunited with his 'wife' as she with him.

While Perk put away our carriage and Cara in the stable some civilized distance away from the charming townhouse where my 'husband' awaited me, I stood with Meg amid our baggage and gawked.

The man standing at the door to our new home was not Lord Blackheart, not a black-clad land pirate, but an elegant figure so dashing it fairly took away my breath to look at him.

"My, aren't you the fine gentleman," I told him teasingly, knowing he was waiting for me to rush up for the embrace we both wanted, but I was too stubborn and proud to accommodate him. High-collared doublet was open at the front, showing elaborate embroidery and lace ruffles at the shirt's wrists. The velvet burgundy overjerkin was of a perfect hue to set off my robber lover's bronze coloring. As I gaped at all this finery, he doffed the matching cap, flashing its jeweled underside with mocking gallantry.

"Welcome, Lady Carnton. Welcome to Carnton House."

I fell into the mood of it, giving him my hand to kiss and holding my head high as I swept past him into my new quarters.

"A decided improvement over our last house, m'lord," I said haughtily. I wandered into the salon, admiring its comfortable simplicity. The oak paneling was beautifully carved, the settle large and inviting. There was a welcoming fire laid in the beautifully tiled fireplace. I took off my fine hat and, in the tones of an elegant mistress of this fine house, said, "The journey was exhausting, m'lord. I would not say 'no' to a bit of refreshment before observing the rest of the premises."

Meg, dimples rampant at all this playacting, gave me a curtsy. "I'll fetch it right away, mum, and then put your things to rights in the bedchamber."

Lian and I smiled at each other over the mulled wine, which warmed my insides almost as much as the look on my lover's face when we were alone again.

"I thank you for all the finery, m'lord." I stroked the fur trim of my wide-cuffed sleeves and touched a rich-hued tapestry adorning the wall. "It's much more than I expected after our little house in the weald." I went on with my lady of the manor prattling, till Lian's face grew dark with impatience.

"Crislyn, will you shut up? I picked out all these things and don't wish to hear you listing all their merits." He came up behind me as I was fingering a fine molded figure on the mantel. His touch made me shiver. "Crislyn, I missed you so. I thought you'd never get here."

I turned and looked up into the handsome face. Had the highwayman been turned meek by the wench of the weald? The thrill of triumph was mixed with something I couldn't define. Disappointment, maybe? I'd thought this man untamable, but now I wasn't sure. "I missed you, too, Lian." My hands drew his face down to mine. Our mouths sought out the passionate depths that were discovered that night in the stream. "Later," I whispered. "In our very own, real bed."

He shed the English gentleman's demeanor and became once more my ruthless captor. "The hell with later," he snarled as he swept me up into his arms. "I want you now.

By damn, it's my house, and if I say it's time for bed, then bedtime it is."

He wouldn't give me time to admire the lovely bed-chamber nor smooth out my costume after it was removed. And I confess I was just as eager as he to relive remembered passion in each other's arms.

There was again the frenzy in our lovemaking. As before, we both knew we had to make the most of every single moment together. My excitement in coming here and the thought of adventures to come made me insatiable, totally uninhibited in learning what there was to learn every which way. When my highwayman lover brought parts of my body to pulsating life in ways I'd never even dreamed of, I felt wonder at love's varieties. And when my turn came to coax even more passion from him, I did so without shame, ignoring moral restrictions imposed by others. We drank from each other's passion, giving ourselves over to new discoveries, new sensations, new heights.

I lay in my lover's arms, at last exhausted and langorous. "Why can't there be only this in the world, Lian? At this moment, I want nothing more."

Lian rolled over on his back, as ready for talk as he'd been for lovemaking a bit earlier. "Remember the wise man I told you about during one of those ridiculous little dinners in the hut?"

I traced a thin scar on his arm. "They weren't ridiculous. I learned a great deal from you, and yes, I remember. Erasmus, wasn't it?"

"Good girl. Cynical philosopher that he is, he's become my hero. 'It's man's leaning toward folly that makes him so fond of women,' he said." Lian chuckled. "There was another part to that. He added if this were in doubt, you only had to 'recall his absurd behavior and the rubbish he talks when he is making love to her.' "

I rolled over and bit his ear. "It wasn't rubbish what you said to me a few moments ago when you were rather carried away. I thought it was sweet. Why aren't there any women philosophers? I don't think I'd care for Erasmus."

"Good." He lifted my hand and touched his lips to each of my fingertips. It was as though he wanted not even the smallest part of my body to go unnoticed. "You haven't said much about our bargain."

"You haven't, either."

"That's because I don't like to think of Hammond doing this . . . or this . . . or . . . no, he wouldn't dare."

I pulled away from him, laughing. "Once you started having a sense of humor, you began to tease at all the wrong times. Are you thinking of dropping your scheme involving me and this handsome lord?"

"I wish you'd stop reminding me how attractive he is. No, I can't drop it." He said glumly, "It's too late. The whole thing's been set in motion, and there are too many people involved. There's no going back now."

"You haven't really told me very much about your plans, or what you and your business cohorts hope to gain."

"True. I won't go into detail, but suffice it to say the charter we'll be given will open the door to huge fortunes for all involved." He sighed. "Foreign imports have been sadly curtailed under the current reign, and there's speculation that wool will be traded in the future far more dearly than now—not in the raw, but already woven into cloths. We hope to be on the beginning of this new endeavor."

"I think I prefer Lord Blackheart the highwayman to Lord Carnton the businessman."

"The highwayman you knew is gone forever. The man you know now will lead a group that could rival the Merchant Adventurers, England's strongest trade group."

"Why not simply join with them, since you and your friends have new, profitable schemes?"

"Because, dear Crislyn, they're a closed group and under the King's thumb. Not only that, they can't see what's happening right under their noses. Bah! Exporting our wool to foreigners and letting them realize big profits is foolhardy. Anyone with a brain can see that England throws away three-fourths of its profits with each shipload of raw wool.

The profit is in weaving it into cloth. Here, in England; not across the water!"

I realized he'd forgotten me and was involved in the plan that had possessed him to the extent of turning him to piracy. "You've given all of this a lot of thought."

"I have indeed." Lian stared up at the fancy molding on our bedchamber's ceiling. "So have wiser men than I. There are uneasy feelings among many, foreign traders as well, that Hal's fickleness will change the world. Scores of changes—political, social, God knows what others—are coming."

Not ready for serious discussion, I reached for the wine flagon at our bedside and poured a bit onto Lian's naked stomach.

He yelled, forgetting his serious mood. "Witch! Just for that . . ."

My penalty was sweet, and we neglected ambition, politics and all else till Meg announced our meal was awaiting us downstairs. England would endure; our passion could not.

Since the maze of London was new to me, I was allowed only a daily ride on Cara within the nearby Lincoln's Inn Fields. It wasn't safe for me to roam too far, Lian warned, and I also mustn't be hoydenish but rather must keep the dainty mien of a well-bred lady. So each afternoon, I carefully donned my riding habit, tucked my hair up under my plumed hat, and prissily cantered on Cara around the wooded square, haughtily looking neither right nor left. Then I would go home to have tea with Lian in the salon, where we carried on conversation like that of an old married couple. He would tell me of the progress for obtaining a charter for his ambitious merchants trading company through Hammond's aid. And he also told me he was recruiting refugees from foreign shores who could teach English workers the weaving skills that would make his exports famous abroad.

Then I would tell him about my mincing ride in the park

or about the fitting at the dressmaker's that day or about Meg's argument with the cook.

Dull, dull, dull! Where was the excitement and adventure, I'd expected to find here?

I complained to Lian, but he only laughed at me. He said I must be patient. Very soon now, he said, I would be hostessing the conclave of men with whom he'd been working. The night would be social on the surface, but in reality be one in which the final loose end was knotted.

The process involved finesse, he reminded me. And when the time came, I would bewitchingly seduce a man who had the King's ear and would see to Lian's charter. But it must seem to all but him that I was an innocent victim to Hammond's seductiveness.

When it came time for my daily ride the next day, I welcomed the drizzly mist with perverse pleasure. My mood was suited to dreary weather and the dearth of other riders in the Fields. I let Cara have her head, leaning into the refreshing gusts of wind against my face, and laughing when the plumed hat left my head and my hair tumbled free.

I nearly ran down a man sitting beside the path Cara and I were galloping down. Contrite, I dismounted and came back to apologize. The man, brushing dirt from his conservative clothes, didn't seem upset. I liked his smile and the way his eyes really saw one.

"Forgive me." I pushed my hair off my face and smiled. "I didn't see you sitting here."

"I'm glad you didn't." The man took the paper he'd been clutching for dear life while I'd nearly dashed over him and held it out to me. "Otherwise, I never should have caught the sheer joy on your face."

I looked at the drawing and saw a hasty sketch of my own face. This was a Crislyn like none I'd seen in my mirrors. Her eyes were wide and full of adventure, her hair flying out behind her, and her horse seemed part of her and the moment. I looked from the sketch back to the man. "You drew this of me?"

He nodded. "Now it's I who must ask forgiveness." The

accent was . . . German? I was still learning about such things. "To use a beautiful lady as a model without first her permission . . ." He shrugged. "But I could not resist."

"It's beautiful." I felt Cara nuzzling at my pocket for her apple and absent-mindedly shoved it at the velvety nose. "Are you a painter?" I grinned. "Now, that's a silly question. I mean, do you do this for money?"

A twitch at the gentle mouth told me I'd obviously said something humorous. "Sometimes. But not in this case." He handed the sketch to me.

"It's mine? To keep?"

He smiled at me. "Just as I'll keep the picture of you riding against the wind in my mind forever." He gathered up his box of charcoals and paints. "I wonder . . ." He looked at me and then shook his head. "No, it would be impertinent to ask."

"Ask what?" Anything new that offered a diversion would be welcome. "Go on; ask me."

"Well, I would be pleased to use you as a model." He smiled a little sadly. "The man whose portrait I'm doing at the moment is a notable gentleman, but he lacks something of your beauty. It would be pleasant to have something to paint on my own, unofficially."

I hoped he wasn't making fun of me. "Is it the King? Is it Henry's picture you're painting?"

"No." He walked over and retrieved my hat from a bush and handed it to me with another smile. "It's Sir Thomas More."

I'd never heard of the man. "Well, are you serious about painting me? Will it take much time?" My face fell. "If my . . . husband will let me, that is."

"Perhaps we could keep it between the two of us. You could come to my room in Lincoln's Inn each day instead of riding."

I clapped my hands in delight. The prospect of any intrigue, even one so innocent as this, was exciting. "I'll do it. When can we start?"

"If you'd promise to keep that look on your face, I'd

start right now." He smiled at me to let me know he was joking. "But since you've already used up sitting time with that mad-dash ride of yours, perhaps we should make it tomorrow."

"I'll be there." My face fell. "But you won't want to paint me in *these*!" I looked at him hopelessly. "And I can't come riding in my fancy clothes."

He said solemnly, again with that twitch, "Come as you are now. We'll improvise something."

As he was walking away, I hurried after him. "I know where the Inn is—Lian showed it to me once from our carriage—but I don't know your name."

"Its Hans . . . Hans the Younger, to separate me from my more illustrious father."

I was so excited over the idea of having my portrait done, I could hardly keep from telling Lian about it over tea, but I managed to restrain my eagerness.

This would be my secret. Perhaps I even would make my lover a gift of the finished portrait.

Meg and I were both nervous over our first entertainment. Lian had instructed us as to the food and drink to be served to the group of men he'd invited, but it was left to us to decorate the house within certain bounds.

There was to be no hot meal, since Lian did not wish his group distracted from their business. We were restricted to trays of cold meat and cheese and plain ale. I was a bit miffed that the fine dishes and goblets with which my house was furnished would not be elaborately shown at a seated supper, but I did my best to present the simple food elegantly. Meg oohed and ahed over my creative touches, saying I had a knack for such things, and I had to admit the results of my efforts were pleasing.

Meg and I told each other proudly, that our cold buffet was far too good for the men who were filtering in our front door even as we finished our preparations.

"Crislyn! Damn it, why aren't you out here to greet our guests?" Lian, looking incredibly handsome in a white shirt, fawn-colored breeches and boots, was impatient with my hovering around the food. "And why haven't you sent Meg out with the ale? These are hard-working men, most of them, with end-of-the-day thirsts."

I peered past him at the people seated in the salon. To my disappointment, they didn't look at all as if they ran in London's higher circles. I decided I wouldn't wear my red silk dress after all.

"I'll be changed in a moment, darling." I patted Lian's cheek, noticing he was grim-lipped and nervous, probably because of my part in the coming evening. I said lightly, "Hammond must be in disguise."

Lian said tightly, "He's not here yet. Now, have Meg fetch the drinks and get yourself ready."

"But how will I know which—"

"You'll know." Lian gave me an ungentle shove. "He's a different cut from the rest, a man of evident rank and wealth."

"Then why is he coming here?" I whispered.

"Because, like most wealthy nobles, he's cautious. Our bribe has already changed hands, and he's ready to . . . close our deal."

I hurried off to dress, after instructing Meg in her duties. Hammond was coming to look me over, of that I had no doubt.

My gown was almost stern, of the palest lavender, with no adornments but its loose-fitting girdle with a single dangling pendant, but its tight-fitting bodice and flaring at the hips accentuated my figure. I knew I looked wonderful. The daily rides had toned my complexion and regular meals had filled out my small-boned body.

My entrance into the salon was confident and my greetings of our guests gracious, though most of them seemed rough and uncomfortable in the presence of one they took to be a lady. Lian shot me approving glances and then signaled when a new guest was shown into the room.

"Lord Hammond." The man who strode in was, indeed, a different story. As we were introduced and he bent over my hand, I felt a tiny thrill of excitement. Here was the man who was to be my adversary in a dangerous game of cat and mouse. "Welcome to our home."

His eyes didn't miss one detail of me or the situation. I realized the challenge Lian had laid out for me. This man was no fool; I could see that in the sharp eyes that looked somehow old and jaded, though the man himself was younger than Lian. Though his lips under the trim mustache lingered at my hand, I sensed his control and cool appraisal.

"The meal was sumptuous, Lady Carnton." Rodney Hammond sought me out in the dining room, where I was replenishing the empty platters. We could hear the buzz of conversation from the salon, but he didn't seem anxious to return to the circle of men. "My compliments on making a simple meal pleasing in every sense."

I daintily coated a bit of fruit in spices and took a tiny bite, then held the remaining morsel out to Lord Hammond. "Thank you, my lord. I hope you didn't miss this special treat."

He bit into the fruit, his lips barely touching my fingers, his eyes never leaving mine. "I would not have missed it, not for the world."

I smiled, letting him know I could play the game. "I'm sure you've tasted more delectable morsels at the court feasts, where I hear you are quite a favorite with the ladies-in-waiting."

He held a honey-dipped berry to my lips. I licked the sweet nectar slowly for a moment, then bit the delicate fruit neatly in half, smiling as he guided the other portion to his own mouth.

"There was not enough honey . . ." Before I could move, he'd bent his mouth to mine and kissed me, lightly, experimentally. He smiled at me. "Such a lovely hostess, seeing to her guests' every need." He glanced over at the opening to the salon. "Your husband tells me you're addicted to riding every afternoon."

I thought about the secret sessions I'd been having with Hans and Lian's observation that Cara seemed to be getting

186

fat and lazy lately. "Addicted? That indicates a weakness of character, Lord Hammond. Let's put it that I choose my daily activities and one of them happens to be riding."

"You wouldn't, perhaps, object to company on some of these afternoons?"

I hastily calculated how much longer it would take for my portrait to be finished. Another week, I estimated. Hans was very swift with his paints, and he constantly told me that I was an excellent, patient subject. "It would be a bit dull for you, my lord, riding around and around the same small area." I smiled at him. "I suspect you enjoy more of an adventure when you go riding."

He chewed up a bit of cheese, watching my face all the while. "Then perhaps I might pick you up one afternoon for a different sort of ride with me. Tomorrow? One o'clock?"

I arranged the slabs of cheese quite deliberately before answering. "I think not. I have . . . other commitments."

"Next week, then. Tuesday."

I looked over at the door to the salon. "Shouldn't you be joining the others? They seem to be quite enthusiastic about something at the moment."

"They can wait. Without my support, their bloody charter and weaving industry are out to sea. Tuesday?"

I plucked a wilted blossom in the bowl on the table. "Poor things, I should have left them in the garden. Lian doesn't even appreciate them, like most husbands who don't notice little efforts."

He put his hand over mine, then lifted the flower I was toying with and put it in his belt. His words were soft, his eyes full of meaning. "I appreciate them, as I value all beauty." He put his finger to the flowers than on my lips. "Tuesday. I insist. One o'clock," he whispered. "Be there." He walked toward the salon, then turned back. He silently took the flower from his belt and stuck it in my hair, then rejoined the meeting.

I took the wilting bloom from where he'd placed it and smiled as I inhaled the dimming fragrance. The man I was supposed to seduce wasn't much of a challenge. If not for my pride, I would have immediately told Lian what he could do without our bargain.

I made my good-nights to the gathering quite soon after Lord Hammond and I had finished our little chat. Very conscious of Lord Hammond's cool green gaze on me as I gave Lian a wifely peck on the cheek, I deliberately avoided the conspiratory look he cast my way as I swept past him. I had no desire to have him too sure of me this early in the game.

Lian awakened me some time later, stumbling over things in our darkened bedroom and drunk as I'd never seen him.

"How did it go?" I asked sleepily. "Did he agree to help you get your charter?"

Lian cursed as he fumbled with his breeches. "I think you know the answer to that. The bastard all but said that he'd cooperate, all depends on you. Does that make you feel smug and powerful?" he asked derisively.

"It was your plan from the beginning, after all, making me part of the bribe," I said, my head turned away from him. "You should be proud of yourself that it worked."

There was a long silence. "Crislyn."

"Damn you, I'm tired. Go to sleep."

He put his hand on my shoulder. "Crislyn, I didn't know how it would make me feel, seeing you with another man, knowing what will happen between you. I was jealous, damn it. I thought I'd never feel that way about another woman again."

I felt as glum about it as he did. But my damnable pride wouldn't let me tell him I found the idea of making love to Hammond perfectly horrible. Except for the hawk-man and Lian . . .

No, I would not allow the hawk-man to enter my thoughts. Why would he persist in invading my mind when I was so intimate with Lian?

"When it's over, I'll find my family in Hastings with your help and perhaps then . . ."

"Then I won't have you anymore." Lian groaned and

reached for me. "Oh, Crislyn, I wish sometimes we were like other people. If I didn't have these things to do, if you could be an ordinary girl waiting for the man of her dreams to come along . . ."

I laughed. "How dull you make it sound."

"Dull isn't always bad. There are times . . ."

I flounced away from him. "There are, indeed." Like now, when I wanted to kill him for not telling me that it was all a joke about Hammond, that he wouldn't dream of letting me go to another man.

As though reading my thoughts, Lian pulled me into his arms. "Crislyn," he whispered huskily. Before I could even respond, his body had found my soft center and made its entry without permission, making me gasp.

"Will it be like this with him?" he whispered. "Never, my darling. Never!"

My trysts with my new friend, Hans, were innocent and light-hearted, if tiring. The simple draped cloth he had me use during my sittings was too scanty for warmth in the bright but cold attic room he used for his work at the inn. I often complained that my portrait, which he would not let me peek at, would have to show my shivering flesh and chattering teeth to be realistic.

But we had fun, more fun than I'd had since my romps in the weald. I delighted in Hans' tales of court life and all the machinations of its players.

"Is she really beautiful?" I asked one day after he'd been regaling me with stories about the king's new interest, Anne Bullen.

"Beautiful?" Hans stepped back, his curved pipe clenched tight in his teeth, its ashes cold as usual, and looked at me. "No." He shook his head. "Yet there's something about her that's compelling, more fascinating than beautiful. Ambitious . . . clever . . . proud. Yes, fascinating more than beautiful." He leaned forward with his brush. "There. It's done." He stepped back. "Would you like to see it?"

I was almost afraid to look. I had the feeling that Hans could see into my soul and knew me as no other man had. "Is . . . is it flattering?"

The painter laughed. "Decide for yourself. Come look, Crislyn, I'm anxious for your opinion."

Clutching the trailing folds of my draping, I walked slowly over to the easel.

My heart stood still. The woman half-smiling at me from the canvas was not Crislyn, and yet she *was* me. I couldn't speak for the impact of the painting. Then I turned to stare at Hans, who was looking at my face, not at the portrait. "How . . . how did you know so much about me in such a short time?"

He reached out to brush off a fleck of color pigment from the mystical background of stars and planets against which he had set my likeness. It looked as though I were suspended between this world and the next. No one could look at the painting and know from my hair or my dress or the background to what age I belonged. Hans said softly, "You're a woman immortal, Crislyn. You've existed forever and will do so always. I'd be laughed out of my trade if this were exhibited publicly. People expect to have every bauble, every current fad of dress, every ringlet of modern hairstyle painted as they are at the moment." He looked at me with those keen, bright eyes. "But with you I dared to delve further. I painted you as I see you—a woman who belongs to no one time, to no one place."

I was shaken to my core—the strange dreams, my wisdom about things I had no wish to know, the strange sense of not belonging. *Who was I?*

I was not just Crislyn. I was every other woman who was part of her, before and after and always.

My head aching from the strain of the afternoon, I refused the ale with which we usually ended our sessions and dressed quickly in my riding clothes.

"Thank you, Hans." I held out my hand to grasp the sensitive fingers of the man who would become famous for his portrait of our incredible king. "There's been no mention of pay, or what you intend to do with my portrait."

The painter sucked at his pipe. "I'd like for you to have it, Crislyn . . . after it has a few weeks to dry, of course."

"But all those other famous people whose portraits you're doing," I cried. "They're paying you great sums, while I . . ."

Hans interrupted me. "I asked you, Crislyn, remember? And do you have any idea how pleasant it is to be able to look at a beautiful woman for a few hours a week, instead of all those notables with their beards and mustaches and medals?"

I leaned over to kiss him. "Thank you, Hans. I shall treasure it always."

He looked pleased. "By the way, I won't put my signature to the painting. It's such a departure from my usual work, no one would believe it to be a Holbein, anyway."

I smiled at him. "I know who painted it, and that's the important thing."

"You'll come back for a visit?"

I thought of my rendezvous with Lord Hammond the next day. "Of course. And as soon as Lian has time from his business, you must come to our house."

We both knew, though, this was good-bye. After telling me that the picture would be sent around to the house on Chancery Lane as soon as it was properly dry, he gave my hand another warm shake.

I took Cara on a quick gallop and then home. I would think of some way to explain the portrait between now and the time it arrived.

"You look very fetching."

I turned at the sound of Lord Hammond's lazy voice. "Thank you." The new riding costume was becoming, I knew. I'd had it made in the rich blue color that was one of my most flattering, and the thick sable trim on my cuffs and hood were a delicious contrast. "You look very well, too, Lord Hammond."

He was quite handsome in attire that I knew to be the

latest fashion. Indeed, I'd heard that Lord Hammond was said to be ahead of the mode in men's wear. He was more daring than most, letting the embroidered sleeves trail unattached, as a mere decoration. The plume on his low crowned hat was too becoming to be fussy, as was the rich, fur-trimmed cape.

I could say without bragging that the two of us made quite a pair as we cantered off together.

As I started on the turn around the park, Lord Hammond caught my rein. "Not that way. I thought you might want more exotic sights to see than this overgrown garden."

I was surprised to see he had a coach waiting on the south side of the fields. He helped me inside as one of his coachmen saw to our horses. Before we were halfway down Kingsbury, he'd produced silver goblets and sweetened wine and made numerous extravagant toasts to my beauty and charm.

I couldn't believe my eyes when our carriage turned into the most beautiful grounds I'd ever seen. I caught my breath and gazed with awe at the arrangement of gardens through which we passed, craning my neck to admire the elaborate fountains. "It has to be where a king lives," I finally managed to get out. Linwood's Bloodstones seemed quite primitive in comparison to this castle.

My companion laughed and waved to the guard at the entrance. "You won't mind if we don't stop and go inside. Wolsey will put me to work if he's around." He settled back and smiled at my gawking face. "You look like a little girl who's just tasted her first sweet," he told me softly. His hand covered mine and pressed it gently. "I think one of the things that attracted me to you from the start is your innocence under such a fulsome disguise." His hand moved to my breast, and I blushed to think how the young guards must view me. I'd been brought here for display as well as to reflect Hammond's exalted status.

Coolly, I went back to the subject of the beautiful house and gardens we were now leaving. "Is it the Cardinal's Court, then? I have heard he has wonderful taste."

Lord Hammond gave another little laugh. "I'm not making fun of you, Crislyn; it's just that everyone knows Henry is jealous of some aspects of his chief minister. It's well-known he covets Hampton Court, and when our stubborn king sets his mind on having something . . ." He stopped, suddenly remembering the driver and the open window. He dropped his voice, putting his mouth close to my ear. "Your husband is a smart man. He knows that I, as a close advisor to Wolsey, could get his charter for him. I think he knows, too, that his money is only half what I require from him and his motley crew of merchants."

I met his eyes squarely. "You're quite right, Lord Hammond. Lian is no fool. Nor am I. I'm aware of my husband's need and the rumors that your favors are available on certain . . . terms."

Lord Hampton, far from being insulted, apparently felt relieved that the cards were out on the table. He put his lips to my throat and chuckled. "I find it abominable to deal only in gold." His arm went around my waist and he tilted my head back so I could not move my mouth even an inch away from his. "When a man has a beautiful wife as well as money, I find it a great deal more interesting to combine unsavory trades with delicious pleasure." He put his lips against mine, and after a moment of exploring little kisses, he forced my mouth open for bolder use of it.

Amazing how much I had discovered of sensual indulgences since that day in the forest with my falcon! How naive I had been, with my chaste views of what lovemaking was like between people of passionate natures!

As I forced myself to respond to Lord Hammond's ardor, I sensed his surprise. I wondered if perhaps he were used to a more dutiful approach from the women he bargained for.

"By God, I've never met a woman like you." He let me pull away from him and stared as I calmly adjusted my hood, waiting for the coachman to hand me down from my seat.

"It's been a most enjoyable afternoon, Lord

Hammond," I told him with a small curtsy, as Cara's reins were handed to me. I mounted and looked down at him, the tiniest of smiles on my lips.

He held my bridle and said softly, so that the coachmen couldn't hear, "When can I see you? Tomorrow?"

"That depends, doesn't it, upon the business transaction you're planning?"

He put his hand on my ankle in its short boot. "It will be done. A week—two at the most. Tell your husband I will send a messenger with the necessary documents."

I flashed him a smile. "Then I'll be here tomorrow, in the same place." I turned and galloped off, knowing he was still staring after me.

Lord Hammond was, I suspected, unused to women who were less than coy in helping their husbands get ahead.

I strode into the house, pulling off gloves and cape as Meg hurried to meet me. "Where's Lian? And please fetch me a cup of tea, Meg; the air has winter in it these days."

"I'm here." A slurred voice came from the salon, and I went to find Lian slouched on the settle by the fire, an empty mug beside him. " 'Fetch me a cup of tea, Meg.' Ah, you learn quickly, wench of the weald." He took the fresh mug Meg brought with my tea and waited till she'd gone before he went on. "You sound like a real lady these days, as well as looking like one."

I warmed my hands by the fire, then sat down and sipped my tea. "That was your intention, wasn't it? Lian, you're drunk. What's wrong?"

"I don't like being cooped up in this smelly, greedy city with all its people crammed together like rats."

"You said yourself you couldn't go on being a highwayman, that it was only a matter of time till you were caught and hanged." I took another sip of tea, not sure I liked this mood of his. And I still had to give him Lord Hammond's message which, I suspected, would make it worse. "You said to be successful at anything, even robbery, a man has to know when to give it up."

"I said a lot of things." He looked at me, his one eye

dark and unreadable. "You've been with Hammond."

It wasn't a question and I saw no need to tell him differently. "He said to tell you all is being arranged. He'll send you the documents."

The silence between us grew heavy. Then, he said, "And that's it?"

I didn't quite meet his gaze. "Not exactly. I'm meeting him tomorrow." I raised my eyes, suddenly angry. "Well, that's how you planned it, isn't it? From the start?" I stood up and smoothed my hair, using the gold-framed mirror at the end of the room both to arrange my ringlets and watch Lian's face. "Then how can you be angry about something that turned out perfectly? If I do nothing to upset matters in our next and, I assume, final meeting, Lord Hammond will be out of both of our lives, I'll be out of yours, and everything can move along as you planned. Incidentally, he has his own wife, a woman twenty years his senior who bought him his place with Wolsey and stays contentedly in her country home while her darling plays."

"How do you know that?"

Hans had told me. "Idle chatter. Meg passes on the cook's gossip. Lord Hammond also, it's said, has no intention of leaving his well-feathered nest since his indulgent, rich spouse makes no demands and will leave him everything."

"Why are you bringing all this up?"

"Because," I said deliberately, "I don't want you thinking I have some ill-conceived ulterior motive in carrying out this farce with Hammond. One night, nothing more, and then it's farewell. I have no notion of his falling in love with me or that anything might come of this." I stopped and thought out loud. "Odd, though, that he doesn't have a mistress instead of these contrived arrangements."

"No doubt you'd like that—becoming his devoted mistress."

"I'd like that less than following my original plan of finding my family."

"Why is that so important to you?" Lian waved his arms

around the room. "You have all of this and probably can have anything else you want—maybe more, with a few additional Hammonds down the line falling over themselves to have you."

"You don't understand, do you?" I cried. "I want to know who I am, where I belong." I sighed deeply. "You gave me Cara and much more, but I need a home, Lian, a place that's mine."

"You can stay here."

I took a deep breath. "And when I have a son or a daughter or both, will they have your name? And know this is theirs, too? Will they feel they belong here?"

Lian had no answer for that. Perhaps he was beginning to realize that my deep need to belong somewhere was really important.

I rang for the cook to see if dinner were ready. It had been a long day and I was hungry and tired. "I have an additional favor to ask." The cook had left after our rapid consultation, and I turned back to Lian. "I'd like to send word to Nana that I'm well and that I'll send for her as soon as I'm settled."

Lian gave a harsh laugh. "Settled where? With a family that obviously turned you and your mother out—not to mention the old crone—to live with a degenerate miller? Or with the father who apparently didn't care enough to try to find you?"

I hated him for speaking the truth. "Will you send word?" I added with gritted teeth, "Or shall I request Lord Hammond's assistance?"

Lian slumped in his chair and said darkly, "I'll see that your grandmother gets word of you. I sure as hell don't want any more favors from Rodney Hammond."

We dined in silence that night, with Lian ignoring his food and drinking himself into a stupor. I got Meg to help me trundle him off to one of the servant's beds downstairs and left her to the task of undressing him and pulling off his boots.

I was through helping Lord Blackheart, or worse, Lord

Carnton, have a more comfortable life. Beyond the next day's assignation with Rodney Hammond, I would concentrate on my own goal of finding a place where I could belong and provide my children and theirs the roots I had been denied. If only that place could have been by Lian's side. . . .

I slept late and was glad when Meg woke me mid-morning, saying Lian had risen early and was waiting to have breakfast with me downstairs. At least I would have a few moments to compose myself before facing him.

She hung around as I dressed, obviously full of questions. "Crislyn, I hope you won't think me nosy, but Perk and I've been talking."

"I'm sure you have," I told her. "Lian and I have been yelling a lot lately. He has a lot on his mind with this charter business, and I guess I've been a bit edgy as well."

She sat on the edge of the bed, taking my hand in hers. "I won't lie to you. I've hoped it would all end like one of those fairy tales you told me in camp. All of us living happily ever after, you know."

"I know." I shoved my tray away and pulled my knees up to my chin. "Meg, I've been thinking. Lian has provided for you and Perk . . ." I saw her swallow back her tears and felt contrite that Lian and I had only been thinking of ourselves lately. What of this young woman who'd dedicated herself totally to both of us? "Meg, I don't know what's ahead of me." I watched the huge tear sliding down her cheek and leaned forward to put my hand on her damp face. "Meg, don't take it so hard. How could I look after you? Lian's much more able. He knows what's ahead of him, and I'd be doing you an injustice to . . . damn it. Do you want to come with me, Meg?"

She nodded, unable to speak.

I pulled the curly red head to my bosom and rocked her. "Then you will. I don't know how or where we'll end up, but we'll be there together." I held her plain face with its wet freckles between my hands. "The two of us, whatever happens, when or where, will always be the dearest, closest friends.''

She raised her head. ''I know we will, Crislyn. Do you feel like that, too? Like we have some sort of bond between us?''

I nodded and hugged her again. ''If I'd had a sister, I'd have wanted her to be just like you. We can take care of each other, Meg, but I have to tell you Lian and I will be going our separate ways. I don't want to make you have to choose between us.''

''I'll make no bones of it, Crislyn. Perk and I . . . well, we both talked about how nice it'd be if the two of you could stay together. But I know how he is—Lian, I mean—and how there's a kind of darkness on him when he thinks of his wife.''

It bolstered me as I went downstairs to confront Lian to think I had at least one ally in this world. Meg was the only girl close to my age who'd ever befriended me. Her choice of going with me instead of staying with Lian would be one, I swore fiercely, the girl would never regret.

10

The gloom that hung over the breakfast table was thicker than the butter that I unsuccessfully tried to choke down with cook's bread. I finally gave up the pretense of eating and pushed my plate away. "Lian . . ." I wanted so much to take him in my arms and tell him that Hammond meant nothing, that between us we could conquer the world without this despicable scheme of seduction, but pride would not let me back away from my part of the bargain.

"Yes?" If I had looked at him at that moment, I should have seen that he no more wanted me to follow through the distasteful business with Lord Hammond than I did. But I was carefully trying to be blase and was busy brushing crumbs from my morning dress, acting as though none of this mattered to me.

"Just please remind Meg that I won't be joining you for dinner this evening."

He scowled down at his plate, then up at me. "You're enjoying this, aren't you? The excitement, the adventure of it. I've become too dull for you, is that it?"

The rush of anger was a relief from the sickness in the pit of my stomach at the thought of what lay ahead of me. "Dull? That's hardly the word for it. Look at you! Already smelling of ale and still in the clothes you went to bed in! If getting your bloody charter for you will get you out of the foul mood you've been in for the past few weeks, I'll sleep with a thousand Hammonds."

His mouth looked white around the edges. "You'd like that, wouldn't you?"

I would hate it. There had been only two . . . no, damn it, one man in my life. The hawk-man would forever be pushed from my mind, if I had any say about it. I shrugged. "If you say so. But the arrangement is for just one night with your friend."

Lian struck the table with his fist, turning over his tankard. "He's not my friend, goddamnit! He's just a necessary tool to get what I want."

I felt a surge of self-pitying martyrdom. "Apparently, so am I."

Lian just looked at me, his face working painfully to hide the jealousy that I would come to realize was behind his moodiness, behind the drinking, behind everything that was wrong between us these days. "Go, damn you, just go. Get it over with."

I looked at him, not knowing how to broach the subject that was lying still and heavy between us nowadays—our unwilling, growing attachment to each other.

Love! The word echoed inside my head, but I would not speak it. Love was for women who were free, and I had not achieved my freedom.

"That I will." I would "get it over with" but not in the way Lian expected me to.

"And send Meg back in here with more ale," he said as I reached the door.

I caught Meg on her way out of the kitchen and passed along our lord and master's request. She clucked disapprovingly but fetched the ale and hurried off with it, leaving me alone with Cook, which was what I wanted.

The woman owed me several favors, so there was no difficulty in talking her into making a quick trip to a certain London midwife's to procure certain powders that I needed for my emerging plan concerning Lord Hammond. The mix of sweetmeats that I would use was already sitting ready on the kitchen table. When Cook returned, there was nothing left to do but add the powders, then mold the delicacies and arrange them in the pretty little basket Cook found in the pantry.

"Wish me luck," I whispered on my way out. "And not a word to anyone, you understand? Not even to Meg."

The ride on Cara was a godsend, relieving me of much of the anger I still felt toward Lian for being so stubbornly obtuse about what was happening between us. My nervousness, though, was increasing at the thought of the risk lying ahead. If Lord Hammond didn't succumb to my trickery, it could be dangerous. Not only would the charter scheme blow up in Lian's face, but I could be the one to suffer the worst consequences. Lord Hammond did not strike me as a man who would take lightly to being gulled, especially by a woman, but more than ever I was determined not to let my body be used again, except in love.

"You look very lovely, Crislyn." Lord Hammond was waiting for me at the south gate of the garden. His eyes showed his appreciation of me. "The air has made your eyes sparkle and your cheeks glow. Most women I know are pale and careful to keep their faces protected from the elements. I see you thriving in the open sun and wind."

With the basket on my arm, I allowed him to help me down from Cara and settle me into the awaiting coach. "I've always loved being outdoors, ever since I was a small child."

He sat close to me, his sweetish scent making me momentarily nostalgic for Lian's strong man-smell, even laced with ale as it had been of late. "Someday you must tell me about the little girl Crislyn. Your mystery charms me, but I long to know everything about you. Perhaps before the night is out . . ."

I took a deep sip of the wine he lifted to my lips and smiled into his eyes. "Perhaps," I whispered seductively, "before the night is out you will know more than you wish to know about me, my lord." I leaned away from his ardor and looked out the coach window. "Where are we?" All I could see was that we were on a narrow lane whose cloistering overhang of shrubbery and trees made the sun very distant. "Is it another beautiful surprise, like yesterday's visit to Hampton?"

"Yes, only a very different kind of surprise." Hammond's hand rested on my knee. "This leads to my very private, very special lodge, where I allow only the most particularly chosen guests to visit."

"Your wife?" I teased.

For that I was cuffed lightly. "Such a little coquette you are, but with such a surprising occasional hint of sharpness. Ah, here we are."

I looked out uneasily, wondering if I ought not to have brought my wheel lock. What if Hammond were a brute? But I had a weapon, I reminded myself, adjusting the basket over my arm and preparing for whatever might happen. Looking out, I could see a massive door, the only visible part of a building virtually covered in vines and wild greenery. "What a queer place," I said, adding hastily as I realized I might be giving offense, "but how cozy and enchanting."

Any further compliments on Lord Hammond's place died unspoken since at this point my gaze fell upon the misshapen little man who was opening the coach door for us. The smile offered me did not improve the ungainliness of the dwarf-sized creature. Only when we were inside the house and out of range of the poor shrunken being did I visibly shudder.

Lord Hammond laughed. "You do not care for my odd little Kreel? He's a pet, a harmless pet, my love. I took him in after he was turned out of court for frightening some of the ladies. His mother was a poor woman who had bound her pregnant body in order to produce a valuable toy for the rich."

My opinion of the rich was diminishing rapidly. I hoped that my family in Hastings were not of the playfully cruel variety. "I should prefer a tour of your lodge to dwelling on the deformities of our society." And I wasn't referring to the dwarf.

"Indeed, and so shall you have it." Lord Hammond took my arm and showed me a large room filled with various animal trophies, pronouncing each kill to be his and regaling me with their histories until I again begged for a change from things I found distasteful.

"Is there not a more relaxing place, a room where we can sit pleasantly and become acquainted?"

"Of course." Lord Hammond led me down a torch-lit corridor to a large sitting room. My stomach lurched when I saw that it held a huge bed.

I carefully avoided looking at it while I wandered about the room, admiring the various tapestries and paintings. When I came to a velvet-topped table in the corner of the room, my interest was sincerely caught by its one ornament—a huge, murky globe. "What's this?"

"Ah, from what I've heard of you, I knew you would find my little collector's item fascinating." He moved closer and stroked the smooth, green ball of glass. "I paid dearly for this. They say Merlin himself used it to increase his all-seeing powers."

I suddenly realized the implication of what Lord Hammond had just said. "What do you mean, 'from what you've heard of me,' my lord?"

Lord Hammond wagged his finger playfully in my face. "Tsk-tsk. I've heard a thing or two here and there, my pretty witch." My insides chilled at that. "You should be less generous with your talents where tongue-wagging servants are concerned."

I cursed my indiscretion secretly. How had I let myself be talked into helping a neighbor's cook with her illness? And why had I allowed my tenderness with animals to lead me to find her child's missing cat?

Well, perhaps I could use my so-called witch status advantageously with Hammond. Perhaps a bit of mumbo-jumbo would give me control of the situation, but looking down into Merlin's crystal ball, I promptly forgot any notion of pretended magical powers. The murky colors made my head spin, and I realized I was in contact with something that was indeed mystical. "They say that to see the future is to see one's own death," I said, my voice sounding foggy to my own ears.

Hammond's tenseness was almost tangible in the quiet room. "You're seeing something, aren't you, Crislyn? Tell me what you see."

My eyes still riveted on the changing shapes and colors in the glass, I asked, "What do you want me to see?"

He took a deep breath. "Wolsey. I've always hated him with his pompous love of power and his place with the king. God, if he knew how I despise him for pretending to be as royal as Henry himself!" He leaned forward, his eyes bright. "What do you see?"

"You must concentrate and see him in your own mind's eye while I concentrate on the same thing."

It was there, in the changing shapes and colors, though my companion saw nothing. I heard myself speaking in a slow voice, not knowing what I was going to say until it came forth of its own volition. "I see this man of whom you speak. I see him sick and deprived of all previous wealth and power, feebly trying to return to London and falling sick on the way. There's an abbey. And death."

Lord Hammond's shout of triumph broke the spell. "Good! So he will fall out of the king's favor as many say is inevitable. I look forward to seeing his downfall, the arrogant old tyrant." He picked me up at the waist and swung me around. "My beautiful witch, you have made me happy. Now it is your turn. Ask for anything, and it shall be yours." As the words trembled at my lips, he cut them off with satanical instinct. "Anything, that is, except the magic globe or release from the agreement between Carnton and me."

"Then there is nothing more I want . . . Wait! There is! I want Kreel." I would take the little fellow with me, and once we were in the country near Hastings, set him free.

Hammond frowned and chewed his hip, staring at me.

"You surprise me, Crislyn. I would have thought you would want Kreel less than anything else I possess. Still . . ." He shrugged, then smiled. "He's yours—body and soul, if he has the latter, that is." He bowed to me mockingly. "Is there anything else you desire, my beautiful sorceress?"

"Yes," I said with a smile. "Some wine and cheese to accompany the sweetmeats I made for us. I was too excited to eat breakfast and am positively famished."

Lord Hammond looked pleased, perhaps at the mention of my being excited. He was a vain man and I knew now that I must do everything in my power to keep that vanity intact.

"Divine." Lord Hammond licked his fingers daintily and looked avidly at the last remaining sweetmeat. "Will you have another, or am I to be allowed the last one?"

"By all means, have that one," I said with a smile. I was glad I had decided to mark the sweetmeats I would eat myself, as Lord Hammond would have wondered had I declined to eat any. "It is the sweetest of all."

"No," Lord Hammond said waggishly, "the sweetmeat sitting across from me is the sweetest of all."

His eyes were getting a glaze that did not come from the wine. As soon as he finished this sweetmeat, he would be ready for bed—but not the way he intended. "May I see that beautiful pendant you're wearing, my lord?" I watched Lord Hammond's fingers miss his mouth by several inches as he put his napkin up to catch the final crumbs.

"See it . . .?" He gave a weak laugh. "You can't . . . have . . . it, though, my pretty." But he took off the dangling medallion he was wearing and handed it across to me, almost knocking over the wine flagon as he did so.

I closed my eyes for an instant and prayed, *Please, Nana, let it work for me as I've seen it work for you so many times.* My grandmother had learned the art which she had only used in times of dire need, such as when a child must have something cut from its stomach, or a diseased limb must be sawed away from the body. I had never tried it but the

205

mind-soothing drug that Lord Hammond had swallowed with his sweetmeats would make him more receptive—or so I hoped.

The candlelight flickered on the table. I started swinging the medallion slowly too and fro while I talked in a low seductive voice about the charms of forbidden love, about how I intended to please my lover, about how I wished him to please me, about everything I could think of that would keep Lord Hammond's mind on my voice and the undulating medallion.

I don't know how long it took, but I do know that when at last I stopped the low monotonous stream of suggestions and gave off swinging the pendant, Lord Hammond was where I wanted him. I snapped my fingers and said, ''My lord, can you hear me? If you can, knock twice on the table.''

This he did, his eyes blank as stones. I wanted to give a whoop of triumph but settled for a quiet prayer of thanks to my grandmother. ''You will hear everything I say until I knock on the bedpost three times and then you will wake up. Your body will tingle with satisfaction from the mad love you will have fancied yourself to have had with me. Your desire will have been so fulfilled by imagined love-making that you will be weak as a kitten and unable to perform further. You will remember none of what I am saying to you now, only remembering our mad passion and dozing afterwards.''

I confess that I was enjoying being in charge of this encounter. After I had led my pliable subject over to the bed and had undressed him, I toasted him with wine. ''So much for victory!'' I boasted.

That's when I started to have the feeling of being watched. Nervously, I searched the room, but there was nothing, no one. Realizing that it would soon be time to rouse him, I put aside my uneasiness and undressed myself, draping myself on the bed next to Hammond. Lying there looking up, I saw the face of a gargoyle and let out a scream.

It was Kreel, watching me from a secret spying-place.

He had seen everything. All right, my girl, I told myself quietly, just keep your head. Kreel belonged to me now. If he had indeed seen and heard everything that had happened in this room, he would be aware of that. Perhaps that was why he had not interfered when he saw what I was doing with his master.

I put my finger to my lips and, with a conspiritorial smile, whispered to the misshapen head that looked down at me, "Meet me at the coach in half an hour, Kreel. Your new mistress has plans for you that she thinks you will like."

With a responding wink and smile, Kreel put his finger to his lips in imitation of my plea for secrecy and smiled so happily that for a moment he no longer seemed the least grotesque. Then he was gone and I knew I had nothing to fear from the little creature.

My rendezvous with Lord Hammond had gone exactly as I'd hoped, but the townhouse in Chancery Lane was strangely quiet when I let myself and Kreel in during the dawn hours. It wasn't like Meg to sleep past the first hour of light. Perk, too, was usually up stirring long before Lian and I arose.

I called softly as I pulled off my cape in the front hall. "Perk! Meg!" No answer. I went into the kitchen, which was also deserted, the fire gone out. My anxiety was quieted by a note from Lian on the kitchen table. I smiled as I opened it, remembering how Lian often teased me about being able to read, thanks to Nana's laborious teachings. "Learning will only get a girl like you into more trouble," he'd said to me more than once.

There was a meeting of his group of exporters, I learned, that would involve his absence for at least a week. Acquiring the new charter had fired up his colleagues, and a trip to inland villages which would soon hold wool-manufacturing industries was vital.

I had a brief moment of resentment that he had apparently not given any thought of my return from Lord Hammond or what my emotional state might be. But then I spied a brown-wrapped parcel and temporarily forgot my pique as I tore it open. It was the painting Hans had sent to me as promised, and I could hardly wait to see the finished result.

For a long time I just stared at the portrait. How had its artist managed to make me look both innocent and worldly at the same time? The woman captured on canvas was both familiar and strange; she made me feel peculiar, as though I were looking at someone who was me and was not me.

The quiet of the house encroached on my thoughts, even before I felt Kreel pulling at my skirt to get my attention. His mouth made its mewling noises and his eyes spoke volumes. He tugged and I followed him upstairs to the source of his alarm.

It was Perk's room, from which groans were coming. I rushed inside to find Perk lying sprawled beside his bed, his head bleeding from a nasty wound. "Perk! My God, what happened?" I knelt beside him and motioned Kreel to fetch water and bandages.

Perk's eyes cleared as he recognized me. "Crislyn. It's you, then, girl. I was afraid it was him come back to finish me off." He moaned, then let out a little shriek when Kreel came trundling in and knelt beside me with the water and bandages.

"It's all right," I said, my hands working efficiently at the wound which, thank God, was apparently a superficial one. "Kreel is our friend. Who did this to you, for God's sake, Perk? Where is Meg?"

Perk managed to focus his eyes on my face. "It was Rolling John did it, Crislyn. We fought, but he caught me by surprise, and just before I blacked out I heard Meg cussing him for dragging her off with him. They were headed to the stables, I think. He was trying to make her tell him where you were." His eyes rolled back in his head, tears squeezing from the corners. "That damned Rolling John! Why didn't you kill him when you had the chance, Crislyn?"

I said grimly, "I've asked myself that question a hundred times, Perk, but it's not too late. How long have they been gone?"

"Not more'n a few minutes." Perk tried painfully to lift himself up, then fell back with a groan. "I . . . I'm no good to you, girl. If only Lian was here; he'd show that bastard a thing or two."

"Don't worry, Perk. I've got the wheel lock, and this time Rolling John won't escape what he's deserved all along." I stood up. "Look after him, Kreel. Keep pressing that wound the way I showed you." The dwarf nodded eagerly and scuttled close to his patient. Under different circumstances, I would have laughed to see Perk's look of uneasiness at being put in the hands of my grotesque little friend, but right now, there was more serious business at hand.

I went to my room and got the wheel lock, loading it with a well-shaped ball that wouldn't roll out at the wrong moment. The black powder was packed as tight as I could make it. I wrapped the pistol in a fold of my cape and grimly hurried to the stable.

I'd brought another load in case I missed the first time. If I could get off two shots, I decided, one of them would be in Rolling John's most vulnerable spot.

The stable door's loud creak made me cringe and slink back against the wall as soon as I was inside. I hoped Cara didn't catch my scent and give me away.

There was a slight sound. I froze, clutching my gun tighter and tensing to shoot at the first shadow that made a menacing move.

The sound came through the darkness again. I moved toward it, realizing it came from Cara's stall.

A soft nuzzle of my hip made me jump. "Damn it, girl, be quiet!"

"Crislyn? Is it you?" Meg's voice was weak but full of relief. I quickly lit a lantern and saw her then. She was lying in the corner of the stall, a bloodied pitchfork held in front of her menacingly. The grin was that of the old Meg. "Tell the truth, I was hoping it was Rolling John, so I could have at 'im again."

"Meg!" I rushed to her, seeing then that she was wounded. The arrow protruding from her chest was ringed with blood, and my heart sank at the sight of where it had struck. Not even a strong man could survive such a wound. "Meg, darling." I knelt at her side and simply wept. "Is there anything I can do to make it easier for you?" I whispered. To attempt to pull out the arrow would mean only a more agonizing death, I knew. It had been shot from a crossbow and was no doubt barbed.

Meg pulled my head down to her good shoulder. "It's easier, just you being here with me. On my oath, I don't feel a thing, Crislyn. I'm just as numb as Perk's brain, and that's a fact." She coughed a little then grinned at me. "My, don't you look fine tonight. Bet you led that Hammond fellow a fine dance."

I grinned back. "You can be sure I did! And it looks like you got in a lick or two on old John, from the blood on that pitchfork. It's not fair, Meg. I wanted to be the one to get the bastard." We were trying hard not to give in to the spectre of death that both of us knew was thick around us and closing in.

"Well, you can have the next shot at 'im, Crislyn. I didn't kill him, try as I would, but I got 'im in the eye—same 'un as Lord Blackheart's." Meg coughed again, and this time there was bright red blood. Meg looked at the pitchfork affectionately. "He came at me and I let 'im squeal like a stuck pig. His crossbow went off crooked or I wouldn't be alive to tell you about it."

So Rolling John was blinded in one eye, a strange kind of justice, but he was loose and more dangerous than ever. I hugged Meg to me. "My brave little sister."

"You smell nice, too," she said weakly. "Crislyn, there's something I got to tell you about Lian . . . something you don't know . . ."

"Don't try to talk, Meg. Lie still, now. I'll get the doctor down here and we'll have you fixed up in no time."

She shook her head. "We both know better, Crislyn." She tucked her head into my chest like a warm little bird. "Say it again about us being sisters."

"Sisters," I said fiercely. "Sisters through all eternity.

Sisters forever. And by all that's sacred, Meg, I swear Rolling John will suffer for this.''

"He already has . . . some," Meg said with weak satisfaction. "It's going dark," she whispered. "Crislyn, don't leave me while it's dark."

I hugged her even more tightly, the tears streaming down my face. "I won't leave you, darling. You're my sister. I'll be with you always, now and forever."

She sighed. "There was something I had to tell you, something about Lian . . .''

Whatever it was, it died untold on Meg's lips.

I stayed with her, cradling her dead body in my arms, until Kreel came to find me. The two of us buried Meg in the soft, rich dirt of Cara's stall, me crying and swearing vengeance on the man who'd murdered my 'sister,' the dwarf looking at me from time to time with contorted sympathy. When it was done and I'd said prayers over the smooth spot, I left Kreel to saddle Cara and went back to the house to check on Perk. By then, the cook had stumbled up from the cellar, where she'd been thrown by Rolling John, and joined us in our grief over Meg.

"I have to go," I told them simply. "Rolling John will just try again if I stay here. You'll both be in terrible danger." I would take Kreel and go in search of my kin. Perhaps they would at least provide protection from the man who would, no doubt, redouble his vicious search for me as soon as his eye healed.

There was much to do, but first I had a need for air. I went out on the steps of the townhouse and said my good-byes to London. I never wished to come back again. As if returning my good-byes, a faraway steeple clock clanged out its bells. I counted along with them.

By seven peals, I found myself far from where I stood, as though I had gone into Hans' painting and the stars were all around me.

11

I sat up in bed, my heart pounding, my body drugged and heavy from the dreams of being in Crislyn's world.

There were no bells. The sound that had pulled me back into the present was the repeated ringing of the phone. With shaking hand, I picked up the receiver.

"H-hello. Oh, Jocko. Yes . . . yes, I'm fine. I must have overslept." I pushed back my hair and looked at the clock. It couldn't be! Almost noon. I tried to listen to what the butler was saying, but it was difficult, since my eyes had lit on the spill of red silk across the foot of the bed. Everything came rushing back—the phantasmagoric love scene with Miles, the sight of myself in the red gown as I looked into the mirror . . .

I rubbed my temple and looked around the room wildly. This time I'd stayed in Crislyn's life much longer. "I'm sorry, Jocko. What were you saying? About Madame Lilah?"

The butler sounded concerned. "Miss Ames, are you sure you're all right? Master Linwood said you were to be left alone to sleep late, but when you weren't down by the time Madame left for her garden exhibit, she asked me to check on you. Shall I bring you a tray?"

I blushed as I looked at the rumpled bedclothes,

remembering last night's excesses with Miles. And a glance at my appearance in the mirror told me I was not ready for the butler's quiet but perceptive eyes. "No . . . no, I'd rather come down, Jocko." I swung my legs to the floor hesitantly and couldn't help a little moan at the dizziness I felt when I tried to stand up.

"Miss Ames, are you sure I can't call Dr. Crockett for you?" Jocko's concern was palpable over the line.

"That's not necessary, Jocko. I . . . I just didn't sleep very well last night." Now that was a classic under-statement if there ever was one! "After a quick bath, I'll feel much better."

"I'll have your lunch ready for you."

The thought of food made my stomach lurch. "Nothing elaborate, Jocko, please. Just tea and maybe a bit of dry toast. I'm not really very hungry." Actually, I still had the smell of the stable (where, as Crislyn, I had buried poor Meg) fresh in my nostrils.

"I'll stir up a bowl of hot porridge for you," Jocko said determinedly. Like most devoted household chefs, he felt food was the universal panacea.

I said weakly, "I've never known exactly what porridge consists of, Jocko."

"I beg your pardon, Miss Ames?"

"I'll be right down," I told him.

The shower indeed had helped, and by the time I walked into the refectory, I felt almost normal. I'd chosen a soft violet sweater and matching wool skirt which down-played my paleness and hollowed eyes. By the time I'd quickly drank half a pot of steaming tea, I was ready to face the toast and marmalade Jocko set in front of me. The porridge might have to wait a bit.

"Jocko, sit down for a moment. Have a cup of tea with me. I want to ask you something."

The butler lowered his considerable height into the chair next to mine and managed to look as uncomfortable sitting as he did standing. "Yes, Miss?"

I pushed my plate back, folded my arms and leaned

across them, my eyes steady on Jocko's. "Tell me about the light in the blood stones at night."

I watched, fascinated, as the bulging Adam's apple went up and down in the elongated throat. "The light?"

"The light. Jocko, I'm not going to make fun of any ghost stories you might tell me. I really want to know if there's supposed to be some disembodied spirit haunting the stones. And why."

Again the Adam's apple made its elevator ride in Jocko's throat. "Some say the ghost of the stones is Anne Boleyn watching the old tower where King Henry liked to sleep. Others think it's the ghost of James Gerald's second wife looking for the precious ruby he hid from her."

"So the former Baron Linwood married twice?" I said that more to myself than to Jocko. "What were his wives' names?"

Something clouded over his eyes. "I'm sorry, Miss, but since the other lady's visit, I've been asked to stay quiet about the family history. If there's more you want to know, you can ask Master Miles or the Madame, or . . ."

I sighed. "Or the elusive Friar Gene, who everyone says knows all there is to know about Bloodstones, but is unfortunately retarded. Very well, Jocko. You're excused from telling me ghost stories. I'll ask Friar Gene when, and if, I see him."

Jocko stood up and cleared my place but stopped halfway to the door. He shook his head, the loose folds at his cheeks wobbling in rare emotional display. "It's hard to say, Miss, what's legend and what's real in a place that's known as many tragedies and terrors as this one has. People may not believe that ghosts haunt the blood stones, but you don't find many walking there after nightfall. So if you saw a light there, you can make up your own mind as to what it was. If you'd been raised in England, Miss, you'd find it hard to explain things away like the lady of the stones."

"The lady of the stones," I mused, half to myself. Had I seen her?

The voice behind me made me jump, and Jocko bent to

his task of clearing up with renewed haste. "Speaking of stones, the tea Miss Ames is drinking looks that cold, Jocko. Bring a fresh pot, if you will, and a cup for me. Also one of my eyeopeners." He raised his eyebrows at me. "One for you as well? I've seen you looking brighter."

I shook my head. "No, thanks."

"Two for me, then, Jocko." Miles sat down beside me and looked at the barely touched dish of porridge with a shudder. "I seem to have frightened you off from your curds and whey, or whatever that God-awful stuff you're eating is."

I waited until Jocko had come and gone and Miles had his cup of tea before saying in a low voice, "I was hoping I wouldn't have to face you today. I'm not too proud of my own behavior, but yours was abominable."

Miles calmly buttered a piece of toast before responding. "I wasn't at my most charming, I'll admit, but I was drunk." His eyes danced mischievously, and he said softly, "What was your excuse? I seem to have forgotten it. As a matter of fact, I scarcely remembered the mad drive back here from the flat of a perfectly luscious lady of the evening. I do recall being furious with you for some reason—I suppose because I couldn't get you out of my head the whole night." He added softly, "I recall quite clearly, too, what happened after I barged into your room. Some of it was quite pleasant, but for the most part, I felt afterwards that we made love like enemies instead of lovers." He leaned closer and whispered, his eyes mocking mine. "Perhaps we could give it another try tonight. Your place?"

I controlled my temper, knowing he was deliberately needling me, and there were some questions I needed answering before we started sparring again. I looked over at the portrait dominating the room. "Maybe the Linwood blood hasn't thinned out over the decades. Wasn't James Gerald something of a lady-killer, too?"

Miles' eyes lost their mockery. "Is that your idea of American humor? It may have gone down in local history accounts that my great-great-great-great grandfather was charged with murdering his first wife, but there was never a confession. His second wife, Meuriel, swore James wrote one in his prayer book before he locked himself in the chapel with the two friars he'd taken in, but the prayerbook was never found. And since James had taken his own life, by the monks' later accounts, the sheriff closed the case."

I was glad he was staring at the portrait and not at my face. I'm sure my shock was apparent over hearing that Meuriel had become the Baron Linwood's second wife. I managed to speak normally, though my thoughts were in tumult. "I'm sorry. When I said, 'lady-killer,' I didn't mean it literally. I meant . . ."

"I know exactly what you meant." Miles' voice was hard. "I just thought you might as well hear that my ancestor was a notorious murderer from me instead of from a gossipy pubkeeper."

I blushed, remembering what Neil had told me about the current Baron of Bloodstones and the cloud of tragedy and suspicion around him and his wife's death. "That's unfair. I've only seen Mr. Willingham three times—once in his pub and twice when he visited me here."

He lifted his eyebrow. "Really? Samantha seems to think the two of you have gotten quite chummy."

I opened my mouth to tell him what I thought of Samantha's opinions, but closed it. There were more important matters on my mind—maybe even life and death matters! "You mentioned a couple of friars that were with James when he died. I thought Henry VIII and the Reformation made monastic orders very unpopular."

Miles said dryly, "As you may have guessed by now, Linwoods have always been known for doing as they wished, king or no king. James decided to shelter the two friars, whose own monastery had been sacked and burned by royal orders. Why he took them in is anybody's guess. Maybe he was repentent. At any rate, he became a secret patron of the Carmelites, and there always has been one of the brothers of that order at Bloodstones since. They've kept excellent records, up till the last generation." He smiled.

"Poor old Friar Gene can't even hold a quill right side up, much less maintain records."

I looked up at the arrogant man in the portrait. His didn't look like a murderer's face, but the brilliant eyes stared back at me in frozen arrogance. "I've heard that many things are passed down century by century, verbally—like Gregory XIII's chants."

Miles was watching me closely, oddly intent. "You've heard Friar Gene chanting anything but gibberish?"

"Not really." I thought of how the little friar had paced up and down as I watched him, his lips constantly moving, his round face puckered as in deep concentration. "It was just a thought."

Miles' face was guarded. "A rather astute one. The famous ruby vanished the night James killed himself. Some think James swore the friars to secrecy as to its hiding place, to spite Meuriel who coveted the jewel above everything. One of them returned to live and die at the castle, till his death wearing the cross that had once borne the ruby at its center."

It was all I could do to ask the next question. "The first wife—you say people think her husband killed her. Why?"

Miles' eyes never left my face. "Officially, it was written that she died in childbirth. Unofficially, it's said James killed her in a jealous rage, denouncing the newborn son as another man's child."

An awful presentiment about Crislyn's ultimate fate was upon me, and I said in a thin voice, "Because the child was born without the Linwood mark?" I felt betraying tears sliding down my cheek and shook my head from side to side. "No one could be that cruel, that arrogant . . ." I turned to Miles, unable to meet the eyes of the portrait any longer. "What about the child? Did your wonderful ancestor murder him, too?"

"You're getting a bit involved in the Linwoods, aren't you, Alix?" Miles asked softly. "No, he didn't murder the child. After his next marriage to the village midwife, which quieted down some of the talk for a while, he had the boy placed with distant relatives. Meuriel eventually gave him 'a true son of Bloodstones' and things went along pretty well until the new Baroness got greedy, making demands that were backed up by threats to tell all she knew to the law.''

I lit a cigarette. Since I only smoke when I'm extremely agitated, Cass once had told me that a carton of cigarettes was the perfect Leap Year present for me; it would last me four years. Miles watched me puffing away for a few moments and then took the cigarette from my hand. ''Enough of that; smoking should be enjoyed. Besides, the habit doesn't suit you.''

I glared at him and immediately lit another cigarette. ''I'm well over twenty-one, Miles, and will choose my own vices, if you don't mind.'' The cigarette tasted terrible, but I smoked it determinedly anyway. ''So Meuriel's son inherited Bloodstones.''

''And a dull baron he was, from all accounts, with apparently few of James' colorful proclivities. I think the people around here were happy when I finally came along; the old stories, and a few new ones, revived. Bloodstones and its Baron were once again the center of wonderful and terrible scandals.''

I had to know. ''Did people really say you killed your wife because she'd been untrue to you?''

The turquoise eyes glinted. ''So you've heard the gossip. Ah, that was a night to build new legends upon, all right! Picture it—a stormy night, with the greater storm inside, where my brother and I had just finished one of our famous fights, with him crashing off to the pub to complain about his war-torn brother. Then the fool went off, half-drunk, to Dover where he had a polo match the next day. He went out on his horse, in the storm, and when lightning spooked the animal, he was thrown.'' Miles eyed his empty glass and reached for the port decanter on the sideboard. ''I'd ask you to join me in a drink, but that would mean less for me, so I won't.''

''So your brother was killed and you blame yourself.''

Miles took a deep swallow and looked at me. ''God, no!

Why should I? Dex was a fool. What else would you call a man who'd get himself killed in such a stupid way? And he was weak, letting my dear wife trap him into siring a child so she wouldn't be turned out by Lilah, who despised her, when it appeared that I might come back in a body bag.''

"She told you it was your brother's child?''

"Only in hysterics, during one of our horrible quarrels. She went into early labor. I had my bad leg and couldn't drive and the phones were out from the storm. Dangerous as it was, Lilah went to the village to get Crock, while I tried to calm Rosalee. I did what I could to help my wife's delivery, but it was no use. The baby was born dead, and my wife died right before Lilah got back with Crock.''

"How awful that must have been for you!" And for Rosalee, I added inwardly. No wonder the Tower room had such a haunted aura! "But surely no one thought it was your fault.''

Miles' face hardened, and he looked significantly at his ancestor's portrait. "There were never any direct accusations. I think the whispers were much worse, especially for Lilah. By then, everyone within a ten mile radius knew my wife and I had quarreled and that the baby wasn't mine. Derek's fatal accident the same night only made matters worse. You can imagine what the gossip-mongers did with that bit of coincidence.''

"At least no one could have suspected you of having anything to do with your brother's death.''

Miles poured out another drink and gulped it down. He was getting drunk, and I couldn't much blame him. These were terrible memories. "No, but the tongues still wagged." He gave me a thin smile. "The ironic thing is that my hero status was elevated. Most of the people around here knew the hell I'd been through to get back here to my lovely wife. By their standards, I was carrying out justice. Even if there'd been an inquiry—which there wasn't, since Crock put on the death certificate, 'death by toxic complications during childbirth'—no jury around Ravensbridge would have convicted me. I was the cuckolded husband, the war-weary soldier who'd fought his way out of a prison camp to get home, only to find that his wife and brother had betrayed him.''

''You sound as though you were disappointed that you weren't openly charged.''

Miles laughed. ''Hell, yes, I was disappointed. An inquiry would have cleared my name officially. As it was, I was 'forgiven,' but people could go on imagining the worst.'' He glanced up at the portrait again. ''The stories about the old man started up, with the delicious addition that I was the living reincarnation of James.''

''Still, rumors have a way of dying down if they're not true.''

''Right you are. And fortunately for me, the young vicar's wife ran off with a London photographer, which provided juicy new gossip. Unfortunately, a few years later, another incident occurred that revived the old suspicions about Bloodstones being an unhealthy place for young women.''

I began to suspect that Miles was leading up to Cass. ''Some other young woman died mysteriously?''

Miles looked grim. ''Nobody knows for sure. While Lilah and I were on a long holiday in the South of France, we let the castle be shown to visitors for charity benefits. Apparently one of the visitors was a disguised terrorist. At the news that a bomb had gone off, causing miraculously little damage and no injuries, Lilah and I hurried home. We were too shocked and exhausted to wonder whose car was parked carelessly in front of the gates. Logically, it belonged to the woman who we had permitted to stay in the castle as guide and caretaker. Though Lilah and I had never met the young woman, we'd trusted the Historic Society's judgment.''

''Where was Jocko?''

''Off with his niece and nephew in Brighton for a holiday of his own. But let me finish. The next morning we were awakened by a pounding on the front door. It was the sheriff on official business. It seemed . . .'' Miles lit another in his chain of cigarettes, ". . . he'd had an anonymous phone call, hinting that the tour guide had met with foul play. And when a thorough search of the castle and grounds turned up no clues as to the young woman's whereabouts, and the missing girl's baggage was found in the locked trunk of her car . . ." The lines near Miles' mouth deepened. "I couldn't really fault Sheriff Bullock for then doing what he had to do. My only objection to having the moat dragged for the guide's body was that Lilah was already upset. When she witnessed the moat business, she suffered her first stroke."

"How awful for her." I added tardily, "And for you."

"Awful is inadequate for what we were put through. Have you ever watched the police drag water for a corpse?"

I shuddered. "No, and I hope I never do."

"Well, it's not a pretty sight. They're in their little boat, casting their lines with those horrible hooks, patiently and thoroughly covering every square inch. People came to watch, as silent as the men in the boat. Everytime a line caught a snag or a root, there was the grim wait to see what would be brought to the surface, not to mention morbid disappointment."

I could imagine the scene. "Did . . . did they ever come up with anything?"

"No. But once more Bloodstones was the target of whispers and morbid curiosity-seekers. We had journalists sneaking in disguised as repairmen, electricians, what have you. That's why I was so reluctant to welcome your cousin to stay with us, but Lilah had been bedridden for so long when Mrs. Coleman arrived, she was eager for company and I gave in. It was a mistake," Miles added shortly.

I took a deep breath, for courage. "Did Cassandra vanish overnight, too? Is that why you're afraid to discuss my cousin and where she might have gone?"

Miles turned his brilliant gaze on me. After a long moment of silence, he said softly, "Crock says my mother can't live through another such episode. I'll do anything I have to," he told me in a tense voice, "to protect her from another ordeal like that." He said more casually, "At any rate, your cousin did leave Bloodstones, albeit unexpectedly, without any good-byes. And, as far as I'm concerned, it was good riddance."

I sensed that Miles was holding something back about Cass. I also knew that he wouldn't tell me what it was until he was good and ready. It was on the tip of my tongue to tell him about Punkin, but I didn't. What kind of credibility could be attached to my firm conviction that Cass would never have left without her beloved stuffed toy? "It seems strange she would leave like that, without even telling you where she was going."

Miles' mouth tightened. "Not strange at all, when you recall your own description of your cousin to me as 'impulsive and restless.' " He shrugged. "Who knows? Maybe she went home. Did that thought ever occur to you—or are you dead set to start another scandal about us?"

I was getting angry. "You know damned well I'm not! And I'm not a complete idiot; I called Cass' home in Nashville two nights ago to see if there was any word from her."

"And?" Miles' knuckles were white as he gripped his empty glass. Was his anxiety deeper than fear of publicity?

"The housekeeper was as baffled as I. They'd heard nothing from Cass since she left for England." I'd been relieved when Phillip hadn't answered the phone. He was in Shelbyville for the horse show, the housekeeper had reminded me, and, as with previous shows, he'd taken a room close to the rings. There was no getting in touch with Phillip even if I wanted to.

As though reading my thoughts, Miles said with a touch of sarcasm, "Obviously, you're more concerned over your cousin's whereabouts than her husband is. We've heard nothing from Mr. Coleman."

I explained about the horse show and how much it meant to Phillip. "Besides, he's used to Cass' impulsiveness after all this time." I turned red to realize I'd just backed up Miles' theory as to Cass' flightiness. I got up to leave. "I thought I heard the car. Your mother will be tired. I'll get her tea and start reading to her as I promised."

Miles' arm shot out to catch my wrist. "You heard nothing. Samantha was chauffeuring today, and you can hear her roaring up a mile away. Sit down."

I had no choice since he was a lot stronger than I. "You needn't belabor the point you've been making, Miles. I still intend to find my cousin, but I won't upset the household doing it." I pulled my wrist sharply from his grip. "And as far as I'm concerned, we have nothing more to talk about."

He leaned over, his eyes mocking, and said softly, "Oh, yes, we do. Last night, for instance . . ."

I hated the slow blush that crept up from my neck. "I don't care to discuss that. You simply took advantage of me. I was confused, tired, and scared."

"And lonely," Miles added, his eyes bright on my face, pausing at my mouth which still was tender from the furious kisses. To my relief, he changed the subject. "The weather's fine today. I think we should have that ride together you promised me."

"For God's sake, Miles, I just got out of bed with this blasted ankle!" I pointed at my foot in its thin nylon and sensible loafer, noting with surprise that the swelling was entirely gone.

Miles laughed softly. "If it weren't for Crock, I'd still think you invented that injury." He cocked his head at the sound of the powerful Rolls. "Now that very definitely sounds like Samantha and Lilah returning."

As I passed him to go and greet Lilah, he stopped me, more gently this time. "Well? About that ride?" He added in a low voice, "They say it's wise to get back on the horse that throws you. Are you afraid to get back on, Alix?"

It was as if he were talking about something other than riding Pandora again, but Miles had no way of knowing about Phillip. Or did he? It increasingly seemed to me that this man knew me too well for such short acquaintance. And, knowing me, he was aware I could never resist a challenge.

I said coolly, "Afraid? Not at all, Miles. Not of

Pandora." Nor of you. "I'll go riding with you."

He threw his head back and laughed. "If you could see the look on your face! All that grim determination to show me how fearless you are! I do believe if the devil himself challenged you to anything, you'd accept in a flash."

"Speaking of the devil, there's Samantha coming down the hall. She sounds angry." The staccato approach of high heels came closer. "She won't like finding us dawdling together like this."

"Samantha knows better than to hold a watch over me and what I do. Around six, then? Just before the cocktail hour?"

I nodded, squirming at the knowledge that Samantha was in listening range. I could feel the pale blue eyes burning with hate as she stared at me from the doorway.

"Lilah's expecting you, Alix." Her glance flicked from me to Miles and back again. "That is, of course, if you think you can spare the time to tend to the duties for which you were engaged."

I said as sweetly as possible, "I'm on my way to do just that, Samantha. Also, after hearing about your driving, I've decided to relieve you of your chauffeuring responsibilities."

I didn't stay to watch the fury on the model's face. With luck, she'd make the mistake of venting it on Miles, and he'd finally see her as the poisonous bitch Lilah and I knew her to be.

I was enjoying the lively farce, *Cotillion*, so much that I forgot I was reading it to Madame Lilah for her pleasure.

She interrupted one of the complex comedic scenes with a drowsy, "That's enough, Alix. I'd rather talk a bit before my sedative takes over."

I put the book down and adjusted the satin coverlet under her chin. "Fine. I can't be as amusing as our author Miss Heyer, but I always enjoy talking to you." I dimmed the reading lamp. "Are you getting excited about your birthday party Wednesday night?"

The old woman shuddered dramatically. "Someone of

my age doesn't get excited over another birthday, which could well be the last. 'Resigned,' I think, would be more appropriate.'' Her right eye opened, bright with mischief. ''By the way, I hope you'll wear something marvelous, to show off that fine figure of yours. Give that emaciated mannequin something to worry about.''

I chuckled. ''I have a dress that would give a girl pneumonia. Will that do?'' And then I remembered the red dress that Miles had bought and ordered me to wear to his mother's celebration. Well, he wasn't my mentor regarding fashion. ''What about you?''

Lilah sighed. ''What possible difference could it make how I cover up this old dried husk of mine?''

I quickly put her hand to my cheek. ''Don't talk like that. You've given me hope that a woman can be beautiful and have fun after seventy.''

The pleased smile warmed my heart. Lilah knew my remark came from honest admiration. ''Sweet Alix. How I wish you and Miles . . .'' She opened her eyes suddenly. ''There's something wrong between you two; I can feel it. Does it have something to do with that Coleman woman?'' I stammered a bit, but Lilah went on without seeming to notice I was uncomfortable with the question. ''I should never have encouraged her coming here, but we'd been through so much, Miles and I, and I thought an American would bring in a breezy freshness to this old place. I loved her letters, and she was a relative, after all.''

I asked carefully, ''What really happened, Madame Lilah? I suspect she must have rubbed Miles the wrong way. Is that why she left so suddenly?''

Madame closed her eyes, but not before I saw the caution there. ''Perhaps. I know Miles was angry with her the day she went away. I heard them quarreling, quite badly, in the chapel where Cassandra worked several hours a day. The door was closed, so I didn't interfere.'' She sighed heavily. ''Perhaps I should have. Miles has a terrible temper and might have done something to . . .''

I was holding my breath. When I saw she wasn't going

to complete the sentence, I let it out slowly. "What were they arguing about that could make Miles so furious?"

Madame's silver head weaved slowly from side to side. "I really don't know, Alix. I heard the shouting, but these walls are all quite thick. All I know is that Cassandra didn't come to dinner that night, and Miles told me without elaborating that she was no longer our guest."

"But surely you must have . . ."

"Alix, my dear, I don't mean to sound rude, but I'm very tired." The brightly-painted lips widened in a smile. "Judging two shows at today's Garden Society exhausted me. If those old fools only knew these ancient eyes can't tell a Diamond Jubilee from a Crimson Glory . . ." Her voice faded, and a delicate snore came from the elegant mouth.

I waited for a few moments to be sure she was resting comfortably, then struck out for the chapel where, it seemed to me, many secrets had their beginnings and their ends. Just as I entered, I caught a fleeting glimpse of an elusive brown shadow disappearing into the woodwork.

Alice had her White Rabbit and I had my Brown Monk. Like her, I was consumed with insatiable curiosity. "Now, let me see, my elusive little friend. Just how did you manage your little disappearing act?"

I knew from what I'd seen that the secret escape hatch had to be concealed behind the carved panel above the stone bench near the altar. Very carefully, I tapped the old wooden panel until I heard the hollowness that I was seeking. "Aha! Now if I slide it sideways like this . . ."

The panel moved easily to the side, revealing a round hole large enough for a man to slip through. "Or a woman," I reminded myself as I crawled through the opening.

The stone landing felt quite safe. The hollowed out stairs that led down from it were a different matter. I had to stoop and brace myself against the tunnel walls as I felt carefully for the next step, but there were not many more steps. As my feet touched solid ground, I realized I was in a sort of cave. "And if I'm not completely turned around," I said aloud, making ghostly echoes all around me, "the outside entrance is right over there, opening out to the safe side of the moat.''

From there, the escaping priest of long ago would have had an easy shot at the river. I stood for a moment, reliving imagined old adventures, then decided it was time to look around and see what I had gotten myself into.

12

The area that opened off from the Priest's Hole was dark, cold and damp. Though I knew it once had been used as an escape route for fugitives from religious persecution, I saw very quickly that it had been put to more recent usage.

There was a moldy old table with a recently used candle. I struck a match to the charred wick and looked about. My surroundings were not impressive; everywhere, on the table and on the dirt floor, were littered papers, most of which had been converted into confetti by trespassing rats.

The telltale scurrying of one of the rodents made me hurry on in pursuit of my quarry. I moved toward the dim light of the outer opening, then stepped suddenly into bright daylight, almost into the moat.

I hardly had time to adjust my eyes to the bright sun before I caught sight of my elusive monk scurrying up the path to the stones.

"Wait! Friar Gene, please wait! Don't be frightened and run away. I only want to talk to you."

'Frightened' was an inadequate adjective for the poor fellow's state. From the chubby toes peeking out from beneath the drab robe to the shining top of his scantily fringed head, the poor friar was visibly trembling. His short, chubby fingers spasmodically clasped what appeared to be an old rusty chain around his plump neck. I held out my hand, slowly, as one does to a nervous animal, and spoke soothingly as I moved toward him.

"There, there. You mustn't run away from me. I'm a friend of the people who care for you."

His round eyes, a childish pale blue, stayed on mine as I approached. It was apparent as I got closer that the monk was quite old; the round face was etched with countless wrinkles, though the eyes were those of a child.

"Pretty lady not hurt Friar Gene. No, no." He shook his head vigorously, smiling hopefully.

My heart turned over. Would anyone deliberately harm such a gentle creature? "Of course not, Friar Gene, I'm your friend. Please don't be afraid."

His look of terror evaporated into childish smiles. "Pretty lady. Pretty lady . . . my friend. Not hurt. Not hurt Friar Gene."

I smiled back. "Friend. Not hurt." We beamed at each other for a moment or two. Then I ventured, "I've seen you here, walking around the stones. Do you come also at night?"

He retreated a step, his eyes wide on mine. "Night? No! Friar . . ." He struggled for the words, then pantomimed being afraid, hugging himself and shivering in a way that might have been comical if I'd been inclined to laugh.

"It's scary here at night? Yes, but someone comes here, someone with a lantern, who walks and looks like this . . ." I swung my arms and acted out my own version of the visitor to the stones whom I had seen from my tower room.

Friar Gene unexpectedly clapped his hands, delighted at my antics. The sound of his childlike laughter seemed incongruous in the cold surroundings. "Ooh, lady of the stones. Pretty lady see her, too?"

It was the second time she'd been mentioned, this 'lady of the stones.' First by Jocko, now by the little monk. I experienced that phenomenon that people define as one's hackles rising for the first time. "This . . . ah, lady . . . Is she real, Friar Gene?"

The monk smiled at me, then performed a pantomime that sent chills down my spine. His motions were clearly those of someone removing one's head.

I swallowed hard. "A . . . a headless lady, then. Tell me, Friar Gene, how is she dressed? Like me?" Blue eyes looked blankly at my modern clothes. "Or like one of the picture ladies in the upper gallery?"

He nodded eagerly. "Big. Headless lady big." He held his chubby hands out wide at his sides, indicating the full skirts of the Tudor women. Our lady ghost was not a modern one, then. My long silence distracted the friar from our topic of conversation, and he wandered over to sniff at a straggling rose. I waited until he'd plucked it and handed it to me before asking, "There was an American lady here, Friar Gene, with long golden hair. Did you ever talk to her?"

The vacuous eyes had a brief flicker of fear, but trust soon won over. The little monk motioned that I should wait while he scurried off, back into the darkness of the Priest's Hole.

He soon reappeared, beaming, but I failed to respond to his eager smile, for I was mesmerized by what he held in his hand.

It was a passport.

Before I even opened the badly watermarked booklet, I knew it was Cassandra's.

The cold significance of the passport being in Friar Gene's possession instead of its rightful owner's was frightening and undeniable. Leaving Punkin behind could have been an oversight; the passport was a different matter. Cassandra would never have left Bloodstones without that all-important document; she was too thorough, too seasoned a traveler.

I swallowed hard and asked as gently as I could, "Friar Gene, how did you get this? Did you find it somewhere? In the Priest's Hole, perhaps?"

The monk shook his head and then took me by the hand. He led me to the edge of the moat and pointed to a bunch of rushes growing there.

I closed my eyes tightly to shut out the sight of the murky water lapping sluggishly at the rushes. "This . . . this was all you found, Friar Gene? Just the passport?"

He looked blank, and I realized that, in his limited brain, the document was just an oddity, a childish keepsake. He held out his hand, and I said soothingly, "No, dear, I must keep this for a while." I rooted around in my pockets and found a shiny travel folder with lots of pictures. "Here; this is much prettier, not all dirty and faded."

I left the little fellow sitting cross-legged by the moat, stroking and cooing over the colorful photos. Guilt over the unfair trade would have to wait, as right now I was anxious to get away from this suddenly ominous spot. I needed a place to mull over this new, disturbing development.

The thought of The Dark Swan with its friendly, sympathetic proprietor gave a lift to my spirits. I needed a friend outside the castle—like Neil Willingham.

I ignored the car Jocko had told me was available for my use when I discovered a trim Moped with keys dangling in the ignition. I needed the whipping wind in my face to clear out the cobwebs.

Neil must have been at the window when I drove into the Dark Swan's lot; he had a pint of bitter and a big, welcoming smile waiting when I walked inside.

"Well, hello! Look at those rosy cheeks! Jocko said you were up and about when I called a while ago, but I didn't expect a visit so soon." He pushed the mug toward me, his eyes alight with pleasure. "But I'm delighted. Linwood was getting pretty sticky about my visits over there."

I pulled Cass' passport from my pocket and laid it on the counter, open to her photograph. "Is this the girl you saw in here?"

Neil peered at the splotched photo. "Yep. Matter of fact, I remember seeing this passport when she was in here." He looked at me, his bright eyes candidly curious. "Like I told you before, she kinda made a point of my taking notice of her, which I obviously did, though she wasn't all that good-looking." He handed the passport back to me and asked quietly, "Now are you going to tell me what all of this is about?"

I sighed. "I think I have to tell somebody, Neil. I'm sorry," I added hastily. "I just meant that you're already my friend, someone I can trust—not a last resort."

"Glad you clarified that." He grinned and got more beer. "Now tell me about this blonde and what she means to you. And what's causing all those worry lines on that pretty face."

I told him about Cassandra and the reunion I'd come all the way to England to bring about. Neil was an attentive listener, but he wasn't nearly as concerned or sympathetic as I'd expected him to be. When I finished my little story of two long lost cousins rediscovering each other in the castle of their girlish fantasies, he shrugged. "So what were you expecting? That Cassandra would come running out to greet you with widespread arms and tears in her eyes, while the Linwoods hummed 'My Old Ancestral Home' in the background?"

I blushed. "That's not . . . Okay, I'll admit it, I *was* hoping for something like that. I wanted us to be close again, without Phillip around to get between us. What's wrong with that?"

"Nothing. But it seems you acted a bit too impulsively since your cousin left before you even showed up."

I waved the passport in front of his nose. "Without this? Without her passport? Neil, Cass may have changed since I knew her, but she would have no more stormed out of here without her . . ." I stopped as my eyes fell on the envelope in my purse where I was stuffing the passport. It held my rental agreement with the London car agency I'd used. "My God," I half-whispered, "how could I have been so stupid?" I raised my eyes to Neil's puzzled face, not really seeing it. "A car. She had to rent a car to come to Bloodstones. And if she really left like everybody says she did, if she went back to London, she might have returned the car." I fished for coins, suddenly excited. "Neil, where's your phone?"

"In the hall. Want me to come with you?"

"No, don't come." I ran for the phone, my heart thumping like crazy. My usual clear thinking had been atrophied by everything else that had happened; maybe now I would be back on the trail of my missing cousin.

The thick pence seemed to take forever to fall through the slot, but finally the clipped accent of the clerk at the first leasing agency I tried came on.

They'd never heard of Mrs. Phillip Coleman. Nor had the second agency. With the third, I struck paydirt. The car rented to Mrs. Phillip Coleman had, indeed, been turned in.

But the circumstances surrounding its return gave me no comfort. The girl told me with some asperity, "It wasn't our regular kind of procedure, Miss—I can tell you that. Her leaving it parked out front of the garage all night, with the keys right there waiting for some thieving bloke to drive off with it—it caused a bit of a stir with my manager, it did."

I finally managed to cut through the indignant complaints. "Then no one at the agency—a security guard, perhaps—saw Mrs. Coleman when she brought your car back."

I was told, with the usual British tolerance for foreigners, that since London streets were not overrun with mobsters and mayhem, there was no need for guards or . . .

I held the phone receiver for some time after our conversation was over, staring into the darkness of the hallway.

No one had seen Cassandra bring the car back to the agency.

The chilling facts closed in, no longer to be denied. No one had seen my cousin since the day before my arrival. The only traces of Cassandra were the soggy passport and a forlorn stuffed animal.

My confusion was compounded with each new fact. Something was all out of kilter, all wrong. I could see Cass arguing with Miles, even stomping off in a fury. She had a fiery temper. What I couldn't accept was her not returning, if not to make amends, then at least to say good-bye to her hostess. Cassandra and I were reared with southern gentility, good manners being drilled into us constantly, without mercy. No matter what we felt about a visit, it would never be ended with such rude and abrupt behavior.

What could have happened to make Cass behave in a way so totally out of character?

There had to be a logical process by which I could find out the answers to all these puzzling questions. Since she'd started with the Linwood family records, I would start there, too.

I left Neil with a promise to call him the next day, since he seemed to be taking his role of protector quite seriously.

When I returned, Madame was still asleep in her room, and Miles was nowhere to be seen. It was a perfect time to do my snooping in the chapel. I found Jocko wielding a giant cleaver over a board of fresh mushrooms in the kitchen and announced my intent.

"The Linwood records? They're still lying about in the chapel where Mrs. Coleman left them, Miss." Though I protested, he insisted on laying aside his apron and escorting me to the chapel. "If you'll be busy with the records, Miss, I should remind you now that the Baron is expecting you for a ride at four-thirty. And Miss Hightower reminded me to tell you she's depending on you for the table settings and place cards for Madame's birthday dinner Wednesday."

Good ol' Samantha, never letting me forget I was on a domestic footing. "Any calls?" I kept expecting to hear from Phillip.

Jocko shook his head and held the door for me to enter the study. "Shall I ring you at teatime? Madame particularly wanted you to have it with her in her room."

I nodded. "My God, Jocko, are those stacks all the family records?" The piles of boxes on the long library table were formidable.

Jocko's mouth twitched, which was the closest he could come to smiling. "The monks wrote everything in sizeable script, you'll remember, and many of the older papers have been encased in glass for preservation." He looked over at the panel over the ancient wooden bench which I already knew was the secret opening to the Priest's Hole. "You won't be startled now, Miss, by the little friar's popping up through there unexpected, like? Madame and the rest of us have spoken to him time and time again about poppng in and out, scaring a body half to death, but you know how the poor bloke's mind is addled. It does no good to warn him as we have over and over about how old and dangerous it is down there."

Some time later, I would regret not paying closer attention to Jocko's parting words about the precarious condition of the Priest's Hole.

Pouring over the family history proved to be more tedious than illuminating. My eyes aching from the painfully careful script, my brain numb from the intense concentration, I leaned back and closed my eyes, trying to get a sense of my cousin's feelings while she sat in the same chair, resting from the same task.

It was a technique I used quite often and usually with success to get into another person's skin, but this time it didn't work. Cass wouldn't come to life in the room where she'd spent all those hours, and I felt further away from her than ever.

I wasn't sorry when the ring of the telephone broke my concentration. I would come back the next day when I was fresh.

I could hear Madame Lilah's lilting laughter all the way down the hall. Crock must be visiting; he was the only one who made her giggle like a schoolgirl. I hurried to join them. Perhaps there'd be a chance to get the doctor off to myself for a few moments. He would be interesteed to learn how far I had come in my spontaneous regression.

"Alix! Oh, my dear, come in, come in! You've just missed hearing the most wicked story. Victor, tell Alix about the Poole sisters and their rhubarb wine."

"I shall—sometime—but right now, Alix looks as if she needs her tea more than one of my silly anecdotes." Crock

236

brought me a cup and asked anxiously, "You look tired, Alix. Are you sure you're not overdoing it, staying on that foot?"

I said with deliberate emphasis, sending a signal. "My foot is fine, Crock, but that other little problem I told you about is getting worse. I may need a prescription."

Madame Lilah looked at me with concern, but her phone rang and she was soon cheerfully gossiping with her good friend, Mrs. Devon, about the morning garden exhibit. Crock and I took the opportunity to exchange a few guarded words.

He sighed after I quickly filled him in on my recent, extended stay in Crislyn's life. "I was afraid of that. You say you woke up nauseated, as though you were the one responsible for and sickened by Meg's death. Alix, has it occurred to you that Crislyn, too, might be destined to die violently?"

I stared at him, fearfully. "I might not be able to return," I whispered. "I could die with Crislyn if something happens to her."

"Not *with*, Alix. *As*. I don't mind telling you I've given this matter a lot of thought, and I keep coming back to the same grim conclusion." Crock suddenly looked his age. "There's a hell of a strong will reaching out to you over the centuries. I'm not sure modern science can offer any protection." He sighed. "If only there were some way I could be there, too. As a friend, if not as a physician."

Lilah hung up and called out, "What are you two plotting over there? Something delicious and totally surprising for my birthday, I hope."

Crock squeezed my shoulder and walked back to the lavender covered bed. "Sly of you to figure it out, Lilah, but will you promise to act surprised if I tell you what it is?"

The whispers and giggles that ensued gave me time to recover from the shocking admission that the doctor might not be able to help me when Crislyn's story came to its inevitable conclusion. With Lian gone, who was left to be the poor girl's ally? Would she find her kin and would they help her?

Don't worry, Alix.

I nearly jumped out of my chair when the voice spoke so clearly inside my head. I looked over at the doctor, thinking it might have come from him, but he was still teasing Lilah about her birthday.

The voice had been familiar, but I couldn't identify it or explain how it brought a sudden peacefulness.

By the time I'd changed for my ride with Miles, my fatigue and apprehension had given way to a springy energy and anticipation of the coming outing.

I had to catch my breath when I walked out the front gate to see Miles astride Shadow. Pandora, saddled and looking eager for her rider, flared delicate nostrils and shook her fine mane in greeting, but I could hardly tear my eyes away from the picture Baron Miles Linwood made against the beautiful Kent countryside which was being bathed in the last rays of the sun.

"I was about to come after you. I thought maybe you'd decided to be stubborn and not show up for our ride."

I bowed mockingly before swinging onto Pandora's back. "I apologize for keeping my lordship waiting. Shall we be off? I don't like riding after dark."

We ambled along the path bordering the Medway, this time toward Aylesford. I could see the tower of the old monastery outlined against the sky. "Tell me, Miles, do people think Friar Gene knows where the famous ruby is hidden?"

There was a long silence, then Miles said harshly, "Your cousin apparently did. That's what prompted our fight in the chapel that day. I caught her bullying poor Friar Gene, trying to get him to tell her what he knew about the Devil's Eye."

I nearly fell off my horse, twisting around to look at my companion's face, which was grim; the remark had not been made jokingly. "Cassandra bullying Friar Gene! You must be kidding, Miles. Cass would never mistreat a gentle little creature like that." Even as I spoke in hot defense of my cousin, I had the uneasy image of Friar Gene's wide-eyed fear at my mention of the 'American lady with long blonde hair.'

"I'm afraid you don't know Cassandra as well as you think, Alix. Or else she's changed since you knew her. She had me fooled, too—until I heard how vicious she could be."

"I still don't believe Cass could ever . . ."

"She told Friar Gene that if he didn't tell her where the Devil's Eye was hidden, she'd see to it that more than his brains were scrambled. And that was the mildest of the threats that I overheard."

I knew Miles was watching my face to see the effect of these shocking accusations against Cassandra. He wasn't disappointed; I could hardly get the words out. "My cousin is a very wealthy woman. Why would she want the king's ruby that badly?"

Miles shrugged. "Greed for rare and unique treasures isn't all that unusual, even among rich people. All I know is that your cousin came to Bloodstones determined to find and steal the Devil's Eye. All those nights we thought she was studying the family records, she was making a methodical search for the ruby. Luckily, I caught on before she got further than the chapel and the Priest's Hole." He smiled grimly. "If she hadn't become impatient, she probably would have found the hiding place eventually."

I said flatly, "I don't believe all this."

Miles didn't seem to hear me. He was frowning. "That was one thing I couldn't understand—the sudden impatience. Lilah and I had extended our welcome for as long as she wished to stay with us. Jocko said there was a phone call for her, a long conversation that left her terribly nervous and upset. It was right after that I heard her with Friar Gene."

I thought of the passport tucked away in my purse and opened my mouth to mention it, but I knew Miles would only come up with some suave explanation. My exhilaration at riding in the brisk country air turned to an impulse to run as fast as I could from this man and his horrible insinuations about Cass. I had my own insinuations to make, though I dared not until I had more solid evidence. *I don't think Cassandra ever left Bloodstones, Miles Linwood. I think the argument you had with her was about something else entirely and that it ended in violence.*

I could bear my own dark thoughts no longer. With a sharp command, I spurred Pandora off and into a swift gallop, not knowing or caring if Miles thought I was challenging him to race as I had before.

There were no hidden walls on this path. I let Pandora have her head and soon felt the tenseness and worries about Cass give way to sheer pleasure.

I was sitting on a rock by the slow-moving river when Miles came thundering up. He first looked at me smoking my cigarette as if I'd been there for hours, then over at Pandora who was munching grass quite casually, then cursed softly.

"Why, Baron Linwood, I do believe I've managed to win another race." I smiled sweetly at him and then became alarmed when I saw the look in his eyes when he swung down off his horse and started toward me.

The bruising grip of his hands as he pulled me into his arms was nothing compared to the furious kiss that held no tenderness. I finally pulled away and hissed into his face, "The mighty baron! Unable to stand being beaten at anything."

"Damn you," he growled and reached for me again, holding me in a bearlike embrace, with my face mashed against his heaving chest so tightly I had to fight for breath. "Damn you!" I could feel his heart pounding like mad and the hot breath against the top of my head as he whispered hoarsely, "I swore there'd never be another woman who'd get under my skin and into my blood. I swore it over my wife's grave."

He lifted my face and looked down into my eyes. "It's the same for you, isn't it, Alix? Hating me and wanting me at the same time; fighting this damn pull between us . . ." His mouth claimed mine again and whetted the rising hunger in both of us. I felt Miles' hands slide slowly under my blazer to push the silk blouse back from my breasts, as my own hands feverishly sought the warmth of his flesh. We stood locked together in our savage need for each other for what seemed an eternity. Somewhere in the part of my brain not fogged by passion, I heard myself thinking that whatever happened with Crislyn and the men in her life wasn't finished. Good or bad, it was left to Miles and me to finish.

Crislyn. Who destroyed her? Instead of completing her love story, we might be continuing the cycle of destruction.

I pulled away from Miles with a little cry. Until I knew all that had happened to my ancestor, I mustn't trust Miles. "Don't you understand?" I sounded hysterical and saw his startled face. "It's not us, Miles. It's Crislyn and someone else. Can't you see?" I laughed out loud at the look on his face. "Don't you see it? It was too strong to die, that passion so long ago. Love . . . hate . . . desire . . . whatever it was, it lives on through us, Miles, through us." I stopped, realizing he was staring at me in utter astonishment. "Why are you staring at me like that? I know what I'm saying sounds crazy, but. . ."

"How did you know the name of James Gerald's first wife? Not a trace of her appears in the archives. Her name was blotted out from all the records. Even her grave was unmarked. Some say she was a witch, who died with a curse on her lips. It was forbidden to speak her name aloud after her death—for superstitious reasons, I suppose."

So it had been Crislyn and James in the end.

"The curse." I found myself whispering. "What was it."

"That Bloodstones would never be at peace until the return of rightful ownership to the flesh of her flesh. Alix, I asked you how you knew the name Crislyn."

I was suddenly frightened. I'd been foolish to stay here, knowing I was the main pawn in some mysterious, dangerous game. I would forget about Cassandra, forget about the Linwoods and go home to America, where I could be free from these insane invasions of my mind and senses.

"I . . . it doesn't matter. I don't know. Maybe I dreamed it."

Miles stepped toward me, looking as if he might shake the truth out of me. He stopped at the mournful sound of a hunter's horn. "We're being called home." He handed me Pandora's reins. "Lilah no doubt is worried that you might have had another accident."

I waited till he was seated on Shadow before asking him challengingly, "One last race?"

Miles raised his eyebrow. "Winner take all?"

I grinned and jabbed Pandora into the quick lead I was learning she excelled at. Several lengths ahead of Miles, I spotted a low-hanging limb on the path just around the bend in the bridle path. With devilish impulsiveness, I swung up on the limb as Pandora passed under, chuckling with girlish satisfaction to see Miles pass beneath me in hot pursuit of the riderless horse. What a good joke on him, I told myself. I could just see his face when he caught up with my horse and found no sight of its rider.

It turned out not to be a good joke at all.

I waited long enough for Miles to have reached the front gate and start wondering what had happened to me, then I let myself down out of the tree and walked back.

Jocko met me halfway between the river and the path through the stones. I knew from his face that something was wrong. "Hurry, Miss, Madame's having an attack, a bad one, and the doctor says for you to come at once."

I broke into a run, my heart racing madly. Crock met me at the front door, his eyes clouded with concern. "Thank God you're all right, Alix. We came out to watch for you, and when Lilah saw Pandora without a rider and Miles galloping up behind like a madman . . ."

I brust into tears. "Oh, my God, no! Crock, she's not . . . oh God, Crock, please tell me she's not dead because of my foolishness."

"No, she's not dead, Alix, far from it. But she refuses to take her sedative until she's seen for herself that you're safe and sound."

I rushed over to the bed where Lilah lay pale and

drawn. The tears from my guilt at having caused this wonderful lady to suffer from my silly prank spilled over both of us. "Oh, Madame Lilah, I'm so sorry that I caused you such distress."

She stroked my hair and kissed me. "There, there, my child, don't take on so. It's I who was being silly, but I was so afraid . . ." The thin arms held me tight. "Alix, you won't ever leave us, will you? I told Miles that nothing would make me happier than to keep you with us forever."

I looked up to find both Miles' and Crock's eyes on me. The doctor gave a slight nod to the unspoken question between us. "Yes, Lilah, forever. That will make me happy, too."

Crock moved over to pierce the delicate arm with his hypodermic. "Lilah, you really should get some rest now. Alix and Miles will both be here tomorrow when you're feeling better." He smiled, though it strained his drawn face to do so. "Your party's only two nights away, remember. If you're going to have the strength to open all those presents, you have to get your beauty sleep."

Lilah's eyes sparkled and showed some of her usual spirit. "No one's asked what I want for my birthday. Lean over, Victor, and I'll tell you."

The doctor listened with a slight smile as the old woman whispered into his ear, then he nodded and gently pulled up the sheet around Lilah's still shoulders. He motioned us to leave, and Miles waited for me to precede him into the great room, where Jocko had a good fire blazing and the brandy decanter set out.

Miles didn't speak until he poured us each a healthy snifter full and downed half of his. "Well? What do you plan for your next stunt?" I winced, but Miles had no mercy. "Filing a report with the Ravensbridge sheriff about your missing cousin, whom you suspect I murdered?" He downed the rest of his drink, his eyes still hard on mine. "That should help slake your thirst for excitement."

"Miles . . ."

"Of course, it might not be the best thing for Lilah,

under the circumstances, seeing the moat being dragged for bodies again, having the old muck raked up as it was with Rosalee and the tour guide.''

"Miles, for God's sake, I love your mother. I'd never do anything to hurt her. I swear it.'' I went over to stare down into the fire. It wasn't fair—to lose Cass and find Lilah, only to learn I would lose her, too. "I'd do anything for Lilah. Anything!''

I could feel Miles' eyes drilling into the back of my head. The silence grew heavy between us. "Alix, turn around and look at me.'' I did. "Do you mean that? About doing anything to make my mother's last few weeks happy?''

"Well . . .'' I hesitated. "Almost anything.''

"Does 'almost' include agreeing to become my wife—for Lilah's sake?''

I almost dropped my glass. "Your . . . *wife*? Miles, you're crazy! We don't even . . . I haven't . . .'' I felt my face changing color. "That's the most ridiculous thing I ever heard in my life.''

"Is it?'' He came over and took the lighter from my shaking hand and held it to my cigarette. "Not so ridiculous when you think of it as a harmless little charade to play out for the satisfaction of a dying old woman.'' He took the cigarette from my numb fingers and threw it into the fire. "Think of the happiness it would bring her, knowing her cherished heir won't live out his days a crusty old, woman-hating playboy. She worries about me, you know. And she loves you—though, God knows why. You're the stubbornest, most convoluted, mixed-up female I ever met in my life.''

"If this is a proposal, why am I laughing?''

"It is a proposal, but not of marriage. And I'm sure as hell not laughing. I love that old woman in there more than anything in the world.''

"Miles, I can't do anything so dishonest.''

"Can't you?'' The turquoise eyes were unrelenting. "You may have taken several weeks off Lilah's life by that little Annie Oakley stunt you pulled. Are you saying you can't play out a harmless farce to add them back?"

"That's mean."

"I can be mean when it comes to things that matter to me."

"How do I know it would really make her happy if we . . ." I stopped at the sound of Crock's brisk footsteps.

"Well, come in, Crock. I'm sure you can use a brandy." Miles got the doctor a snifter and refilled his own. "How is she, Crock? And be straight. Alix knows about Lilah."

The doctor's cherubic face was filled with sadness. "Not good, Miles, I'm afraid. Not good." He sighed heavily. "I'm afraid we'll be lucky if those damn bells aren't ringing out a castle death before Guy Fawkes Day." He looked at Miles and then at me with a little smile. "Too bad the two of you get along like a pair of Welshmen in a London pub. You know what she told me she wanted more than anything in the world?"

I didn't dare look at Miles or ask Crock what Lilah had said. I felt both men looking at me as the doctor said slowly, "She said that nothing would bring her more happiness than hearing that you two were planning marriage."

Miles and I looked at each other, and I opened my mouth but not soon enough.

The next thing I knew, Crock was slapping Miles on the shoulder and kissing me and a bottle of very good champagne was being popped open. I was now the intended bride of the Baron of Bloodstones. Numbly, I heard my 'fiance' explain to Crock that the announcement would be saved for Lilah's birthday.

To say that I found falling asleep difficult in my isolated tower would be putting it mildly. With all that had happened, sleep was impossible. I finally gave up the pretense and got up, putting on my heavy dark robe against the night chill, and paced up and down the room.

How had I let myself be talked into such a foolish commitment? Though Miles and I agreed before parting that mention of a firm wedding date would be deliberately vague, our engagement would be made official at Lilah's party.

I stood at the archer's slit, looking out over the blood stones, absent-mindedly noting the shimmering of the moonlight on the river and hearing the distant sound of a motor boat.

The castle was quiet as death. I had begged Crock to let me sit with Lilah during the night, but he refused, saying she recovered quickly from her attacks and would be more distressed than aided by my keeping a vigil over her.

I shivered and hugged myself for warmth, thinking I heard a creak on the stairs. Surely Miles wouldn't come to me tonight!

I stood listening, half-dreading, half-wanting his visit, but there was no repetition of the sound. Silly to be so jumpy. I turned my thoughts to other matters, like Cass and the passport Friar Gene had found.

Jocko had told me once that the monk was like a little pack rat, forever collecting bits and pieces of things, scraps and colored bits of glass.

Where would he keep them, I wondered?

In the Priest's Hole, no doubt. That's where he'd gone for the passport. There might be other clues to Cass' disappearance somewhere in that awful place. The thought of entering such a creepy place this time of night didn't appeal to me at all, but it seemed the logical time to explore undisturbed.

Friar Gene was asleep in the little room off the chapel. I heard his gentle snores as I made my way over to the Priest's Hole opening. The tiny flashlight I'd brought offered more security than light. Easing my way through the dark entry, I wished I had a larger torch.

But my flickering light found the very old table I'd noticed on my earlier visit. The candle atop it was fat and new, and I struck my lighter to it, looking around and shivering in the dampness of the cavernous place.

Dust and cobwebs were everywhere. I saw a couple of

boxes full of pictures and scraps of paper—undoubtedly the friar's treasure trove. I lifted one of the boxes to the table and started sorting through the mess.

When my hand closed on a furry spider, I didn't scream but jumped away in horror, tilting the table dangerously and barely catching the candle before it set fire to the scattered debris.

Trying to keep the table from crashing over and balancing the candle, I watched in fascination as a concealed drawer slid open.

I had, it seemed, found the secret hiding place of my little pack rat friar. After I'd righted the table and candle, I saw the pitiful collection of the childlike little monk—pictures cut raggedly from magazines, bits of yarn and colored glass, rusted nails and scraps of metal.

And a very old book bound in sheepskin. I knew at once that it had to be the prayer book that hadn't been found after James Gerald's lonely death.

Very carefully I opened the rotting cover to the faded, almost illegible inscription: *James Gerald Linwood, October 23, 1495.* The date of his death was added in flowery script, no doubt by the attending monk: *Died June 7, 1553, may God have mercy on his soul.*

The yellow parchment crackled as I opened it a page or two more. I felt guilty about tampering with what could be a precious family document and was about to return it to its hiding place when I felt a lumpish inconsistency on the back cover.

I slit open the false cover and pulled out the well-preserved packet that held, I was certain, the famous confession James Gerald Linwood had written from his deathbed. The candlelight wavered, and I heard something behind me. Flicking my flashlight about, I pinpointed the source of the noise—a cracking timber in the shored-up ceiling. "My God," I said aloud as a shower of soil came down, "this place could collapse at any moment." As if to corroborate this, there was a loud groan from the ancient rafters. Even more chilling was the sudden wind that whipped through the tunnel from the opening on the moat side. The candle was extinguished, and the letter dropped to the floor as I groped for my flashlight.

The soft curses I was murmuring made me feel better. The feeling that something terribly evil had swept into my presence was frightening and overwhelming.

There was another groan of straining timbers. I heard a clear little voice of instinct telling me to forget James' letter and get the hell out of this dangerous place.

About halfway to the outer opening, to which I was closer, I stopped to listen. There was the slightest sound of something that was definitely not connected with the ceiling faults.

It was, I realized with an icy chill, the sound of human breathing. Someone or something was waiting for me near the tunnel's opening.

Very, very quietly I felt my way along the damp wall, back the way I'd come. When I reached the opening to the chapel, I abandoned caution and scrambled for refuge from the frightening, evil-smelling place.

Just as I wriggled through the opening to the chapel, I heard the crashing timbers of the cavern walls and felt the floor beneath my trembling knees shake with the impact. Friar Gene, his robe rumpled and his sparse fringe of hair awry from sleep, appeared at the door to his room and ran over to me, his face full of terror.

I put my arms around him, as with a child, and said soothingly, "It's all right, dear. Don't be frightened; it's all right." The sounds of the crashing timbers subsided and everything was still again. I stood there holding the little friar's trembling form and waited for the house to react to the disaster.

It took longer than I thought for people to come running into the chapel. Jocko was first, with Miles right behind him, and then Crock, who'd spent the night to keep tabs on Lilah.

They all came to an abrupt halt just inside the door, staring at what I'm sure was a ludicrous sight. There I was—wild-eyed, hair askew and dust streaks on my face, in my robe and slippers—holding the whimpering, terrified little friar.

Miles' eyes went to the panel opening and back to me. "Didn't anyone ever tell you about curiosity and the cat?"

Crock gave Miles a stern look. "Never mind that." He came over to me. "Are you all right, Alix? I've been telling Lilah for years they should shut up that damned hellhole. It hasn't been safe since that bomb went off and weakened some of the main supports on the lower level."

Miles wasn't going to let me off the hook that easily. He said sternly, "I thought Jocko said he'd warned you about going in there. We've tried to keep Friar Gene out, too, but you know how ineffective that's been."

I looked at Jocko with apologetic eyes. "I'm sorry. He did try to warn me about its being unsafe, but I . . . Look, Crock, don't you think you should forget about me and do something about this poor man? He's still shaking through and through."

Miles spat out a couple of commands to Jocko about boarding up the moat entrance to the Priest's Hole while Crock went off with Friar Gene. I was left alone with my newly betrothed.

He looked at me, sighed and shook his head. There was a sparkle of humor in the brilliant eyes. "Can't I even leave you for a few hours without your causing some kind of upheaval?"

I didn't think it was humorous. "That cave-in would have happened whether I'd been in there or not." I sniffed in righteous indignation. "Doesn't it even concern you that I might have been killed?"

"It concerns me more that you were up and about, prowling where you had no right to be. What were you up to this time, Alix?"

I tried my best to look innocent, but since I wasn't, it didn't come off too well. "I . . . I came down here for something to read and . . . I heard a noise." I was back in honest territory now and said with more vigor, "Miles, I swear there was someone down here. Somebody . . . evil.''

"Hmm, evil. No doubt, one of the ghosts that haunt the blood stones, looking for new territory. Alix, I suggest you leave your fantasizing to your novels. And if you say anything to Lilah about a prowler, I'll wring that luscious neck of yours.''

I lifted my chin. "I have no intentions of telling your mother about this." I added anxiously, "I hope none of this ruckus upset her.''

"She's still sleeping like a baby. I looked in on her before I came here.''

"In that case, I'll go back to bed." I pulled my robe close around me and started past him.

He put an arm across the door, not letting me through. The turquoise eyes mocked me as he said softly, "So you couldn't sleep, either.''

I took a deep breath. "I think I can now.''

"I'll see you to your room.''

"No need. Miles, I'm tired. Don't give me a hard time. I've already had one hell of a night.''

He unwound his long length from the doorjamb and smiled down at me. "I insist on seeing you up to the tower. With your record, I might lose my fiancee between now and breakfast.''

I glared at him and stalked past. "This may be the shortest engagement in history if you start playing games with me.''

He caught up with me at the end of the hall. "Alix, you're getting hysterical. Calm down. Come in and let me get you a brandy.''

I wheeled around to face him as I came even with the door into the refectory. I was acutely aware of the cold painted eyes of the portrait watching the scene below. "Listen to me, your Lordship. I don't want any brandy. I most particularly don't want a brandy with you. All in the same day, I've learned my cousin is a monster, wherever she is, gotten engaged to a man I neither understand nor like very much, and nearly got smashed under a few tons of rubble." To my disgust, my eyes were filling with tears. "And to top all that, I had the answers to a lot of terrible questions right in my hand." I held out the hand that had held the famous confession letter and shook it in front of Miles' nose. "And . . . and . . ." My face crinkled up. "I lost it. I *lost* it, Miles!" I could see from his face he had no idea what I was talking about. Sooner or later, I had to tell him about the prayer book and James' unread letter that was lost forever. "Maybe I will have that brandy after all."

The tense happenings of the day—or the brandy? I could blame what occurred that night on either or both—or the fact that by the time I had told him about discovering the confession, I found it hard to leave Miles. There was something different in the air between us, something very different from the old antipathy.

We kept falling into little silences, during which neither of us seemed to be able to stop looking at the other. Once I lifted my eyes suddenly from the flames of the fire and caught Miles looking at me with such a combination of tenderness and vulnerability that I almost ran to him, to take his face in my hands and smother it with kisses.

Every start at conversation dwindled off, neither of us aware of anything but each other and what was happening to us.

I wanted his arms around me. I wanted him next to me in my bed, but this time without the anger, without the fighting. My heart was hurting. Deep inside me, something very old and locked away was uncurling and making its warm, licking way to long-suppressed emotions. "Miles," I whispered shakily, "I don't know what's happening to me."

"I don't either," he whispered back as shakily, "but I know I've never felt quite like this before."

Still, we stood there, just looking at each other, not moving. Then, Miles spoke so quietly I could hardly hear him. "I want you tonight, Alix. I want you in my arms, in love."

"I want that, too." I was unable to say more before he

swept me into his arms and we kissed with a passion that transcended the centuries.

He was a man who wanted to forget, and I was a woman who was desperate to remember. Suddenly, love seemed the balance between us.

We lay in the dark, both oddly silent, considering how much we had just shared, but I was beginning to see that Miles and I communicated better on a different level. There was so much unspoken understanding between us that words seemed almost superfluous.

"You can see why I didn't want to have that brandy," I said finally, in a voice still shaky.

"I'll have Jocko lay in a case tomorrow," Miles said, with his voice not much steadier.

"Miles . . ."

"Alix . . ."

The simultaneous address accompanied by a joint move to face each other made us both burst out laughing. "You first," I said.

"No, you." He kissed the tip of my nose. "I like your three freckles."

"I was thinking about the war . . . Don't laugh. Let me finish."

"The one between England and the upstart colonists, you mean?"

"No. The one between our south and the Union. All those terrible, bloody battles all day, and then at night . . ." I had a pang, suddenly feeling the loss of Uncle Porter, who'd been a Civil War buff. "The men would sit in their separate camps and sing, often in unison, North & South together."

"Is that what we were doing? Singing?"

"I told you not to laugh, but yes. Miles, whatever you think about tonight, we still have some fighting to do."

He was very still. "Is there any hope of surrender?"

I slipped from his embrace and pulled on my gown. "Perhaps." Once I find out the truth about Cass—and about Crislyn.

The attraction to Miles was strong. So was the affinity for Lilah and the people I'd met since coming to England.

But the pull from Crislyn's past was stronger than anything else. I knew I could never leave Bloodstones without letting her story unfold, whatever its conclusion or effect on me. Miles and I falling in love would have to wait its proper turn.

13

You could hardly label me an old-fashioned girl by any means, but waking up alone in my own bed has been (since my affair with Phillip) a die-hard rule. Miles had scoffed at my primness about appearances, but left at my insistence long before dawn.

The sound of hammering came in through my little window, waking me, and after a few groggy minutes, I realized that Miles' instructions about having the opening to the Priest's Hole boarded up were being carried out. Jocko, bringing up a tray of tea and muffins, corroborated this.

"I can't say I'm sorry about that place being closed up for good, Miss. I've always worried when the village children come for their apples and candy on Old Hallows. They wander about, exploring and such, and could have been buried this next time as you came close to being."

I thought about the menacing shape that had been furtively sneaking toward me when the tunnel had caved in. Should I tell Jocko he ought to have the workmen search for a body under all that rubble?

I decided against it. I was already credited with too vivid an imagination. "Jocko, I hope you won't take offense, but I have to ask this. All of you—Crock, Miles and yourself—came rather quickly to see what all the fuss was about.

I was too excited about the cave-in to say anything at the time, but something struck me as being mighty peculiar.''

'' 'Mighty peculiar'?'' I didn't know if the butler was making gentle fun of my colloquial southern speech or buying time to think of a response. 'About our wasting no time getting to the scene of the disaster?'' He stooped to pick up and fold a blanket that had slipped to the floor. ''I'd just come in from a game of cribbage with Mrs. Hightower who often suffers insomnia, and I'm sure the good doctor and Baron Linwood were still wakeful from the earlier business with Madame.''

I sighed. ''Which accounts for all of you being wide-awake and fully dressed.'' So much for my brief suspicion that it could have been one of the three lurking in the shadows while I made my search of Friar Gene's treasure trove. ''And how is Madame Lilah this morning? I hope the news about the Priest's Hole hasn't been upsetting.''

''Oh, no, on the contrary. She's been after the Baron for years to have the thing filled in. Gives her the creeps, she says. and, I might add, Dr. Crockett left this morning on his regular rounds, pronouncing her quite recovered from her attack. He put the two of us in charge of seeing that she gets her rest before the festivities tomorrow night.''

''I'll look in on her as soon as I'm dressed. And after that, Jocko, perhaps you and I should go over some plans for the party. Unless, of course, the Baron wants to do that himself.''

Jocko shook his head. ''Oh no, Miss, the Baron gave me specific instructions this morning before he left for London that you were in charge. Just draw up the lists of what's needed, and I'll see to it everything's delivered.''

''So the Baron is out for the day, is he?''

''And the night. He has a flat in Mayfair that serves him when he's in London on business.''

I hated myself for pumping the butler but couldn't help myself. Up to this point, I wasn't sure Miles pursued even a pretense of an occupation. ''He has a business in London?''

''Baron Linwood is associated with one of the finest

barrister firms in London, Miss, though he can only provide limited time to the practice, by necessity." Jocko added proudly, "You may not be aware of it, Miss, but the Baron is quite well received in some exclusive, high government circles. There was even some discussion of his being knighted, as recognition of his courage in leading his compatriots to safety out of some dreadful war camp in Korea. But then there was the bombing here, and . . . ah . . . a bit of unfortunate notoriety that made him feel he could best serve the crown as a simple countryman."

"I see." But I didn't. I was beginning to wonder if I would ever be able to piece together the mass of complexities and contradictions that made up the whole of the man with whose life my own had become inextricably tangled and with whom I was falling in love.

Samantha intercepted me on my way to Lilah's room. Since there was no one else around, she made no attempts to gloss over her dislike. "You're quite the little schemer, aren't you, love?" The thin scarlet mouth curled in a contemptuous smile. "The old woman won't let anyone tell her anything about her new pet, but after that stunt yesterday, I'd guess you won't last much longer than the other one."

I was surprised at the reference to Cass. Had Samantha figured out that we were closely related? "Watch yourself, Samantha. Your fangs are showing. The competition's getting a bit rough, is it?"

The pale eyes held cold fury. "Don't look so smug, love. Before you start thinking the Linwoods are keeping you around because you're irresistible, ask around a little bit about why they're so eager to entertain their wealthy American relatives."

I walked past her and sat down. "So you know that Cassandra Coleman and I are cousins. How? Did Miles tell you?"

She came around and sat on the end of the sofa, consciously arranging her thin form in a graceful pose. "Not directly. I overheard him speaking with one of his colleagues at—what's the firm's name, the one that keeps up with all the rich Americans?''

"Dun and Bradstreet," I told her. "But they wouldn't have me listed, since I only recently came into any kind of inheritance. The Manning fortune is huge, true, but it all went to Cass, not to me." Uncle Porter's legacy was paltry, compared with the steel holdings of Cass's name.

"Ah, but I overheard an interesting little tidbit." Samatha's eyes were gleaming with malice. "Your cousin, it seems, has two heirs—her husband and you."

"Correction. Cass has only one—her husband, Phillip."

Samatha lit a cigarette, her eyes on mine as she blew out a silver curl of smoke. "Interesting, isn't it, that Miles has taken the trouble to find out more about your closest relative than you know yourself? You see, love, Miles found out from a particularly thorough investigative source that your cousin's trip to England wasn't altogether for pleasant family research. It was the first step in a legal separation from her husband."

I stared at her, forgetting to be cool and unperturbed. "Separation! But Phillip never said . . ." I stopped, remembering the keen interest on his part in learning what, if any, contact I'd had with Cass. If Phillip had fallen from grace, Cass was capable of cutting him off without a dime. Uncle Porter had told me Cass had willed everything to Phillip. Had she since changed her will?

"I don't think you know what you're talking about, Samantha. In the first place, I don't see any signs of the Linwoods hurting for money, and in the second place, there wasn't any way they could get their hands on Cass' fortune—certainly not through Phillip. Nor through me, even if I were in line for it, which I'm not."

Samantha held out her hand and looked at the long, curved nails painted the same scarlet as her mouth. "For one who's well past girlhood, you're awfully naive, Alix. How many servants do you see running around this huge old mausoleum? Just one—poor old creaky Jocko, who probably spends his salary to keep the old woman in sherry. And if it weren't for the rent I pay for the cottage and the summer tourists, the whole household would be on the dole.''

''I don't believe you.''

''As for getting their hands on your cousin's fortune, you're right that it wasn't too likely. Your Cassandra didn't hit it off too well with Miles; besides she was already married.'' Samantha raised her eyes slowly to mine and I saw the malevolence that told me we'd come to the core of her hatred. ''Then you popped in—beautiful, sexy . . .''

''Thank you,'' I offered dryly.

''. . . and most of all, available.'' The pale eyes gleamed. ''There'd be enough to tide them over until your full inheritance from Cassandra was settled on you.''

I smiled at her. ''You see what comes of eavesdropping; you apparently didn't get all the facts. You see, it's not I who'd inherit the steel fortune, even if Cass were dead, which she's not. Whatever you heard about Cass leaving her husband, it's still Phillip who gets everything.''

''Oh, but you're mistaken, love,'' Samantha said softly. ''You see, I had the opportunity to . . .ah . . . glance through dear Lilah's correspondence from your cousin before she left America. She was enthusiastic about providing the Linwoods with ample funds for restoring Bloodstones to all its earlier splendor. And she made it clear that her new will would insure that support would be continued by her cousin who was equally dedicated to the family heritage.''

I stared at Samantha, still not knowing what to believe. ''But Cass never wrote or said anything about this.''

''Ah, let me finish. She further indicated that her husband and she had agreed to separate due to various . . . differences. Phillip would have his farm and a large sum settled on him, but you, love, would inherit the bulk.''

I tried not to think of Miles' steady, step-by-step seduction that had led to our convenient betrothal. ''I don't believe it. You're making all this up. Cass hated me. She was leaving everything to Phillip. I saw the will, or a copy of it in

Uncle Porter's—''

''She may have hated you then, but the letter I read to the old woman said things had changed. She was changing her will, as I've repeatedly explained to you, and was planning to send for you after she'd worked out things with the Linwoods.''

''But she left without so much as a good-bye. If you know so much, tell me what happened? And where is she now? What happened to my cousin Cassandra?''

Samantha gave an elegant shrug. ''Ask Miles. He was the last one to see her. As for me, I hardly saw the girl at all. I was off in Paris on an assignment until the day before your cousin left.'' She looked at me with a cool smile. ''I shouldn't make guesses about a girl I knew so briefly, but my own speculation is that Miles rejected your Cassandra.''

''Rejected her?''

Again the casual shrug. ''I told you I was guessing, but what woman doesn't fall in love with Miles?'' Her eyes challenged me to deny my own reluctant attraction, and she'd certainly never made any effort to hide her own. ''As for the rejection, by then Miles was probably aware of the more attractive, more available cousin. I'll admit I'm surprised he risked losing the promised support of his precious castle's restoration, but Miles can be rather cold-blooded about women. Quite frankly, love, Miles can be something of a snob. He'll settle for a woman who's beautiful or rich, but never for either unless there's also that all-important breeding.''

I wanted to box those neat little ears, but somehow I managed to maintain my . . . breeding. ''It amazes me that a girl who worked her way up from a slum in Liverpool can recognize breeding, or the lack thereof,'' I said sweetly. Later I would chastise my below-the-belt use of something Samantha had let slip to Neil while in her cups. I watched her blush but felt no compunction whatever. The blood running through Cass' veins, as well as my own, might not be as blue as our English relatives but we'd done as well.

I realized I was contradicting the one thing in this whole

damned mess that I knew for certain—I was as much a part of Bloodstones as the present Linwoods. And, if there was any substance to the facts that were emerging through my periods of alter-consciousness, my blood was even bluer.

If Crislyn's mysterious parentage held aristocracy, so did mine.

Samantha was coiling to strike back, but I didn't give her time to gather her forces for some new attack. "And while we're being honest with each other, Samantha, there's one thing I've been wanting to tell you. I am not," I said sweetly, "and never have been, nor ever will be, a friend of yours. Therefore, I'd appreciate it if you will refrain from addressing me as 'love.' "

She glared at me for a long moment, her mouth working to form the vituperative reply I was sure she was thinking, but she finally settled for silently stomping off.

I winced at the sound of grinding gears and screeching tires as the model vented her fury on her rather worn old Mercedes convertible. Better the car than me. And better to have our enmity out in the open rather than hidden behind false smiles and tissue-thin civility.

"Alix, I was about to ring Jocko to see if you'd been swallowed up by some new misadventure." Lilah held out her arms and I went into them gladly, more shaken by my encounter with Samantha than I had realized at first. It was good to see my best friend in the castle looking rosy and happy to see me. I hugged her as tightly as the delicate bones would allow. "Darling, I do believe you're crying." Lilah pushed me away and looked into my face. "Dear Alix, did Victor scare you so awfully about that silly attack I had? Why, all you have to do is look at me now to see I'm fit as a fiddle and no worse for wear." She wiped the dampness from my cheek gently. "Don't cry, child. I can't bear it. Is it because you're still concerned that I suffered my attack because of you?" The hammering had resumed, and Lilah frowned delicately. "Those workmen! No doubt taking more breaks than necessary like all the modern laborers these days. I'm glad that fool hole finally caved in, though, without harming anyone."

She didn't know I'd been close to being caught in the cave-in, apparently, and I was glad. "Lilah, there's something I simply have to tell you. I'm sure Crock, and Miles, too, would be furious if they thought I was selfish enough to unburden myself at your expense, but I can't keep quiet any longer."

Lilah stroked my hair back from my forehead. The beautiful eyes, so much like her son's, were full of quiet laughter. "Ah, Alix, women need their secrets. Don't tell any of them that should be kept to yourself, child."

"But this one's eating at me. I'll leave after I tell you, if you want me to."

I'd turned my face away. Look at all the trouble I'd caused this dear woman, and now I was bringing more distress, about to tell her the truth about who I was.

Her fingers went softly to my chin, turning me back to face her. "If it's about your silly little masquerade, child, dry your tears. I've known who you are from the start, though I went along with Miles' little game for the fun of it."

"You knew all along? But how . . . ? Did Miles tell you?"

"No, not until I confronted him. My son had some ridiculous notion that you might be here to cause trouble, but I think I've finally convinced him of my fondness for you. But you asked how I knew about you. It's quite simple, Alix. Your cousin wrote me about you not long before she came, even enclosing an old snapshot of the two of you, young and smiling, with your arms entwined." She smiled at me. "You're even lovelier now, my dear." Her smile faded. "It was very different, that last letter from your cousin. She was worried and unhappy; I think about you, mainly. At least, she kept saying how she was setting things right again between the two of you, and that once the two of you were back in England together, all would be as wonderful as you'd always dreamed."

"Back in England? We never came here, either of us,

though we always planned it.''

"She probably meant more of a geneological reference. Alix, I shouldn't mention this, since your cousin said nothing when she was here and it's probably quite confidential, but she wrote in that strange letter I mentioned that she was leaving a great deal of money to you.''

"So that I could keep the family castle up as she planned to do.'' I felt a sudden sense of loss. "Lilah, listen to us. We're talking about Cass as though she were . . . were . . . dead!''

Lilah dropped her eyes from mine. "I'm sure Miles regrets his quarrel with her as I do, but Alix . . . about your cousin . . . I really don't know quite how to put it. There was . . . there was something missing from Cassandra.'' She shuddered. "You've seen the suit of armor in the front hall. God help me, that's how your cousin struck me. All . . . hollow . . . inside.''

I didn't know what to say, but I did feel a streak of anger. Damn Phillip for doing this to the joyful, sweet and wonderful girl I'd grown up with!

I'd been lucky; it could have been me instead of Cass.

"Alix, dear, I hope I haven't offended you by speaking critically of your cousin.'' Lilah looked anxiously at me.

"No, you haven't offended me. It's unrealistic of me to expect to find Cass unchanged after all these years and everything that has happened to both of us. I'm beginning to accept the fact that when we do meet again, it'll be as strangers.'' *If* we meet again, I said to myself, thinking of the passport. But I had no intention of upsetting Lilah with that little item. "Now, are you in the mood for a few more chapters of *Cotillion*, or are you ready for me to leave you alone to rest?''

Lilah's hand covered mine. "I love hearing you read, my dear, and love even more hearing you enjoy the same things I enjoy. It's no secret to Crock, and Miles, too, that I've grown very fond of you, but no more of that. Read on.''

Our pleasant reading session was interrupted by a visit from Mrs. Devons, a town matron and friend of Lilah's, who reminded her of a promise to contribute to a local charity benefit.

Lilah frowned as soon as her visitor was gone. "I'd completely forgotten about the auction next weekend. Ada reminded me I'd pledged a box of old junk from here."

"Tell me what to do and I'll take care of it."

"Oh, the box is all packed and waiting to be delivered. Perhaps I could have Jocko take it over since they need it today. All of the old historic houses for miles around are sending stuff to be sold. It's incredible the exorbitant prices people will pay for mementos from old castles."

"Jocko is up to his ears in food preparation for tomorrow night."

"But the box is quite heavy, my dear."

"I'll call Neil to give me a hand. I need to go to the village on some errands for Jocko, anyway." And to buy my birthday gift for Lilah, I suddenly remembered. "Will you be all right if I leave for a couple of hours?"

"Victor's coming by later. My dear, are you sure you don't . . ."

I kissed her cheek. "I'm sure. Now, get some rest. And don't let Crock overstay, even if he is your doctor."

Jocko took the box out for me so that Neil would only have to load it into his car. The list he handed me held only two items yet to be purchased. "The pate mold from the Royal Oven is one of Madame's favorites, and the Baron made arrangements for the cake with the bakeshop only two doors away."

He peeled off the money I'd need from a thin roll of pound notes he pulled from his apron pocket. I thought about the butler surreptitiously providing for extras from his own pocket and determined to pay for the pate and cake myself and see that Jocko's money found its way back to his pocket.

"I'll order the flowers, too, while I'm in town, Jocko. Oh, and what about the workmen who've been here all morning? Shall I see to it that they're given their wages?

Madame Lilah can reimburse me later," I added, seeing the slight flush on Jocko's face. I should remember he had the Linwood pride as much as any of the family.

"No need, Miss. Baron Linwood saw to that before he left." With a look of reprimand in his stiff posture, Jocko went back to his kitchen.

I decided to stroll down to the Priest's Hole and see how the workmen were doing. Neil had said over the phone that he would be at least half an hour arriving.

The carpenters had done a good job, using old timbers and hardware that blended well as a sturdy barricade to the tunnel. I saw Friar Gene standing forlornly at the edge of the moat. Realizing the poor little fellow was no doubt mourning the loss of his favorite passageway and the contents of the secret drawer, I called out to him cheerfully. "I'm going into the village, dear. Can I get something for you—maybe something sweet from the bakery, or . . ."

He wasn't listening to me, but was staring down into the rushes at the moat's edge. I thought he was still sulking, but then I saw him stoop down to pick something out of the tangle of brush.

The dripping scrap of orange silk that Friar Gene held up, his eyes alight at finding a new "pretty" to replace some of those lost to him, was obviously an expensive scarf. I came closer, my eyes riveted on the bedraggled accessory, telling myself there was no need for the sudden sick feeling in my stomach.

Just because Cass had always kept a drawerful of colorful designer scarves, one to match every costume . . . Just because she's always loved that burnt-orange color . . .

That didn't mean the scrap of silk the little monk held was Cassandra's. I looked down at the sluggish water lapping at the rushes, morosely wondering if the moat held more, even darker secrets. Would it slowly, tantalizingly give up one clue at a time to my cousin's disappearance? First the passport, then the scarf.

Would the next thing be a tangle of long, blonde hair in

the murky water amid the rushes?

"Alix! Alix, where are you?"

I came to my senses at Neil's call. "I'll be right there." To Friar Gene, I said gently, "Please don't lose that, dear. I may . . . I may want to show it to someone."

The friar tucked the scarf into his voluminous robe, nodding happily. "Pretty. Very, very pretty."

I left him carefully picking up tiny, round stones to add to his new treasure trove and singsonging the soft chant that sounded like it might be some sort of nonsensical nursery rhyme.

"What were you doing down there?" Neil held open the car door for me then got behind the wheel, looking at me curiously. "I'd think, from what I heard about your close call in that medieval hideaway, that you'd be poking around almost any place else but that one."

"How did you know about the cave-in?"

Neil grinned at me. "Carpenters talk almost as much as bartenders. Where to, fair lady? This beast of a car is at your command, as am I."

"Village Social Center first, to drop off the stuff for the charity auction, and then I have to pick up a few things for the party. Plus, I'd like to pick up something special for Lilah."

"The old woman has taken a real liking to you, hasn't she?"

"It's mutual, believe me. Maybe because I lost my own mother so early, and she never had a daughter . . . There, Neil. There's a parking place right in front."

Mrs. Devons bore down on us as we pulled in, directing Neil with the box and talking to me simultaneously. I saw there was no decent way to get away without at least taking a look around the crowded room where the hundreds of items were being auctioned the following Saturday.

"Good heavens," I said, picking my way around a table stacked shoulder high with musty old pictures, most of them in disrepair. "Will people really pay dearly for all these old things?"

"You'd be surprised, my dear," Mrs. Devons told me cheerfully. "These old paintings, for instance; why, they'll sell at prices to shock you. The *nouveau riche* buy up such things in a minute, then hang them up in their own homes, claiming they're pictures of blue-blooded relatives . . . what's the matter, dear? Something in that stack take your fancy?" She laughed. "Well, don't expect to find an Old Master's work or anything. This batch came from an old house in London, one a patron of ours bought to restore and use during the season . . ."

I didn't hear any of her other prattling. I was too busy rubbing a thick layer of dust off the shiny dark hair of the figure in the painting that had caught my eye. When I saw the silver streak emerge, I stopped, my heart pounding.

I was almost certain it was the Holbein portrait of Crislyn. "I'm looking for a present for Madame Lilah. Would you sell me this?"

Mrs. Devons gave her tinkling laugh. "But, dear, the box you delivered has a hundred things more valuable than this old painting. Why, look at the frame. It's all broken, and there's not even the hint of a signature."

"A hundred dollars?" I smiled at the wide-eyed look Mrs. Devons was giving me. "I know it's not worth it, of course, but Lilah told me about your cause, and I'd already planned to buy something at that price."

Mrs. Devons hugged me and took my American dollars since I hadn't that many pounds with me. "Well, thank you, my dear, and don't let Lilah be angry at us for accepting your donation for such a . . . such a . . ." She looked at the painting again which did, I had to admit, look sad and valueless. "Are you sure you won't let me sell you a more exciting souvenir, like the Earl of Warwick's shaving mug or . . ."

"No, this is just fine." I hastily tucked my prize under my arm and went off to do the shopping. When I didn't respond to Neil's teasing remarks about my sorry purchase, he gave me an odd look and started talking about something else.

As we were walking back to the car with the mountainous cake for Lilah's celebration, it occurred to me that the gift of the portrait would require a complex explanation that I wasn't sure I was ready to provide. "Wait a moment while I duck into this little antique shop, Neil. There's a brooch in the window that I think Lilah would love."

The hand-painted pin with its lilac and mauve colors was tucked in my bag, and I seconded Neil's suggestion that we stop in Ravensbridge's quaintest little tearoom.

He looked at me over the delicate service that was set before us. "All right, let's have it. You've been out to lunch since we got to town. What's going on in that pretty head of yours?"

I looked at the honest, open face of this man who'd befriended me from the beginning and wished I hadn't insisted to Madame Lilah that my Neil be invited to her party. What would he think when it was announced that Miles and I were engaged?

I couldn't do that to him. Every woman knows when a man is beginning to care for her, and I knew this was happening with Neil, though I'd never given him any reason to think we might become more than friends.

"Neil, there's something I need to tell you. First, let me say that I value your friendship more than anything I've found in England."

"I don't like the sounds of this, but shoot."

"You're coming to Madame's birthday party, so I feel I should tell you there'll be an announcement made about my engagement to Miles."

His teacup clattered to its saucer, and Neil put his hand over his eyes. "Damn, damn, damn! I was afraid of something like this. Samantha stopped by to cry in her beer yesterday, saying something was brewing between you and the war hero. I told her she was full of beans, that you're too smart to trade good ol' American independence for a romantic title."

I wished for a moment that it were that simple, that I

had not fallen in love with Miles. Then I said, "I didn't know the two of you were such good friends."

"I run a pub and listen to anyone who buys my beer." He leaned across, his worried eyes on mine. "Look, I probably shouldn't say this, but maybe you should watch yourself a little closer with that one. She's definitely becoming an enemy of yours, and I'm not sure you want Samantha for an enemy."

"I'd find it difficult to want her for a friend." I poured another cup of tea for both of us. "But go on. Why's she staying out here in the provinces? A high-powered model, from what I hear. Hiding out from the law?"

"Not exactly. She was acquitted, thanks to Miles." I looked up, startled, my fingers frozen on the milk pitcher. "She was accused of murdering her husband's mistress. You could find it all in the tabloids, so I'm not being disloyal to a customer's confidences. Miles felt sorry for her after it was all over and let her come out here to ride out the shock waves."

"Neil, why are you telling me this? Do you think Samantha might try to harm me?"

He took the fourth packet of sugar from my hand. I'd been unconsciously filling my cup to overflowing. "All I know is that there was some doubt left as to Samantha's guilt. Miles, apparently, is a helluva lawyer. And given that and the fact that she's nuts about him and can't stand the thought of competition . . ."

"Good God, she's going to be at Lilah's party, too."

Neil looked at me with a thin smile. "Then you won't need to buy any fireworks for the celebration. Do you love him, Alix?"

His direct gaze would brook no lies. "I . . . I'm afraid I do, Neil, but there's so much standing between Miles and me . . . Neil, someday I'll try to explain it all to you, that is, when I understand what's happening myself."

Neil paid our bill and led me out to the car. "The cousin you were so worried about—has she turned up somewhere?"

"No." I looked out the window, silent for several minutes. Then, noticing we were on the lane that ran beside the Dark Swan to a deserted sheep farm, I said, "Neil, what are you doing? I have to get back."

He turned off the motor. "This may be the last chance I have to kiss you. I've wanted to do that since the day I met you. Maybe before. Like I said, I feel like I've known you a long time."

I didn't try to pull away from the kiss; I didn't have to. Any man knows when he's not being kissed back. My affection for Neil was just that—affection and nothing more.

He finally let me go and started up the car with a savage curse. "So that's how it is," he said, staring ahead with a grim look. "God, how I hate the Linwoods of the world—with their bloody smooth ways, the damn silver spoons they're born with, the snobby schools, the powerful cars, the money, the women . . ." He gunned the car onto the main road, and I held onto my seat for dear life. "Well, I guess I know where I stand with you."

"You stand ten feet tall with me, and you always will. It's just that . . . believe me, Neil, I did not want to fall in love with Miles Linwood. I've fought it as hard as I've ever fought anything, but it . . . it was meant to be. Neil, slow down. That cake will topple if you don't."

He calmed down, once again the affable pub owner. "I'm sorry. I shouldn't have made that pass at you back there." He grinned at me as we pulled up to the castle. "If I put my lust away for good, can we still be friends?"

I grinned back and kissed him lightly on the cheek. "I'm counting on it—forever and always."

After checking with Jocko to be sure Lilah was resting comfortably, I left him to unpack the birthday cake and hurried off to examine my purchase in private. My heart was beating erratically as I carefully cleaned off the years and years of accumulated dust and grime.

Bit by bit, the startling image of Crislyn emerged. It gave me goose bumps, sitting in my ghost-filled tower, staring at a portrait that might have been a mirror image of myself.

It was not a painting I wanted to share with anyone just yet. I hid it in the back of the old wardrobe holding the red silk dress along with Punkin and Cass' passport.

The edge of the portrait was still visible, so I propped the package of books I'd brought to autograph for Cass against it and freshened up to go downstairs.

Miles had left word that he wouldn't be returning until perhaps an hour before the party. With Samantha nowhere around and Lilah staying close to her bed, Jocko and I decided on sandwiches. I was on my way with Lilah's tray when the phone rang and I heard Jocko saying in the overly loud voice that we all use for long distance calls, "Coleman, you say? Just a moment and I'll fetch Miss Ames. Manning? I'm terribly sorry but there's no one here by that . . ."

I hastily took the phone from him. "That's me I mean . . ." I was too excited to explain or to wait for the caller to say hello.

"Oh, Cassandra, I knew you'd call as soon as you heard where I was! Oh, darling, I've been so worried about you, Especially after finding your passport and . . ."

The voice on the other end finally got through the crackling static. "Alix? Alix, can you hear me? We've got a terrible connection, but I think we can hear each other now. What's all this you're saying about a passport?"

My joy plummeted as I recognized Phillip's voice. How stupid of me to jump to conclusions that the Coleman calling was Cass instead of her husband.

"Have you heard from her, Phillip? I'm really getting concerned."

He hadn't, and there was no way I could avoid telling him about the passport. He was concerned but not alarmed. "You know Cass, Alix. She leaves a trail of her belongings everywhere she goes. Look, if you're really all that worried, I'll come over there as soon as this thing is over."

"What good will that do? Unless you have some idea where she might have gone. Or . . . or unless you expect to report her missing to the authorities here."

"I don't think it's time for anything that drastic." Phillip hesitated, then said with a touch of embarrassment, "I didn't quite tell you the truth about Cass and me, Alix. There was . . . well, we made a bargain right after I left teaching. She bought me the ranch and the horses I wanted. In exchange, I gave her the freedom to travel and do as she pleased."

"You agreed on divorce?"

"God, no! Neither of us wanted that, but we were growing apart." He gave a little laugh. "Even our one mutual passion, the love of fine horseflesh, wasn't enough anymore. As a matter of fact, Cass started leaving all of the ranching matters up to me a while back. She started getting involved with this geneology thing. Then, the death of Dark Satin, our best horse, seemed to bring back her old restlessness. She really didn't care any more about Dark Satin Two, or the shows, or anything around here."

"Phillip, I'm sorry if this sounds blunt, but I have to know. Is it possible Cass never had any intention of returning to you?"

He was silent for a long moment. "I honestly can't say, Alix. I hope she did. We still cared for each other, even with all our differences." We were both silent then, I thinking about the case this made for the new will Samantha had mentioned, Phillip thinking God knows what. "I'll come, Alix. Give me about a week or ten days to get things wrapped up here."

"Why, Phillip? What can you expect to accomplish by flying out here? Madame Linwood's not well. You'll just upset her and . . ."

"I have to be in Oxford anyway. My book's in its final draft stages. I won't impose on your precious relatives. I'll just call you from London when I arrive."

I stared at the phone long after it had gone dead, wondering what on earth I would say to the Linwoods about Cassandra's husband suddenly deciding on a visit.

Well, I'd deal with that later, I decided. Right now I would take Lilah her tray, come back to finish up the party preparations with Jocko, and then plan what to wear the following evening when it would be announced that I was to be the next mistress of Bloodstones.

I walked into the kitchen, seeing the tray of vegetables arrayed on a wooden slab with Jocko's paring knife alongside.

The dizziness began again.

"In the kitchen?" I heard myself saying from afar. "It's going to happen to me here."

And the whirling strangeness was all around me as the kitchen became a place of the past. And the knife being waved about was in a plump hand that definitely wasn't Jocko's . . .

14

Despite our sadness about Meg, we had a bit of a laugh when Cook took after Kreel with a carving knife when he walked into the kitchen. Fortunately, Perk and I caught the woman's hefty arm before she could do any damage to the dwarf.

Since we would be riding double on Cara, I had to limit my traveling pack. The painting from Hans would have to remain. I thought about leaving it as a gift for Lian, but decided it would only be a thorn in his side. At Cook's suggestion, I let Perk pack the painting away in an old trunk in the attic with some of my other things. Someday I would send for it.

Kreel and I would mainly fend for ourselves, I decided, letting Cook load me up with only minimal provisions. "Just dried meatskins and manchets for us, Maud. I need room for my wheel lock." At the last moment, though, I packed the red silk dress; I couldn't bear to leave behind that one memento. It was bad enough that I was leaving behind my heart.

Maud, the ever practical cook, had some concern for herself. "The Lord Carnton'll be holding me responsible for letting you go off like this, my lady. What shall I tell him? Where will you be headed?"

I pulled my fur-lined hood up over my hair. "Toward the sea, toward Hastings. But Lord Carnton won't come after me, Maud, he's too busy with his own concerns." I felt a tinge of resentment that his part of the bargain had not yet been completed. He'd promised to help me find my kin, but I couldn't wait for his return. Rolling John was vicious enough to have Linwood and the law down on me in a flash. "You can tell him for me that I look forward to meeting him again someday, in some other weald."

With a final good-bye to Perk, who was recuperating nicely, I went out into the cold dawn and mounted the patient Cara. Maud, with a hearty grunt, swung little Kreel up behind me. She stood waving until the last echo of Cara's hooves on the cobbled lanes had faded.

All I had to help me find my kin was the knowledge that they were highborn and living near Hastings. Lian had tried to trace the crest I'd copied crudely from my memories of the mugs my mother had brought to the mill cottage, but he'd found no record of its origin.

I knew if I stayed he would make good his promise to help me find my relatives, but I couldn't risk remaining where I would be a helpless target for the men who sought me.

I was not holding my promise to Meg lightly, but finding Rolling John and killing him would come later. Right now, it was vital to find a new protector to stand between myself and the Baron in case he should still be searching for me, even though I had no cause to think this was so. A man of Lord Linwood's power and resources would have captured me by now if he had really been determined.

The skills of living in the woods came back readily. Even after weeks of soft living, I relished being on my own once more. The biggest problem was finding safe places to hide Kreel, Cara and myself during the day. I finally figured out that the safest thing to do was to free Cara of her saddle and gear, find a villager's field of grazing livestock, and simply let my horse pose as a local inhabitant, while Kreel snoozed under a nearby hedge and I foraged for food.

When I stumbled upon a small abbey near East Grinstead, we were sheltered graciously by a serene order of monks. Undoubtedly they were aware, as I was from my time in London, of Henry's growing lack of consideration for monasteries. At any rate, the kindly brothers fed and sheltered me without any questions, and gave me a parchment map of the best route to the sea as well as provisions for my journey. They took such a fancy to Kreel and he to them, that I knew I'd found the perfect home for the little fellow.

One of the monks, Brother Jubal, who had a keen sense of people and instinctively knew I was a fugitive, gave me the name of an innkeeper in Hastings who would help me till I was safely with my kin.

He helped me onto Cara when I set out after a much-needed rest. "If any should come seeking you, sister, what should we tell them?"

I thought about that with great guilt. What if these gentle people should suffer from the likes of Rolling John or the Baron?

"It would be best, Brother Jubal, if you could forget you ever laid eyes on me. Already one dear friend has died protecting me."

The monk crossed himself and looked up at me with his kind old eyes that saw through clear to one's soul. "Forget you? Impossible, little sister. But I do find my memory dimming as to the direction in which you galloped off on that mare of yours."

I grinned and patted Cara's shining chestnut neck. There were a few tears that would have fallen easily if I hadn't been sure Brother Jubal would have been horribly embarrassed by them. "I hope I see you again someday, Brother."

The dwarf patted my foot in its dust-streaked boot, then tucked his head into the monk's robes. Brother Jubal smiled at me. "You will see me again—if not in this world, then in the next. The good live on forever, if only to see justice finally done. Now, be off; I hear the call to matins and I must be going.''

I felt the warmth of his blessing on me as keenly as the early rays of sun.

The route he'd shown me was safe for daytime travel. There were no villages between me and Bodiam and, besides, people in Sussex were well-known for minding their own affairs and no one else's.

I felt my heart lift when I topped a hill that King Harold might have rested upon, while watching for the fatal, final onslaught of the Norman conquerers led by William. And soon, there was the restless, mighty, wonderful sea.

It was my first view of such an overwhelming body of water. I drank in large gulps of the cleansing sea air and hoped that my relatives would welcome me with as much peacefulness as had this beautiful sea.

The innkeeper at the Bull and Bear looked like a cross between the two animals. I approached him boldly in the dark tavern. ''Mr. Peavy? Mr. Hull Peavy?''

''That's who I am, lass.'' His voice was more the growl of a bear, I decided. ''And who might you be, showing yourself in a place where men'll soon be coming for their ale?''

At the mention of Brother Jubal, his tone and manner changed abruptly. I might have been a long lost daughter come home at last.

He definitely was a bear, I decided after being enfolded in a hug that barely left my ribs intact. But it was the hug of a fatherly, warm human being and the first of its kind I had ever received from a man.

''If the good Brother sent you to us, then there's not enough we can do for you here, lass.'' Mr. Peavy bellowed for his wife and led me to one of the rough long tables, eyeing me with the shrewdness of a pubkeeper who'd seen every form of misfortune. ''First, it'll be a tall ale for you, though I don't usually hold with women drinking, and then one of Lizzie's meat pies to round out some of them hollows in you.''

Mrs. Peavy was just as cordial to this waif who'd

appeared with nothing to recommend her but the name of an aging monk. She clucked over me, fussing over my dusty clothing and tangled hair till her husband sent her off to see to my horse.

"There, now we can talk, lass. The wife is a good soul but never gets over missing her six birdies that flew away, the last this summer." He waited till I'd swallowed half my ale and inhaled the meat pie before saying, "What might your trouble be?"

With my mouth half-full, I said, "How did you know I was in trouble?"

Mr. Peavy gave a deep chuckle. "Even when he was a commoner here in the village, Brother Jubal collected people in trouble. He helped us many a time when we were having ours, and I never turned away anyone he sends our way." He put his huge hand under my chin and tilted my face up, so that my hood fell totally off my head. I stopped chewing and was completely still while he took his measure of me.

He said softly, "I was about to ask your name, lass, but now I see no need. I'm a simple working man, with little to do with the folks in the castle, but I know a spittin' image when I see it."

I whispered, "You knew my mother?"

He nodded. "That I did, though it was as a lowly pub-keeper knows all the high-ups in his town." He drew himself an ale and refilled my mug. I was aware of a new kind of deference toward me, though I knew it couldn't be due to anything other than his longstanding knowledge of my family's status. "She didn't get fair treatment from her kin, some say—like myself and my wife—but her brother's wife was no one you'd want to lock horns with. They turned her out, saying the child she was big with was the devil's, which only a fool would believe, knowing the nature of Lady Amanda."

"Lady Amanda." I savored the sound of it. "And my uncle—has he a title?"

He looked at me sharply but didn't question the oddity

of my asking a stranger about my own uncle. "Don't know that it matters, since he's not in favor with the king for raising organized resistance against one of Henry's greedier ideas. Your uncle, being a tight-fisted soul, wasn't happy about the 'amicable loan' business Henry was proposing. Seems King Hal had no plans for paying people back."

"He's rich then, my uncle is." It really wasn't a question, but Mr. Peavy took it as one.

"That he is, since your mother's properties became his, as well as his own mother's. And not only that, he managed to confiscate a few large holdings when the sheep-grazing fury cropped up some time back. Made himself some enemies then, he did. Folks don't much like the idea of small farmers being turned off the land for the benefit of a few large sheepherders. Or taking a family's homeplace by crooked politics when they refuse to go along with the notion of inclosures."

I had the flickering memory of what Lian had told me about this same thing happening to him. But, no, it would be too much of a coincidence for his troubles to have come about through my uncle.

I said ruefully, "It doesn't sound much like you like my uncle."

He was silent for a long moment. "Let's put it this way, lass. If Lord Sheffield was to catch on fire over there . . ." He waved his tremendous arm toward the slumbering blaze in an oversize hearth. "And I'd had my daily bucket of ale . . ." He grinned at me. "Well, I might piss on 'im to put out the blaze, and I might not—depending on the mood I was in."

I felt disloyal about laughing, but couldn't help it. Hull Peavy was apparently a man who spoke his mind. "You sound like Nana, my grandmum. She didn't want me to come here."

The shrewd blue eyes were steady on mine. "She was thought to be wiser than most of us, not just because of her laying hands on the sick and healing 'em. Why *did* you come here, lass?"

"Because I needed help from somebody and I couldn't imagine anyone cold enough to turn away family. Because I've never belonged anywhere and there's this terrible need in me to know who I am.'

"Going back don't always help, lass. Go forward instead. Get married, have your own children and give them what you've wanted."

I lifted my chin stubbornly. "I'll do that, but after I've satisfied myself."

Hull sighed. "I could tell when you walked through that door looking like you owned the place that you had a stubborn streak. Well, first off, why don't you stay here a while and look things over? Your uncle's not one of my best customers, but he drops in here now and then to lord it over a few others."

I grinned, feeling suddenly cheerful. "Oh, would you let me stay? Just for a few days? I'll earn my keep. I'll serve ale and scrub tables and . . ."

Hull shook his head slowly, looking at me. "I have the feeling Brother Jubal sent me a package of trouble this time. All right, lass, but have Lizzie give you a kerchief for that hair of yours and one of them sacks she calls aprons. I don't want the men knifing each other over the new barmaid and staining up my good tables."

The days I passed with the kindhearted Peavys at The Bull and Bear were filled with hard work, but it was a time as near to being a real part of a warm, loving family as any in my life. Lizzie fussed over me as much as if I'd been one of her three daughters, and Hull growled formidably at any customer who tried to make free with me as I served ale. Many times they pressed me to forget my longing for a reunion with my relatives, but I still waited patiently for Lord Sheffield's appearance in the pub.

I spent many an hour dreaming of our reunion. He would stride in, see my face and recognize me as his long lost niece. We would embrace tearfully, then my uncle would bear me off to the castle for a joyful homecoming with his family. And then Nana would be sent for, there would be more rejoicing, and all of us would live happily ever after.

"I say, wench, are you dozing at the keg?" I came out of my daydream and found myself in the midst of a nightmare.

The rough voice belonged to Rolling John. He had a dirty patch over the place where his eye had been till Meg put it out. He hadn't seen my face yet and I thanked God that I still wore the homely kerchief over my telltale hair. But I was alone in the pub just before closing time as Hull was off fetching his wife from their daughter's lying-in at a nearby village.

I hung back in the shadows, making my voice croaky and sullen. "There's another pub a half-mile down the road. This'n is closing, mister."

He cursed, and I kept my face down, praying he'd leave and not come closer. My wheel lock was tucked away in the little bedroom Lizzie had fixed up for me; I was defenseless.

"The hell you say, girl. Go fetch your master and let me tell him to his face what I think of being turned away from a pint after I've ridden all this way on a rainy night."

I mumbled something about the owner being in his room and inched my way toward the door leading that way, but Rolling John moved as quickly as a snake to block my way.

"What's all this shy hiding away from a customer, wench? I never saw a barmaid yet who . . ." He reached out a hand and grabbed my arm, pulling me up against him under the lamp.

I couldn't contain the blazing hate in my eyes as they met his startled ones. Nor could I keep from hissing in a voice filled with loathing, "You filthy bastard, I should have shot you when I had the chance."

He stared at me, hardly believing, then he ripped off my kerchief so my hair tumbled to my shoulders. My apron was next, and then he threw back his head and filled the empty room with his evil laughter.

"Well, if this ain't a lucky break for old John. Here I

thought our little fox had burrowed out of sight forever, and I find her filling mugs in the last wayside tavern I stop in before turning back." His laughter stopped and his hand dug into my arm painfully. "Little bitch, I've got you now."

I didn't flinch from his grasp or the evil eye. "After what you did to Meg, you filthy slime, I hope you're hanged and quartered!"

He sneered down at me and held a grubby finger up to his eye patch. "Look at this! Look at what that scrawny little chicken done to my eye! If I'd had my way about it, the little bitch would have suffered a lot more, but I couldn't hang around to see to it with all the commotion she made." He moved toward me menacingly, and I backed away. "You're the one. You're the root of all my troubles. Lord B. would have set me up like the others, but, no, you had to turn him against me."

"When he finds out you murdered Meg, you'll be smart to stay out of his way. God help me, I wish I'd killed you both times when I had the chance."

"Just goes to show you couldn't bring yourself to kill the only real man in your life." Rolling John looked me up and down and licked his lips.

I then said the worst thing I could have to a man like Rolling John. "You one-eyed bastard—that's the only way you remotely resemble Lord Blackheart. You could never take his place in my bed."

He slapped me so hard my ears rang. "We'll see about that, wench." He was breathing hoarsely now. "They say even a fine baron traded off land for you but you ran away. He wouldn't have you now, after your fine highwayman's had at you, but Rolling John's not so proud."

I backed away from him, up against the front window. "If you touch me again, I'll . . ."

The sound of a coach rolling to a stop in front of the pub made us both freeze. Rolling John hissed viciously, "Lying little bitch, you said the place was closed."

I gave him a triumphant grin. "To scum like you." I glanced out the window, and my heart skipped a beat. My mother's family crest was on the side of the fine coach. How fitting that my kin should appear for the first time as a means of rescue! I turned back and said smugly, "Now you're in for it, John. That's Lord Sheffield, who's as good as the king here. And he's my uncle, to boot. You'll be lucky if he has you thrown into gaol instead of shooting you on the spot."

A flicker of fear crossed my tormentor's face, but he quickly covered it with the hateful grin. "That's still to be seen, wench. Let him in before he batters the door in."

I opened the door and was nearly knocked off my feet by Lord Sheffield's angry entry from the driving rain outside. "Where's the proprietor, where's Peavy? I demand an explanation for being kept outside like this! And not only that, but I . . ."

He caught sight of me and visibly blanched.

My uncle's face changed back from stark white to mottled gray, and I could see, then, that he was not the handsome, affable relative of my fantasies. His features were regular enough, the clothes fine, but there was a pinched look of discontent around the full mouth, red veins from overindulgence, and the pale blue eyes held not a whit of warmth.

"God help me," he finally managed as he stared at me. "We'd heard you died when the child was born."

The disappointment in his voice cut me worse than any knife ever could.

"I'm not Amanda, my lord." I curtsied and held out my hand, which soon fell back to my side for lack of response. "I'm Crislyn, her daughter. Your niece, my lord."

"Good lord," he said, with obvious growing distaste for what he saw before him. I realized then that I looked anything but the niece of a fine lord. My hair was mussed, and my blouse was torn and smudged from my tussle with Rolling John.

Rolling John stepped forward and blustered, "She's a piece of baggage, m'lord, as you can see. She's not fit to call herself kin to the fine likes of you. I'll just be taking her home now, her being so addled and all from our little family spat."

Rolling John would have taken my arm, but Lord Sheffield's icy eyes turned on him, stopping him cold. "And who are you, my man?" My uncle's open contempt was effective; Rolling John's blustery attitude turned to sniveling.

"It's your servant I am, m'lord . . ."

"It's a murderous rogue he is, one who should be handed over to the sheriff," I spat out.

"Wait." Lord Sheffield's gaze turned back to me, and I saw a new cunning in the icy blue of his eyes. "Crislyn, is it, the daughter of the Ravensbridge miller?"

'Your niece, my lord," I said weakly, not liking the direction this was taking.

"Then you're the one Baron Linwood said to be on the lookout for." He lost interest in Rolling John, concentrating on me now in a way I didn't care for. "The runaway bonded servant." His nostrils flared as though he did not like the smell of me, as if I were a shabby horse bought for a full-blooded animal. "It seems the baron has some intention of retrieving you and making you his bride."

Rolling John and I, for once, were in accord—we were both flabbergasted, Rolling John at the news that the baron still wanted me and I at Linwood's uncanny tracking of my whereabouts. "My lord, I have made a dreadful mistake, burdening you with my troubles. I will just leave a note for Hull Peavy and be on my way."

Lord Sheffield moved to block my escape. He smiled down at me in a way that was somehow even less attractive than Rolling John's earlier leering. "Nonsense! As my niece, you will be taken in by my wife and me with the greatest pleasure. We shall see to it that you are prepared for your liaison with one of Kent's finest houses in a manner properly befitting a true Sheffield." He put his arm around my shoulder and led me toward the door. "I shall send word to Linwood at once that, as your guardian, I shall be amenable to negotiations. Consider yourself now under the protection of Sheffield Manor, my dear.''

At last I had gotten the protection of my kin but was more trapped than ever before. My uncle apparently saw me as something to be bartered for gain. I pulled away from my new captor. ''You don't understand, my lord. I refuse to be given to a man, any man, baron or no, marriage or no marriage.''

''Don't be ridiculous, girl.'' The pale eyes flicked over me, then showed their contempt for a raggle-taggle half-wit who would rather toil in a pub than be the mistress of Bloodstones. ''Besides, you shan't be 'given' away. When Linwood learns of your connection to the Sheffield family, he will come through with a fitting offer.''

I said sarcastically, ''Only a few moments ago, you wouldn't claim me. Now I'm a 'connection to the Sheffield family.' I may be naive, my lord, but I fail to understand how you expect to profit from me. Linwood claims to have bought me already. Why should he pay twice?''

Lord Sheffield patted my shoulder. ''Now, Crislyn, don't worry that pretty head about business matters that rest with Linwood and me. We'll work out the details. The important thing is that the baron will soon learn that I can drive a hard bargain when I have something that another man wants a great deal.''

I shook off the plump hand. ''I'm glad Nana isn't here to see what kind of man her son's become.''

My uncle's eyes turned hard. ''My mother never even liked me when I was little. It was always her precious Amanda that counted, never dull little Cecil.''

Rolling John, seeing that he was being left out in the cold, mustered a last burst of bluster. ''Now, see here, governor, you can't be taking the girl off without she wants you to.''

As an answer, Lord Sheffield called in one of his men from the waiting coach. ''See to it that the sheriff knows this man is leaving town within the next half-hour. If he's found in the vicinity after that, the fellow's to be charged with assault and battery.''

Rolling John went out between two of my uncle's men, cursing and protesting the whole way. When he passed me, he spat, "Little bitch! The next time we meet it will be very different. I swear it."

"The next time we meet," I told him softly, "I intend to put a bullet in your brain." When the door had closed, I turned back to my uncle and said coldly, "Don't expect me to thank you. I'm not sure Rolling John is the worse of the two of you."

I abandoned any plans of escape when I learned from Lord Sheffield that his lien on the Peavys' pub would be moved upon if I tried anything unseemly. But I did insist that he allow me to say good-bye to the couple who had taken me in with a thousand times more warmth and love than the relative I'd come so far to find. While my uncle sat sipping ale, I waited grimly for Lizzie and Hull to come home.

Lizzie cried when I gave her the red dress. "I'll treasure it always. But you'll need something fine, love, for your stay at the Sheffields."

I told her truthfully, "I'll wear my rags proudly, reminding them of the life of poverty they condemned my mother and grandmother to live."

"Keep the dress, Crissie," Hull said in his gruff way. "Lizzie'll just pack it away in her chest with the few other pretties she's collected."

"I want her to have it."

The Peavys were grim and dignified as they waved me off in the carriage with its Sheffield crest on the side. I know they would never have allowed the trade-off I was resigned to making. I knew, too, that I could do nothing less for the people who had treated me with warmth and decency from the moment I'd walked into their pub.

The Peavys' warmth was the last I was to encounter for a while. Sheffield Manor held all the warmth of a frozen cave. Its master's character I already knew only too well; I was in for an even more unpleasant encounter with its mistress.

Madelina, my uncle's wife, naturally hated me on sight. She reminded me of a great, gaudy spider in her silks and satins in which she vainly sought to make herself look slender. The layers of brightly colored sashes and ribbons and shawls trailed about her like a web. I wasted no opportunity to let her know that her loathing was returned. In fact, we arrived at a sort of truce during my forced interment at the Manor. I avoided her as carefully as she avoided me.

Though I never spoke another word to my uncle, he made sure I was kept apprised of the negotiations with Baron Linwood. Finally, one day, he pronounced the bargain made. I was to be sent to Bloodstones as soon as my trousseau was ready. My uncle had the gall to produce a bottle of his finest claret at table that night in celebration.

I poured mine out on the fine linen tablecloth.

Madelina took charge of readying me for marriage. Oddly enough, she chose becoming colors, fabrics and styles. Morning after morning, I stood silently while the dressmaker measured, cut, poked, tucked and hemmed.

Just before the final fitting of my wedding gown, my uncle called me into his study. "No use your continuing this sullen silence of yours, Crislyn. I have questions for you from your intended husband."

He hemmed and hawed for a bit then finally came out with it. "Lord Linwood seems to have some reason to think you are, er . . . not completely chaste, Crislyn."

I forgot my embargo on speaking to my uncle and let out a roar of laughter. "Then will he insist on checking me out first, like a man checks a horse's teeth and hooves before buying?"

"No call to be vulgar." Sheffield cleared his throat. "There are two conditions Linwood insists upon. One, that you marry immediately upon your arrival at Bloodstones. Second is a rather boorish condition. It seems Linwood forbids myself or my wife to accompany you or attend the wedding."

I gave another hoot of laughter. "Why, the man has some taste after all!"

I was even somewhat cheerful when I tried on my wedding gown. It was a lovely thing, of creamy silk and lace, its tight bodice embroidered with gold stitching that also decorated the small cap I was to wear.

When the day for my departure came, I was almost relieved to be leaving, even if it were for a marriage to a man whose reputation and life style had never earned anything from me but contempt. I watched from my window as the coach rumbled up to fetch the bride of Bloodstones. And when I was inside the carriage bearing me away from the splendor of my mother's ancestral home, I never once looked back.

15

I endured the ride to Ravensbridge, knowing my fate to be unavoidable. Even though I had the wheel lock in my lap, hidden under my cloak, the fight had gone out of me.

I could not risk the harm that might come to the Peavys if I resisted Baron Linwood's plans for me. And, in all honesty, I simply was getting tired of running away.

We rode through Ravensbridge, and I craned my neck to catch my first glimpse of the old mill. When we reached it, I pounded on the back of the driver's seat. "Please stop for a moment." The man Linwood had sent to guard my trip home rode up to my window. He was polite, but obviously nervous about this departure from his instructions.

"I'm sorry, Miss, but the Baron was most emphatic. We was not to stop for anything till we reached the castle."

He was a sympathetic little fellow, though, and when I explained that I simply wished to call upon my old grandmum, he let me have my way. "Thank you, Noddy." I remembered his name, and I think that influenced him even more than my obviously sincere desire to stop at the mill. "I won't be very long at all." In fact, I planned to insist that Linwood allow Nana to come to the castle to attend me for my wedding.

I swept past the guard out the carriage door, noticing

with a dart of apprehension that the little herb garden by the cottage entrance was overgrown. It was Nana's pride and joy, and she tended to it serupulously.

My alarm increased when a strange woman opened the door. She curtsied as I pushed by her, obviously impressed by my fine clothes and the waiting carriage.

"Where's Nana? Where's my grandmother?"

She had a kind face, as did the stocky man who joined her. They exchanged glances and then looked back at me.

"My lady, the village had need of a new miller when Roark Scotney died and . . ."

I felt a rising panic, seeing Nana's room bare of anything recognizable. I turned back to the couple, gripping one arm of each. "Please, I have to know if she's being cared for. If she left here, where is she?" I knew my fingers were digging into their flesh, but didn't care. "Where's my grandmother? Where's Nana?"

They looked at each other again and then at me with pity in their creased, kind faces. Then, without a word they led me between them to the kitchen and to the open window there.

"She's there, lass, under that tree by the mill wheel. That's what she wanted—to be able to hear the soothing sounds of the water and have the birds nesting above her."

I stared at the neatly marked grave, not believing my beloved Nana could be gone. The new miller's wife was squeezing my hand, and I was grateful for the touch, glad of someone to hold onto in my shock.

"Was she . . . did she suffer?" I whispered.

The miller cleared his throat. Like most simple, hard-working men, he wasn't built to deal with feminine grief. "We took good care of her, the wife and I did, and told her she could stay with us as long as she wanted."

"We don't have no family of our own," the woman said softly. "And don't you be fretting about her suffering. She was real sick all right, but real cheerful up to the last. And when she got a letter from somewheres in London, about you being safe and all . . ."

I let the tears have their way, but they were less from grief than relief that she'd received word that I was still alive. "I . . . I don't know how to thank you. I . . . the headstone must have cost you something. Here . . . I . . ." They tried not to accept the two gold coins I still had from Lian's gift for the trip to London, but I pressed them into the honest hands, wishing I had a trunkful to give them.

They tried to thank me, but I stopped them with my own thanks for making the final days of my dear Nana comfortable. I hugged them both, saying I'd be back with flowers for the grave as soon as I could. The miller was a little embarrassed by the embrace, but managed to hug me back.

I took a long look around the room which no longer had any traces of my former life there and then took a deep breath. Another link to my past had been dissolved, another place left behind forever. With a lump in my throat, I said, "I wish I had something of hers to keep, but I suppose . . ."

The miller's wife put her hands to her mouth. "Oh, my, I almost forgot. She left a little box for you that she said we was to tell you came down from your mama for you."

"She left a box for me?"

The miller had disappeared while his wife was talking and reappeared with a plain, wooden box. "We never once opened it," he said, "though the lock's not much to keep a body from it."

I smiled at him as I took the little chest. "I know you didn't open it." I kissed each of them on the cheek. "Bless you both. I'll see that you're rewarded for your kindness when I'm . . ." I almost said "when I'm mistress of Bloodstones," but I caught myself in time. Saying it aloud would make it come true.

Noddy helped me back into the coach, his eyes going to the little chest I was settling carefully onto my lap. "Is it a treasure from your grandmum, Miss?"

"That it is, Noddy," I said, the tears dropping to my lap where I clutched the one memento of my mother's life. "That it is."

The knowledge that I was now alone in the world was bad enough, but my reception at Bloodstones only added to my sense of isolation. It was headed by Meuriel Farnsworth, the last person in the world I wanted to see. She had always looked upon me as a rival and hated me. "Ah, m'lady," she said, curtsying with facetious exaggeration. "Such a long way we've both come since you left Ravensbridge." She preened herself as she directed the servants about the coach and my scant luggage. "You, the intended bride of Lord Linwood, and I, his new chatelaine."

"I thought you specialized in your mother's old trade, birthing babies," I said wearily, not really caring why she was here.

She flounced through the gates, waiting for me to catch up with her. There were some late roses blooming beside the steps leading to one of the parapets, and something in my heart lifted at the sight of the lovely pink blossoms. "Come with me. I'll show you to your room." She jangled the heavy ring of keys at her side as though to emphasize who was the jailer and who was the prisoner. "I came to help with the cook's daughter when she 'ad her firstborn; the good baron asked me to stay on to see to you getting settled in."

All this time she was leading me down a great hall, only stopping when she reached its end, which led to a narrow staircase. I felt something like real fear catch at my heart. "But . . . but you can't be taking me to stay in the King's Tower! Not the very room where they say King Henry likes to sleep!"

Meuriel chortled. "Don't worry. You'll not be bothered by the great man's royal hunger. The king is too busy these days pacifying dark and hungry Anne on one hand and Queen Catherine on the other. He'll not be staying with us in the near future."

I was up at the landing by now and looked down the steep stairs, remembering all the strange stories about our monarch's eccentricities. Meuriel chuckled again.

"If you're wondering if Hal's famous wall will be put up

to seal you in here, I wouldn't be surprised if the Baron's not considering it. You've given him a merry chase, girl,'' she added as I passed her, and I could feel the withering hate and jealousy, "And now you're to be his bride. They always said you were clever, but I never realized how clever.''

I set my bag down on the huge bed and turned back to her with a haughty look, reminding her who would be mistress here. "Since I've never met the Baron, I could hardly practice my so-called witchcraft on him, could I, Meuriel?" I pushed back my hood, flinging my hair loose and knowing she was watching me with those luminous dark eyes. "And what about you? You never answered my question about how you wound up here instead of in your chosen field.''

She took my cloak, hanging it up on one of the wooden hooks, but not before stroking the luxurious fabric lovingly. "Ah, there's a good reason for that, m'lady . . .''

"Call me Crislyn as you have before, Meuriel," I said coolly. "I'd prefer it.''

"Very well. Anyway, *Crislyn*, the Baron is in London frequently. He needed someone to see to his household here and entrusted that position to me. Unlike you, I have always wanted a place at Bloodstones Castle.''

I kept my hands tight on the bag, not allowing Meuriel to unpack it. Otherwise she'd see my hands were shaking, and I didn't want that.

Meuriel smiled at me as she flung open the curtain to a short, angled passage in the wall, "Thanks to the king, who insisted on his royal privvy chamber, you'll find no need to leave this room.'' She closed the nook off again and looked at me speculatively.

Her envy was palpable, dangerous. I said coldly, "That will be all for now, Meuriel. I'm very tired and wish to rest.''

She bowed slightly. "I'll send a maid to unpack your trunk.''

I followed her to the great, carved door, hardly able to wait for her departure before closing it. "Never mind. As you should know, I'm not used to being cosseted."

"But you must get used to being waited on." Her dark eyes gleamed with malice. "For instance, on your wedding night, I've been given the pleasure of preparing you for the bridal bed. And, should the night's rigors bear fruit, I've already promised his lordship I'll help birth the first child." I pity you if the baby doesn't bear the Linwood mark. His lordship already has doubts about your purity!"

I closed the door in her face. There were too few hours left for me to enjoy my privacy. I certainly didn't want to spend them listening to Meuriel's sly insinuations.

I bathed my face with water from the bowl near the wardrobe and stood at the room's one window, an arrow-slit, letting the cool wind waft over my face.

Then I got the chest Nana had left me and sat on the huge bed before opening it. My mother certainly had not known her legacy would be a wedding gift.

I lifted the lid with trembling fingers. Inside, there lay a delicate locket, inlaid with tiny jewels that glittered like the tears in my eyes. I knew it had been my mother's, and I pried open the catch, weeping openly when I found a lock of dark hair that matched my own—my mother's, I was sure. I put the locket around my throat, happy to have something of hers close to me to carry me through the coming days. And I would always treasure the folded piece of needlework with my mother's name laboriously added under the family crest.

It wasn't much, but it meant the world to a daughter of a woman who'd risked her world to bear her child safely, dying in the process. I could hardly see to read the fine writing on the folded letter beneath the piece of tapestry. My tears fell copiously for the woman who hadn't lived to see my face.

My dearest daughter (for I know you won't be a son, as I know so many things in advance, and I am glad),

I won't live to see you grown and beautiful as I know you will be, but my heart will be with you always, along with my hope that your life will be happier than mine.

But I had my joyous moments, as I hope you will. The man who fathered you was the giver of those moments. A handsome German prince (whose name isn't important, since it couldn't legally be mine or yours), he came to Sheffield Manor as part of an official visit to the county and to several prominent land-owners' homes. We fell in love, and he begged me at the end of his visit to return to his country with him. But I knew he was destined to rule and that his bride was already chosen. I knew, too, that he would be a good ruler, that the sovreignty would suffer without him, and that my return with him would have forced his abdication from his inherited and rightful role.

So he left, never knowing about you or how I would suffer from the consequences of our love for each other.

But, dear daughter, I never regretted one moment of my life, even knowing as I write this that I won't see you grow into a strong and beautiful woman.

Be proud of who you are, my daughter. Though my weak, cruel brother Cecil would seem to contradict it, the Sheffields are a strong family, as were your grandmother's relatives. And now you have the blood of a great royal family flowing with that of our ancestors.

Live well, my darling. Be proud. Be happy. And may the locket, which bears the mark of your real father and a tender remembrance of your mother, keep you from harm.

I sat like a stone, weeping silently, but the tears were from happiness in knowing who I was. And my father had loved my mother, truly loved her! That was more important to me than knowing he was a prince.

As I traced the letters scratched into the back of the locket, I realized this was not the first time I'd seen that mark.

I took the wheel lock from its wrappings and examined the elaborately carved handle. It bore the same mark, and I sat transfixed, knowing at last my father's name.

Hapsburg.

Though the prince who'd presented the gun to Lian wasn't the same man who'd made love to my mother, he'd been part of the same great family.

I held the locket and the silver-handled wheel lock to my damp cheek and walked to the arrow-slit, looking out on the rich, sprawling countryside and the strange arrangement of stones. My pride filled me to bursting. I was an offspring (illegitimate, but no matter!) of one of the world's greatest aristocracies. This would be my son's, all of this. I could claim no one place, no one heritage, but my heirs would rule Bloodstones and would inherit the legitimate honors that went with the land.

My heart swelled to bursting as the conviction grew within me that Bloodstones Castle would be my eternal home. The Baron and his notoriety didn't matter; the important thing was that I now had a fitting place where my son and his sons would belong.

It was a strange wedding, the one which bound me forever to the Baron of Bloodstones. I hadn't yet looked on his face, nor he on mine (or so I believed) until the exchange of vows.

There were very few others in the small chapel where our marriage took place. The shadowy figure awaiting me at the altar might, have been Satan himself. I could discern none of his features through the thick veiling Meuriel had draped over my face, saying it was the Baron's wish that his bride be shrouded in mystery until the moment of consummation.

It seemed suitable to me, this phantomlike wedding. I stole nary a look at my groom during the vows. Even if the scarce candles in the chapel and thick veiling I wore had not prevented it, I had no wish to look upon the face of my new husband. I would look upon it soon enough, when we were alone in the tower room for the first time.

Meuriel accompanied me, not bothering with any pretense of joy any more than I. The sounds of the wedding feast being held in the refectory receded as we grimly made our way to the bridal chamber. I was glad I'd been excused from the drunken revels, though Meuriel told me many found it strange that the Baron's new bride was whisked out of view as soon as the vows were said.

"There's some saying, since your veil is so thick and the marriage was held in such a poorly lighted room, that the new mistress of Bloodstones is hideously scarred from the pox."

Her sidelong, malicious glance to see how I took this slur was wasted. I kept my tongue, not wishing to feed her hate of me any further. Secretly, I planned to get rid of the woman as soon as I could.

My shrug was nonchalant. "Is that so? Well, I suppose they're in for a disappointment." I flung off my cap and veil as we entered the room and stood under the brightest candle. "See?" I told Meuriel with a smile. "My face is unflawed."

I knew my own beauty, without conceit. Meuriel's face contorted with jealousy and frustration that nothing she could say seemed to bother me.

She got herself under control again and said cloyingly, "Ah, you're a beautiful woman right enough, Crislyn, but you'd do well to remember what my mother said of you and that wild beauty of yours."

"I can hardly wait, Meuriel," I said.

"She said men's lust for you would keep you from ever having an honest man's love."

"I didn't realize the good woman was a prophet, Meuriel." I handed her my gown. "Here, take this as a gift."

I could not have said or done anything more cruel. Meuriel was, perhaps, a good third bigger than I, and though she looked very well in the dark clothing she inevitably wore, she couldn't have worn my gown, even unfastened.

But Meuriel hid her fury. She thrust at me the filmy nightgown that was apparently to replace the more decorous one Jane had made for me. "It's time for your bedding, m'lady," Meuriel told me with a humorless smile.

I was too weary to fight with her. "Please go. I can dress myself."

"Suit yourself." Muriel pointed to the pomades on the

table and gave me a nasty smile. "I'd advise you to sweeten yourself up for him. The Baron's one who likes his women sweet rather than tart."

"Then it's as well you did not land him yourself," I said to her, drawing a satisfying wince from her. "Now will you leave me to myself? I have no way of escape but that arrow-slit over there, and I'm not quite that thin."

She turned her head at the burst of laughter that drifted up from the tilting yard. "'They're getting drunker. They'll all be bringing 'im up in a little while."

"I hope they hurry, then." I gave an exaggerated yawn, though I secretly cringed at the prospect of the Baron's guests bearing him inside the nuptial chamber as was the custom. I could do without their advice, good-natured or otherwise.

Meuriel finally left me alone. The first thing I did was check my hiding place for my treasures behind a loose stone near the wardrobe. If Meuriel ever found out about them, she would, I was sure, tell the Baron their whereabouts.

The candle beside the bed flickered. Someone was coming up the stairs. I could hear the measured treads which kept time with my beating heart. I sat on the bed, my eyes on the door, dreading the moment when it would be pushed open and I would be faced with my spectral bride-groom.

Slowly . . . slowly . . . the door opened. And when I raised my eyes to the man who stood there looking down at me, I let out a little scream.

It was the hawk-man, the man who had won my body in the contests of falcons. Suddenly I began to understand why the wedding had been so secretive, why Baron Linwood did not insist on the presence of his bride at the wedding feast. And when he ripped off the mask and stared toward me, the flickering candlelight caught the strong planes of his face and yet another image flashed through my consciousness. Except for the lightness of beard and hair, except for the absence of the black eye patch, it might have been my Lord Blackheart coming toward me.

"Why do you stare at me so, my bride?" he asked me softly, his hands going to loosen his tunic.

"It . . . it is because you remind me of someone, my lord."

He seemed unconcerned. "Oh? It is said my cousin in the high country is like enough to be my twin, except for the shades of hair, but I have not seen Lian in lo these many years, not since he sought a harsher path than the one I chose."

Lian! He was kin to Lord Blackheart, then. Was that why I had always had the phantom of the hawk-man in my mind when Lian and I were in the midst of loving? "My lord, I do not know how to say this except to say it. I do not love you, nor do I see how you can love me. When you won our contest, I forfeited my maidenhead to you, as I promised. Why have you continued to pursue me?"

He moved steadily toward me the while I spoke. Finally, I was caught in his arms and his lips were at my throat with a familiar ardor that my mind confused with nights in the stone cottage as well as in the forest. "Beautiful, proud Crislyn, my wife, my bride. You still do not understand, but you will. You were destined to be my wife, my bride. Now you are all mine at last."

His mouth on mine was devouring, insistent, and I felt my own mouth opening to the relentless hunger of his. And when he pulled the flimsy gown from me and lifted me in his arms, holding me against his maleness, I realized my own passionate weakness was my enemy now.

I realized, too, that my heart had never been free of my hawk-man and never would be so again.

16

How can I describe the way things were between my husband and me? I only know that there was a strange bond, a deep similarity of our souls that I could no more explain than fly to the moon. James was too complex for me to understand. At times, I sensed depths in him that the self-indulgent Baron Linwood could not possibly have. Other times, I found him exasperatingly shallow.

Such as his demands on me. He knew how much I despised his hedonistic London friends, yet he insisted that I play hostess to them. Once I defied him by riding off to the men's hunt instead of sitting primly with the ladies as the hostess of Bloodstones was expected to do.

"They're boring, James," I told him later, when he complained of my outrageous behavior. "Boring, boring, boring! And sometimes I look at you and sense you think of them the same way as I do."

James turned that aside. "I thought you adored hearing the latest London gossip."

"I'm bored with that, too. All those chattering magpies want to talk about it how Catherine has lost her king to the fascinating Mistress Anne of the sallow complexion and flat bosom and fascinating eyes and wit. They're all so nasty, James." Even as I fussed, I wondered what was happening

303

to me these days. When Hans had prattled on about my royal favorites, I had loved it. Now it just irritated me. I was restless and malcontent for reasons I could not pinpoint.

My husband smiled at me. "Those same nasty tongues will start wagging about you if you're not more careful. For instance, last night you shocked everyone by mingling with the men over the ale down in the great room instead of staying above in the gallery with the other women." At my sound of disdain, James shook his head. "Well, I do hope you will be more discreet with our guests this weekend. Lord Hammond is not a person one wants to offend."

Fortunately, he had gone to refill his goblet and did not see my face. I sensed, though, that he was intently interested in my reaction. No doubt he was aware, as everyone in London was, of Hammond's reputation with married women. "My lord, let us not plan anything for a week or so. I am so weary of it all." I went to drape myself about my husband's neck. It was an unusual show of affection and I could feel his surprised reaction. "Let us just have our own pleasures, just the two of us. How long has it been since we raced Cara and Gallows? Or swam in the secret place by the rocks?"

His arousal was apparent. "I really had no intention of having Hammond out here," he whispered. "He's a scoundrel from all accounts, and I want no rivals for my beautiful wife's attentions."

He kissed me, and I had the usual strange feeling that I had experienced often since my wedding night—that the man I had married was a man of many secrets.

We were like two children in our chase along the narrow path beside the river, James on his powerful horse, Gallows, and I on my faithful Cara. I spurred my horse well on ahead of James and devilishly pulled one of my old highwayman's tricks. With newfound agility, I swung up on a low-flung limb, letting Cara gallop forward, riderless, while James on Gallows came thundering beneath me not a moment later. How I laughed as I watched James catch up to Cara and realize I'd outwitted him! When he came back looking for me, I swung down into his arms and teased him unmercifully for the rest of the day.

That night our lovemaking was especially tender. I think the bracing, naked swim we'd had in our private spot in the Medway after our ride had awakened new channels of passion. Later, snuggled against him, I brought up a subject I had been longing to explore since first he had mentioned it. "Tell me about your cousin Lian."

James stiffened. "Why?"

I automatically became cautious. My husband could not know that his cousin was the notorious Lord Blackheart; such knowledge would be dangerous to both men. "Because . . . I feel that I know him somehow."

He sat up in bed and looked at me intently. "As I told you, Lian and I were once as close as brothers, but then he went away, to live with his mother's people, whose estate passed to him. There was a woman . . ." James's face darkened. "We both loved her; she chose Lian. She was a faithless, selfish woman. She turned us against each other, but that wasn't the worst of it. She later betrayed Lian with the man who tricked him out of his lands and holdings." James's mouth worked painfully. "Lian was a brave man. He stood up to the people who were encroaching on the small landowners. They called him their champion. After fighting for their rights, he fought the man who stole his land and his wife, losing an eye in the process." James's eyes were dark with pain. "I don't know what happened to him after that."

I did. But how could I tell James that his cousin had not died, but had reemerged as Lord Blackheart, highwayman to most, hero to a few? Then I would have to tell him the rest of it.

We did not make love again. James was restless and full of his own thoughts. I had the feeling he wanted something from me, but I had my own thoughts to deal with as well, so I turned my back to him and lay wide awake till sleep finally came to me near dawn.

* * *

When I awakened, my husband was gone, not just gone from our bed but from the castle as well. He had left word with the staff that I was not to be awakened or bothered until he was well on his way.

Meuriel, whose dismissal I had still not been able to bring about, took pleasure in telling me about James' departure. "He said he had business, m'lady, business that you would only be a hindrance to. He'll be back in one, maybe two weeks."

I knew James had said no such thing about my being a hindrance to him, but allowed Meuriel her spite. If the spots I'd seen before my eyes on arising and the accompanying waves of nausea meant what I thought they did, I would be in need of the village's only experienced midwife in a few months. How I hated the thoughts of Meuriel being the one to attend my lying-in, but I had no alternative. Besides Nana and Meuriel's late mother, there was no one else who was equally skilled.

Meuriel's sharp eyes didn't miss a thing. "You're pale this morning, m'lady, and I think there's a roundness to your bosom that's new. Would you, now, be expecting a bairn, say, five months from now?"

I smiled at her with a touch of smugness. "Seven," I answered, correcting her firmly. Even so, sure as I was that the child I was carrying was James', I found myself recollecting the passionate night between Lian and me before I went to Hammond's. No, the babe would be a Linwood. It must. "Seven," I repeated flatly.

Meuriel did not defy me, but she looked at my thickening middle with practiced eyes and made it plain she had her suspicions.

The thought of greeting James on his return with the news that Bloodstones would soon have its heir made me break into happy laughter at the smallest provocation. Adding to this happiness was the absence of Meuriel, who had gone to a relative in the Cotswold for a lying-in. I found myself wandering about the gardens, smelling roses, smiling at the shy castle children. Though I missed James, it was pleasant having time to myself, without the endless rounds of entertainment.

It would soon be time for me to give up my daily rides on Cara, so I took advantage of a balmy evening to take a canter along the river. As I passed under my favorite tree for my old riding trick, I looked up into the branches . . . and let out a scream. Cara almost bolted but finally came under control of my reins.

"Perk! Is it really you?"

The little fellow put his hand on his lips. "Shh, Missy, they'll be down on me in a minute if you're not careful."

I looked around but there was no one in view. "Perk, what on earth are you doing here? Is Lian with you?"

Perk scampered down out of the tree. Even for Perk, he was a mess—grimy, tattered, travel-worn. "No, Missy, but that's what I'm about. Lord B. He's been hurt, he has."

"Hurt! Perk, for God's sake, where is he? How badly is he hurt?"

"It's a fever from the cut he took from Lord 'ammond, Missy."

"From Lord Hammond!"

Perk nodded, not quite meeting my eyes. "Lord B., he got me all set up in another place where I couldn't be got at, then he went after 'ammond." At my perplexed look, he explained further. "I came back to 'im, Missy. Just wasn't much use in me trying to settle down to the normal life, not with Meg gone and you away and Lord B. needing help . . ."

"Perk, take me to him." I slid forward and patted the saddle behind me. "Get up here with me. There's no time to try to sneak you your own mount."

Perk didn't move but only shook his head slowly. "Missy, you don't understand. Lord B.'s *here*."

I looked around wildly. "Here? For God's sake, Perk, where?"

"I left 'im in a copse back a piece till I could find you. Missy, 'ammond knows Lian's the same as Lord Blackheart. He's got every hot-blooded bloke in England looking for us.

Rolling John, too, if I know the scum. If any of 'm followed us here . . .'' Perk shivered. I hate to bring our troubles to you, but I don't know where else to turn. 'E's out of his head, 'e is, and . . .''

"Never mind that, Perk. I've been in danger before. The important thing is for us to get Lian somewhere safe so we can care for him.'' I slid off Cara and paced up and down, furiously thinking. Thank God James wasn't here—and Meuriel! It sent a shudder through me to think of what she would do with this new development. For that matter, anyone would betray me for the king's ruby, which was the price on Lian's head.

Except . . . "Noddy!" The little gate guard's loyalty had been unswerving. I had discovered not long after my arrival that my grandmum had saved Noddy's little sister from permanent blindness, and he had transferred his un-swerving gratitude to me. "Perk, take Cara and fetch Lord B. back to this spot. I'll have Noddy waiting for you. It'll be dark by then and I've just thought of where Lian will be safe. Did you notice the cave a few yards from the blood stones? No, of course you didn't come in that way. But Noddy will show you.''

It would be perfect. I could use the secret hole in the chapel to get to Lian a little later without anyone suspecting. I was grateful for the superstitious nature of our castle staff. The story that a medieval priest had fled through the hole, swum the moat, only to be washed back into the cave by a sudden flood of the Medway, had led to general avoidance of the place. Most people thought the cave was haunted, and more than one report of a little brown ghost popping out of the Priest's Hole had made the rounds of the kitchen.

I could hardly sit still at dinner for being so anxious to see if Perk and Noddy had brought Lian to safety, but I could not afford to vanish into the chapel until the staff was safely abed. I laid the groundwork for my visit below, how-ever. I wrapped half the meat and cheese from the platter in my neckcloth and made sure a full jug of ale did not make its way back to the kitchen. To the scullery maid cleaning up the last of my dinner, I said, "Tell my chambermaid that I'll not be needing her tonight. I've some prayers to learn by heart, and I'll be keeping myself late in the chapel."

At last I could go to them. Once inside the chapel, I felt safe. I also felt nervous about seeing Lian again. After all, I had run away. And I was married to his cousin, his one-time rival.

I approached the smooth, carved bench that concealed the secret opening to the space below and stopped, making sure that no one was outside the chapel.

Everything was utterly quiet. I approached the stone bench near the altar and carefully put my hands against the carved panel that I had learned concealed the secret exit to the cave below. Sliding it aside, I cautiously eased myself through the hole. "Tight fit," I murmured. "Lian, if you'd waited another month, I should not have been able to make it."

The stairs were dusty but quite sturdy. I soon found myself in the chamber and could make out a glimmer of candlelight over near the wall closet the opening. "Perk," I whispered, my voice husky in the close space. "Perk, is he all right?"

"Better than all right," came back a weak but familiar voice. "Come give me a kiss, wench of the weald, and I'll bound up from here like deer faking its hunter."

"Lian!" I rushed to his side but staved off the embrace. "Here, none of that till I've had a look at you." I examined the mottled area of the wound. From what I saw, another day out in the woods would have relieved Lord Blackheart of the worry of being captured forever. "It's badly infected and spreading. Noddy, I must have scalding water. You'll simply have to manage it somehow in the kitchen without making Cook the wiser. Perk, it falls to you to get the herbs I'll need. They're in the southern corner of the tilting yard garden. Remember the little bright olive-colored leaf that I showed you back in the forest? And the mandrake root I taught you to boil for fevers?" After a few additional, terse instructions, my two little friends went scurrying off, leaving me alone with Lian.

"Bossy as ever, I see," he said with weak laughter in his voice.

I went right to the heart of my chagrin with him. "Lian, what kind of damned fool would pick a fight with Rodney Hammond?"

Lian turned his head away from me. "I didn't plan to. I went to him to tell him I was leaving London, that his precious charter wasn't needed, and wound up calling him a goddamned bastard. Your name came up once or twice, too, and not with any flattering adjectives attached." He turned back to look at my face in the shadowy light. "I had to know if you really went through it," he said simply. "Somehow, I thought you wouldn't. Right up to that moment, I would have sworn you couldn't go through with it." He gave a cynical laugh. "God's bells, Crislyn, if you did have to go through with it, did you have to enjoy it? Every word Hammond said was like this damn knife wound. I thought at first he was lying, just bragging, but then he told me some of the things you . . . the way you . . ." He turned away from me again. "That's when I saw red. That's when I hit the bastard, and he pulled his knife on me. That's why I didn't kill him. I thought you were the one woman I'd found who was worth dying for, but you weren't."

"Oh, Lian!" I put my head in my hands and wept. My trick on Hammond had worked only too well. There was nothing I could say, no way I could convince Lian . . . but, then, why should I owe him any explanation? I was not his wife; I was married to James and, although King Henry might be looking for ways to make his own marriage invalid, to me a marriage was forever. "So you tested me and I failed the test," I said in a hard voice. "Lian, enough talking." I bent over him so that my breasts, no longer bound by their neckcloth, nearly spilled forth.

Lian was looking at them and at me with such odd speculativeness that I blushed. "Yes, it's as you think. I . . . I am going to have a baby."

Lian's face was such a mixture of feelings that I would

not have dared try analyze it. Then it changed into a new hardness that matched my earlier coldness. "Whose? Mine? Hammond's? Or Linwood's? Of course, there's no way you could know for sure until the baby comes, is there?"

I could have slapped his handsome face, but I just gritted my teeth and reminded myself that Lian was convinced I was promiscuous and enjoyed being so. "Just so it doesn't show up with only one eye," I said cruelly. But Lian just gave one of his grim little smiles and turned his back on me.

I eventually forgot my anger when I realized the temple I touched from time to see if the fever was abating remained scorching hot. I could see that the herbs and poultices were helping the wound; already the spreading red streaks were fading. But Lian's body was not resisting the terrible fever, and I was afraid I knew why.

"All right, you stubborn ass, if you won't fight for your life, I will. Perk, get me water from the moat—lots and lots of it, the colder the better." I hiked up my skirt and gave Noddy one end of my chemise. "Don't be so bashful. Tear the damn thing off. We don't have time to be delicate." With his help, I ripped the cloth into squares. By then, Perk had brought the water and I could go to work.

I was exhausted long before Perk and Noddy finally dozed off, the latter posting himself as guard just inside the cave, but somehow I kept going. The dawn was coming up, and I decided to get more water before the castle servants awoke; it also would give me a chance to rinse out the cloths.

I blinked at the daylight, then set my tub down and reached for the cloths with which I had bathed Lian's head and face all night. "What the . . .?" I stared at the dark stain covering many of the white rags. "What on earth did Lian have all over him?"

Nut-brown stains. I remembered Meg hiding her hands from me once when I teased her about not washing before supper. I remembered a dark smear on the pillow next to me after a hot, sweaty night of lovemaking in the London townhouse. I remembered Meg's trying to tell me with her last breath what I had been a fool not to realize by now.

Lord Blackheart—Lian, Lord Carnton, whatever the hell his real name was—and James Linwood were one and the same! What a fool I'd been!

I marched back to the cave with my telltale bundle and strode over to the limp body on the blanket. I knelt and, without a great deal of tenderness, snatched Lord Blackheart's eye patch from his head. Lian's eyes flew open in shock. I noted they were clear and free of the dazed, feverish look that the one exposed eye had held earlier. "You bastard," I said, waving the patch in front of his nose. "And to think I went to all kinds of trouble to keep from disturbing this last night, so I wouldn't offend your precious pride by seeing that marred eye socket. To think I saved your rotten, suspicious, deceiving, worthless skin at the risk of my own, and Perk's, and Noddy's."

Then I simply burst into tears.

"Crislyn . . ."

I was finally able to speak. "Why did you marry me? Why did you want me in the first place? If you hadn't traded for me with Roark, I never would have run away and left Nana."

He gave a deep sigh. "I had to get you out of that scum's reach. I knew Scotney, knew the moment I saw you that he would put his filthy hands on you sooner or later. After our night together in the cottage, I couldn't bear the thought of that. And the masquerade as Lord Blackheart was too important to a lot of people to risk trusting you. I haven't had much luck with trusting women. Every one of them I've loved has turned out to be unfaithful in some way."

"So the real Lian, your cousin, never existed." There were so many questions buzzing around my head, I hardly knew which one to choose.

"Of course Lian existed. He was like a brother; I told you that. What I didn't tell you was that after Suzanne betrayed him with his enemy and he was left for dead in a

copse, Meg and Perk came to find me, to beg for my help."
James's voice shook. "I refused to go. Or at least I refused
the first time. The second time they came, I went to him,
but it was too late. When he died in my arms I knew I had to
do something to ease my conscience. He'd lost an eye, so I
put a patch over my own eye, had Meg color my hair and
beard black with bark dye, and went to a rally of the small
landowners who were getting such raw treatment from the
big wool dealers. It changed my whole outlook. I looked at
what I had done and what Lian had done and the different
kinds of men we had become, and I didn't like the way I fell
short."

By now, Perk and Noddy had come closer to listen
solemnly as James talked. "Perk will tell you. Something
happened to those men out there that night when I rode up
on Lian's black horse. It was like a wave of hope went out
toward me; in their minds, their hero had come back from
the grave to help them again. I got what Lian had gotten from
those men—respect, love, loyalty. I'd never before had
those things in my life."

He sighed. "So, anyway, you know the rest. I kept up
the pretense of being a brainless, pleasure-loving baron. The
parties I had at the castle proved an invaluable source of
information about shipping schedules, rumors of land
takeovers, London business deals." He looked at me.
"You're taking this a lot better than I could have ever
hoped."

"That's because I'm waiting for you to get around to
answering the question I asked you. If the bargain we made
about Hammond was just one of your devious tests of my
faithfulness and I failed it in your eyes, why would Baron
Linwood force me to marry him?"

"Because I couldn't stand to be apart from you, Crislyn.
I convinced myself that you gave yourself to Lord Blackheart because you were attracted to the side of me that you
didn't know when I was Linwood. Only Hammond stood
between us, and he's the only one who stands between us
now." He covered his eyes in agony. "If only I could be sure

the babe you bear will be a Linwood.''

I was sure, but I had no way of proving it to James. Kreel was the only one besides myself who knew the truth of the night at Hammond's lodge, but he was mute. Besides, I was too proud to protest. After all, I was the deceived one, not James Linwood! ''You will know when my son is born with the famous sixth finger.'' I shook my own finger in his face. ''And, mark my words, James Linwood, on that day I shall revel in your crawling on your knees to my side and apologizing for all the lies, all the accusations, all the lack of faith.''

''I shall do so ecstatically, my darling,'' James said in a low voice, his face pale. ''When you give me a true heir to Bloodstones, my life will be yours.''

We fell silent after that, James still weak from his fever and I deep in thought. The four of us divided up the last of the wine and cheese for breakfast, then Noddy went back to his post and Perk left for Brother Jubal's monastery. I'd decided he would be as safe there as he would be here, probably safer.

''Tell Kreel to look on you as my friend,'' I told the little fellow as I hugged him. ''He will stick to you like glue and be your friend forever.''

To James, when we were alone again, I said, ''Well, at least there's no more danger of your being shot for an outlaw. Once we burn the last remaining rags of Lord Blackheart, you can simply reclaim your place as Lord of Bloodstones. Only do not,'' I said as I buried the stained cloths in the cave floor, ''expect to reclaim your place in my bed. Until this child is born and forever proves his ancestral rights, I have no desire to lie beside you.''

James managed a wan smile. ''I shall miss him, you know.''

''Perk? He's much better off without us.''

''Lord Blackheart. Shan't you miss him, too?''

I thought about that for a minute. ''Yes. Now go to sleep. I shall be back after dark, this time with fresh clothes and hot soup.''

314

James rolled over, but before I left, he turned back to me. "Crislyn."

"Yes?"

"Thank you. You saved my life, but my debt to you doesn't change anything. Can you understand how it is, my torment about the babe? It's a part of my blood, the desire for a son and heir; it's centuries old. I can no more change it than those stones out there can change themselves into cinders."

Maybe I did understand, I thought grudgingly. Hadn't I been born illegitimately? "Go to sleep."

Don't ask me why a sudden presentiment of danger made me return to fetch my wheel lock from its hiding place. I had fretted all day about someone accidentally discovering James' hiding place. Though he no longer bore the physical marks of Lord Blackheart, the knife wound would cause questions. By the time night rolled around and I could go to see about him, I was jittery as butterflies.

"James?" I called softly as I descended the stairs.

There was a sound halfway between a moan and an acknowledgement. "James?" I kept my hand in my pocket where I'd placed the wheel lock and hurried down toward the huddled form illuminated by the candle.

"Crislyn, look out, he's got the crossbow on us."

I whirled then and saw the tall shadow silhouetted in the opening to the cave. Even before the hated voice spoke, I knew who it was. "Rolling John!"

"Yes, wench, and this time there'll be no coach stopping, no tricks, no pitchforks." As my eyes adjusted to the darkness, I could see that Rolling John had his crossbow trained on James. "I'm taking this'un in for the reward, and then we'll see what happens to you for harboring a criminal. And if I don't get you as part of my pay for bringing in Lord Blackheart, I'll be coming back privately to collect on my own."

"This isn't Lord Blackheart," I blustered. "It's Lord Linwood, and you'll have a lot to answer for, Rolling John, if you loose that triger." All the time, I was positioning my weapon. If I could distract his good eye away from his crossbow, I'd have him.

"Oh, no, you don't. I tracked 'em here. Sort of suspected it all along, him disappearing like he did and all. Then when I saw Perk sneaking out this morning . . ."

"Run for it, Crislyn," James said calmly. "He can't get off but one shot."

"Don't worry, James," I said coolly. "I guess Rolling John thinks he's smarter than he is. I sent for the sheriff not an hour ago, telling him I saw a dark-haired, one-eyed man lurking about the moat. They've probably got the opening surrounded by now." Suddenly I raised my voice shrilly. "Sheriff, he's in here! Lord Blackheart's in here." When John jerked his head toward the opening to the cave, I threw the jar of soup I was carrying as hard as I could and saw John swerve his aim toward where it crashed against the hard wall. Then I raised the wheel lock and took careful aim.

The ball would have gone through the back of his head, but John turned toward me just as it reached him and smashed into the middle of his face. Blood and fragments of flesh went everywhere. "Just hope it left his bad eye intact," I said out loud, not even realizing what I was saying.

I let him lie there for a long time before I walked over and nudged him with my foot. The lower face was a mess but the black eye patch was intact and clearly visible. I noted coolly that the hair and beard and lean, muscled body were about as close to "Lian" as I'd remembered.

I looked over at my husband, who was staring at me as though I were a total stranger. "There's your Lord Blackheart, all ready to be signed, sealed and delivered. Shall you collect the king's ruby, or shall I?"

The sounds of bells startled me, but James made no sign of hearing them. Were they inside my head? Why would the bells be ringing for evil Rolling John? And then the dizziness came. *My baby*, I thought confusedly. *I mustn't let anything hurt my baby. . . .*

17

What a ludicrous sight I must have been as Jocko walked into his kitchen—standing with his paring knife frozen in my hand, my eyes round and fixed on the Austrian bell clock. What must he have thought?

"Miss Alix?" He rushed to my side. "Are you all right?"

I gave a shaky laugh and carefully put down the knife. "I'm afraid I got to daydreaming and left most of the work for you, Jocko. And when the clock sounded, I realized I've still got to dress for Madame Lilah's party."

He looked at me oddly but was too polite to argue that I seemed upset if I claimed I wasn't. "Don't concern yourself about the vegetables, Miss Alix. I've plenty of time to finish."

He watched me out of the corner of his eye while he went back to his chopping, most likely on the lookout for further odd behavior.

Back in my tower room, I sat down and stared at the red silk dress, hand-cleaned and back for me to wear tonight.

As I slipped it on, not daring to look at my reflection even while I arranged my hair Empire-style and applied cologne, I realized I had no appropriate jewelry.

The painting was real; maybe the locket is, too.

Almost in a dream, I walked over to the alcove where

the bath facilities were and had always been.

The loose stone came out easily in my trembling hands, as did the chest. It was almost all I could do to open the clasp, so poignant was the sensation of holding the same chest in almost the same spot as Crislyn had.

When I lifted out the locket with its delicate engraving, I felt the tears sliding down my cheeks. And as I shakily fastened it around my throat, felt it cool against my flesh as it had been against Crislyn's and, before her, Amanda Sheffield's.

The compulsion to look at myself was growing stronger. My hesitation came from knowing that when I did, I would once again be Crislyn.

"It's too soon," I whispered, my eyes tightly shut, my hand at the locket. "Too soon. I was just there. Please . . . not now."

But I couldn't keep my eyes closed forever, nor did I really want to. Opening my eyes, I saw the woman in the mirror and nothing else. As I watched, the glass seemed to move in waves, making me dizzy and I felt myself sliding back into the past. . . .

The image was not of a woman in red silk with modern makeup and a stylized hairdo but of Crislyn in a loose-fitting dress of soft material which accommodated her growing girth.

As I so often did these days, since the approaching birth of my son made me think constantly of my mother and what her feelings must have been before I was born, I fingered the locket at my throat. Like the wheel lock, which was a sort of memento of my unknown father, the locket made me feel close to those who had conceived me in love.

I walked over to the arrow-slit and peered at the blood stones. Soon, very soon, my own child would be a participant in the ancient ceremony. My anger at James for doubting the parentage of our child had evaporated gradually as I pondered the inheritance that would someday come down to my son, then pass to his son, and so on. James was justified in wanting his own son to inherit. Without a proper Linwood, the castle and its surrounding properties would revert to the king's roster of estates to be offered to court favorites. Allegedly, the land would go to the village of Ravensbridge, but everyone knew who would claim Bloodstones should its heir be in question.

At any rate, I had nothing to fear. I patted my bulging stomach and smiled. "You, my son, are a Linwood through and through, and none shall be able to say otherwise."

Meuriel came in. She had been more meek and pliable of late, as most of the servants were these days after hearing of how Lord Blackheart was killed by the lord of Bloodstones. (James and I had agreed it would be best to let it be known he had actually done the deed. I certainly needed no attention from London!) "M'lady, will you be dining up here as you've been doing since Lord Linwood's departure?"

"Yes, Meuriel." James was in London, ostensibly to be presented the king's reward for producing the head of Lord Blackheart, but actually to tie up any loose ends that might connect him to the highwayman. "The stairs are getting to be a bit much for me."

"It won't be much longer," Meuriel said with fake solicitude, her eyes going to my middle.

I'd given up trying to combat the rumors that Meuriel had spread all over the castle and town about her lady having a secret lover. The birth of my son would forever dispel them, and I saw no need to lower my dignity by refuting Meuriel's vicious tongue. "I certainly hope so. The babe has been tilting inside me for weeks now, like a full-grown knight." The size of the growing child was beginning to alarm me. I knew, now, that my thought of sending Meuriel away at the time of labor was impractical. It could be a dangerous birthing, I sensed.

"Will our Lord Linwood be coming home soon, m'lady?"

I shrugged. Meuriel watched us too keenly for me to pretend James and I were blissfully married and jubilantly exultant over the coming event. "I fully expect him to be here in time for the arrival of his son. Now, Meuriel, would you mind going down to tell Cook I'll not be wanting a heavy supper? Just fresh milk and some of those pears with perhaps a bit of pudding."

Once I was rid of her, I sat dreamily at the window, looking out at the reaches of fine land, and thought about my son inheriting all of this.

"Madame." The whisper at the tower door was soft but insistent. I'd slept like the dead, but came wide awake when I realized the voice was that of my loyal little Noddy. "M'lady, it's Noddy."

"I know, I know," I said, struggling to my feet. "It just takes me a while to hoist myself up out of bed." I opened the door. "Why aren't you at your post, Noddy? You know what the Baron said about keeping a sharp lookout while he's gone."

"Yes, m'lady, but there's two odd ones come to see you. The big one nearly caught the head of my ax when I saw him, but he says he's a friend of yours."

God knows I could use another friend, I thought. "Where are they?" I opened the door wider, prepared to go out.

"Right here, behind Noddy," a deep, rich voice answered. "And Kreel's hiding in my skirts as usual."

I embraced the hooded man who smelled of the fields and had the gauntness of a beggar. "Brother Jubal! And Kreel! How glad I am to see you, but what danger you're in! You know the sentiments of King Henry these days about the Orders . . ."

"I know them only too well, but my fear is little compared to my joy in seeing you in such bloom, little sister. I kept hearing you call to me in my dreams."

"Noddy, bring a basket of food and a jug of wine. These men look starved."

The monk stook his head. "Not for me. For Kreel, perhaps, who has not yet mastered the art of fasting. But for me, I shall fast until I've seen your needs clearly."

"My needs?"

"For my teachings, little sister. Your knowledge must be expanded so that it will be useful to you in dire times."

I nodded eagerly. "Yes," I whispered. If I could learn this man's secrets of calmness and peace, I could survive anything in the future. "I'll arrange for you to stay here as a gardener. And you, Kreel," I said, laughing, "we'll have to think of a job for you, too."

"Cook was complaining of needing someone in the kitchen since the little wench who was helping her ran off," Noddy offered helpfully.

"Fine. I'll see to that in the morning. Brother Jubal, I shall be spending a lot of time amongst the roses. We shall have much time for talking."

Brother Jubal fit as quietly into the life of our castle as anyone could. I was grateful for his gentle presence and the calmness he managed to bring to my life.

We would talk as I piddled about with the roses and he weeded the nearby vegetable and herb garden. He understood my uneasiness and often tried to set my mind at ease, reminding me anxiety was not good for me or my coming child.

I learned from Noddy what Brother Jubal had never spoken of—he and his fellow monks had been evicted without warning from the monastery. The stained glass and furnishings had found their way to royal coffers, while the property was quietly confiscated in the name of King Henry.

"Jubal, you never complain of the unfairness of things. You always seem at peace with your world." We were sitting cross-legged on the bank of the Medway, watching the sunset as we often did together with James away. "Often, when we sit together like this, not talking, I feel that way, too. Then I can feel myself floating, light as air, and that wonderful peacefulness comes over me. Nothing in the real world hurts or matters much."

Jubal looked at me sadly. "I hoped you would learn that, my child, though I had no idea you would learn so quickly. Remember the secret well; it will help you when your time comes."

"You mean the baby?" I laughed. The child inside me was lively and strong, and I had never felt nor looked better. "Jubal, I'm not frightened of the birthing ahead of me."

He put his hand on my shoulder. "I'm not talking about the labors of giving life to the child, Crislyn. I don't mean to frighten you, but I've felt ill feelings around you since I've been here."

I frowned and, pulling my cape closer about me, held out my hand for my friend to pull me to my feet. Such a big fellow my son would be! "That's easy to explain. Meuriel still can't stand me nor I her, but she's quieter now, anyway. And James refuses to dismiss her since she's the only competent midwife in the province." I brightened at a new thought. "Jubal, could you . . . would you be willing to stay close at the lying-in? I should feel so much better knowing you were nearby."

Brother Jubal nodded. "But your Meuriel would forbid my being in the chamber during the birth. It's a superstition that these midwives guard with steel wills that theirs should be the first hands on the newborn—not a man's."

Still I felt better knowing that Brother Jubal would not be far away when my time came. I feared the danger he sensed was more real than fancied.

Later that day, I had my first scare as I started up the stairs to my room. A sharp pain went through my middle. Meuriel was close behind me and caught me as I stumbled. "It's all right," I told her after a moment or two in which the pain subsided and did not return. "Still, I think it's time we sent for Lord Linwood. It could be the babe will be a few weeks early." Even by my secret calculations, I had at least two weeks to go, but the babe might not decide to adhere to its schedule.

"They're taking bets in the village about the babe,"

Meuriel threw out suddenly.

"Then bet on a boy if you wish an edge on the odds," I told her.

"The betting's not on boy or girl; it's on whether it'll have the mark."

"You'd like it to come out with pointy ears and red eyes and two horns, wouldn't you, Meuriel?"

I curbed my anger at that but coldly sent the girl off to see about having someone sent to London. James might be busy with important business, but this business at home was far more important—to all of us. As I turned to go up to my room, I was overcome with dizziness and dropped to my knees. "Oh, God, not now. Brother Jubal!" My knees buckled as I tried to rise, but suddenly there was a strong arm holding me up and a kind voice in my ear that told me my cry for help had been heard.

"You'll be fine, Crislyn, just fine. I'm right here."

"The baby . . . it can't come yet." I felt my mind trying to grasp where it was that I needed to go so urgently, but there was a confusing fading in and out of my consciousness that curbed coherent thinking.

"Try to relax, Crislyn. Here's the bed. Close your eyes . . . relax . . . remember the peacefulness of the river . . . the flowing water . . . flow with it, Crislyn . . . relax. . . ."

I felt the tenseness go out of me, my breathing resume regularity, and I knew the baby would not come now after all. "Jubal. Dear sweet Jubal. You are always here when I need you. How do you do that?"

He may have answered, but I was too far away to hear.

"Crock." I opened my eyes to the doctor sitting next to me, his face full of concern. "I was so scared. The baby . . . I was afraid it was coming early. It would have, too, except Brother Jubal was there and . . ." I stopped, staring at the lined face that was watching me. "You were there. It was you helping me. You were Brother Jubal!"

Crock patted my hand and shook his head slowly. "I

don't know what you mean, but okay, I'm a brother Jubal, whatever that is. I came up here to check on you when Jocko told me you might still be upset about some call you had. I saw you were in—whatever it is you go into—a trance and agitated. I tried hard to reach you, but I couldn't get through."

I squeezed his hand and said excitedly, "But, don't you see? That's exactly what you did do. You did reach me, did get through. As Brother Jubal. And thanks to you, Crislyn's baby didn't come too early."

Crock chuckled. "I don't know about this jumping around from one century to another, Alix. I'm a quiet fellow; never been much further than Brighton." He patted me. "Ask anybody in town. I'm as much a home-loving, conservative old sawbones as you'll ever meet."

My response to that was to take his freckled hand and press it to my lips. I silently thanked Brother Jubal and then remembered that I must face Miles soon, and I left Crislyn's world behind for Alix's.

18

The steady stream of well-wishers who stopped by to pay homage to Bloodstones' matriarch dissipated at the same rate as the champagne punch and trays of hors d' oeuvres.

Miles ushered out the final visitor and clapped his hands together with exaggerated glee. "Ha, the last of the village sops has gone." He smiled around the room at those of us left—Crock, Samantha, Neil and myself. Madame Lilah was lying on the sofa, tired but apparently happy. "Now I'll have Jocko bring out the good champagne." He waited until the old Waterford goblets had been passed around, then held his glass high. "To my mother, whose vintage improves with each passing year."

We all drank and offered our own toasts and good wishes. Samantha, a picture of willowy elegance in a black one-shouldered gown, took the tray holding our presents when Jocko brought it in. She put it beside Lilah. "Open mine first. It's on top."

"Oh, my." Lilah lifted the heavy baroque pearl choker from its box and chided, "My dear, you shouldn't have done this. Why, it must have cost a fortune." She replaced the pearls carefully in the case and reached for my present.

"Oh, Alix, my dear!" She held out her hand and pulled me over for a kiss. "Just the kind of thing I love—and my very favorite colors." I could feel Samantha smarting as the old woman pinned the ornament I'd given her on her dress. The fact that the model had probably spent a small fortune hadn't helped a whit to gain Lilah's approval.

Crock's music box that featured an exquisite little harp on its lid was an instant hit, as were Neil's imported box of chocolates and Jocko's leather-bound volume of Keats, Madame's favorite.

"Everything is so lovely." Lilah's eyes shone like a young girl's and then looked at Miles with pretended hurt. "And what's your excuse for not giving your poor old mother a present, you ungrateful fellow?"

Miles looked at me over his mother's head and I felt my heart leap. He was about to announce our engagement. "I've saved the best for last. And though my gift is wrapped in a pretty package, I beg you not to unwrap it." He took my hand and led me over to stand in front of the fireplace at his side. "Lilah, my darling mother, I hereby offer you the present you've wanted most from me for many years. A new bride for your son—and Bloodstones!"

The happiness on the old woman's face was indeed something to see. "Oh, my darling children, if you only knew how much joy this brings to me." She motioned us to her and, as we knelt together, put her arms around both of us. "This calls for more champagne. Jocko, bring another bottle." She hugged again, so tightly I could breathe in Miles' light scent and could feel my shoulder pressed against his.

After we'd all drunk to the engagement and the others had made appropriate remarks (even Samantha, though I'm sure it choked her to do so, offered insincere congratulations), Lilah looked from Miles to my unadorned hand holding my wine glass. "Why, Miles, I do believe you've been negligent. I don't see Alix wearing a ring. My dear, that simply won't do at all, not at all." She pulled off her own huge diamond solitaire and handed it to Miles. "Here. I'd always meant you to have it someday." She held the dazzling ring out, and Miles took it, then bent to kiss her.

"Lilah, I can't accept it." I felt awful, knowing I was part of a deception. How could I ever have consented to such a dishonest thing? "Miles, tell your mother that we're not getting married . . ." I looked from the ring being slid onto my hand to Miles.

". . . until my lovely fiancee has had time to let her American friends know about the wedding." He stood aside while Crock and Neil kissed me and clapped Miles on the back.

Even Jocko was affected. I could swear his eyes held tears when he bent over my hand, but I wouldn't him get away without a real kiss. "I've never seen the Madame so happy," he whispered.

Predictably enough, I was soon cornered by Samantha. "I knew you were devious, all right, but I underestimated you. I watched your face when Miles was telling us about your engagement. It wasn't that of a smitten bride-to-be." She leaned closer and hissed. "I don't know what he's up to, but I'm willing to bet it has something to do with the money your cousin's leaving to you."

I said impatiently, "I told you Cass never said anything to me about a new will or even hinted she was leaving me any money." I heard my own words with horror. I was doing it again—talking about Cass as if she were dead! "And if she hasn't said anything to her husband or me, how could Miles possibly know about a switch in beneficiaries?"

Samantha lifted the smooth shoulder that was bare, making the thin gold snake ornamenting her upper arm look as if it were alive. What an appropriate choice of jewelry, I thought nastily. "Miles is an excellent barrister, love, with fantastic resources. He probably knows more than you think he does." She added slyly, "He probably knows all there is about whatever dingy little past you might have had, too."

He couldn't know everything. Even Cass didn't know the far-reaching effects of Phillip's callousness on my life. In anger, I struck back. "He must be an excellent lawyer, indeed, to have convinced a judge and jury of *your* innocence.''

The scarlet mouth opened and shut several times, but for once Samantha was speechless. Finally she managed, in a strangled voice, ''How did you . . . who told you about me?''

I felt like a heel, but there would be no point in apologizing. At least I wouldn't incriminate Neil. ''I guess I read about your case somewhere.''

''Well, Samantha, what do you think of the news that Bloodstones will soon be ringing out wedding bells?''

The possessive arm at my waist didn't escape the model's eye, and I found myself feeling sorry for her again. The pinched look around her eyes and mouth told me Miles' affair with Samantha had been casual on his part, perhaps, but much more serious on hers. I felt angry that he didn't even realize he was being cruel.

But Samantha wasn't bashful about using any weapon at hand. She put her hand with its mandarin nails against Miles' cheek and smiled sweetly. ''So romantic! Like that sweet old-fashioned dress Alix is wearing.'' She tapped Miles' cheek lightly. ''Now that Alix is practically in the family, darling, you really should allow her to have a say in family matters.'' Her smile faded. ''Like which heirloom should go to pay for that fairy tale wedding Lilah will want.''

There was murder in Miles' eyes, but Samantha was already halfway toward the door. Miles rubbed his cheek as if to erase her touch and said lightly, though his eyes still burned with anger, ''Hell. hath no fury . . .'' He looked down at me with a little smile. ''Only this wasn't a case of 'a woman scorned.' I never led Samantha to believe there could be any serious relationship, and she has no right to be so vicious.'' Miles, catching his mother's adoring eye on us, lifted my hand to his lips. ''But, here, why am I discussing another woman with my betrothed?'' He turned my hand with the large diamond over and kissed the palm lightly. ''There are a great many things I'd rather be doing.''

I actually blushed. If only things had started off

differently for Miles and me; if only I did not feel we were caught up in something that would not allow us to discover love and passion in a more natural way! "Miles, please . . ." It was torment, knowing I was falling deeply in love and not knowing if he was doing likewise. "Let's not shock Lilah any more tonight."

"Shock her?" Miles laughed softly, happily. "Look at her. Look how happy we've made her."

I looked over to see Lilah beaming at us from the sofa where Crock and Neil were paying her court. She blew me a kiss and went back to her animated chatter with the two men. She did look happy, and I wished I were that happy, too.

"Promise me that you won't mention Samantha's remark to Lilah, about selling something to finance the wedding."

I met his eyes gravely. "It's true, then, that there's no money."

Miles' mouth twitched. "Ah, now we come to the truth. You're marrying me for my money."

I did not find that amusing. "Miles, please don't joke about such things."

Miles' humor vanished. "Jocko and I have done a good job of keeping our . . . ah, cash flow difficulties from my mother. She would insist on giving up her extravagances and the little luxuries she loves, and Jocko and I would hate that. We don't want her scrimping in the short time she's got left."

"Don't worry. I won't say anything, but I wouldn't trust Samantha not to."

Miles' face hardened. "Don't worry about Samantha. Her lease on the cottage expires at the end of this week, and I intend to see that she's out of our hair for good. Unless," he added teasingly, "you had her in mind for a bridesmaid."

"No, thanks. Broomsticks are out of fashion at weddings these days." It was difficult for me to be flippant about this, and I sensed that it wasn't that easy for Miles, either. "Will you forgive a little American directness and explain why there is no Linwood fortune?''

"I confess I am having a bit of trouble adjusting to that directness, though in you it's rather adorable. To delude you of the notion that I probably squandered all our money on gambling, women and—what else?—the horses, I'll tell you.'' The teasing tone was gone now. "My brother Dexter was responsible for the mess we're in. He bet heavily on his damned polo matches and steady lost. Some unsavory gamblers got hold of the notes, and Dex put this place in hock. I've managed to get things back on a more stable level, but it hasn't been easy.''

"You sound like someone who didn't like his brother very much.''

"That's putting it mildly. I'm not a hypocrite. Dexter's dead and I'm very glad of it. If he had lived, I would have eventually had to shoot him.'' I could tell Miles wasn't joking. "But not to worry about wedding expense, love. The Linwoods always come through.''

There he was again, talking as though we really were getting married, that there really was no barrier to our love.

I said a little shakily, "Where I come from, the wedding is the responsibility of the bride's family.''

Miles rubbed my arm up and down, bringing the usual goosebumps. "But, my darling, we're your family now. We're all you've got.'' Miles stopped at the look on my face. "Darling Alix, I'm sorry. Of course, you've got Cassandra.''

But I didn't; that was the trouble. I changed the subject. "Miles, Crock is helping Lilah to her room, and I'd like to say good-night.''

His eyes were warm on mine. "And then we can be alone at last.''

I had turned into a blushing bride-to-be. Every sensual innuendo Miles made went directly to the quick of me and ignited little flames. "I'll be right back.''

After saying good-night to Lilah and Crock, I stuck my head in the kitchen where Jocko was putting away the last of the canapes. For some reason I thought of Cass and me sneaking chocolate cake and milk late at night, promising each other that one of us would marry the prince and the other would come live in the castle always.

Jocko was a bit embarrassed at being caught in his bathrobe, but I very carefully averted my eyes from the pink bunny fur slippers as I thanked him for the evening.

He very warmly welcomed me into the family, then exclaimed, "Oh, Miss Alix, in all the excitement, I forgot to give you your letter."

"My letter?" I took the plain white envelope, noting it had a London postmark. Who on earth would be writing me from London? But Miles was impatiently awaiting my return and the aperitif he had ready, so I tucked the letter away for the time being.

Once we were alone, I very quickly forgot my mysterious missive. Miles had a way of making me forget everything but churning emotions when I was with him. He pulled me into his arms, and we watched the fire until neither of us could bear the thought of not being closer. He looked at me and saw that there was no need for words. Silently we rose and moved arm and arm toward my tower room.

But once in our private bower, I felt the need to speak of the things that we both had begun to accept about our relationship. "What's happening to us, Miles?" I asked. "Are we caught in some sort of endless cycle of old and new love?"

"I don't know," he said gravely. "All I know is that we have never been strangers, not even from the first moment."

"It's as though there were a thin curtain between us and them."

"Them?" Miles raised an eyebrow.

He knew who I meant, but like him, I wasn't eager to name the uneasy presences in our lives. It was too scary. "By the way, I should warn you that Phillip, Cassandra's husband, may be paying you a visit any day now."

"Fine." As Miles was nibbling my earlobe, I was having my usual trouble concentrating on what I was saying.

"He's quite capable of causing a big fuss if he decides there's anything fishy about Cass leaving here."

"I'm capable of throwing him out on his ear, too."

I pulled away from him. "Miles, don't ever look on Phillip as a joke. He isn't one, believe me. And even though he finally broke down and confessed Cass wasn't planning to come back to him, he's not ready to give it up."

Miles looked at me for a long moment. "Are you sure this Phillip isn't coming here to find . . . someone else?"

I reddened. "There's something I haven't shown you." I walked over to the wardrobe and dragged out the stuffed elephant. "Punkin."

"So?" Miles wasn't impressed.

I smiled. "Punkin is sort of . . . well, to Cass he's like Linus' blanket."

"Linus' blanket?" Miles was totally befuddled by now.

"The 'Peanuts' character, you dope. Good lord, is it possible you people don't have comic strips? Or teddy bears?"

Miles laughed. "I'm educable, my darling, and very willing. But tell me more . . ."

I did. I told him about the passport and the scarf, and Miles stroked my arm as I talked. When I'd finished, he asked quietly, "Is that it?"

I stared at him. "Isn't it enough?"

He smiled. "No, but I tell you what. When your Phillip arrives here, I'll give him a name and number of a fellow I know at Scotland Yard, and he can check this thing out for good and all."

"Maybe I ought to be the one to call Scotland Yard. Now."

Miles tossed Punkin back into the wardrobe. "Not very practical, darling. You said you hadn't seen Cassandra in years. Could you describe her accurately? Provide the necessary data? Credit cards and personal information as well as clothes and traveling habits?" I shook my head and Miles said reasonably, "Then let the person who can be most helpful to the Yard people be the one to report her

332

missing. That is, if the fellow really decides he wants her back.''

We always came back to this. Cass did not mean to Miles what she meant to me. I felt isolated and suddenly very, very tired. "Miles, I guess I'd rather not let you stay, after all. I'm exhausted.''

He wasn't as upset as I thought he'd be. He just traced my mouth lightly with a gentle finger, then kissed me. "We have a thousand and one nights ahead of us, my darling, at the very least." He looked around the room and then back at me. "Is it all those ghostly nights our forebears spent making love in here? Is that why you've suddenly turned shy on me? But I won't tease you about it." He kissed the tip of my nose and left. I heard him whistling "That Ol' Black Magic" all the way down the stairs.

Smiling at his new boyishness, I opened my bag for my cigarette case and saw the envelope Jocko had given me. It was almost all I could do to open it. Like a telegram, it bore the aura of the unexpected.

Inside was a theatre ticket to the Fortune Theatre for Thursday night's performance of Agatha Christie's "Murder at the Vicarage." That was unexpected enough, but the badly typed message that accompanied the pass was even more strange. "I can help you find C. Enjoy the show, it's a real killer. P.S. Don't leave your seat. I'll find you."

My heart leaped with new hope. It could be from Cass herself. It was just the kind of intrigue she loved—the theatre ticket, the secrecy.

Thursday . . . tomorrow night! I looked down at the note and felt a little chilled. *I'll find you.*

I'd go, of course. Even if it were some kind of terrible joke, I still had to do it.

"It couldn't be dangerous—not in the theatre, with all those people."

Or could it?

"Brace up, Alix o'l girl. You have to go. Cass would do the same for you."

Or would she?

There was the problem of what to tell the Linwoods, of course. It might look a bit odd, my dashing off to London the day after I became engaged to Miles, and he'd insist on going with me.

I laughed aloud at the simplicty of my solution. I would tell them all the truth—or what could be the truth. I would say I was going in to meet Cass and take in a show with her, as she'd requested by mail. She could get the news about my upcoming marriage, and perhaps I could smooth things over about her tiff with the Linwoods.

"And I could start shopping for my trousseau." I grinned, thinking how much that would satisfy Lilah. I'd even buy a few frilly gowns just to give her pleasure.

A sense of my own cleverness obscured the underlying question that I refused to let surface until just before I fell asleep.

If it turned out Cass hadn't sent the ticket, who had?

There was one other uncomfortable thought that reared its head before I startled everyone the next morning at breakfast with my announcement of a visit to London.

If someone at Bloodstones had harmed my cousin, how would that person react to the news that I'd heard from her?

Miles' reaction was predictable. He stared at me over his cup and then broke into laughter. "So all that dark drama last night was just a show for my benefit, was it?"

"I hadn't read the note then," I told him brightly.

"I'll drive you in, though I won't be free to join you. I have a client staying over who'll want a business dinner."

"It's just as well. There's the awkwardness between you and Cass, and anyway she only sent one ticket."

"What's the play?"

Jocko came in just then and was very flustered over having forgotten his longstanding commitment to Neil Willingham today. "I promised to take him about to some of the best catering places to do business with, but if the two of you are leaving and Miss Hightower's not to be found . . ."

"Don't worry, Jocko, I'll give Mrs. Devons a call. She offered to stay with Lilah any day that was necessary." I got up to phone the matron. "And I'll let Crock know we'll all be out, so he can check by later."

I came back a moment later. "Well, Mrs. D. was delighted to keep Lilah company, and Crock's partner said he was on call if she needed medical attention." I sat down very slowly, mulling over the information that the good doctor was already on his way to London for a consultation at a hospital there.

Except for Lilah, everyone I knew would be in town today.

"I've just had a marvelous idea, Alix. You can stay at my flat tonight, since there are no late trains and I doubt you'll want to impose on your cousin."

My heart fluttered. Miles and I had never been alone together anywhere but the castle. "Shall you join me?" I asked shyly.

"I'll be staying at my club. There's a special game my client wants in on and no doubt we'll be up all night." He reached in his blazer pocket and pulled out a key. "Here you are; the address is on the tag."

My pride wouldn't allow me to show how disappointed I was. "So gambling takes precedence over one's fiancee."

I would have seen the twinkle in his eyes if I hadn't been busy collecting the shopping list Lilah had given me. "Strictly business, my darling, I assure you. Now, shall we be off? That list my mother gave you looks wicked."

The trip into London was actually pleasant, without a single fight or insult. Miles and I chatted and laughed like any normal couple. Maybe it was because we were away from the atmosphere of the castle that seemed to have such a strong influence on me.

It was only near the very end of our journey that Miles changed suddenly into one of his moods. "Are you sure you hadn't rather have a ring of your own instead of that secondhand one of my mother's?" he asked unexpectedly.

I waved my hand airily so that the huge stone caught the light. "I like wearing a Linwood stone."

Miles looked so gloomy that I decided I had disappointed him by allowing his mother to part with a family heirloom of such obvious value. Since he was already pulling up to Harrod's to let me out for my shopping, I could not delve into possible reasons for his sudden gloom. "Shall I really not be seeing you tonight?" I asked, ignoring the bobby blowing his whistle at us for blocking traffic.

Miles' mouth twitched slightly. "You have no idea how flattering I find that, especially since you kicked me down the stairs last night."

"I did not . . . all right, all right!" The bobby was getting hysterical about us, so I blew Miles a kiss and ran for the entrance to Harrod's. Unfortunately for the man coming out, my umbrella caught him right in the stomach. Even so, the famous British politeness prevailed, albeit through contortions of pain. "Sorry!" the poor man managed, tipping his derby.

I burst into tears in the midst of this ridiculous and unfair exchange. Suddenly the problem that had plagued me from the first moment of realizing I was falling in love with Miles Linwood came flooding in on me. Until I found Cassandra I could not completely commit my love and trust to him.

The man with the derby got many wilting looks from people, thinking he'd upset me, and he hurried away. I rushed off to find the tins of pate that Lilah had on her list, then headed to the jewelry department to retrieve the pearls she was having restrung. While leaning over admiring the gorgeous rings and brooches, I was offered a free appraisal of the ring I was wearing. "Why not?" I told the jeweler.

Over a sausage roll and beer at the wonderful Sherlock Holmes Pub on Baker Street, I started laughing so hard two handsome young Oxford students came over to see if I was all right. "Yes," I assured them and "No, I can't join you for another beer; one's my limit."

At least I now knew what Miles's very peculiar mood had been all about.

19

Though I was entreated by my youthful admirers to spend the rest of the afternoon pub-crawling, I parted from them with the truthful excuse that I had more shopping to do.

The meaningless little interlude of flirtatiousness and fun had successfully taken my mind off Miles and the approaching meeting at the theatre. I set out to complete my shopping excursion quite cheerfully.

Lilah had predicted I would probably relish the Chelsea and Kensington boutiques far more than her traditional Simpson's and the like. She was right; I adored the flair and daring styles of the exciting little shops. Falling into the mood set by the head-turning fashions, I impulsively bought a gown and negligee of apricot satin with ostrich plume trim, more appropriate for a 30's sex symbol of the silver screen than a blushing bride-to-be.

But then I reminded myself as I hailed a cab for Aldwych, Miles and I were not really headed for the altar. That reminder brought back the earlier sadness that too much was unspoken between Miles and me to openly say to each other, "I love you."

By the time I had finished shopping, eaten a quick supper and found my seat in the tiny theatre, I was feeling quite morose.

Even so, Christie's genius has a way of drawing you out of the real world. I 'was so engrossed in the play by intermission that I was startled when an usher handed me a note. It occurred to me as I thanked him that my end seat on the first row balcony made me quite visible.

Was someone watching me as I opened the note and read it?

The terse message ended my enjoyment of British humor. *Wait until the maid brings the family tea in the next act. When she exits, go to the phone box just outside the door to your section.*

I sat nervously waiting for the hilarious Mary to deposit her tea tray in the Vicar's living room, then I exited as she did.

The phone rang just as I got to it. Even expecting it, I jumped. "Hello?"

The voice was a curious mixture of at least five accents. I know now that that was a technique used to force me to concentrate on the message so as not to identify the voice.

"Cass, if it's you, please say so. Please!"

"I'm not your . . ." The static was awful; I strained to hear. ". . . could be dangerous for us."

"Dangerous? You mean to you and to Cass?"

"No, I mean to me. And I guess to you, though I don't think . . ." The static again. ". . . can't talk any more, not now."

"Oh, don't hang up! Look, if you know something about my cousin, anything at all, I'll pay you!"

The voice was a loud whisper. "I thought I heard someone at the door. I have to go . . ."

I cried, "Please, can't we meet somewhere and talk? Somewhere safe?" I was encouraged by the listening silence. "I'll bring the money. Cash."

"How much?" I named a figure. "Five thousand is cheap for the risk I'm taking, but at least it's enough to . . ." The crackling static blotted out the next words but then I heard with chilling clarity, ". . . meet you at the blood stones. Tomorrow at midnight."

338

"I don't know if I can . . ."

I heard the sound of a door opening and my caller saying sharply, "What are you doing back here? I thought we agreed that . . ."

The line went dead; either my mysterious caller had hung up the phone—or the visitor had.

The sound of laughter from the balcony reminded me I would soon be in the middle of milling people at another intermission. I hurried down to the street and hailed one of the cruising black taxis, drawing a blank when he asked me where I was going.

"Are you all right, Miss? You look a bit pale, if you don't mind my saying so."

"I'm . . . I'm all right." I fished for the key Miles had given me and read the address off to the cabbie.

He was obviously impressed by the Bloomington Square location. I could see why when I was let out at the charmingly renovated Georgian residence.

The flat was distinctively masculine in flavor, but exquisitely furnished in period pieces. A mirrored bar with a crystal array of decanters stood welcomingly at the fireside whose logs awaited only a match.

And a drink. But first I wanted to shed the suit and shoes I'd been in all day.

Trying on my new movie star ensemble was just another way of delaying the thinking I knew I had to do, but like the fire, it boosted my spirits, as did the record of Van Cliburn I found on the phonograph.

But nothing could hold back the questions and the fear swirling through me. I stared at the fire but knew it didn't hold the answers. Where was Cassandra? Was she alive or dead? Who was the person who'd sent me the theatre ticket?

If I could force myself to go to the stones the next night, I'd find out all these things. But the mere thought of creeping down to that haunted, dreadful place in the middle of the night made me weak.

"You could tell Neil. Or Crock." But I knew even as I heard the uncertainty in my voice that I no longer trusted anyone. My caller had known about the blood stones; whoever had walked in while we were talking could be someone from the castle who . . .

The scrape of a key in the lock made my hair stand on end. Someone had followed me. Very slowly I reached over and wrapped my hand around the handle of the fireplace poker. "Who . . . who is it?" I waited for the figure to step through the door, my weapon drawn up in striking position.

"Alix, for God's sake, it's me." Miles came in, his face aglow with the fun of his little trick. "If you insist on hitting something with that poker, please spare this thirty pound bottle of hock."

I was torn between the desire to strike him for giving me such a fright and the longing to throw myself into his arms and feel safe again. I compromised, giving him a quick kiss before sincerely saying, "I have never been so glad to see anyone in my life. And I love your place."

Miles did not fail to show his appreciation for the way I was dressed; the admiring looks at my satin and feathers were warm enough to melt the chill of fear I'd had since the theatre. "It's not my place, my darling, not exactly. Will you hold everything, including that luscious look of being truly glad to see me, while I put this away?"

I poked up the fire and had brandy waiting when he came back. He stopped in the doorway and looked at me, his eyes full of softness. "To see you like that, to have you all to myself like this . . . Alix, I've been like a kid all afternoon, dying to be with you."

He sat beside me and kissed my hand after taking his brandy, and more of the cold apprehension inside me melted. "What about your client? Or was that part of your little tease?"

Miles sighed and rubbed his eyes tiredly. "That part was all too real, I'm afraid, but I finally left him at the club with his large stack of chips to keep him happy. I play a good game of making my clients think I can gamble along with the wealthiest of them, but it's a facade. The manager and I have an arrangement . . ." He stopped and ran his hand softly over my cheek, down to my shoulder. "God, you look beautiful."

"Thank you, kind sir. But, Miles, are you saying none of this . . ." I waved my hand to include the flat and expensive furnishings. ". . . none of this is really yours?"

"Uh-uh. It used to be, but quite a long while back I sold the flat, the Club membership, the expensive sportscar to the firm; it was leased back to me for modest sums so that I could keep up the facade of blueblooded wealth that our clients expect. It's all business." He put his lips to my ear and blew lightly, making me shiver. "This isn't." After a moment or two, he pulled away and lifted my hand with the ring on it. "This morning when I asked you if you really wanted this ring instead of your own . . ."

I put my finger against his mouth. "Miles, I know the ring is paste, and that Lilah probably doesn't know it. It doesn't matter to me—and I certainly have no intention of breaking the news to your mother."

The look of relief on his face made me laugh. "Alix, you little devil, are you telling me that you wasted no time getting our family's heirloom appraised?"

"Shh. It's not the way you think." I told him how it had happened. "As a matter of fact, the jeweler told me it was such a good copy that it would take an expert to tell the difference."

"It had to be a good copy. My mother is quite a connoisseur, but when I had this done to finance her treatments in an Austrian clinic, I was desperate enough to take the chance. I hated fooling her, but . . ." He stopped and said softly, "And you, my sweet, how I hated the thought this morning that you were bound to me by a fraud."

I knew there was nothing fraudulent about the way Miles and I were bound together. "I think it's one of the loveliest things that could happen to me, wearing something that may have given Lilah more years on earth."

Miles looked sad for a moment. "I wish to God it had. The treatments weren't successful, but we had to try. Now, my beautiful darling, I cannot afford to let that expensive wine breathe any longer . . . or shall I save it to go with breakfast?''

The last of the coldness melted. ''Breakfast?'' I whispered with a smile. ''Miles, please tell me you can't cook. It would destroy my image of you completely.''

He kissed me. ''There are many, many things about me that you will find surprising as you get to know me better. Which brings me to something I noticed the moment I walked in—after I noticed that illicit way you're dressed, that is.'' His face was concerned now, all teasing gone. ''Alix, I'm getting so I can see things in your face now. You're upset. You didn't find her, did you?''

''No,'' I said, the coldness coming back at the memory of the theatre incident. I wanted so much to tell Miles everything, but I couldn't. I just couldn't! Damn you, Phillip Coleman, would I ever be able to trust again, as well as love? ''It was just someone's idea of a joke, I guess.''

He looked at me for a long time without saying anything. I knew he was aware I was lying to him. After all, as he'd just said, I couldn't hide my feelings from him any longer. ''Come here,'' he finally said.

I didn't need any more urging to go into his arms. I whispered against his chest, ''Oh, Miles, just hold me. Don't ask me questions. Don't make me think about anything but being with you. I need you. I want you.'' And I love you, my heart added, although I could not say the words. Not yet. Not until I could offer the trust that must come with love for it to be worth anything.''

He held me so tightly I felt as though nothing outside his embrace could ever get to me again. ''Oh, Alix, I don't think I could ever let you go again.''

He didn't even notice the 'again.' But I did.

I once told an editor who was a good friend that if I could come back as a man, I would have every woman I wanted at my feet. ''It's so simple. We can get everything we want by ourselves—and most of us like doing that on our own—except for one thing: romance. Romance! We all yearn for it, everyone of us.''

Phillip had been masterful at providing romance, no question about it, but his motives had been selfish.

Miles, however, sensed that tonight was a time apart from all that had happened between us and set out to make our evening together beautiful and romantic. His motive was simply to make me happy for the moment; mine was the same.

We danced to sentimental band music Miles found with magical ease on the radio, deliciously savoring the leisurely build-up to the pleasures ahead. Miles murmured into my ear after a good deal of enjoyable swaying to the music, ''Do you mind if we dispense with the ostrich feathers? They're lovely but get in the way of nibbling your neck.''

A coal in the lingering fire and the candles Miles had lit flickered over the lovely room. The lace topping my gown did little more than hold up the satin. Miles took a deep breath. ''That may have been a bad move, but it is getting a bit warm in here, don't you think?''

I laughed softly and moved back into his reach. ''Perhaps if you took off your shirt . . .''

His bronze chest caught the dying fire flames. I shivered as he pulled me back into his arms, and the inconsequential barrier of lace between my breasts and his warm flesh only heightened the intimacy.

He lifted my chin and lightly put his mouth on mine. ''I'm almost afraid to move,'' he whispered, ''for fear this mood will end and we'll be at each other throats again.''

I smiled up at him. ''I don't think we'll have time for that, Miles.'' The music began again and our mouths came together, but this time we couldn't part, and the music seemed very far away. I didn't protest as my lover's hands gently slipped the straps of my gown off my shoulders. Nor did I hear the shivery rustle of satin as my one and only trousseau purchase slipped to the floor.

The pretense of dancing over, I slid out of Miles' arms and led him by the hand to the window of the bedroom. ''Look, even the night is full of magic, like this place and us." I watched the moon clear a wispy cloud and pulled Miles' arms around me. "I used to wonder if the world were in a huge volcano, with the moon being the opening to the rest of the universe."

Miles was less interested in my fanciful concepts than in continuing the night's sensual perfection. "In a moment, Big Ben will remind us it's the witching hour. You can hear him this far when the wind's right, telling us we're wasting time talking the night away."

"Silk sheets," I murmured a moment later. "Miles Linwood, you are positively decadent."

"Yes," he whispered, touching his tongue to a hollow on my shoulder that I'd always thought a flaw until now. "Isn't it wonderful? But the silk is no softer than this." He touched his mouth to my breast and captured its tender peak, lingering to enjoy its response to his teasing. "Or this." I felt his mouth softly graze the flatness of my belly, and still lower, it left me trembling weakly.

We held each other for a long time after the act of love had drained us of everything but contentment. "Do you realize," I said sleepily against Miles' chest, "I didn't even hear Big Ben when he told the city it was midnight?"

"Umm. You'll be a true Englishwoman yet. All the things you tourists make such a fuss about will be as normal and ordinary as your heart beating."

I smiled and snuggled closer as I realized Miles had no way of knowing the special effect the sound of bells could have on me. After all, it had been the bells at my uncle's funeral that had started the whole mysterious process of Crislyn and James.

But this had been Miles' and my time, without intrusion. Soon the day would dawn, bringing us new problems and old complexities. But this night had been ours—as lovers, sweet and tender, rather than enemies.

"What are you doing still awake?" Miles kissed me sleepily, but then opened his eyes wide when I returned the kiss without any doubt as to why I wasn't asleep. "I hope you know what you're doing," he whispered, pulling me to him.

I did. I was trying to keep morning from ever coming.

Miles had been modest about his culinary skills. The sausage-rolled crepes were divine, and I felt wonderfully sinful, having wine with breakfast.

We were quiet driving home. "Miles," I finally broke the silence. "What would you do with the Devil's Eye Ruby if it were found?"

"This may surprise you, but Lilah and I feel the same way. We'd donate it to the Crown Jewels for display, as was done with the Black Prince Ruby." He said with a sidewise glance, "Disappointed?"

"No." I shook my head vigorously. "I wouldn't want such a tainted jewel around." I held my breath as we created a third lane to pass one car and avoid a second oncoming one. "I don't suppose I'll ever get used to British driving, Miles."

He laughed. "You have to get used to it, darling. After last night," he clasped my hand warmly and smiled at me, "you can't pretend any more that things aren't real between us."

"Last night was very special, Miles, but it was more unreal than any other part of what's happening." I looked at him levelly. "I have to find Cass before I can have anything real with you, Miles. She's between us, like a thin wall."

"You won't find the cousin you lost long ago. Give it up, Alix, before you get hurt again."

I was silent and withdrawn, hardly aware of the beautiful countryside. When Miles pulled over for gas, I opened up the newspaper he handed me and read it as if it were the most fascinating thing in the world, though I hardly knew what I was reading.

A picture, far toward the back, caught my eye. It was from America's Celebration, showing the famous Tennessee Walking Horse Champion. Dark Satin II! I peered more closely at the photo, surprised to see a stranger atop the horse. Phillip must be thrilled, I thought, forgetting Miles for the moment.

"Alix." I finally came back to hear Miles talking to me. "I just asked you if I can tell Lilah we'll be married before Christmas."

The beautiful night we'd spent in each other's arms had enshrouded me in its magic, but now that I was outside the circle of Miles's arms, other forces were pulling at me. "You're making our sham engagement sound very real," I told him with a flippancy that wasn't real at all.

Miles grabbed my hand and squeezed it hard. "You know as well as I do that it's no more sham than last night was. Not any more."

"Miles, I can't marry you," I said quietly. "Not until I know about Cass. You see, she married someone I didn't trust before I had a chance to tell her my side, and . . ."

Miles jerked his hand away. "Are you saying your cousin and you can tell each other who to love and who isn't worth it? I resent what you're implying here, Alix."

"And I resent the way you act whenever Cass' name comes up. You make no bones about not caring whether she turns up or not and, frankly, I'm beginning to think you'd prefer she didn't. Oh, Miles, let's not fight again. Help me find Cassandra. Go with me to the police."

"You know how I feel about that," Miles said grimly.

"And you know how I feel about Cass," I replied just as grimly. "Besides, I've known my cousin for a hell of a lot longer than I've known you."

Even as I said that, a chill went over me from head to toe. I had known Miles for a long, long time. . . .

Jocko took the brunt of Miles' pique. I cringed when I heard Miles barking at the poor man for the empty port decanter and couldn't help butting in. "Miles, it's not fair to expect one man to take care of this whole, huge mausoleum."

I was in for my share of his irritation. "Alix, when I do decide to turn over the management of my estate to someone, you can be assured it won't be to a colonist." With a little bow to me, Miles got the bottle from the bar cabinet and stalked off to his study.

His limp was quite noticeable this time.

Jocko whispered, "Don't be upset, Miss. I'm used to his moods, but for someone like you, I suppose it's a bit off-putting. Is there anything I can get you, Miss Alix?"

I sighed. "No, Jocko. Except, perhaps, answers to a hundred questions."

"I beg your pardon?"

"Nothing, thank you. Is Madame still asleep or can I look in on her now?"

"She's still asleep, Miss." Jocko's mouth twitched. "She and her friend stayed up and talked and played cards, she said, till quite late." His mouth twitched a touch more. "The sherry decanter, I might add, is rather the worse for it."

I laughed. "Then I think I'll make a quick call to my housekeeper in the States and maybe take a stroll in the garden. The ride made me a bit stiff." Liar, I told myself, that wasn't at all what made you stiff.

Mrs. Goody sounded euphoric over the phone. "Miss Alix, if you could only be here. You wouldn't know the place, with all the goings on. Mr. Axtell painted the upstairs bedrooms like you said, then fixed up those swings in the garden you and Miss Cass used to love so much . . ."

I explained that I still wasn't sure when I'd be back, but Mrs. Goody assured me things couldn't be better at home.

The waning roses in the garden were sad. I saw Friar Gene hard at work, pruning and snipping, and walked up to him. "Good morning. You're very busy today."

The monk grinned and handed me one of the prettiest remaining blooms. I sniffed it and pinned it in my hair, then sang with dramatic pathos for the little fellow's amusement, " 'Tis the la-a-sst rose of summer . . . left bl-ooomm-ing alone . . ."

Friar Gene clapped his hands and laughed gleefully when I'd finished, a tribute I didn't deserve. He screwed up his forehead, and then, in a most remarkable tenor, he sang a perfect imitation of my exaggerated ditty.

Pleased at my applause, he went humming back to his work. As I was about to return inside, his tuneless humming changed to a distinguishable singsong refrain, obviously mimicked.

I froze, not missing a word, knowing I was hearing a riddle, a chant, passed down from James Gerald's time. And after listening to it, I knew it told the hiding place of the Devil's Eye.

> *The one who peers through cross upright*
> *Where once was shot a shaft of might*
> *And eyes of death saw their last light,*
> *Will know where hides a king's delight.*

"Friar Gene." I turned slowly and spoke gently, so as not to startle him, "That's pretty, very pretty." I walked closer. "I like the part about the cross. I like that very much."

He smiled and nodded, then he pulled at the rusty chain around his neck and a heavy cross appeared from under the voluminous robe. With a sigh, he lifted the chain from around his neck and, with a dignity that I had never seen in the little man, knelt, holding the cross out to me. As I felt chills like none I'd ever known go up and down my spine, he intoned in a voice that was not his, but was dearly familiar, "For the next Lady of the Castle, the Cross dear to James Gerald of Bloodstones."

I gave an awkward little curtsy and took the cross. Friar Gene beamed then looked blank for a moment, before getting up and returning to his roses. He was soon happily humming away, as though nothing out of the ordinary had happened, and I was left with the cross and the question of whether or not I had imagined the voice of Brother Jubal.

With the cross nestling against my skin under my suit and blouse, I stopped by to report on my London excursion to Madame Lilah. "Would you believe Cass and I never got together? We chatted on the phone, but there was no dinner and . . .''

I couldn't tell from her bright gaze if she believed me or not. "So you and my son had some time together after all? Perhaps dinner, just the two of you?"

"Um, yes. Well, a drink. I'll confess to eating my way through the pubs of London. And we had breakfast together this morning."

"Ah." Lilah's smile faded. "Poor Alix, working at keeping up that lovely front so I won't know you and Miles argued."

"Lilah, I swear I don't even know what this one was about."

"Jocko said he was into the port. Drunk before lunch . . . tch, tch."

"And we had wine with breakfast."

"How nice," Lilah said abstractedly. "Alix, dear, perhaps you could set the wedding date. I have an idea that's what has poor Miles so woebegone and dejected. What's to stop you from setting the day right away?"

"Well, there's Cass, my cousin."

"But you said she rang you up for this London thing." She looked totally confused. "That's why you drove there yesterday."

"Well, her husband is coming to England."

"I rather got the impression the two of you aren't on very chummy terms."

"We aren't. Phillip and I are definitely not . . . chums."

"Then what's to stop you? You said there was no other family."

"Yes. What's to stop you?"

I whirled around to see Miles leaning against the doorjamb, his eyes bright on mine. "Miles . . ." He knew the ghost of Cass was between us, but I did not want that brought up now to worry Lilah. "Your mother needs a visit from her son. I'm going up to rest for a bit and leave you two alone."

I blew them both kisses and went up to my tower.

I sat on the bed, wishing with all my might that Cass

would suddenly appear in this room, then all my doubts would vanish.

A beam of sunlight shot through my little arrow-slit and the friar's doggerel came to mind. Beam of light. Shaft of might. *"Shaft of might!* An arrow! The 'shaft of might' would be an arrow.''

Where eyes of death saw their last light. Crislyn's eyes. She'd died in this room. ''This room holds the key.'' I pulled the cross from under my blouse and walked as if in a trance to the window and held it ''upright where eyes of death saw their last light.''

It fit into the archer's slit perfectly; no doubt, it had been crafted to do so.

The hole where the ruby might have been set into the cross was the keyhole through which I looked to see the exact spot where the Devil's Eye was buried.

Appropriately enough, it was beneath the altar stone on which countless Linwood heirs had lost their tiny sixth fingers to the lord of the underworld. I closed my eyes, knowing that this final sacrifice had been made for the dead Crislyn, no doubt by James, who knew how she'd hated the ruby, which had been soaked in a century of evil. ''What do you want me to do?'' I whispered to the room. ''What should I do?''

It wasn't going to be made that easy for me. I put the cross with my hidden cache and wearily removed shoes and stockings. At least whoever was haunting the stones at night had something to guard—the Devil's Eye.

My hand paused at my blouse tie. ''Guard? Damnit, that's not a ghost roaming those stones at night. It's someone who's figured out where the Devil's Eye has to be hidden.''

Miles was too bright not to have figured this out by now. I puzzled over what reason he might have for allowing the so-called lady of the stones to haunt his premises un-challenged.

I lay down on the bed, staring at the ceiling and thinking. Should I tell someone about cracking the riddle? Lilah? Miles?

"No, first I must find Cassandra. Then, we'll see about the Devil's Eye." I had all the bad luck I could stand at the moment.

It had been a busy 48 hours. My brain worn out, my body exhausted and the midnight rendezvous still ahead of me, I closed my eyes and slept deeply, neither moving nor dreaming nor remembering that I should be afraid.

20

I suppose Lilah warned Jocko not to disturb me for dinner. When I appeared in the kitchen as he was clearing up, he told me that Miles hadn't made an appearance, either.

I fixed a tray of sandwiches and milk to take back up to my room. "Jocko, I haven't heard anything out of Mrs. Hightower lately. Has she gone off on another modeling job"

"Not that I know of, Miss. She's an odd sort, though, sometimes keeps to herself for days. Other times, she's up here every minute, or after me to play cards with her. She's a nervous lady, no doubt about it. But the Baron tells me she'll be giving up the cottage quite soon."

I added some fruit from the bowl on the kitchen table to my tray. One needed a good deal of sustenance for visiting haunted shrines at midnight. As a matter of fact . . . "I think I'll trouble you for one of those small carafes of wine, Jocko;" I handed him back the glass of milk and made the substitution, knowing he undoubtedly was convinced I was going downhill.

While I waited for the hours to pass, I wrote letters to friends back home, washed out undies and stockings and cleaned out my little closet. Coming across the little cache I'd collected, I laid out everything, each with its own little mysterious meaning, on the bed.

The collection certainly was a curious one. There was the portrait of Crislyn whose face was as much my own as any twin's could be, but there was no mystery there since I knew whose artistry had immortalized her. I also knew the origin of the locket and who had put it in the chest. The cross had divulged its long-hidden secret through Friar Gene.

I looked at the more modern additions—Punkin, with one button eye gone and his mistress God knows where, the passport with Cass' faded photo staring up at me as if in rebuke, and the package of books for Cass.

Crock called right after I'd hastily stuffed everything back into the wardrobe. "Alix? I just talked to Lilah and she said you were totally exhausted. Are you all right?"

"I haven't been on any more unexpected 'trips,' if that's what you mean." I hesitated, then decided to ask a question that might rightfully infuriate the doctor. "Crock, I know I haven't any right to, but do you mind if I ask you a personal question?"

"You ought to know physicians are the only ones allowed to do that, but carry on."

"Well, it's silly, but I have a reason. Is Lilah the only woman in your life?"

Crock chuckled. "Why, no, there's my housekeeper, and my chief nurse who's been with me since the Norman conquest, and my aunt in Cornwall . . ."

"Not that kind of woman, Crock."

"How many kinds are there?"

I laughed. "Well, you know what I mean—a romantic attachment, or someone you occasionally see in town, or take to dinner or . . ."

"I'm fascinated. Well, quite honestly, I'm afraid I'm not what you'd call much of a swinger, Alix. Occasionally, my friends trap me into squiring a widow to something or other, but aside from that . . ." He chuckled. "I'm quite available, if you're asking." At my silence, he added, "I take it you weren't."

"Did your consultation go well yesterday?"

"I was too tired afterward to see anyone, if that's what you're getting at, Alix. Sometime you'll have to tell me why you're asking this, but right now, I'll let you get some sleep. Oh, but first . . ." He asked casually, "How was your evening? Lilah said you didn't get to see your cousin after all. That's too bad."

"Yes, it was too bad."

As I hung up the phone after Crock had wished me a good night, I thought about how no one so far had seemed in the least surprised that Cass hadn't showed up for our 'meeting.'

I had the distinct impression that the surprise would have been if she *had* met me in London!

There wasn't a light in Samantha's stone cottage as I'd hoped there would be. I would have to use the small flash-light I'd stuck in my dark trousers' pocket, but making my way over the uneven path to the stones wasn't much easier with the tiny light. Several times I stumbled and nearly fell.

At the edge of the shrine I stopped, my heart pounding. Was that a shadow behind the altar? I must have been insane to agree to this.

"Put the light away and don't come any closer."

The whisper was sexless and might have come from the night itself. I turned off my flashlight and strained to see the source of the hoarse words. A shadow stepped from behind the tallest stones, and I caught myself before letting out a scream. The moon came out from its cloud cover just then and caught a gleam of brocade and satin and elaborately piled platinum hair. Though the face was shadowed, I knew the figure was flesh and blood.

"You're no real ghost," I said accusingly.

The laugh was a whispery one. "An astute contradiction of terms! Go home, Alixandra. Leave this place, leave England."

"Who are you? Did Cassandra send you to warn me?"

"No matter. Just go. Your cousin's lost to you forever."

I forgot that I might be in danger and moved forward. "Please, just tell me if Cass left England."

The whisper sent shivers through me. "Your cousin will never leave England."

I moved again, and the figure suddenly turned a powerful flash in my face, blinding me. I put my hand over my eyes and stumbled backwards, blinded and disoriented. When I opened my eyes, blinking against the darkness, I saw a movement and as my vision cleared made out the shape of the person I'd just encountered.

The creature was gliding and swaying away from me, through the stones, the wide skirts whispering in the night. And . . . I blinked my eyes again, wondering if I were hallucinating . . . *it was removing its head.*

I moved back, horrified, my eyes shut tight to keep out the terrible vision. When my foot hit a stone and I fell to the rough ground, the breath knocked from me, I was conscious of relief at the welcome blackness that engulfed me.

It couldn't have been more than two minutes before I'd caught my breath and was back to normal, but when I looked around me, there was no sign of the strange figure. Forgetting the nature of my surroundings for a moment, I sat on the altar stone to let my knees stop their knocking and to think. There were a couple of sounds that didn't belong to the quiet night, but I was distracted, at that moment struck by something that threw the whole encounter out of kilter.

"She never asked me for the money," I said aloud. "That doesn't make sense; that doesn't make sense at all." I'd had no intentions of bringing that kind of cash to the rendezvous, but was prepared to arrange for its exchange once I had the information about Cass. But the person in the stones had never once mentioned the money.

I couldn't sit here all night, even if I wanted to. Besides, the thought of the Devil's Eye, not to mention my sacreligious perch on the altar, was creeping up, making me uneasy. A misty rain started to fall, making my egress more imperative. I looked at the towers of the castle jutting against the moody sky, with the hazy moon the kind that inspires howling instead of love songs.

"I can't go back in there tonight. Not now." The idea of mounting the dark stairs to my haunted tower was unthinkable, but I certainly couldn't sit out here till dawn.

I saw then that there was a light in the cottage that hadn't been there before. Samantha must be there after all. Perhaps she'd gotten up to use the bathroom, or . . .

I tried but couldn't make myself go in there, even though my werewolf moon had vanished and a steady rain had begun to fall. If the person parading as the lady of the stones was hiding inside, waiting her chance to leave or . . . just waiting . . .

If it were Samantha, she wouldn't be exactly thrilled to see me, especially in the middle of the night.

I made a quick decision and walked back to the castle, heading for the parking area, wishing my shoes didn't crunch on the gravel quite so noisily. The Ferrari was gone, which wasn't surprising since Miles hadn't been in evidence all afternoon or at dinner. I was quite wet by now and decided the Rolls would just have to put up with the indignity of a sopping driver.

I thought my banging on the door would wake everybody in a five mile radius, but it was a good ten minutes before Neil showed up. I could hear him cursing through the door and saying what he'd do to anyone wanting a drink at this hour. When he flung open the door and saw me standing there, looking like a half-drowned rat, he couldn't say anything.

I grinned through my straggling hair. "Just one teenie-weenie brandy? I know it's a little early—or is it a little late?—but I . . ."

He pulled me in roughly. "Get in here, woman. What the devil are you doing out like this?" I'd started shaking, and he rubbed my hands in his warm ones, then set me in front of a smoldering fire, throwing coals on and looking at me and talking at the same time. "Jesus, you scared me

when I saw you standing there! My first thought was someone's gone and thrown her in the moat."

"The brandy, Neil." My teeth were chattering, and I
drank the burning liquid he brought me gratefully. "What
took you so long to come to the door?"

Neil ran his hand through his already tousled hair. I
noticed the candy-striped pajamas with an inner smile.
"Have you ever heard of folks going to bed and to sleep? If
the dogs hadn't started barking out back, I never would
have heard you. I sleep like the dead." He put his robe
around me. "Christ, you're still shivering like crazy."

"I can't get warm." I didn't tell him it wasn't just
because I was cold from the rain.

"Look, there's no two ways about it. You gotta get into
some dry clothes. Wait here . . ."

"I'm not going anywhere," I called after him.

He reappeared with a fuzzy blue kimono. "This . . .
uh . . . is one of Susie's. She left it when she stayed overnight to look after the place once."

I grinned but didn't tease him. He deserved an
occasional overnight girlfriend. "Umm, feels wonderful.
Mind turning your head for just a minute?" He did and I
was out of the soggy clothes. The blue robe felt warm and
wonderful, like Susie probably did when she warmed Neil's
bed.

"Thanks, Neil. One more tot of brandy and I'll explain
all this."

"Maybe I'd better get one, too. I have a feeling this isn't
going to be a story about you liking to walk in the rain."

You had to trust somebody. And a man who'd just
warmed you inside and out and wore candy-striped pajamas
was a good place to start. I told him about the rendezvous in
town. I told him about the meeting in the stones. I started to,
but didn't, tell him about the Devil's Eye. ". . . so you can
see why I didn't want to go in. I wasn't sure which way the
lady went. It could have been toward the river or into the
castle."

"Jesus. You say there was a light on at Samantha's?"

I stood up from where I'd been leaning into the fire to dry my hair. "Yes." I sat down and stared at Neil. "You think there's a chance it could have been Samantha in that getup?"

"Like Lizzie Borden, our Sammy's not what you'd call a girl scout type. Truth is, I'm surprised she's been so quiet, after the bombshell you and Linwood dropped on her."

I evaded the candid eyes on mine, fussing with my clothes, which, like my hair, had dried by the fire's heat. "I'm all right now, Neil. I'll go back to Bloodstones now. Can I dress in your bedroom?"

Neil reached out and touched my hair, still warm from the blaze. "You're so beautiful, so goddamn beautiful."

"Neil, please don't . . ."

"Oh, I'm not going to make a pass, Alix. You're a . . . a princess, and I'm just an ordinary fellow, a lowbrow that's content to admire you and adore you and wait on you and . . ."

"Neil, cut that out!"

He grinned and dropped my hair—and, to my relief, the serious tone in his voice. "Sorry. It's just that with your hair all fluffy and loose and no makeup and that dumb robe, you're a helluva lot more touchable."

I bent to pick up my shoes that I had warming on the hearth and noticed Neil's feet were incongruously shod in sturdy loafers.

Muddy loafers!

I straightened up slowly, hoping Neil hadn't noticed me staring at his shoes. He hadn't; he was too busy looking out the window. "Thought I heard something . . ." The dogs started. "Those damn mutts! I fed 'em late, just before I went to bed."

The pen was far back in the woods, so there was my explanation for the mud-caked loafers. I sighed. "Neil, if you'll be kind enough to drive me back, I'll send Jocko for the . . . what is it?"

"There's someone at the door. Wait here; I'll be right back. I don't think I locked it after you came in . . ."

He patted my shoulder absently when I leaned close, my earlier fright returning. "Neil, for God's sake, don't leave me. Don't leave me!"

I guess I was prepared for anybody or anything to appear in the door to the room where Neil and I were huddled together in front of the fireplace.

Except Miles.

He wasn't surprised to see me for a logical reason. "Rather indiscreet of you, wasn't it, love, leaving the car parked right out front?" His eyes went from the brandy glasses intimately touching each other to Neil in his boyish pajamas, and then to me. The gaze flickered scornfully over every guilty detail—the flyaway hair, the informal robe, the undies and hose I'd neatly folded and placed in full view on a chair. His words were surprising. "And to think I came out here looking for you. I should have guessed you and Willingham were too cozy to have just met."

Neil stepped forward. "Now look, Linwood, I don't know what the hell you're getting at, but I'll set you straight on one thing. Alix and I are friends, and we were from the first moment she stopped in here to ask how to find your castle. I won't deny I'd sure as hell like to think we could be more than friends, but I'm smart enough to know that's not in the cards." He looked at the protective arm he'd put around me and dropped it suddenly, muttering, "Sorry, Alix."

I leaned over and deliberately kissed Neil's cheek. "Don't be sorry for anything. If Miles chooses to believe the worst, there's nothing we can say to make him change his opinion." My heart sank with the heavy pain of realizing that Miles and I were still far from having the trust that goes with love.

Miles said furiously, "I have a choice about what to think, when I walk in and catch the two of you *in flagrante delieto.*"

Neil put his arm back around my shoulder. "I'm a country boy who doesn't know what that fancy language means, but I get a general idea. And I don't like it worth a . . ."

"Neil, please, I can speak for myself." I turned to Miles. "I was 'in the act' of getting ready to drive back to Bloodstones. I'll get dressed while you apologize to Neil for charging in without so much as a knock." I sailed past my furious fiance into the bedroom and deliberately locked the door behind me.

When I came back out, fully dressed, I found Neil sitting alone in front of the fire.

"Where's Miles?"

Neil lifted his face then, and I saw anger that equalled that I'd seen in Miles. "God help me, probably off somewhere to try to figure out the woman he's in love with." He made a low sound in his throat and jabbed at the coals in the fire. "And I'm trying to do the same thing." He looked up at me. "Why the hell didn't you tell him what really happened instead of letting the poor bastard go off with his heart tied in knots over you?"

Before I could answer, Neil pointed the poker at me accusingly. "Well, I was sitting here trying to figure it out, and I think I've got a handle on you now, Alix. Somewhere along the line some jerk made spaghetti out of that big vulnerable heart of yours, and now you're out to do unto others. Only Linwood was done unto, as well, and you'd better watch out—especially since you're crazy for the guy, like he is for you."

I let the silence go on so long I could hear the coals falling and the hard lump in my throat when I swallowed. I was stunned by the truth in what I was hearing.

"I thought you didn't like Miles."

Neil threw his empty wrapper of Players into the fire, and I handed him my half-pack. "Thanks. I didn't. Maybe I still don't. But that doesn't keep me from admiring some of the things I know about him. Or feeling sorry for him when I see the woman he loves playing soccer with his ego."

I said weakly, "He was the one jumping to conclusions." Neil looked at me without speaking, and I went over to him and put my head on his chest. "You're right. I've been like that with Miles from the start—challenging him on the smallest thing, daring him to do his worst, believe the worst, making no concessions. Neil, what in the world's wrong with me?''

He patted my back like the brotherly friend he had become once again. "Whatever it is, I think it's on the mend. Now, before anyone walks in and misunderstands and we're back on another merry-go-round with me in the middle of two stubborn people, do you want me to go back with you?"

I shook my head and picked up my bag. "No, I'm not frightened any more. Except for what Miles and I might do to each other before it's over."

Neil kissed my temple gently. "I have a feeling it's an even match." He called out softly as I reached the door. "Hey, lady, I love you."

I knew what he meant. "I love you, too—for being here." I smiled at him. "And for calling me a princess, even if sometimes I'm a crazy one."

It was getting light as I drove into the castle's parking grounds. Miles' car was nowhere to be seen, and I guessed he'd gone into London to spend the night at his flat. The rain had given way to a magical half-mist that was made of sparkling dew and mini-rainbows, dispelling the gloom of the previous night. I was getting a stuffy nose but impulsively delayed going up to my room to check on Samantha.

Something about the deserted little cottage bothered me. I knocked and waited only a couple of minutes before going in the unlocked door. "Samantha? Samantha, it's Alix, not a burglar. Yoo-hoo." The room was a mess, with clothes and shoes and suitcases strewn to kingdom come. I could picture the fiery model flinging things hither and yon while cursing the American 'bird' who'd loused up her chances with Miles for good.

"Samantha, are you in there?" I walked noisily back toward the bathroom, where I could hear water running. I raised my voice. It wasn't the shower or the tub running; I was sure she could hear me. "Look, I just wanted to see if you were okay."

Either she was ignoring me or . . .

I looked down and saw that water was seeping under the door. "Oh, my God. Samantha! Open up!"

Assuming the door was locked from the inside, I nearly fell into the room as I pushed the door open. The sink was running over, and I turned off the faucet, noticing the clutter of makeup and toothpaste. Either Samantha had left in a terrible hurry, or . . .

"Thank God," I breathed, not seeing any signs of . . . well, I wasn't sure what. Blood, maybe? I took a final look around before leaving and saw something that brought me to my knees on the tile floor.

It was mud, like what the person in the stones might have tracked in from the shrine.

I got up slowly, looking at the scattered makeup with more interest. Had it been Samantha dressed up as the lady? But how could she have known about the meeting, unless she was the mysterious donor of the ticket?

I knitted my brows, remembering the sharp interest that had suddenly been shown by my mysterious theatre caller when I offered a substantial payment in exchange for information about Cass. With modeling jobs scarce because of her notoriety, Samantha might have needed money badly. She was leaving Kent, maybe even the country.

I walked slowly to the castle and up the stairs to my room, suddenly aware this was the second night in a row I hadn't gotten a normal night's sleep.

I looked at the time, groaned, and fell onto the bed, thankful that Lilah was a late sleeper and Jocko too polite to wonder about guests who slept disgracefully late.

The stuffy nose had progressed to full-blown sniffles, but I decided not to humor the penalty that I fully deserved for running around all night in the rain. I dressed and went downstairs, sure I was the last of the stragglers and ready to apologize to anyone who cared.

There was no need. As I warmed myself at the cozy fire in the great room, Jocko informed me that Madame was a bit under the weather and staying in bed all day.

"Oh, Jocko," I wailed, "I feel awful that I slept late again and haven't been in to see her today."

"She asked me most particularly to tell you she was content dozing off and on without company and that Doctor Crocket had positively exhausted her with silly tests all morning."

I didn't like the sound of that. Sometime later, I must catch Crock alone and find out if Lilah's condition was worsening.

It was difficult, but I casually managed to ask if Miles was around. Jocko shook his head. "I'm sorry, Miss, I don't know quite how to put this, but the Baron never came home last night at all. I'm afraid we can't expect him for lunch, since he hasn't called, as he does when he's returning from London." He looked sideways at me as he tidied up some magazines, I suppose to see if I were shocked by my fiance's unreliable behavior.

If Jocko only knew that my behavior wasn't much more reliable! "Then, if I'm the only one around for lunch, I'd love a tray by the fire."

The bisque and hot popovers were divine. The newspaper Jocko included on my tray provided less appetizing fare. I read about the Queen's loan of her private china to the Royal Pavilion for an exhibit on one hand and about a razor gang attacking a group of tourists on the other.

There was also an unpleasantly detailed account of an unidentified woman's body flound floating in the Thames. Apparently there had been some damage to the limbs, I read with a shudder, when a boat bound for the Winchester landing caught the corpse in its engine.

I put the paper aside with another shudder and tried to forget it by staring at the fire, but the words leaped out from my brain as they had from the page.

. . . *slight build and fair coloring, police have determined the dead woman to be in her late twenties or early thirties. Positive identification has not yet been completed as the fingers were too badly mangled in the motor launch . . .*

. I pushed my bisque away, feeling suddenly nauseated, but forced myself to read further.

. . . for fingerprint study, nor has anyone reported a missing person answering the description. Authorities are attempting now to learn how long the woman has been in the water. Current temperatures in the Thames make it more difficult to fix accurately a time of entry into the river . . .

I threw the paper away from me, fighting the insiduous, horrible suspicion that was uncoiling at the back of my mind. "No, it couldn't be. Not . . . not . . ." I couldn't, wouldn't say her name, for fear the coiled suspicion would become truth if I said the name. I got up, feeling dizzy and depressed by the awful account in the paper.

Not only depressed, I was overcome with guilt at that part saying 'nor has anyone reported a missing person . . .' The body probably wasn't my cousin's, but I should have gone to the authorities, damn it, in spite of Phillip, in spite of everybody. Lilah would have understood, despite Miles' concern for her.

My head started to ache dully from trying to think what I must do. I wanted suddenly, more than anything in the world, to have Miles' arms around me, to have him take care of me. But he hated me now, probably looking on me as an ill-tempered trollop who went from one man's arms to another's.

"Miss Alix, it's Baron Linwood on the phone. He wants to speak to you." Jocko looked at my flushed cheeks with concern. 'You look ill, Miss. I'll ring the doctor as soon as you've spoken with the Baron."

I took the phone from him. "It's all right, Jocko. I'm just catching a cold from the change in weather."

"Well, I'll see to getting you an extra heater for your room and extra blankets."

He hurried off, and I said timidly, "Hello?"

Miles was silent, then said, "I think I must have the wrong party. The lady to whom I wish to speak is firm and assertive."

"Miles, I . . . look, about last night, I didn't . . . ."

"Alix, let's save that for when I see you, the part about us, I mean." Miles sounded bone tired. "This is about something . . . someone else." He paused. "Have you, by chance, seen this morning's papers?"

The burning heat I'd been feeling turned to cold ice. "Miles, if it's about the . . . the body in the river . . ." I took a deep breath. "I've already decided to go to the authorities." He didn't say anything, and I knew he must be trying to think of some tactful way to tell me the body had been identified as Cass. "It's . . . it's Cassandra, isn't it? I can feel you trying to say it."

Miles said heavily, "I'm afraid so, Alix."

I leaned against the cool stone of the wall. "Oh, God." I'd known she wasn't ever coming back. Deep down, I'd known it all along. Numbness held back grief. "How . . . how did you find out about it? You're not even . . . oh, God!" I closed my eyes, seeing staring eyes, tangled hair, mangled hands. "They'll want the next of kin to identify the . . . the remains, won't they? I'll have to come and tell them it's Cass."

"No, Alix. Thank God, you won't have to do that. Phillip is there right now, filling out the papers. Poor guy is still suffering from jet lag and doesn't know what hit him."

"Phillip."

"He got to his hotel here early this morning. I tried to get him at his house in the states after I saw the . . . left the morgue. His housekeeper told me he'd left for London the day before, not even going home first. He started worrying about the passport business and thought he'd better get over here." Miles added tiredly, "I caught him at the hotel she'd mentioned to me."

I couldn't hate Phillip any longer now. "Poor Phillip. I should be there with him."

Miles said quietly, "He told me he was glad you were spared the ordeal. I am, too."

I closed my eyes, blocking out the newspaper account. "She wasn't . . . you could tell it was Cass?"

"Without a doubt, Alix."

I took a deep breath, closing my eyes. "Oh, God. I was afraid of that when I read the description." I tried to pull myself together but found it difficult. "You saw it and went down there so it would not have to be me who . . ." My voice caught. "Thank you, Miles." He had done that, had gone over to a cold morgue and made that hideous identification so I could be spared, so I could be sure at last. "Thank you, Miles," I said again, in a whisper.

Jocko rushed up just then and helped me to the sofa, his jaws quivering with worry. "I'll call Dr. Crockett, Miss. Or do you want me to drive you right over to his clinic?"

I just wanted to lie there and not have to think or decide anything. "No. He can give me something, I'm sure. And don't look so upset, Jocko. I'm not dying. I just have a low threshold for sickness, even a bad cold." The chills started, and I could barely talk for my teeth chattering. Jocko piled on another blanket and heaped more coal on the fire. "I don't know which is worse, Jocko—freezing to death or roasting alive with fever!"

By the time Crock arrived, I was back in the fever stage, and he wasted no time giving me a shot. "There, you'll go to sleep and we'll have this thing licked in no time. I don't ordinarily give high voltage treatment for what you have, but under the circumstances . . ." He patted my arm and got up. "We'll move you upstairs as soon as Jocko has that icebox warm enough."

"I . . . like it down here. You heard about Cassandra, then? How? Have you told Lilah?"

"Not yet. She's had a bad enough day already." He put his hand on my brow, which was already sweating off the fever. "Miles called me right after he talked to you. He was worried and feeling badly that he couldn't break the news in person."

I licked my dry lips. "Crock, did Miles tell you . . . did the police say it was . . . murder?"

"He said they were releasing the remains to your cousin's husband as early as tomorrow. I don't think they found any suggestion of foul play."

I cried out, "Crock, someone killed her! They can't just let it drop."

He said quietly, "Alix, don't get overwrought. Your cousin's husband was wise to let things go without making a big fuss. It's difficult enough having to deal with the most natural death in a foreign country, believe me. Something like this . . ." He spread his hands in an entreating gesture. "It's best to let it go."

Upset as I was, the drug was getting a deep hold on me. "I . . . still . . . think . . . it's crummy."

"That there won't be an investigation?"

"That . . . Cass . . . was   murdered . . . and . . . nobody . . . cared."

"But you cared." Crock tucked the blanket around my chin. "And since you're the one, Lilah tells me, who will benefit from her death, she must have known how much you cared."

"I'm not . . . it's Phillip who . . . get . . . all . . ."

I was too sound asleep to hear Crock tiptoe off to check on Lilah and then return to sit up and keep the fire going while I slept.

There were whispering voices all around me. I kept my eyes closed and said clearly, "Crock, am I in the present? Am I Alix?"

"You are," the doctor said softly. "I'm sorry we woke you." His voice changed. "Professor Coleman was just letting us know that he doesn't think you're being properly taken care of."

My eyes sprang open. "Phillip!" And then I saw a large shadow near the fireplace. "Miles. I didn't know you'd be driving back this evening."

"Oh, yes. But it's not evening, darling; it's almost midnight. Are you feeling better?"

I felt rather than saw Phillip's twitch at the 'darling.' Had no one told him of the Linwood/Manning betrothal, I wondered? "Much, thanks to Crock." I could feel Phillip staring at me and made myself look at him. "I'm so sorry,

Phillip. You know how much I wanted to see her again and make things up between us.''

He cleared his throat. God, the man was tired. ''Me, too. More than anything, I wanted the same thing.'' He cleared his throat again. ''Linwood says he can arrange for the memorial to be held at Hever Chapel.'' He smiled a grey smile. ''Anne Boleyn's old place of worship. I think Cass might have liked that, don't you, Alix?''

''I guess so.'' My eyes closed again. ''You aren't thinking of an . . . open casket, are you, Phillip?''

''It's a memorial, Alix, not a funeral. Cass was . . . cremated this afternoon.''

''I want the bells,'' I said suddenly. ''When we hold the service, I want the bells to sound for Cassandra.''

Crock moved toward me. ''Alix, you know how that can . . .'' He stopped and said less vehemently, ''I don't think that's a good idea.''

Phillip said sharply, ''Alix is tired. And we haven't had a chance to talk. I'll take her up to her room.''

Miles said coolly, ''You missed your chance, Coleman. I'll look after Alix from now on.''

I looked at him in surprise. How long had Miles known about Phillip and me?

Phillip looked from one of us to the other, totally bemused. ''Alix, I don't understand. Everyone's talking as if you're planning to stay in England. After this terrible tragedy, I'd hoped we could go home together, be of some comfort to each other in our loss.'' He moved closer and knelt at my side. ''With your uncle gone, and now Cass lost to us both forever, you have no family, no one but me.''

I expected Miles to make more of a scene about it, but he only stated mildly, ''Lilah looks on Alix like a daughter, Professor Coleman.'' His eyes met mine with a question. ''If all of us here have our way, she'll be part of our family from now on.''

Phillip acted as if he hadn't heard. ''Alix, leave with me tomorrow, after the service. I'm leaving my wife here; I can't lose you to Bloodstones, too.''

369

Crock said firmly, "Professor Coleman, I don't think Alix needs this at the moment, nor is there any question of her leaving tomorrow. Not only is she ill, she's had a tremendous shock. And you look none too well yourself," he added, eyeing Phillip's haggard, though still handsome face.

Phillip's eyes stayed on my face. "If it seems I'm not as grieved by Cass' death as I ought to be, Alix can tell you we've had . . . problems. We lived together, my wife and I, but we parted emotionally years ago. And my wife's trip to England may have been the official final step. I'd already adjusted to Cass' loss before I came here, but I never can adjust to losing you again, Alix. I didn't the first time, and I can't now."

Crock stepped forward, his blue eyes full of indignation. "Professor Coleman, this is most inappropriate under the circumstances! I must insist, on the grounds of human decency, that you . . ."

Miles put a steely hand on the doctor's pudgy arm. "Take it easy, Crock. The man's just emotionally and physically wrecked from his ordeal. Let him have his privacy with Alix."

The doctor looked as incredulous as I'm sure I did. "Miles, what do you think you're . . ." At a look from the younger man, the doctor said more calmly, "Very well. Why don't you come with me to look in on Lilah. I know she's still awake after sleeping all day, and it's probably time we caught her up on things."

Phillip didn't seem to think it unusual that the two of us were left alone, but I was both baffled and indignant. "Phillip, I'm totally outraged and disgusted at your behavior."

He caught my hand in his. "I don't care about these people, Alix, and neither should you. You and I can have a fresh start now. Cass would want it, too, Alix."

I jerked my hand away. "Phillip, you're insane! And talking about this, about you and me, after Cass has just been . . ." I turned my face away, but not, I'm sure, before he saw the revulsion there. "I'm sick, Phillip, and you're . . ." I almost said "making me sicker," but didn't. Phillip heard them anyway, I think. "Just leave me alone. And for God's sake, don't talk like this anymore, if not for Cass' sake, then for mine. After the service tomorrow, you can go back to your life, and I honestly hope never to see you again."

Phillip got up slowly, and I could feel a change in him without looking. It was in his voice, too—a resignation, a finality perhaps. "I see. I'd hoped you'd feel differently now. I thought that anger you showed when I saw you at your uncle's house was just injured pride, loyalty to Cass, perhaps."

With a deep sigh I said, "Phillip, you've always managed to think what you wanted to think."

As if he hadn't heard me, he said, "It's really too bad. I never felt right about the money—Cass getting it all and you getting a pittance, which your uncle's place is, after all. Compared to our horse farm, it's nothing."

"I don't believe this," I whispered. "What on earth do you think you're doing? Trying to buy me back with Cassandra's money?"

"You're overreacting, as usual, Alix. I only meant that I had fantasies of sharing everything with you, since it's mine now." His hand went to my hair, sending a shiver of revulsion through me. His voice was soft, though I still heard the odd note of regret, as though he were speaking of the past. "I could see you, at my side, on Dark Satin, your hair flying in the wind, your eyes sparkling. That horse is a champion, Alix, a thoroughbred like you. I could see you in riding habits of rich suedes and velvets. How often I thought of how you'd look riding in the ring, the beautiful darling of the shows and . . ." He stopped. "Why are you staring at me like that?"

I said slowly, "I'm remembering the picture I saw of you and Dark Satin II riding up to collect the Grand Championship trophy. Only, it wasn't . . ."

Crock came in just then, so I didn't see the look on

Phillip's face. "Sorry to break up your little chat, but Alix needs some rest and quiet if she wants to try to make the service tomorrow."

Phillip said quickly, "I'll take her up."

Crock said amiably, "That's good of you, Professor—may I call you Phillip?—but Jocko is waiting to do just that. Besides, Miles and I would like to have a little talk with you about something that concerns us, something we can see you share our concern about." Crock winked at Phillip over my head and indicated me as the 'concern.' I didn't know whether I was more bewildered or furious.

"Crock, what on earth are you . . ."

The doctor soothed me in the voice one uses on mental patients that are being coaxed back into their padded cells. "There, there, my dear, I know how upset you can get. And you'll be happy to know Lilah and I discussed the business of the bells and will see they're rung at the memorial for your cousin—though we know how much they upset you."

Before I knew what was happening, I was bundled into Jocko's care and on my way to bed in the tower.

"Jocko," I said about halfway there, "please stop for a moment. I'm . . . I'm . . ." I groped for some reason to send him to the kitchen without his being suspicious. ". . . dying for some of that herb tea you keep in the fridge. You know, with the mint, and lots of ice if you can spare it . . ."

The butler stopped. "I can bring you some after we have you settled, Miss."

"No! I mean, I'll be asleep the moment I hit the pillow, Jocko, but how I crave just one wee glass of that tea. I'll wait right here while you fetch it and then we can go up. Jocko," I added in a voice of authority, "I'm not budging till you bring me that tea."

The poor fellow went off, having no idea I knew the pitcher stood near-empty and more would have to be brewed, giving me time to do what I wanted to do.

There was a perfect spot, next to the huge fern just outside the door the great room. I had a view of everyone and could hear perfectly.

The first voice I heard was Crock's. "We're very worried, Phillip; that much we can tell you. Poor Alix has gotten deeper and deeper into her sad delusions since I've known her." He lifted his brandy and smiled. "The dear girl fancies herself some sort of . . . ah, link to the past."

Miles added to the perfidy. "We've humored her, of course, in this strange compulsion of hers to follow my ancestor's first wife's tragic course. There are similarities between the two which, I'm afraid, poor Alix has exaggerated out of proportion."

Phillip had an air of deadly stillness. "She was always unstable emotionally, always looking for something or someone to cling to. But you mentioned something about the bells, how they have some sort of bizarre effect on her."

Crock said solicitously, "There are other things, too. The poor child think she's living the tragic life of Crislyn step by step to its end. All sorts of things can trigger the unfortunate young woman's hallucinations." He looked down into his glass. "Miles, at my suggestion, showed a romantic interest, and there was even some talk of marriage. It seemed the reasonable way to keep her from doing something rash."

"Poor Alix." Phillip looked so pitying I wanted to run out and choke him. "But it's not really her fault, you know. She and Cass were brought up on pap about fairy tale princesses and living forever happy in some beautiful castle." Phillip took the new brandy Miles brought him and looked around the huge room. "Easy to see how her over-active imagination could go to work in a place like this."

Miles said quietly, "Phillip, it's more than a grown-up child's leftover fantasies. Alix really thinks she was Crislyn, and that I was James. She could . . ." He looked at the doctor. "Tell him Crock. I still can't accept it."

"Alix is so deeply convinced that she's living the past at times that she could, through the strength of her own delusion, reenact her own murder!"

"She's acted out many of Crislyn's other tragedies," Miles said sadly.

"Reenact her own murder!" Phillip's hand was white on his brandy snifter. "But how?"

A new voice spoke from the highbacked chair facing the fire. I couldn't believe it. "It's said that James smothered Crislyn in her bed when the infant son was born without the Linwood mark. He used a pillow, even as the newborn baby cried in a nearby cradle, and the midwife, who helplessly stood by, was later quieted by his marrying her."

I let out a little gasp, but no one heard it. My horror was not so much for the story I heard as the fact that its narrator was Madame Lilah.

Crock put his hand on Phillip's shoulder. "Don't worry, old chap. Knowing how her cousin's death might send her off again, might even cause her to do something dreadful to make her identification with Crislyn hideously real, I took precautions."

I froze in my concentrated stance. Precautions?

Phillip said it for me. "Precautions?"

Miles said, watching Phillip's face with those vivid eyes that were part of every dream I had, waking and sleeping, "We decided it was best to sedate her, Crock is sending something up later with Jocko."

Phillip said huffily, "I'm not sure I care for this high-handed treatment of my wife's cousin."

Miles said in a velvety voice, "We just want her to be safe and well when we send her home to you, Coleman."

I took a deep breath, wishing I would hear Jocko returning so I could leave this horrible eavesdropping.

"Poor Alix." Phillip's voice oozed sympathy. "Cass and I always felt badly about her exclusion from the Manning fortune. I'll see to it that she's cared for properly back in the States. As a matter of fact," he burst out with a patronizing tone, "I know she had some modest plans for seeing to it that this place was preserved. Perhaps when things are settled." Bribery, I thought, with gritted teeth. Pure bribery.

Lilah said in a thin voice, "That's very kind, Professor Coleman. You can be sure we're very grateful." I saw Phillip leaning over Lilah's hand, all that was visible of her, just as I heard the squeak of the kitchen door.

As Jocko came to retrieve my drooping form, I decided I would have been a spectacular actress if I had not decided to write novels.

No one—not even the sensitive butler who was, as far as I could tell, the only non-traitorous friend I had left in the castle—could tell my heart had crumbled into a million pieces that sitll lay just outside the great room under a large fern.

"Jocko." I looked from the glass of tea back to the long face that bent over me like that of a solicitous father. "Did Dr. Crocket give you anything to give me before I went to sleep?"

The butler shook his head. "Why, no, Miss. Do you think you'll be needing something? If so, I'll just . . ."

"This tea you fixed for me." I held it to my lips, my eyes holding his. "It has only the usual ingredients."

Jocko looked a bit odd, then nodded. "Only the mint, Miss."

I drank it down and handed him the empty glass. "Good-night, Jocko. I wish you'd do me one last favor."

"What's that, Miss?" He paused at the door.

"I wish you'd seal in the bottom of the stairs like they did for Henry VIII. I feel very much alone here tonight."

He gave a slight smile. "You've only to call or ring, Miss. Good-night."

If there was a sedative, I wasn't feeling it. My dozing was fitful. I knew I was still a little feverish, but I had no intention of calling Crock.

There was a sound on the bottom stair, and then on the second. I stared into the darkness. My God, who would be coming up here now—worse, why?

I willed myself not to count the approaching footsteps, but though there was no sound from the person who stood just outside my door, I turned my head at the exact time the knob turned. "James? James, you've come at last. Our baby—our son—is born!"

21

It hadn't been an easy birth.

I looked at the woman bending over the crib. "Meuriel, tell him to come in. Tell him I want him to be with me, to see our son. Tell James I need him, please."

She straightened up and came over to tower over me. I could see the triumph in her face now that she was strong and I was weak.

"He can't come in now. I'm not finished with the dressing." Still looking at me, her eyes bright with evil, she called out loudly, "I'm sorry, my lord, but it wouldn't do for you to come in now. Your lady is quite weak and in great pain."

I struggled to call to him, but no sounds would come. Meuriel smiled and said with fake concern, "I sent Brother Jubal for medicine. Your wife is . . . not doing well."

The strength it took to will James to enter in spite of what he heard drained me of my last bit of energy. I fell back on the pillows, weak and defeated. "Liar! You sent Brother Jubal away so he couldn't protect me from you."

The silence from the other side of the door was heavy. Meuriel walked back over to me. "See? Your loving husband has gone back to his ale and, no doubt, the new pastie cook, whose bosom, I'm told, rivals her strawberry tarts.''

I lay back upon my pillows, exhausted. ''Meuriel, by all that's merciful, if you will not allow me to see my husband or have Brother Jubal as I'd asked, at least let me see my son.'' I looked over at the crib eagerly. ''Is he marked?''

''The tiniest suggestion of the Linwood extra finger.'' Meuriel leaned down to the small figure in the crib. ''Though he looks like you as well.''

''Let me hold him.'' I turned my head and watched, unbelieving, as Meuriel calmly picked up a sharp knife from the table beside the bed. ''What are you doing? Meuriel . . . my God, no! You can't . . ! What are you doing to my son?''

She straightened up, laid down the knife, and dropped a small bit of stained white linen in the basket of soiled cloths. ''Don't worry; he didn't feel it in the least. Not even a whimper. Such a tiny shred of flesh . . .''

I screamed at her, ''You're a fiend! A madwoman! My son is the heir of Bloodstones, damn you! I'll tell them what you did; you'll never get away with this.'' She was coming toward me, and I saw with horror that there was saliva at the corners of her red mouth. How she loved being in control of my life, of hurting me through my son and my destroyed hopes for him!

''You'll never tell anyone,'' she said in a menacing tone. ''Your husband won't tell anyone, either, because he won't know exactly what happened. He'll never be sure the child's hand wasn't injured during birth, as I will tell him. You see, I put a bit of a potion in his ale. He's down there now getting stewed like a nervous rabbit because he doesn't know what to expect.''

''Why? Why are you doing this? It must be more than hating me, surely.''

''I want your place, Crislyn. I want it to be my son who has this castle, my dresses that sweep grandly down the stairs, my body that warms your precious James.'' The pink tongue licked the scarlet mouth, and I felt sick. ''I've heard the two of you up here, yes, rutting like two pigs in your own love bath." I looked at her in horror. "Oh, yes, I sneaked up here many a night and lay against that cold door, hearing the pair of you. And every time you moaned when he drained his seed in you, it was really me it was happening to. *Me!*"

If only I had the strength . . . but I could only lie there, knowing my time was ebbing. How I strained to reach the quiet, strong part of me that Jubal had taught me to know. I willed my mind to fight, though my body was useless. "You knew my grandmum, Meuriel," I said quietly, as she approached, her face full of venom. "Like her, I know many secrets. Though I've never turned my talents to hurting others, I won't rest until I avenge my death at your hands and the theft of my son's birthright." My death? Why did I say that?

The handsome face showed fear, then resumed its hateful expression. "You're not at full power, witch. You can't hurt me. You're weak and powerless and . . ." She lunged at me, and the pillow at my side was now choking the life from me, causing sparks to light to float and explode in my head. With all my strength, I cried out the curse of a mother whose son has been cheated of both his mother and his property.

The black void in which my head was encased was tempting, so tempting. I felt the urge to stop fighting, to let this wondrous nothingness seep into my soul and heal every pain.

It was like being in Hans' picture of shooting stars and floating planets and heavenly peace. There was no pain, no worry; all I had to do was wait. The sound of the bells from the chapel blended with the floating peace. Someday, somewhere, they would be heard. No need to hurry. Time has no meaning nor claim on me.

I hear the voice and I know my time has come to awaken.

"Alix! Alix, for God's sake, say something!"

I opened my eyes, noticing the strange little sparkles

weren't there against the black nothingness anymore. But whose hoarse, croaking voice was the one that called me as if from far, far away? "James?"

"It's Miles, my darling. And Crock is here with us to make sure you're truly all right."

I smiled at him. "Miles. Then I didn't die after all. I'm back here with you."

He kissed me. "Forever and always. Just try to get away."

"Miles, it was awful. That dreadful woman, that midwife, Meuriel, killed Crislyn. It wasn't James, as everyone thought. And the baby she had—he really was James' own son, only that dreadful woman took a knife and . . ."

"I know, darling, I know."

I stared at him. "You know? But how?"

Miles said quietly, "We found—or rather the police did—the prayer book among Phillip's things, with the letter you found that day in the Priest's Hole. He got his hands on it just before the cave-in."

"Phillip's things?"

Miles looked at the doctor, who nodded in answer to an unspoken question. "It was Phillip all along, Alix, but more of that later. The so-called, famous 'confession' James Gerald Linwood was alleged to have left wasn't a confession at all."

"I know. Meuriel was the one who murdered Crislyn." At Miles' questioning look, I said hastily, "Just a feeling. Go on. Tell me what else is in the letter from James."

"Well, thanks to Brother Jubal, he finally realized it was Meuriel who had betrayed his trust, not Crislyn. God knows what the poor man suffered when he realized the whole truth."

Crock broke in. "It was too late, of course. Meuriel wasn't taking any chances. She sent for the sheriff, but not before poisoning her husband so she could explain how he confessed everything and took his own life. But she didn't count on James locking himself in the chapel to write the true story and entrust the secret of where he'd buried the

Devil's eye to Jubal. He wrote that it would separate the good from the evil from then on, the greedy from the honest.''

"There wasn't any mention of Crislyn's child?"

Miles put his hand on mine. "There was too much guilt, no doubt, and the boy was part of a new family that wanted to get far away from the scheming Meuriel. Brother Jubal made all the names part of the records, though. It's all there." He smiled at me. "That new family, of course, became your ancestors."

I turned my head away. "Poor James."

"The hell with that," Miles said. "He didn't know much about women, damn him, and I seem to have inherited that failing."

I put my hand on his cheek. "I think you're a decided improvement over James."

He put my hand against his lips and looked at me in a way that made Crock clear his throat and shuffle his feet. "I have to ask you, Alix. When you learned where the ruby was, why didn't you go for it? You could have, easily."

I shuddered. "I never even want to see that awful thing. I know it's evil."

Crock said with a smile. "Miles held his breath when he found out Friar Gene had divulged the hiding place to you. And when he saw you leave the blood stones that night and go to Willingham . . .''

I gasped, "Oh, no! You thought I . . . oh." I smiled at Miles and said softly, "You thought I was a thief as well as unfaithful."

"Not for long," Miles told me.

"By the way, you two haven't told me how you happened to be up here just in time to rescue me from . . . from . . ." I met Crock's eyes and finished, ". . . that awful nightmare about Meuriel."

Miles said quietly, "Phillip was trying to smother you, Alix."

I closed my eyes, remembering the smothering blackness, the strong hands that were Meuriel's—and somehow

Phillip's, too. "Oh, no. It's because of the picture I saw. He wasn't riding Dark Satin; it was another man. I could point out that he could have been away from the States at the time, though he pretended he was an ocean away from all of us and even had his housekeeper believing it." I opened my eyes. "I knew when I saw the publicity photo of the Championship that something was all wrong. Phillip is too much of an egomaniac to have let someone else ride Dark Satin for that important event." I rubbed my head wearily. "There's so much I still don't understand. Like, for instance, where Phillip is now."

Miles said tightly, "If it were left to me, he'd be in Hell where he belongs, but Crock wouldn't let me throw the bastard down the stairs like I wanted. Something about a Hippocratic oath or the like forbidding our doing that, even to someone who's just tried to smother the woman you love."

I felt afraid again. "He escaped? Phillip is out there somewhere?"

Crock chuckled. "He headed straight for the Medway, where he stashed the little motorboat he's been using to get here along with his accomplice. The police are planning a bit of a surprise for the chap."

"Wait a minute, Crock. Slow down. Back up to 'accomplice.' Let me guess—Samantha; right?"

"Wrong." Miles kissed me on the tip of the nose. "You always were anxious to prosecute that poor woman, but she's alive and well, somewhere in Cannes."

"But she left all her clothes, even her makeup."

"I think she's found someone to provide a new wardrobe for her, a gentleman with far more ready cash than I." Miles grinned at me. "Are you bound and determined to have us drag the moat?"

Crock said, "Tell her about the Wainwright woman, Miles, and stop teasing Alix."

"You're right; it's not a teasing matter. It seems, Alix, that Phillip had been mixed up with some pretty grim types over here. I don't know how serious his book research every summer in Oxford really was. We do know now he may have been indirectly responsible for the bomb attack here and maybe some others on country estates like ours."

I gasped. "Phillip? Are you saying he joined a terrorist group?"

'Not exactly 'joined.' 'Supported' is a better word—with Cassandra's money, which may be one of the reasons things weren't too rosy between the two of them." Miles paused. "Or maybe she found out about his mistress, the Wainwright woman. She was not without charm, though she had a deadly poisonous hatred for British gentry shared by her American lover. Phillip somehow felt that by supporting his anti-establishment friends with his aristocratic wife's money he was providing a moral equivalence. It gathered momentum in his head. Maybe it even became a cause justifying murder."

My mind wasn't up to this. "Wait a minute. You said murder. Do you mean Phillip killed Cassandra?"

Crock looked at Miles and back at me. "You'll have to know this sooner or later, Alix. We're pretty sure Phillip did kill your cousin, but the woman in the Thames was not Cassandra Manning Coleman. It was Phillip's mistress, Patsy Wainwright, a top member of an underground group of terrorists. She went by other names, of course." He paused. "One of them was that of Cassandra Manning Coleman."

I gasped. Then, I looked at Miles. "It wasn't Cass who came here, then? It was this Wainwright woman? But why did you accept her as Cass? And when you identified the body . . ." I shook my head to clear it. "But of course Phillip made the official identification. And I'm beginning to see why it was in his best interest to say the corpse from the Thames was Cassandra's."

"I accepted the woman as Cass because that's how she came here. She was an actress, a trained Shakespearean one, with the extra advantage of two things. First, Phillip was coaching her to appear here in Cassandra's stead so that she could search for the Devil's Eye Ruby. She had the same general coloring, features, hair. Southern accents are the easiest for English actress to imitate. Just think of Vivien Leigh as Scarlett O'Hara. Second, she had posed as a guide here, learning enough about Bloodstones, before she disappeared after the bombing, to appear to be a serious Anglophile.''

"But why would Phillip kill her after everything went so smoothly? I'm guessing the woman took advantage of the ghost legends to search the stones at night. What advantage would Phillip have if she were dead?''

Miles put his hand on my shoulder. "Can't you guess? She found out about you, my darling. And she'd already heard from Phillip about Cass threatening to change her will and leave most of her money to you. Patsy Wainwright desperately wanted to find the Devil's Eye Ruby; it would give her wealth that Phillip couldn't touch. Patsy wasn't dumb; she knew her lover was capable of rewarding her almost perfect masquerade by killing her off as the pseudo-Cass and being free then to marry you, thus covering all possibilities.''

"You keep talking about a new will, but there wasn't one—or not one I know of.''

Crock said, "The police have followed through on Miles' suggestion that your cousin's lawyer be contacted. he said he helped her draw up the new will in your behalf. Unfortunately, she took both the original and the copy with her. The lawyer—and Miles and I—are positive Phillip made sure they'll never be found.''

"Like Cass' body,'' I said dully. "That's the one thing you both have been skirting. If the body we were planning to memorialize tomorrow is Patsy Wainwright's, that means Cass is lying cold and alone in some spot, God knows where!''

Miles pulled me to him, his lips warm on my hair. "Darling Alix, we're so sorry, but maybe Phillip will tell us where—''

The explosion rocked the tower room and left us gaping at one another till the pounding on the stairs turned into the young police officer in charge of the investigation.

"Captain Linwood," he said breathlessly, "the target was duly tagged and kept within apprehending distance, but I'm afraid he got away in the end, sir."

"He blew himself and his boat to kingdom come," Miles guessed, and glanced at the officer for confirmation. "I'm sorry, Alix."

"Don't be sorry," I whispered. "The Phillip I knew never existed. And the one Cass knew shouldn't have."

Miles said to the young officer. "It might be better and simpler, Jenkins, if we gear the post-mortem reports to the Wainright woman and her gang. The American wasn't ever a registered part of it, after all. And he's dead."

I whispered, "Thank you, Miles." He couldn't know how much it meant not to have Phillip made internationally infamous.

Crock said softly, "Alix, I wish we could hold out hope that your cousin is still alive somewhere, but we all know better."

I wanted to weep. "Poor Cass. God knows what he did with her body." I wiped my eyes. "You said she—I mean the woman we thought was Cass—was cremated. How did they find out it wasn't my cousin after all?"

"Our research on Phillip had turned up his connection with the Wainright woman. After Phillip left the morgue, I suggested that they contact some of her kin. A relative gave us a positive identification. Once we were sure Phillip had lied, we decided to stay quiet and find out why. After that, it was easy enough to put the pieces together."

Crock said with apologetic tones, "I hope you don't mind the fact that we painted you as a bird one foot out of the cage to Phillip. The police told Miles we needed more of a case and that you might do well as the bait for trapping him."

I sighed. "It's true, eavesdroppers seldom hear good about themselves."

Miles kissed me soundly, not paying attention when Crock whistled and sang and did everything possible to cover his embarrassment at our undisguised passion for each other. "That's for not even asking about the Devil's Eye."

"Oh, dear, I keep forgetting about that dreadful thing. Did I let everyone down terribly by not going out and digging it up in the dark of night? You keep bringing it up, as if you're disappointed in me."

Miles laughed. "Disappointed isn't the word I'd choose. I have to confess, though, Lilah and I—and, yes, Jocko, too—kept holding our breath to see if you'd find some creative cover like the fake Cassandra's 'lady' to search for the ruby. It's been our secret that it's safe far from here."

I didn't laugh with him. "It was Phillip I met that night in the stones, wasn't it? He'd heard Patsy making our assignation over the phone when he walked in on her. God, I should have remembered the static had the same quality that was in his so-called call from Tennessee."

"He knew then he couldn't trust Patsy any longer. Just as she'd decided her life wasn't worth much to Phillip any more, now that she'd established Cass' disappearance, You offered money. She probably would have told you everything."

"So Phillip killed her that night, after he'd found out she was in touch with me." I felt a heavy weight inside. "In a way, I caused Patsy's death, didn't I?"

Crock said gravely, "She was a terrorist, Alix. One of the bombs she helped set in some harmless tourist center killed seven people, including two children."

Miles looked at me and said to the doctor, "I think Alix has had all she can handle for now, Crock. Let us have a little time by ourselves, now, if you will."

Crock kissed me, and I said softly, looking into the eyes that were at least as old as mine and Miles', "You were there like you promised, Crock. I thank you for that."

After he squeezed my hand and left, Miles came closer. "It's over, Alix." He kissed my fingers, one by one. "It's just you and me now. No more Crislyn. No more James."

I sighed. "I know. I'll miss her, Miles. And James, too."

He gave me a long kiss that made it hard to think of anything else, even the two dark parts in my mind that still restricted my joy in finally reaching the end of the tunnel. "Miles." I waited until after the breathless kiss from necessity. "There's something I have to tell you. We each have a right to our pasts, but there's something in mine that has to be out in the open."

"Umm. You posed in the nude for a notorious magazine."

"Besides that. This concerns Phillip. And, well—you, too, I suppose."

He pulled back and looked at me, his eyes serious on mine. "You don't have to tell me, Alix. I already know about you and Phillip. And beyond that." He lifted my hand to his lips. "He never knew, did he? What he missed by losing you?"

I took a deep breath. I didn't have to tell him! "Maybe that's why everything happened as it did—because he wasn't meant to know." I took another deep breath. "What will Lilah think about it?"

He held my hands in the tight warmth of his. "She knows. And she may have decided to stick around another year or two—or even a decade—to see how things go. We both love you very much, Alix," Miles said simply. "Like the inscription James had on his tombstone: 'Let Death not be the great divider.' "

I breathed out, unable to contain my inner happiness. "That's beautiful. Poor Crislyn, never to know the sensitive soul of James. They had so little time together, after all their battles."

Miles took me into his arms. "Don't you think we can make up what they missed in our lifetime?"

I said softly as his lips closed over mine, "Make that two lifetimes—theirs and ours!"

The other dark part in my mind, the part that grieved for Cass and longed for an answer to many questions about her disappearance, overshadowed the preparations for my wedding. There would be a very special guest or two flying in soon to help celebrate, but I still agonized over Cass' body lying cold and forgotten in some unmarked grave.

A few days before my marriage, I took all of my contra-band from the bottom of the wardrobe—or what was left of it. The police had been given Cass' passport, since Patsy had used it to carry out her impersonation, and the portrait of Crislyn hung in the refectory in a handsome gilt frame, right next to James.

I confess to a tear or two when I held Punkin to my cheek and thought of Phillip's callous attention to detail in such things concerning Cass. When I put him back, I saw the books I'd been meant to autograph and, on a sudden impulse, decided to sign them for my cousin now. When we found her secret grave and buried her properly, I'd see that were sealed away with her, along with Punkin, as a symbolic gesture of final peace between us.

The knot on the package had become too tight. I finally took my scissors and snipped and all of my books went tumbling to the floor. *Daughter of Loneliness* fell open as it struck the floor.

How could I have forgotten all those games Cass and I had played, pretending we were spies, foreign agents, clever detectives? Our favorite way of sending messages had always been straight out of a "B" movie. We'd cut out a square of pages from an old book, making a perfect hollow space for our secret papers.

The letter taped neatly in the hollowed-out square had my name on it in Cass' writing. I read it and, after a numbing moment to collect myself, called Miles. "Darling, will you have someone contact the Williamson County Sheriff's Department in Franklin, Tennessee?" I swallowed hard. "I know where they can find Cassandra."

The will was with her letter, but that didn't matter to me.

The call came several hours later and Miles held my hand while the authorities told me they'd found Cass' body, right where I'd told them it would be—in the dark, rich soil floor of the first Dark Satin's stall.

Small comfort it was, but I learned I couldn't have saved Cass even if I'd remembered about the book trick. She'd been beaten to death with a shovel at least two days before Uncle Porter's funeral.

Like Meg, I thought suddenly. Cass had been buried like Meg.

This part still brings me pain. It's all I can do to force myself to read Cassandra's last words on this earth, but Miles and Lilah urged me to include them in my account of everything that happened. Only the Devil's Eye will be made public on exhibit in London; after this, Cass' letter will remain private.

Incidentally, the tearstains are mine.

Dear, dear Alix,

> *After reading your books (especially this one), I know you have not changed. Nor have I, and if that is so, neither has our love for each other. Only the circumstances have altered, and I am at last determined that you shall be my close confidante again, as you were so many times in the past. We've been so foolish, Alix!*
>
> *I grow more miserable with each passing year. My life is empty, my marriage a mockery. And now, at last, I am forced to take steps to change both.*
>
> *It's Phillip, Alix. You did try to warn me about him. Just think how much he influenced our lives from the beginning. First, he ruined your academic dreams (yes, I finally learned about that, years after you'd gone and the hurt between us was too deep to heal—or I thought it was). Then he made my dream of marriage a nightmare of lies and disgust.*
>
> *Lies, lies, and more lies. Even Phillip's doctorate came as a result of a plagiarized dissertation, Alix, but that was not the worst . . .*
>
> *I finally threatened to expose him to the Board*

at the University. He reluctantly decided to resign, especially after he found out his contract was not going to be renewed anyway.

By this time, I had learned by accident that he was involved with a fanatical group of activists in Oxford. The sabbatical leaves and all his time there had been just an excuse to visit his mistress, one of the underground terrorists. (Alix, she was one of those who helped blow up a busload of children!).

I happened on a letter from this woman and confronted Phillip. We quarreled horribly, right there in the stable with the thoroughbred horse which was the only mutual interest we had at that point. I became actually frightened, physically, and leapt on Dark Satin I (Phillip's pride and joy, though I paid for him) and rode off madly, with Phillip screaming at me from behind.

It was foolish of me. I knew better than to ride a potential champion animal that hard, but I rode like the devil—jumping fences and ditches and treating Dark Satin like any ordinary horse.

I won't go into the rest of it, how I was crying and cursing and spurring poor Satin into greater and greater speed, since that part still makes me weep. But the upshot of it was that I jumped a fence that was too high and the exhausted horse caught the barbed wire as we went over.

Just a scratch, it was. He didn't even stumble or limp when we cantered back to the stable. And I was calm by now (Phillip was nowhere around) and rubbed the beast down and cooled him off properly.

Then a dreadful thing happened. The scratch on Dark Satin's leg got infected; tetanus set in, and twenty-four hours later Phillip's prize horse was dead. Phillip's fury was incredible. I let him rage and rant about my mistreatment of his horse and how inconsiderate I was of his needs, etc. etc. then calmly told him that I wanted a separation. I said I was going to make some changes in our financial arrangements, that his having free rein with my money had spoiled him. I hinted that after I returned from England (oh, I forgot to tell you that the Linwoods issued me a very cordial invitation to visit. Do you think you could come, too? Think about it when you read this.) that I might be changing my will. In fact, I've already done so, though Phillip doesn't know about my clandestine meeting with my lawyer this morning. I left the invalid one, the one that shows Phillip as sole heir instead of you—yes, you, my much-wronged cousin!—in the desk to throw Phillip off. If he discovered it missing, he might give me trouble.

Do you suppose blood kinship does last over the centuries? For some reason, I wrote to Lilah Linwood about my plans. I said that I wanted to contribute funds to maintain the family castle, and that if anything happened to me, I was sure you would keep it up. I feel so close to that lady. I even confided that I might be separating from my husband.

Actually, I have every intention of divorcing Phillip when I get back, and I'm pretty sure he suspects it, maybe because I closed out most of his charge accounts the day after our fight. At any rate, things have been very cool and strained between us. I think Phillip is as glad about my leaving the country as I am. He's had a new horse trained, Dark Satin II, and he's been busy getting ready for the upcoming horse shows. I hinted that he'd better win, since this would be the last one I bankrolled for him. Mean, huh? But you know how Phillip likes to play at being Bigshot Squire!

That night we got a call about Uncle Porter's death and it seemed like a sign of some kind.

I don't expect anything to happen between now and the time I see you at Uncle Porter's funeral, but something keeps urging me to let you know what I've been going through and why.

It would be foolish to trust Phillip with my letter, so I've been racking my brain for a way to get *it to you without his suspecting anything. Don't worry; I'll think of something.*

Later. The old 'letter in a book' routine; how could I have forgotten? If something does happen to keep us from having a private talk, I can just hand you the books, asking that you autograph them at your convenience. (I can hear you laughing now, Alix, at your crazy cousin's love for intrigue)

Later still. Phillip saw the package of books on my dresser and asked about them. I told him something to the effect that it was silly, keeping up a grudge match with someone as celebrated as you, and told him how I would seek your autograph and, hopefully, a renewal of communication.

He asked me a lot of questions, like when had I heard from you, or had I written you or anything. When I said "no," he got downright amiable, like the old charming Phillip.

He makes me sick, but I'm trying my best to be pleasant until I get him out of my life forever. As a matter of fact, I agreed to help him decide on the tailset for Dark Satin II's show. The championship trials are Phillip's favorite; they were mine, too, before my husband's intensity about winning spoiled everything for me.

Well, he'll be getting impatient, and since he's already down at the stalls waiting for me, I'd better close this and "mail" it. I'm enclosing the new will, too, since you're the only person I can trust.

I'll be leaving for England right after the services. Phillip has made all my travel arrangements. Maybe—just maybe—you'll join me. I hope so.

It's a shame to think it's taking a funeral to bring us together again, isn't it?

Love, Cass.

We planned a small memorial after the news about Cass

came from Tennessee. There was more peacefulness than sadness about the tiny service in Bloodstones Chapel. I knew Cass would want to be in the plot next to Uncle Porter, as she would be, but I knew, too, she'd be pleased to know we were remembering her in England.

The eleven bells were beautiful, and my only reaction this time was to shed a few tears.

"Lilah says if you don't come down for tea before all the rehearsal fuss starts tonight, she's going to elope with Crock and leave you with no adopted mother of the bride." Miles' eyes danced like an imp's and I knew there was more to his invitation than he was letting on.

"Maybe I'll elope with him instead of marrying you. Very convenient, having a doctor around. Lawyers are a dime a dozen and much too expensive. Look at what your firm charged me for setting up the trust for the castle—and Crock's clinic. You'd think a simple . . ."

"Will you come on, woman?" He pulled me out of the room with the briefest kiss.

"Miles, seriously, have you checked with the airport? It seems to me the plane should have landed by now."

"Crislyn, I thought Americans did nothing but rush around. You're positively creeping along."

I didn't point out that he'd called me by the wrong name. It sounded fine with me.

I stopped him halfway down the hall. "Miles, there's something I must ask you. I know how proud and stubborn you are and how you've kept things from Lilah about your money problems." I looked at him worriedly. "Does it bother you terribly, my having all that steel money?"

"I'll try," Miles told me with his eyes laughing for even suggesting that such a silly thing as one-sided wealth mattered with us, "to adjust to this terrible flaw in my beautiful, delicious, sexy, wonderful bride." He picked me up and swung me around, almost knocking Jocko down as the butler made his way from the kitchen with a tray of cheeses. "Now come on, Missus Moneybags, and let's see what Lilah's having for tea.''

Lilah was having a wonderful time, for one thing. And when I let my eyes go from her radiant face to the handsome boy sitting mesmerized at her knee, I felt the happiness that mothers do when at last they know their sons are home with them.

"Brian!" I turned to Miles, my eyes shining. "You devil! You sneaked out to the airport without telling me." I hugged and cried and hugged my beautiful son again.

"Dolores was sick on the plane and asked if you minded her sleeping for a while first." My oldest friend, the widow of my very first editor, had never left my side from the time Brian was born. Between us, we'd given Brian as much security as a boy could have without a father.

I beamed at Lilah. "Isn't he a fine-looking fellow? And so big to be just eleven!"

"Mo-*ther*!" But Brian kissed me and beamed at Lilah, too.

"How do you feel, Brian? About Phillip, I mean. I hope you understand that I asked Miles to tell you about your father because he could talk to you man-to-man."

Brian shot an admiring look at Miles. "It's okay. Phillip had some problems, I guess, but Miles explained how he got mixed up about things. I mean, growing up poor and wanting things and seeing people having things so easy . . ." Brian looked around the high-ceilinged room, his eyes—turquoise; yes, turquoise!—shining. "He didn't grow up knowing he had a castle in his family like me."

I had the grace to blush. "Dolores was the practical one in this little family. I was the one with the fairy tales."

Brian tried hard to remain adult in his reaction to everything, but it was awfully hard to hide his excitement over being in a real, live castle. "Mother, Jocko promised to show me the secret place in the chapel. And Miles said you're going to rebuild it like it was and I can have some stuff down there and . . ."

Jocko, not to be cheated of his time with the liveliest

spirit we'd had around, took Brian off, still chattering, leaving Miles to fetch Lilah's contraband sherry from beneath the tea tray. Lilah beamed at me from over her glass. "Alix, he's wonderful. A Linwood through and through. I'm so pleased you both feel good about the name change, as Miles and I do. He has as much right to it as any of us."

Miles took my hand and held it to his lips, looking deep into my eyes. "Brian held out his hand when I met him at the airport. I noticed he still has the sixth finger. It surprised me, knowing American children and their sensitivity to their peers' opinions. Somehow, I wouldn't think it was 'cool.' "

I smiled at my future husband. "He's always said it made him feel special—different from the other boys."

Miles said, "I think Crislyn would be very happy about Brian. She'd be proud to know he's 'flesh of her flesh' and the future heir of Bloodstones." He took me in his arms. "And like you, he belongs here as long as he's happy."

"That will be for always," I whispered, "but what about the talk?"

"What would Bloodstones do without a scandal?" Madame Lilah asked impishly, and Miles and I joined her in happy laughter.

We would keep the Nashville horse farm and the country house in Alabama, we decided, so Brian could have the broadest heritage of us all. At the wedding reception held at the Dark Swan, Crock teased Lilah about the visit we all planned to make to Alabama. "What will a dowager do in the south?" But Neil assured him that Lilah would "take to it like ducks to a June bug."

I'd wept through the ceremony in Hever Chapel, overcome by having my marriage officiated in a place that held the bones of Anne Boleyn and countless other historic figures.

Once back in our tower, I whispered, "Would you mind awfully if I turned Henry's face to the wall?" The sketch of the famous monarch was leering at me and try as I would, I couldn't ignore him.

"Let him eat his heart out, or cake—whatever makes him happy." He then set out to make me forget there'd ever been a Henry or a James or any other man but my husband, Miles.

To tell the truth, all eight Henrys could have sealed the door to our happy tower like in olden days, and Miles and I wouldn't have even noticed.

Or cared.